The Woman in the Cupboard

Merry Jones

Published by Bloch Books, 2024.

This is a work of fiction. Similarities to real people, places, or events are entirely coincidental.

THE WOMAN IN THE CUPBOARD

First edition. May 27, 2024.

Copyright © 2024 Merry Jones.

ISBN: 979-8224397792

Written by Merry Jones.

To Robin, always

Prologue

December, 2018

    The slash comes from nowhere. Fast, unexpected. At first, the old woman cannot understand why blood is spraying from her, shooting in thick spurts. She clutches her throat, feels the thick warm eruption, sees it spattering her shelves, her carefully preserved vials and jars. She stumbles against the wall, struggling to stay on her feet, wondering how she'll clean it all up. Where is her son? Why isn't he helping her? She strains to call out his name but can make no sound. Careful to not to slip in dark puddles, she staggers the few steps from the kitchen to his bedroom. He will get help. He will save her. She thrusts herself into the room but he doesn't jump to her aid. He lies limp, his body drenched scarlet on his hammock, a gash in his throat, his only eye dangling from its socket.

    She blinks, but the scene does not change. The old woman lets go of her wound and sinks to the floor, perhaps sensing a filmy, slender figure just out of sight. Fading, accepting defeat, she grasps what has happened.

    So. She thinks, sinking into the growing darkness. *She has come back.*

Chapter 1

May, 2018:

I took the call first thing Monday morning, before I'd even taken a bite of my jelly donut.

"Already?" D'Angelo sighed. He looked tired, the bags under his eyes darker than usual, but he stood, wrapped a napkin around a couple of donuts and grabbed his coffee.

Neither of us talked in the elevator. It was, after all, Monday, and neither of us was happy about being awake, let alone at work.

I drove, mostly so D' could eat.

"So, what is it?" His mouth was full, the sugar bringing him to life.

"A double. Apparently pretty bloody."

D'Angelo swallowed. His eyes popped. "Wait, what? You're saying there are two vics?"

"Yes, two. What else would 'double' mean?"

"Mother of God." D'Angelo shook his head and swallowed. "Unbelievable."

What was unbelievable about a double homicide? I pulled out of the Roundhouse parking lot.

D' watched me, clutching his donuts and coffee. "You won't believe this, Mo. Last night, Teresa woke me up, scared from a nightmare. She dreamed I was twins."

"Two of you? That is a nightmare."

D'Angelo was always going on about his wife and her dreams, as if they had some kind of meaning. I made a left, hoped Vine Street wouldn't be backed up.

"No, listen. My twin and me—Teresa said both of us were wandering around covered in blood. How do you explain that, Mo? She has that dream and, Bam, the very next morning, we get the call about two blood-soaked victims." He was convinced that her dream had been a premonition.

I told him that his wife was always having crazy dreams and that he was looking for connections where none existed. I said what I always said, that dreams were just our brains firing random messages, sorting themselves out. But D' kept repeating that the dream foretold trouble, that he had a bad feeling about this call.

"Mo, it's no coincidence. We get a double homicide right after she dreamed I was twins? If that's not a premonition, what do you call it?" He took a sip of his coffee.

"I call it Monday morning." I drove through a red light. "Besides, if you were covered in blood, you wouldn't be wandering. You'd be flat on your back." D'Angelo didn't do well around blood, had been known to pass out at grisly crime scenes. He was a burly bear of a man, fifty-two years old. Had been in homicide for decades and seen it all, but when massive quantities of blood were involved, he took a dive.

"That's a vasovagal response, Mo. It's neurological. Nothing I can do about it."

"I'm just saying. Either the guys in her dream aren't you or they're not bloody. Forget about it."

I swerved past a guy who was straddling two lanes. D's coffee splashed. He scowled, holding it high as if that would stop it from spilling. "Jesus, Mo."

I ignored him, pulled onto the Vine Street Expressway, which was jammed. Damn.

"Siren? What do you think?"

"Sure. Won't do much good, though."

I turned on the flashing light and siren, but the cars around us had no place to go. I nudged them over to the right, one by one, inching ahead, cursing my decision. I should have taken Arch Street, even Market.

D' talked over the siren. "Teresa said the dream was a sign that something bad's coming my way. She wanted me to call in sick." He stared at his sloshing coffee, bounced a leg.

"Relax, would you?" Teresa's cataclysmic dreams popped up every few weeks. Probably linked to her hormones, maybe change of life. "Seriously. Let it go."

"So, you're saying she's wrong?"

"No, she's right. Something bad is going to happen. Something bad always happens. D', we work in homicide."

"Mo. I'm serious—"

"D'. You do this every time Teresa has a dream."

"I don't—"

"You do." I started listing them, the dreams I could recall. Dreams of kidnappings, train wrecks. Of people being tossed out of skyscraper windows. Of arson and mayhem.

D'Angelo finally quieted down. But I could tell he was still contemplating the dream because his leg kept bouncing, and he didn't say another word the whole way to the crime scene.

Chapter 2

The report was that the scene was gruesome. Not that it mattered. I wasn't like D'Angelo, didn't swoon at violence and gore. What killers did to their victims didn't affect me much. No matter how grisly the crime or sympathetic the victim, I regarded scenes without emotion, in a state of objective detachment. I clicked into "detective" mode, switching gears, shutting off my feelings, seeing only evidence.

D' thought my attitude was unhealthy. "You're gonna get cancer, Mo, you keep bottling up your feelings. All that anger and revulsion builds up. It'll sit inside you and fester and balloon until it bursts and makes you sick."

Maybe he was right. But it didn't matter. As a female in the Philadelphia Police Department, my career demanded that I be tougher and calmer, steadier than my male counterparts. I approached that new double homicide in my usual way, by shifting from Mo Sterling the woman to Detective Sterling the cop. I straightened my shoulders, set my jaw, numbed my emotions, and headed into the study of the elegant old house off Rittenhouse Square.

The 911 had come from a guy named Timothy Saunders, a paralegal working for the homeowner. He'd shown up to accompany his boss to a meeting in New York, used his key when no one answered the door. When D' and I got past the crime scene tape and gaggle of uniforms surrounding the house, we found him cowering on the front steps with a not much steadier Tom Reynolds, the first cop on the scene. Saunders was bug-eyed, his skin sallow. He hugged his briefcase against his belly. D'Angelo charged inside toward the crime scene. I stopped to introduce myself and ask Saunders if he'd be okay for a few minutes. Then I followed D' and Reynolds into the house.

The foyer was domed, marble-floored, topped with a multi-tiered crystal chandelier. Reynolds led us to the bottom of a majestic winding staircase. "It's on the left. Second room." He pointed the way.

We passed a set of carved double doors leading to the first room. I glanced in, saw a living room—or did the rich call it a parlor? A sitting room? Whatever, it was beige—everything was beige. Sofas, love seats, walls. Even the rugs were in tones of pale neutral brown. The only color came from a monster green plant and a huge painting over the mantelpiece—something abstract, smears of red, yellow and purple.

Even with booties covering them, our shoes clacked on the marble. A long smear of red led from the second room to a doorway up the hall. Drag marks? An aborted clean up attempt? Maybe both? As always, D'Angelo walked too fast for me. At six foot two, he was eight inches taller than I was, his legs longer. I'd have to jog if I wanted to keep pace, but if I did, he'd only speed up to stay ahead. As usual, he got there first, went in first.

And came out looking green.

I put a hand on his shoulder, and went on in. Recognized the fresh stench of death. Took in the scene while D'Angelo hung back behind me.

Dixon Granger, aged 61, high profile attorney and philanthropist, sprawled on an Oriental carpet, almost decapitated. His suit jacket was folded and draped over the back of a leather sofa, his necktie on top of it. Granger's head dangled at an impossible angle from his body, his eyes peering through not quite closed lids. The cut on his neck was clean, exposing tissue and bone. The blood on his body was so thick that it had caked, cracking like rivers of dried red lava. The carpet was stained but not drenched the way the body was. The murder had likely occurred elsewhere.

The other victim was Judith Granger, aged 54, art collector, Philadelphia socialite, and charity fundraiser. She had been hacked in the face so severely that it would be necessary to use fingerprints or dental records to confirm her identity. She'd died wearing an ivory silk robe, now soaked with crimson. Her arms and hands were striped with defensive wounds. Matching slippers had slid off her feet and lay abandoned on the carpet. A blade had entered and exited an eye socket. Probably that was the lethal wound.

Not that it mattered.

Judith Granger's body still wore diamond earrings, a jumble of gem-studded bracelets, a roped gold necklace, a mammoth diamond ring set. Dixon wore a signet ring and a heavy gold watch.

A small fortune in jewelry, not stolen.

The study was chilly. I shivered, looked away from the bodies to the walls of bookshelves, the mahogany partners desk. The paintings of hunting dogs. The crystal bottles on the bar along the far wall. The crimson drapes, closed around the windows. CNN playing on the big screen television. The spilled glass of what smelled like bourbon on the coffee table.

"Looks familiar, doesn't it?" D'Angelo hefted his pants up, looked at the walls, the ceiling, the door. Anything but the bodies. "It's just like the others."

In fact, the murders resembled two of our open cases. Sylvia Blake had been a secretary at Dixon Granger's law firm, a divorcee who'd lived in a nearby luxury condo. She'd been stabbed to death nine days earlier. And just days before that, J. Steven Richards, one of Dixon Granger's law partners, had been found in his Porsche with his throat slit.

"Let's look into the relationships," I said. "See if they're connected."

"*If?* Obviously they're connected. All of them were stabbed. Three of the vics worked together. And all four were killed within—what? Two blocks of each other? They're connected, Mo. It's the same guy."

D'Angelo was probably right. But as always, he was ahead of himself, making assumptions. And as always, I pulled him back. "Before you close the case, Sherlock, we ought to find out a little more."

D' harrumphed. "It's one guy. You know it as well as I do, Mo."

"I don't know anything yet."

He shook his head. "You wouldn't know the nose on your face unless we tested it for DNA."

I smiled. "But I would know your ass, which is where your head should be."

"Okay." D' smirked, as he put a hand up. "But you'll admit it sooner or later. The same guy did them all."

I didn't answer. Didn't have to. We both knew that we had to do the legwork. Look into the relationships between Granger and Blake, Blake and Richards, Richards and the Grangers. We had to find out who had reason to kill them, who might benefit from their deaths. And we had to see what the techs pulled in—the killer might have left blood or prints.

About then, Franks arrived with the medical examiner's team, and D'Angelo went to catch up with crime scene techs and take a statement from poor Timothy Saunders. I stepped out of the ME's way but stayed close, studying the wounds. Estimating the strength and rage it would take to inflict them. What had driven that amount of rage? I imagined being the killer, seeing from his eyes, his mind. Obviously, I'd have killed Dixon first, eliminating the larger, stronger victim. And because Dixon had no defensive wounds, I must have struck him suddenly, surprising him, not giving him time to respond. My weapon would have been sturdy yet sharp as a scalpel. And I'd have struck with not just force but also precision, the first blow accurate enough to halfway detach his head.

Unlike her husband, Judith Granger had many wounds, so I couldn't tell which had been intended, which had occurred in a frantic struggle. But clearly, Mrs. Granger had fought. She lay on her back on the Oriental carpet, one knee bent and one arm extended over her head as if she'd been doing the backstroke, trying to swim away. Again, I pictured myself as the killer, chasing after her, pouncing onto her as she crawled across the rug, rolling her over, fighting her, stabbing and slashing until my arm ached, until blood spatter blinded me.

"Mo," D'Angelo called from the doorway, gestured for me to join him. "Let's move."

He was always rushing.

"There's stuff you need to see."

Franks looked up from Dixon Granger's body. "Go on, Mo. We got this."

Reynolds stood at the study door like a palace guard. As I stepped past him, D' started walking, talking to me over his shoulder. "I sent the paralegal home. He doesn't know squat."

Really? How could D' be so sure? "D', he must know something. Saunders worked with three of the vics, and he has his own house key."

"The key doesn't mean anything. He just used it to pick things up for his boss." D'Angelo led me along a trail of dried blood down the hall, into a vast kitchen of white tiles and stainless steel. "Granger often traveled at the last minute, needed a suitcase. Or he worked at home and needed files delivered. Seems like Saunders was his personal lackey. Trust me. The guy might be worth talking to later, but for now he's a mess, better off at home."

He stopped, pointing out the blood trail behind us, spatter on the walls, traces of wide pools on the floor. "Probably Mrs. Granger was dragged to the other room. But the action happened in here. Someone tried to clean up." He moved on, swung a door open, revealing the laundry room. Crime scene techs were in there, collecting evidence. "This, though, is interesting." D'Angelo nodded to one of them. "Show her, Al."

Al lifted the lid of the washing machine, revealing a tubful of dark pink water and soaking clothes. Blood soaked?

"The load was running when Reynolds got here. He noticed it while he was checking to see if anyone else was here."

"And he looked in the washer?" Had he thought the killer was hiding in there?

D'Angelo jingled change in his pocket. "He looked inside because he thought it odd that someone was doing the wash right after the people who lived here were killed. It's a good thing he did. He stopped the cycle."

I didn't get it. I stared at the load. "So, the killer was washing his clothes here?"

D' shrugged. "Wait. There's more." He guided me back into the kitchen. Another tech stooped beside the open dishwasher, pointed out a meat cleaver and a long steel carving knife. Dark brownish red matter blood clotted around the handles.

The murder weapons? I stooped to get a better look. Why had the killer left everything in the house?

"How about the rest of the place? Anything else interesting?" I stood, scanned the cabinets, the fridge.

"You and I should take a look. Reynolds and the uniforms cleared the upper levels and the basement. Upstairs, there's a media room, bedrooms, bathrooms, an office. Downstairs, they've got one of those infinity pools and a sauna. A complete fitness center. Also a small cubby with a head, day bed and closet with some white dresses, size six. Looks like a maid's room."

"Yeah?" I stepped around him, opening cabinets, checking out plates and bowls, noting that the Grangers had about a half dozen brands of high fiber cereals. "Any sign of the maid?"

"Nope. She might not live in."

Right. Or she might be stuffed in some closet, dead. I opened the refrigerator, saw yogurt, bags of kale, a head of broccoli. Lactose-free fat-free milk. Had the Grangers been health nuts? I thought of Dixon Granger's beefy frame, the glass of spilled bourbon. Maybe the wife had been the health nut. Or she'd been trying to get him to eat better.

"So, let's do a walk-through." I shut the door, wondered if food had been a point of contention between them.

"Let's make it fast. We need to get to the partners, find out what Granger's been working on." D'Angelo was already on his way out of the kitchen, as always in a rush. Wherever he was, he had someplace else to go. Bounced a knee when he sat. Jingled the coins in his pockets, fidgeted. Had to move constantly.

I didn't rush after him. I took my time, resisting D'Angelo's pressure. I opened a cabinet full of dishes. Another full of pots.

"Mo, nothing's in here," D' said. "Let's move."

I ignored him, looked into the cabinet under the sink, stepped over to the pantry and opened the narrow door.

And faced a striking dark woman with large blank eyes. Wearing a white uniform, she sat on a case of canned seltzer beside a wall of shelves stocked with bottled water, paper towels, and twelve-packs of canned tuna. The other wall was bare, painted a deep sky blue.

***

The woman concentrates on the color before her. It reaches high and wide, and does not move. It remains steady, without sound or edges, plain flat blue.

She watches the color, and the blueness deepens, expands like a cloud and dissolves into the air where it reaches out to her face. She takes it in as if it were a breath. But she knows it is really a color: blueness.

A voice—Is it her teacher's? M. Roger's? Is she in school? The voice asks her name. Her name? The voice floats away, comes around again, asking again. She must respond, and so she does. But then it asks more, and more again. She reaches into the blue, trying to pluck out answers, missing some, grabbing others, not sure if they are acceptable or correct. Is it an exam? She hasn't studied—doesn't know how to respond. She speaks to avoid speaking, says what she cannot say. The air is heavy. Maybe she is not speaking and no one is asking. Maybe the wall isn't blue, and there is no wall, only her own breath. Or maybe there is no breath and she is herself the air, because she is gone like a deep blue cloud, no longer alive.

Chapter 3

I blinked at her. "Ma'am?" I finally managed.

D'Angelo dashed back and stuck his head in front of mine. His hand was on his weapon. "Holy Mother. What are you doing in there? You want to step out? Come on now. Hands on your head."

The woman didn't move.

"I got this." I nudged him away, spoke to her gently. "Ma'am, we're the police. Are you okay?"

She didn't answer. Didn't budge. Her eyes didn't register that she'd heard us.

"Ma'am?" I stepped into the narrow closet, knelt in front of her. Her legs were long and sturdy, her cheekbones chiseled, eyes large. Hands slender, callused and dry. I couldn't guess her age. Maybe forty. Maybe twenty-five. I took her wrist. Still, she didn't stir, maybe in shock? Her pulse was slow but steady, her skin cool. "Can you tell me your name?"

She didn't speak. Sat with her back straight, perfectly still.

I looked back at D'Angelo who stood with crossed arms, impatient as usual. "What's she doing in there, hiding?"

I shook my head. Maybe she was terrified. "Ma'am, do you work here?"

"Of course, she does. She's the maid. And she knows what happened," D'Angelo whispered. "She was cleaning up the mess, washing the clothes."

I held up a hand, gesturing for him to be quiet. "Ma'am," I asked. "Why are you sitting in here?"

No answer. Nothing. I waited a beat. Maybe she didn't speak English? Or needed time to process the questions. But D'Angelo was shifting his weight, letting me know he wanted to move things along. And pausing didn't help. The woman still said nothing.

So I went on, keeping my voice low and non-threatening. "How long have you been sitting in here?"

She didn't answer, but slowly turned her head, aimed her eyes at me. I looked into them, trying to connect. But her gaze seemed unfocused, as if looking past me. Or through me.

I turned to D'Angelo. "She needs a bus. She's not right."

D'Angelo adjusted his pants, shook his head. "Let me try. She'll answer me."

"No, D." I stood, blocking his way. "Don't push. She's in shock or traumatized. Catatonic or something."

"Bullshit," he muttered. He stood at the closet door and barked. "Yo. Lady. We're the Philadelphia police. You want to step out here and tell us who you are and what you're doing in there?"

The woman didn't seem to notice him, kept staring at air.

"Really, D'?" I scowled at him and turned back to the woman, speaking softly. "Ma'am. You're okay now. You're safe. Just wait here a minute." I stood, put a hand on her shoulder and then, shaking my head at D'Angelo, stepped out to call for an ambulance.

***

She waits beside the blue, but Miss Judith does not appear, nor does Mr. Dixon. She sits while darkness, then light pulses through window slats. A new voice floats by. You are safe, it says. She doesn't know the voice. Maybe it's her own? And then there are clashes of rough metallic sounds, but not biting like the slashing of blades. She doesn't resist when hands reach for her, but watches while colors whirl and the air sweeps, chilly and raw. Voices murmur, and she is lifted, separated from the blue. Still, she doesn't resist. She lets strange hands do their closing and gripping, raising and lowering, rearranging and fastening, and when they release her, she notices that the colors are changing, moving. And when they settle, they are pale green with dull tan. Nothing is vibrant, nothing alive. After some time, the green splits open and a figure emerges. Maybe it comes close to her. Or maybe it remains behind the green, and only its voice emerges. Or maybe it is the pale color green itself, and not a figure at all. But a voice comes to her and rumbles soft words, "I am Dr. Vogel."

The voice says more, but she lets go of the words, not convinced that they are real, suspecting that the voice is only a mirage. Or maybe it is lost and wandering, searching for an ear to enter, a body in which to root. No. If she lets it in, it might soak into her bones until it owns her. She tries to shut it out, and she listens for the voice of Miss Judith or Mr. Dixon even though she is convinced she will not hear those voices again. She looks at the green and the beige and watches the slats of light. She stays still, waiting.

Somewhere, not far, she hears softness—Is it music?

Chapter 4

The next morning, I was up before dawn, still tasting the cheese and pepperoni I'd ordered about one a.m., unable to sleep, unable to stop thinking about the woman in the pantry. I'd tossed. Turned the television on, then off. Walked around. Done planks and pushups. Tried to read. To look at Facebook. No matter what I did, her empty gaze wouldn't release me. She was everywhere, in my head, hollow-eyed and dazed.

Who was she? Why couldn't I shove her out of my mind? I scolded myself. I knew better than to take the job home, much less give up sleep. But there I was, wide awake, contemplating the woman's empty eyes. The emptiness felt personal, and I had no idea why. Unless it was because it reflected my personal life, which was similarly blank. It had been almost three years since my divorce, and I hadn't moved on. Hadn't gone on a single date. Hadn't even moved my stuff into Dan's still-empty closet. No doubt, at a basic level, the woman in the pantry reminded me of myself, all alone and hiding from the world.

Okay, no. I was exaggerating. My situation wasn't anything like hiding alone in a pantry. Probably, the woman just reminded me that I needed to move on and start over, have a life beyond work. Around eleven, I'd texted Evie, my oldest friend, sure that we'd have our usual conversation.

"Log on, Mo," she'd say. "I'll walk you through it."

And I'd answer. "I'm not that desperate. I don't need to beg random men in cyberspace for a date."

And she'd say, "Yes, you are. And yes, you do."

But Evie didn't answer my text. Might have been asleep. Or busy with her boyfriend Joe who lived with her.

They'd met online.

I'd dawdled, opened a beer, tried not to think about the Grangers and the maid. Finally, I'd taken a seat at the computer, logged onto the dating site Evie had been pressuring me to join. Maybe I'd actually sign up this time. Weeks earlier, after a few Cosmos, she'd helped me start my profile, sitting with me while I filled in a bunch of information. Age: 33. Eye color: hazel. Hair color: brown. Height: 5' 8". Body type. This question offered a list of choices.

"Curvy?" I'd suggested.

Evie tsked. "You are not curvy, Mo."

I wasn't? "You're saying I'm flat?"

She rolled her eyes. "Just check 'athletic and toned.'"

"They'll think I'm an Amazon."

"No. They'll think you're athletic and toned." She was ready for the next question. "You're in shape, so advertise it. It's a selling point."

A selling point? I was a product on the market. Like prepackaged burgers.

I'd resisted, but Evie had urged me on. We'd checked boxes saying that I was divorced, had no kids, no religious beliefs. A college graduate, raised in Philly. Declined to share political views. And then I'd come to the stumper, the question that had stopped me: Occupation.

"What's your problem?" Evie had asked. "Type it in."

But I hadn't. What kind of guy would want to date a woman who carried a gun and spent her days with corpses and murderers? Especially one who claimed to be athletic and toned? I'd hesitated, chewed my lip. Felt exposed. Why was I sending all this private information to strangers, telling them how I liked to spend my spare time, what books I'd read, how often I worked out? Why was I describing myself by filling-in-the-blanks? Being divorced was lonely, but defining myself by my hobbies, hair color, and height—Well, it felt demeaning. Less personal even than a singles bar. At least there, you could make eye contact.

Despite Evie's encouragement, I'd closed the site at the career question, convinced that my product wouldn't appeal to the marketplace. And last night, I'd closed it there again. I'd eaten pizza and thought about the mystery woman, mentally compiling her profile: hair color, height, body type. I'd wondered where she'd grown up, where her family was. What music she liked. Finally, around five a.m., I'd given up, showered. Turned on the television again.

And saw pictures of the Grangers. They were smiling.

Chapter 5

Their murders were the big story of the morning. The anchor talked about their prestigious lives, narrated clips about their charitable work, and I revisited their bloodstained marbled floor, the wounds on their corpses.

The woman hiding in their pantry.

Why couldn't I stop thinking about her? What was it about her that haunted me so? Her vulnerability? Her stunned lack of emotion? Never mind. I was a cop, needed to reclaim my objectivity. Focus on concrete facts, ask questions. Had she actually witnessed the murders? Tried to clean up the blood? Seen—Or been seen by the killer?

And then, on the screen, there she was. A shot of the maid, being taken from the house. I froze. How the hell had the media gotten that footage? The anchor was asking anyone who could identify the woman to contact the police. How had that happened? Now the killer would know there was a witness—And what she looked like. Who had let the media so close to her?

Furious, I pulled on some clothes and went into work early, without even stopping for coffee. Passing the newsstand, I grabbed the morning *Inquirer*. The Grangers' murders were the headline story, their faces on the front page, the mystery woman's watchfully below them. A caption asked readers to contact police if they could identify her.

I cursed, gaping at the page. No one had consulted me or D' about the release. It was our case. What had happened to protocol? Who'd authorized this without our involvement?

I jumped onto the elevator fuming, but by the time I got to my desk, I'd cooled down a bit. Despite the glitch in procedure, it might not be a bad idea to ask the public for help. Maybe someone would identify the woman and give us a lead. I sat at my desk, watching the phone. Waiting for someone to respond to the news and call. No one did.

But it was still early. Not even seven. Calls would come.

The first call that came, though, was from the press. Mike Vega, a crime reporter. He'd figured out that there must be connections among the Grangers', J. Steven Richards', and Sylvia Blake's murders. I told him I couldn't discuss the cases, referred him to the public affairs office and hung up, rattled.

The media were ahead of us. Already linking our four murders even though we had no definite proof that they were connected. Never mind. I couldn't think about the media, couldn't control what they said. The reporter had deliberately avoided authorized channels, had called homicide directly to talk to the investigating detectives. Which meant he should have expected to get nothing.

Except that I'd given him something: my name. I'd introduced myself when I'd answered the phone, before I'd realized who was calling. Great. I was probably going to be embarrassed by the press, singled out as rude or obstructive or uncooperative or just plain dumb. Damn. Why had I come in early? Why had I picked up the phone?

Never mind. It was out of my hands. Vega would write what he would write. It was his job. Meantime, I needed to do mine. To focus. I wanted coffee. And a cheese Danish. Or a donut. Some caffeine and sugar to kick-start my brain. Instead, donutless and coffeeless, I sat alone at my desk, waiting for phone calls, avoiding the stare of the mystery woman on the front of the newspaper. Soon, D'Angelo would be in. He and I had an appointment with the psychiatrist who was evaluating her. Meantime, I had some time. Decided to follow up on Vega's questions, review my notes, looking for links between the Grangers' murders to Sylvia Blake's and J. Steven Richards'.

I took out my file on Sylvia Blake and looked at the phone interview I'd had with her daughter in Maine. The daughter had said that Sylvia and Judith Granger were longtime friends, roommates at Vassar College. Six years ago, Dixon Granger had handled Sylvia's divorce from investment banker Stadler Blake, and soon afterwards, he'd hired Sylvia as his secretary.

My notes continued with information on Stadler Blake. Early on, we'd ruled him out as a suspect. After the divorce, he'd retired with a fortune, married his longtime mistress, and moved to California. He'd had no financial or emotional motive for killing his ex-wife, and had cooperated, supplied an alibi for the time of her murder, seemed genuinely upset by the death of his ex. If we were looking for a serial killer, Stadler Blake wasn't it. He'd had no connection whatever to the first victim, J. Steven Richards, or, except during his divorce, to the later ones, the Grangers.

Blake wasn't our guy.

The next interview in the file had been with Dixon Granger, Sylvia's boss. When he'd learned of her death, he'd been shaken, distraught. He'd had no idea who would kill her. Didn't think she had a boyfriend. Didn't know about her current personal life, except that she had an ex-husband and a grown daughter, and that she was a close friend of his wife. He'd been home with his wife at the time of her murder.

The interview with Judith Granger had also led nowhere. She'd been almost too upset to talk, but said that Sylvia had been seeing someone. A married man, but she didn't know anything else, couldn't give us a name.

I closed the file, frustrated. The victims had known each other, but I had nothing but dead ends. I picked up my file on J. Steven Richards, put it down without opening it. I already knew what was in it. Reading it was just wasting time.

Looked at the clock. Not even eight yet.

The phone still wasn't ringing.

Maybe I could run outside to the coffee truck, get a cup of black. A donut. Last night's pizza flashed to mind. Maybe I'd skip the donut.

Then again, why should I? What was the harm in one lousy donut? After all, wasn't I "athletic and toned."

But I wouldn't stay that way if I kept downing late-night pizzas.

The clock crawled, my stomach grumbled. D'Angelo would be in any minute, probably with a box of glazed. I could wait.

The phone was silent. I opened the file on Judith Granger. Found a photo of her fricasseed grimace. Her fancy negligee, ragged and stained. D'Angelo had suggested that Judith Granger might have been collateral damage, killed just because she was present. That the law partners and Sylvia Blake might have been the intended victims because of something at the law firm. I'd made a note of the theory, but it didn't feel right. Not with the viciousness of Judith Granger's wounds. If I were the killer, I wouldn't plunge a blade into the eye of someone who'd just wandered into the scene. I'd have to have a pretty deep personal grudge against her to do that. For me, she was a targeted victim. Maybe even the main target.

I rifled through the folder. Noted that Judith Granger's personal computer was being examined for frequent contacts and recent appointments. Lists of neighbors and friends were being compiled. Blah blah blah.

I checked the clock again. Only a few hours until our meeting with the psychiatrist. Maybe he'd gotten the maid to talk to him. Maybe she'd talk to us.

Maybe her eyes wouldn't be so blank.

People began to wander in, grunting good morning. Most of them carried coffee. The aroma wafted around my head, taunting me. When the phone rang, I grabbed it.

A woman asked if she'd called the right number. She had information about the woman in the newspaper. She recognized her from her water aerobics class, didn't know her name, but she was certain that she belonged to the Roxborough YMCA.

I was making a note of the information when a Styrofoam cup and a muffin landed on my desk.

"Yo." D'Angelo's way of saying good morning. "You see the papers? The media are all over us."

I reached for the coffee, breathing my thanks. "Any idea who leaked it?"

"New guy in public affairs. Asshole didn't even try to follow protocol."

I opened the lid, felt the burst of steam.

"Fair warning, Mo. Between the news and Teresa, I'm steamed."

"Another dream?"

D'Angelo rolled his eyes. "She's got us in the grave, Mo. Literally. Come on. We gotta get." He jingled coins in his pocket, hurrying me.

The phone rang again.

"Someone else'll get it." He grabbed the car keys as he started for the elevator.

I watched the phone for a couple of seconds, then grabbed my muffin and coffee, and followed. D'Angelo stood jingling his change, waiting for the doors to open.

Chapter 6

"Rough night?" D' pulled out of the Roundhouse parking lot. "You look beat."

I did? "Couldn't sleep."

D' frowned. "You need a man, Mo."

What?

"You need to get out there again. You're alone too much."

Oh great. He was starting again. I wondered about the guys in the department. Did they see me as poor lonely Mo, the horny divorcee who had no life? I took a breath, preparing for a D'Angelo sermon.

"You need to let people close, let yourself feel things, Mo. It's no good cutting yourself off. I told you Teresa wants you to meet her nephew—"

"D. I'm fine." I cut him off.

He eyed me.

"Really. Men aren't a problem."

"This is me, Mo. Don't fake."

"I'm not faking. You're making assumptions. I said I didn't sleep and you immediately figured it was about my love life. It wasn't."

"No?"

"No. It's because of the case."

"Bull." D'Angelo shook his head. "You? You never take a case home."

He was right. I didn't. Except now I had. "I kept thinking about the maid." Again, I pictured her liquid eyes.

D' swerved, cut off a Septa bus. "Yeah, I agree. She looks good for it."

Wait, what? "You think the maid killed the Grangers?"

He stopped at a red light, let out a sigh. "It's not about what I think. I know, on the surface the case seems like it'd be connected to

J. Steven and Sylvia Blake. But look at the facts. There was no sign of forced entry. We got her bloody clothes, the cleaver and knife. And most of all, she was the only one there."

I pictured her huddling in the pantry. "She might have opened the door for someone."

"Yeah, but who? And why didn't they kill the maid, too? Why leave a witness? Besides, who would want to kill the Grangers? They were model citizens. Patrons of the arts. Philanthropists. Their foundation gives money to hospitals, food banks, scholarships, museums. They had no enemies."

No enemies? "D', the guy was a lawyer. He had to have enemies." I wasn't sure why I was resisting. The maid might well have killed them.

I saw her staring at the pantry wall, completely without expression. Was that the face of a woman who'd just slaughtered her employers?

"I don't know, D'," I told him. "I still think the same guy killed all four. How could that be the maid?"

He didn't answer. We were quiet for a few minutes, driving.

"I mention Teresa had another dream last night?"

I chewed my muffin, sipped coffee, closed my eyes. "What. This time you were triplets?"

"No, worse. Our daughter went missing. Teresa dreamed someone took her and buried her. And when I went looking, I got sucked into the ground, too. So, what do you think?"

D'Angelo's daughter was about thirty, newly married. Maybe Teresa felt that the new son-in-law had taken her daughter away, that the marriage would bury her? That D' was too heavy? Who knew what the dream meant, if anything?

"I think Teresa shouldn't snack before bed. Indigestion gives you nightmares."

"I don't know, Mo. Yesterday, she dreamed of two bloody people who looked like me, and I got two bloody murder vics. Now she dreams our daughter's kidnapped and buried—"

"Stop. Just stop. How can you keep taking this seriously? Teresa is always dreaming something, and somehow we've all survived."

D'Angelo snorted, looked out at traffic. "Yeah," he finally said. "I guess you're right. But the thing is, when she first woke up, she wasn't sure that the girl in the dream was our daughter."

I gazed out the window, sipped coffee.

"What I'm saying is. You know how she feels about you, Mo. You're like family. At first, she thought the kidnapped girl—She thought it was you."

"Me?" I blinked at him.

"She's worried about you. And so, when I saw how you looked this morning, I got worried, too. I don't like you being alone so much."

I reached over, squeezed his arm. "D'. I'm fine. Really. Tell Teresa not to worry."

He glanced at me. "Right. You know how much good that'll do."

I leaned back, felt my face heating up. My life was making problems for other people? What was I supposed to do, invent a husband? I thought about the dating site, the snapshots of single men searching for love. Reminded myself that I was on the job. Needed to focus on the case, the maid. The murders.

As he pulled into the hospital garage, D' said, "Do me a favor, Mo. I know you don't believe in this stuff. But Teresa's got a gift. Maybe the dream wasn't about you—maybe it was nothing. But just in case, what's the harm? Just be extra careful. Try not to be alone for a while. And when you are, watch your back."

Chapter 7

D'Angelo hated hospitals. Maybe because they reminded him of when he'd been shot a couple of years ago. Maybe because he associated them with blood. But whatever the cause, his discomfort with hospitals was intense. Whenever we had to visit one, he complained.

"Why do they all smell so bad?" He muttered all the way to the elevator. "There are a million products out there. They make kitty litters smell like flowerbeds. Why not hospitals?"

I didn't engage. I said nothing, letting him vent. Wondering if the maid had spoken yet.

Dr. Matthew Vogel waited for us near the elevator. He was gangly and thin with a mustache that was also thin. We introduced ourselves, and he led us to his office in the psychiatric unit. Offered us seats and coffee.

We accepted seats, said no thanks to the coffee.

"Has she said anything?" I asked.

Dr. Vogel sat at his desk, opened a folder, reviewed the contents. "Not a word."

"Do you happen to know her dress size?"

Both Dr. Vogel and D'Angelo raised their eyebrows at me.

I explained. "The Granger's maid wore a size six. I'm just confirming her identity."

"No, I have no idea. Wait a moment." Vogel read something, smoothed his mustache. "Her belongings are listed here. Let's see. Yes, the dress she was wearing when she arrived was white, size six." He read on. "And she has a healthy appetite."

"She's eating?" I remembered how skinny she'd looked, huddled on the case of seltzer. Long and waif-like.

"Apparently, yes. Especially sweets." He crossed his arms. "Last night, after a meatloaf and mashed potato dinner, she put away six containers of pudding." He smiled.

D'Angelo harrumphed. "Doctor. This woman may have killed two of our city's most prominent citizens. Other than her dinner choices, have you learned anything about her at all?"

Vogel's smile vanished. "We've run a number of tests, detective. So far, her blood work has come back normal."

"No drugs?" I recalled the vacant look in her eyes.

"Not so far. But we've just run a standard screening for common substances—"

"We know what it tests for, Doc." D'Angelo shifted in his chair, unable to sit still.

Dr. Vogel bristled. "I've ordered more specific tests as well, but they take longer, and it's difficult to test when we don't know what she might have been exposed to, if anything. After all, her condition might not be drug-induced. She might be suffering from catatonia."

"You mean like schizophrenia?" D'Angelo tried to sound knowledgable.

"Catatonia covers a wide spectrum and can result from many different conditions," Vogel leaned forward, rested on his elbows. "Schizophrenia is one of those conditions. But so are depression, bipolar disorder, drug overdose, and post-traumatic stress disorder, not to mention certain infections and lesions. And of course, sometimes alcohol or drug withdrawal—At any rate, there can be many causes."

D'Angelo bounced his knee.

"Is there a treatment?"

Vogel turned to me. "Antipsychotics, but they sometimes worsen the symptoms. Plus, they have side effects. For the short term, I recommend we continue monitoring her physical condition, stabilizing her environment, testing. We'll need some time. She's been here just one day."

Not great news.

D'Angelo thanked him and stood, ready to go.

I didn't move. "Can we see her?"

Vogel sat back, rubbed his mustache. "I don't think that would be wise."

"Why not?" I asked. "Worst case? She won't respond."

"But your presence and tone, your questions might adversely affect her," he eyed D'Angelo. "We want to prevent disturbing her further—"

"Disturbing her? Doc, with all due respect, the woman is a person of interest in a double homicide. Do we really care if we disturb her?" D'Angelo couldn't help himself. He was out of his element. And frustrated.

Vogel looked up at him, spoke slowly. "Let me rephrase: If we pressure her, we might further complicate her condition, pushing her more deeply into catatonia. That would certainly not help your cause."

D'Angelo stepped back, shoved his hands in his pockets. Jingled coins.

"What if I went in?" I asked. "Just me. I can talk to her a little, not mention the murders or ask questions. I'll just sit a few minutes and let her get used to having me there."

Dr. Vogel tilted his head, crossed his arms. Pursed his lips. Looked at me. Finally, he stood. "Only you, alone. We'll observe through the window. And if I think you're pushing her, you'll have to leave."

Chapter 8

The room was sparsely furnished and small. Just room enough for a nightstand, a hospital bed, a wardrobe, a bathroom. The woman sat in a vinyl chair by the window. Her hair had been brushed: A couple of gray hairs coiled among black. Her limbs and fingers were long, bent under a creamy knit blanket.

I sat facing her in a straight back chair. Sunlight shone on her face, highlighted the high curve of her cheekbones, the fullness of her lips. She didn't move.

I watched her, assessing. Was she strong enough to wield a knife? A cleaver? She was slim, but wiry like me. Built strong like a runner. The skin along her fingertips and cuticles was cracked and dry. Nails short and filed. Her arms and hands bare, exposing no cuts accidentally inflicted while stabbing her employers.

We sat. After a while, I couldn't help it. I spoke. "My name is Mo." She didn't react. I waited a while before I went on. "We met yesterday. Do you remember?"

Silence.

"You're in a hospital. You're safe here. Don't be afraid."

Nothing.

"Can you tell me your name?"

Still nothing.

I waited.

"Ma'am? Do you know why you're here? Can you remember what happened?"

Damn. I was questioning her, what was wrong with me? I was bringing up stressful topics. Needed to stop.

I followed her gaze out the window. Saw forsythia bushes, their buds popping bright yellow. "It's spring," I said. "Isn't it nice to see all the flowers coming back to life?" I sounded idiotic, expected no response. Sat quietly for another moment.

"I'll come back another time," I said. "Remember, you can talk to me."

Nothing.

"I wish you would at least tell me your name."

I was about to stand up and go.

"No."

The voice was so small and sounded so far away that I thought I'd imagined it.

No? Had she actually said, "No"?

I was sure she had. But "no" what? I sat still, rewinding my rambling commentary, replaying what I'd said. I'd asked if she liked seeing spring flowers. If she remembered what had happened. If she could tell me her name. "No" might be the answer to any of those questions. She might even be telling me not to come back again.

But what she'd meant didn't matter. What mattered was that the woman had spoken. I looked at the observation window near the door. Had Dr. Vogel heard her? Had her voice been too low?

The woman stared out the window, listless and unmoving. But despite her stillness, she knew I was there. And she'd tried to make contact with me.

I tried once more. "Please. Tell me your name." It wasn't a question this time. My tone was gentle, but insistent.

Seconds later, she mumbled an answer that made no sense. Her voice was low. I must have misheard.

"Say that again?"

Without looking at me, without expression, she repeated, "No name."

No name?

I took a breath, didn't let myself move. Didn't want to startle her by reacting to the substantial event that had just occurred. The woman had responded, had actually answered a question. Was she coming out of her catatonia? Dr. Vogel was observing from the other side of the glass. He might come in and stop the visit as soon as he realized her condition had changed. I was making progress and had little time, so I hurried on.

"No name?" I spoke patiently, in a low voice.

She didn't respond.

Maybe I should change the question. "Where do you live?"

Again, silence. I rephrased it. "Do you live with the Grangers? In the house near Rittenhouse Square?"

This time, her eyebrow did a nano-wobble and her lips puckered slightly. "No."

"No?" Okay. Good. She didn't live with the Grangers. "So. Where do you live?"

Nothing.

Dr. Vogel tapped on the glass, signaling me to end the visit. I held up a hand, signaling that I understood.

"Ma'am?" I asked again, "Can you tell me where you live?"

She didn't move. She just said, "No." Negative. She could not tell me where she lived.

No? Was it possible that she didn't know her own address?

The woman's gaze remained fixed on the window, at trees and yellow buds beyond the glass. Seconds passed.

Dr. Vogel rapped on the window again, insisting that I end the visit.

I stood to say goodbye, and the low soft voice spoke again. It was almost a whisper, but the words were crisp. "I do not live there," the woman said. "I do not live."

Chapter 9

"We got nothing," D'Angelo grumbled. "That was a complete waste of time." He went through a red light, heading back to the Roundhouse.

"Don't whine."

"I'm not whining. I'm just pissed we got nothing."

"You're whining. Let's get an early lunch." I focused on D's mood so I wouldn't think about the woman's answers. The gooseflesh that had risen on my arms, the tingle on my neck.

"It's too early for lunch." He jerked to a stop at a red light.

Okay. I took a moment, collecting myself. "It wasn't a complete loss, D'. We found out she's definitely the maid—she's the same size as the dresses at the house."

"Big whoop. We already knew she was the maid."

"Not for sure. And look—she's emerging. She talked to me."

"Yep, she talked to you," D'Angelo acknowledged. "She said she's got no name and she doesn't live. What is she saying, that she's an effing zombie?"

"Come on, D'—"

"Look, Mo. We found no ID, no driver's license. Nothing about her identity at all. Obviously, she's an illegal, playing dumb to avoid getting caught."

I said nothing. Had nothing to say. D' might be right that she was here illegally. The Grangers wouldn't be the first wealthy couple to hire illegal aliens. But I didn't think it was that simple. The maid hadn't seemed coherent enough to be deliberately evading my questions. She'd seemed genuine. Her comments echoed in my mind as we drove through Chinatown, inhaling the aroma. I could almost taste Peking Duck.

D' went on. "Her being an illegal isn't what bothers me. What bothers me is that our only witness, and likely suspect, is a complete and utter loon."

We drove past pedestrians, restaurant signs, groceries. Traffic. Normal daily life. But it all seemed altered. "Normal" seemed distant, out of reach. I kept hearing the woman say, "I do not live." Why had she said that? Why did remembering it give me the chills?

"Maybe she's just been drugged," I told D', "Give her time for them to wear off. Vogel's doing more tests. And he said she might be getting clearer."

D'Angelo wasn't convinced, kept complaining about our lack of leads, our dead ends on the other two homicides. I stopped listening. His voice faded into a persistent pulsing baritone. We crawled along Race Street, stuck in traffic. I kept seeing the cracked skin on the woman's fingers, the distance in her eyes. Kept hearing her say, "No name."

How could she have no name? Everyone had a name. Everyone alive, anyway. "We need a name for her," I interrupted D'.

"What?"

"Until we find out who she is, we can't just call her 'the woman' or 'the maid.' We need a name."

"How about Jane Doe."

"No. Something real."

"Zombie Queen?"

I ignored him, pictured her cheekbones. Her perfect skin. "Vanessa? Natalie?"

He took his eyes off the road, blinked at me. "Zombie Queen's better."

"Olivia? It's just for us to use. Nothing official."

He drove on. "Whatever you want, Mo." He pulled to the curb. "You win."

I won? Olivia?

"Get me pork lo mein." He held out a twenty.

I grabbed it and dashed into a take out restaurant. Decided on General Tso's chicken. And Vanessa.

Chapter 10

The voice sounds like cotton and asks the woman what her name is. It asks where she lives.

Shadows, figures move. The woman hears shuffling, the rustling of cloth. The voice floats by, promising that she is safe. That it is okay to remember.

Remember? As if the past were contained in a box. As if the box could be opened at will. What is she supposed to remember? She waits for the voice to guide her, but it has changed. Now it offers her lunch. It is different, musical, and it says, Open.

She feels a tickling at her mouth, parts her lips, and tastes something warm and soft. Chew, the voice says. It tells her she is doing well. That she must keep eating.

Faces and scents appear, drift away. She doesn't know sleep from waking, dream from actuality. Shapes take on human forms, and then dissolve into abstract fluid blurs.

Sometimes she hears music, delicate and fine.

A flat, blank, square stretches in front of her, and a voice says that she should fill it with what she thinks, what she feels.

Colored sticks appear, lined up like school children, and she watches them until a red one melts and puddles over the others. It stands, splashing as it jumps up, spinning and leaping, and it flies, fogging the air with droplets that enter lungs and skin, mouths and eyes. Fabric rips, flesh tears, and gushes of red bathe the walls, the roof, even the sky. After a while, the rampage ebbs. The color red lies flat, exhausted. She notices the screaming only after it has stopped.

The voice sounds disappointed when it says that it's not a problem. That she can wait until she is ready, that they will try again later. And then, like all the others, the voice drifts away.

Chapter 11

D' and I had only a short time until we had to interview the Grangers' son. We brought lunch to our desks, found Reynolds waiting for us.

"Phone hasn't stopped all morning."

In fact, it was ringing as he spoke.

"Everybody seems to know our mystery woman. She's a model from Europe, a movie star from Brazil. Dixon Granger's lover, his illegitimate half-sister. Look. Read for yourself." He showed us the list.

So far, the maid I'd dubbed Vanessa had been recognized by dozens. She was a couple's runaway daughter who looked mature but was really only fourteen. A homeless woman who hung around the Pine Street Baptist Church. A former employee of a boutique on 18th Street who'd run off with the proceeds of last summer's sidewalk sale. Maxine Something-or-other, the long-lost childhood friend of a Mount Airy woman.

Those were the more feasible calls. There were others. People said the woman was a fugitive who'd robbed a liquor store in Jersey, killing the clerk in 1987. She was an Islamic terrorist, a would-be suicide bomber from ISIS, or Iraq, or Somalia, or Syria. Carlotta, an international drug smuggler who operated out of a duplex in West Philly. Aliantra, the ex-girlfriend of a hitman, escaped from the witness protection program. Sgt. Sally Stone, listed as a casualty in Afghanistan, actually the victim of a secret government biological weapons experiment.

The list went on.

"And then there's this one," Reynolds pointed to an entry. "The guy's called about six times."

The calls had come from Haiti, from a man named Kenny Wadd.

"We've had lots of yahoos, but in my book? This guy wins," Reynolds didn't smile when he chuckled.

Weirder than an extra-terrestrial? I chomped on a bite of General Tso's and read the log. The man had insisted that the woman he'd seen on the news was his former fiancée, a Haitian woman named Ja Vala Boudin. He was certain of her identity.

"What's so weird?" I asked.

"Read on." Reynolds pointed to a detail.

According to the caller, his fiancée had died almost nine years ago.

Reynolds hooted. "Can you believe that? He wins, doesn't he? The guy keeps calling to say the maid is a dead woman? Like a zombie? I've heard it all. I really have."

D'Angelo and I exchanged glances. I recalled the woman's small voice declaring, "I do not live." I rubbed goose bumps off my arms, trying to laugh along with Reynolds. Clearly, the woman I'd dubbed Vanessa was alive, and the man from Haiti was a crackpot. Even so, for just a moment, D' stopped swallowing lo mein noodles, looked at me with raised eyebrows, and I was sure that the room had become chilly, that D' looked a little pale.

Chapter 12

Sometimes the shadows declare that the woman is in the afterlife, neither awake nor asleep, neither moving nor still. A soul alone among murmurs. Yet, she has sensations. She feels cloth on her skin, sees light far away, glowing. Is it the sun? She smells vegetable soup, pungent and thick, the aroma moving in and out of her, carried by her breath. Or is it her breath? Does she breathe? She considers her chest, the way it draws itself up and down, as if taking in and pushing out air. But maybe it is a useless motion, performed out of habit only.

In fact, nothing she touches seems solid. Her world is fog, thin clouds that hide the sky. The rooms she sees are pictures in her mind, places that used to be, or might have been. Sounds muffled, distorted by the fog and clouds. She tries to understand. Does she dwell in memory? In a dream? Is her confusion permanent, with every sensation just out of reach and without definition?

Maybe the distance from her hand to the armrest is the length of a lifetime. Maybe that aroma of soup, warm from a stove, is meant to comfort a spirit unaware that she's passed.

Maybe she lingers close by, just beyond the reach of the living, not because she wants to return, but because she has no place else, doesn't know where to go.

Chapter 13

D'Angelo was driving. "You gotta admit it's weird, Mo. The maid says she isn't alive, and some guy from Haiti identifies her as a dead woman. If I didn't know better, I'd think Zombie."

"But you do know better," I said. "There were tons of calls, D'. Another guy said she was his mentally ill wife."

He wove between lanes, not paying attention to traffic. "I got a feeling about this. The guy called too many times, all the way from Haiti. And it's not just that."

"No?"

"It's also Teresa. Her dream. She saw a woman getting buried? Maybe that woman wasn't our daughter or you. Maybe it was the maid, buried in Haiti."

Oh God. "D', are you listening to yourself? You sound crazy—"

"I'm serious, Mo. I know you don't put stock in the spiritual."

"I think you're effing losing it."

"Mock me all you want. I've got a feeling about this."

A feeling? "So, you're saying you think the guy from Haiti is for real? And the maid is his dead fiancée? That's absurd." I gaped at him.

He shrugged. "I don't know what I'm saying. I've just got a feeling. Over the years, I've learned you got to trust your gut."

"Your gut." Great. I'd worked with D' for six years. His "gut" was accurate about fifty percent of the time. Same odds as a coin toss.

"Go on, Mo. Make fun of me. But I'll bet you fifty bucks that Haitian guy isn't just some crackpot. He's connected to this somehow." He pulled into the driveway of The Ritz Carlton.

Before I could reply, the doorman stepped over to let me out of the car. For the second time in half an hour, I shivered with chills.

Chapter 14

Lance Granger was lanky, deeply tanned, wearing tight jeans and a V-neck sweater that revealed a smooth, probably waxed chest. He was in his mid 30s, had a couple days' growth of fashionable golden stubble. He opened the door to his suite at the Ritz and ran a hand through unwashed light brown hair. His eyes were gray, outlined in raw red.

"Come in, come in." He led us into the sitting room. "Have a seat. Have a seat."

We sat. I took a love seat, D'Angelo a wingback.

"Coffee?" Lance looked at me, then D'. "Coffee?"

Why was he repeating himself? D' shot me a "don't ask me" look. We declined coffee. Lance sat on a sofa, crossed his legs, uncrossed them, crossed them again. His eyes darted around. His hands traced paths through his hair.

D'Angelo started by expressing our sorrow for his loss.

Lance leaned forward, then back against the cushions. "I just talked to them."

We waited, but he didn't say it twice. Instead, he stopped talking and stared at air, his mouth half open.

"You just talked to them," I repeated it for him.

"Yes." He turned my way. "Yes."

"And when was that?" D'Angelo asked.

It had been around ten, the night before they'd been found. He'd talked to his father, suggesting that they visit him in South Beach. He'd wanted them to get away, since they'd been so tense. Arguing a lot.

Really? "More than usual?"

"More?" He smirked. "Detective, I don't think that would be possible. My parents bickered constantly. Constantly. But, yes. Lately, since their friends' murders, their arguments were more heated. They'd been close with Sylvia Blake and J. Steven Richards. I assume you know what happened to them—the murders." He paused, waiting for us to nod. "But fighting? My mother and father considered it a sport. And they were both quite adept at it—Masters level ball busters."

D' and I glanced at each other. Was it possible that the Grangers weren't the perfect couple after all?

"Who could do this?" Lance's voice was ragged. "And why? Why would somebody kill them?"

D'Angelo waited a beat, leaned toward Lance. "That's what we're trying to find out, son."

Son? Wow. Their eyes met. They were bonding. For once, D'Angelo wasn't hurrying. He was being patient, paternal. Using a soothing tone. I felt out of place, like an intruder. Eventually, the tender moment ended, and the men sat back and straightened up. Lance cleared his throat.

I asked Lance what his mother had told him about Sylvia Blake's murder.

"Why? Is that relevant?" He looked at the ceiling, then at me. "Oh, obviously. You think the same guy killed all of them."

I told him I didn't know, was simply gathering information.

"Well, Sylvia's death positively destroyed mother," he said. "Actually, father too. Sylvia was father's secretary and one of mother's dearest friends, even though mother had long intimated that Sylvia was—How should I put this? A slut?" Lance's eyes twinkled for a nano-second. "Mother said Sylvia made 'bad choices'. In other words, she slept around. With men she shouldn't have."

"What men?"

Lance glanced at me, answered D'Angelo. "Dangerous men. Unscrupulous men. Powerful, abusive men. Married men. I don't know. Mother said Sylvia was all about impulse. She had no boundaries or morals."

Nice way to refer to your best friend. I asked if Lance thought that J. Steven Richards might have been one of Sylvia's men.

"Oh." His eyes widened. "Interesting. You think that's why they were killed? Because of an affair?"

I tilted my head. "Do you?"

"Do I?" His hand went back to his hair, pushed through it again. "Let me think about that. You see I'd assumed J. Steven got killed because of one of his shady high-profile cases. Because who would care if he was boffing Sylvia? According to mother, everybody was boffing Sylvia. Unless that's the point—" He straightened up, gesturing. "Let's say Sylvia and J. Steven were sharing pillow talk—That could be it! The lawyer shared confidential information with Sylvia and she blabbed it—or threatened to. So, somebody shut both of them up."

Lance was on a roll. But he stopped, shook his head. "But, no. That doesn't explain my parents. Whatever did or didn't happen between J. Steven and Sylvia wouldn't have involved them—Especially not mother." He stared at the carpet, a hand resting on his head. "Who would kill them? Who would kill them?"

We waited a moment. "Lance," I tried a new topic. "Do you know this woman?" I held out a photo of Vanessa.

He took the picture. Looked at it. "Who is she?"

Apparently, he hadn't been in town long enough to see a paper or watch the news. That face had been splashed everywhere.

"Did your parents have a maid?" D'Angelo asked.

Lance shrugged. "I assume so. Is that who this is? Their maid?"

"We hoped you could tell us."

Lance handed the photo back to me. "Afraid not. I'm not acquainted with their help. I've lived in Florida for years. When I visit, I need my space, so I stay here in the hotel."

"You wouldn't know if they'd hired anyone from, say, Haiti?" D' asked.

I shot him a glare—he made a slight shrug.

"No idea. No idea."

"So," I persisted, "you have no idea why that woman would be in your parents' house?"

"Well, if she was in their house, then I'd assume she's the maid."

I didn't answer, just met his eyes.

His darted away. He crossed his legs and folded his arms. "Why don't you ask her?" He looked from me to D'Angelo. Waited. Looked from D'Angelo to me. "Unless—Oh God. Oh God. Is she dead, too? Is she dead, too?"

D'Angelo's knee began bouncing. He'd been in one place too long.

"No," I assured him, "she's not dead—"

"But wait," Lance sat forward, held up an arm. "She was in the house? During the murders? Is that what you're saying? Because if she was—If she was, she might have seen what happened. She might have seen—"

"We're on it, son." D'Angelo stood. His hand found his pocket, started jiggling coins. "So, we won't take more of your time right now." He asked if Lance had family and friends around, if there were people, we could contact for him. Lance assured us that his parents had been so loved by so many that he was being deluged with visitors, invitations, phone calls. His father's surviving partners were coming over. He'd heard from the mayor, judges. News reporters. His parents' priest. A list too long to recite.

As we walked to the door, he asked when he could get into his parents' house, when he could bury them. D'Angelo said we'd let him know.

At the door, Lance leaned against the doorframe, slouching, hugging himself like a frightened little boy.

"We'll be in touch," D' shook his hand, met his eyes.

"Thanks for coming by," he said. As we headed toward the elevator, we heard him again. "Thanks for coming by."

Chapter 15

The news that day continued to be all about the Grangers' murders, and the photo of Vanessa, the unknown woman who was probably the maid, once more splashed across the front pages of both the *Inquirer* and the *Daily News*. Uniformed officers had canvassed the Grangers' neighborhood but nobody recognized her face.

D' was intrigued by the caller from Haiti, but still suspected that Vanessa had killed her employers. On our way back to the Roundhouse, he went with Lance's theory.

"We might have two separate killers, Mo. Someone might have done Sylvia and J. Steven for reasons connected to a legal matter. And someone else, namely the maid, might have killed the Grangers. I think she did it. Nothing else made sense."

"I don't know," I argued. "At first, you thought it was all the same guy."

"Now, I don't think so."

"But maybe Vanessa just found the bodies."

"Mo. She was the only one there who wasn't dead. And her clothes were covered with blood."

"Maybe because she was trying to to help them."

"And didn't call police?"

"Because, like we said, she's probably an illegal. And if she's illegal, she'd be afraid to call. Besides, she wasn't able to talk—You saw her."

"Fine. So why did she try to clean the murder weapons?"

The cleaver and knife had been retrieved from the dishwasher and tested. Indeed, blood from both victims had been found on each. They had likely been the murder weapons.

I didn't have an answer for him. Maybe cleaning was just her automatic reflexive response to a mess. Maybe she'd picked up the weapons to clean them without thinking, the same way she'd put her clothing into the washing machine.

Or maybe he was right that Vanessa had killed the Grangers and had been washing up, trying to get rid of evidence.

I pictured her committing the murders. Coming into Dixon's study. Running at him so he wouldn't have time to react, swinging the cleaver at his neck with all her strength.

It would have taken all her strength, for sure, to cause that wound.

And Judith Granger? The maid would have attacked her in the kitchen, maybe while pretending to wash dishes. She'd have turned the knife on her savagely, unexpectedly. Would have chased her, jabbing and swiping.

And then, after she'd killed them, she'd have dragged Judith Granger into the study, methodically changed into clean clothes, run a load of wash, put the weapons into the dishwasher, and hidden in the pantry?

"It makes no sense," I said to D. "Those murders took strength and passion. They were brutal, personal. But when we found Vanessa, she was completely passive."

"Vanessa. So, we're sticking with that?"

"Until we have something better."

"What about the dead Haitian woman? What was her name? You can call her that."

I ignored him. "My point is that she wasn't either strong or passionate. She was physically limp and emotionally flat. And she still is. She barely talks. She sits without moving hour after hour, staring at walls. She has to be spoon fed. How could a woman like that have committed—"

"I don't know, Mo," he turned into the Roundhouse lot. "But there's nobody else. So, unless we find another suspect, she's it."

I sputtered. "So, if the only one in the house was a dog, you'd think the dog killed them?"

"What's with you, Mo? Why are you so testy?" D'Angelo turned off the ignition, faced me.

Testy? I got out of the car, slammed the door. Was I testy? Maybe. Probably. Okay, yes. I must be overtired.

"Think about what I said before, Mo. Let Teresa fix you up. You need a guy."

Really? I was "testy" so that meant that I needed a guy? I simmered, glaring at him.

"I get it, Mo. You have needs like anyone else. Going too long without someone, well—"

I punched his arm, hard. "I swear I ought to file harassment charges."

He laughed. On the way inside, we stopped at the lunch truck and got coffees.

"Hey, Mo," D' asked. "What kind of coffee beans do Zombies like?"

I shook my head.

"Human beans." He grinned, proud of himself. "I made that up."

I took my coffee and walked away, leaving D' to pay. He meant well, was trying to lighten my mood. But I couldn't stop thinking of Vanessa. I pictured her huddled in the pantry. Except for a large scar on her forearm and chapped skin on her fingers, her hands and arms had been pristine. Uninjured.

And I wondered: If she'd repeatedly stabbed Judith Granger, how had she managed not to cut herself even once? Had she worn gloves? I couldn't imagine her being that methodical. Maybe I just didn't want to believe that she'd done it.

I headed to elevator, wondering if more calls had come in. Maybe someone had identified her, providing her real name. In a way, I hoped not. I liked 'Vanessa.' It suited her.

Chapter 16

A man appears from the green wall, moves closer, his eyes on her as if she is a delicacy to be devoured. She recognizes his voice. She's heard it before, though she is not sure how many times or exactly when. Again, his voice declares his name and says he is there to help her, that she can trust him. That she is safe.

She has the urge to laugh out loud. How absurd he is. Does the man really believe he can help her? That he can keep her safe? Can he not see the darkness swirling around her, holding onto her, darting out towards his head? Is he blind?

She stares at black tentacles coiling from her body toward his head. She holds still, barely breathing, imagining his eyes bleeding, punctured by the creature that has hold of her. As if oblivious of danger, his voice keeps on, a rhythmic sound, not deep like Dixon Granger's. No, it is higher, raspier. A thinner tone.

You can keep it with you, the voice says. *Use it to draw. Or to write down your thoughts. Whatever you want.*

His lips stretch into a smile, show even, white teeth. The edges of his face fade, leaving only the teeth, shiny and sparkling. Unease slides through her. She tries to remember the word for it—this unease has a name. M. Roger steps before her, scolding. She should have studied better, he scowls. She should remember his vocabulary lessons.

This way, the voice says, *you won't have to wait for me to visit. Whenever you want, you can put your thoughts here. Your memories. Your feelings. What you see in your mind. You can keep it here until I see you again.*

She glances at his hands, sees what he holds. She recognizes it. It is the same kind of notebook she used at the school. Black binding, a black and white pattern on the cover. Inside the pages are marked by wide blue lines. Without effort, clear and crisp, a memory comes to her. The voice of M. Roger: *Ecrivez vos reponses.*

Again, unease washes her bones.

"*This book is yours to keep. Use it. Write in it.*"

Is this a command?

The man is standing. Ready to leave. His face is still dim, and his smile is gone. Lips cover his teeth. She looks down, avoiding the probing rays of his eyes.

Finally, he disappears through the slit in the green. She is alone again with silence. With nothing. With whispers and dots. The notebook. And a fat pen, too thick to cut with.

She watches these objects, solid and defined, until the black and white designs on the notebook cover begin to dance, daring her to catch them, and, as they twirl and spin, she recalls the word for her unease. Peur. M. Roger nods, yes. Very good. Peur, in French.

In English, fear.

Chapter 17

Tuesday night, driving home, I thought of my mother. Remembered her in the television room of her nursing home, propped up in a wheel chair. Asking me my name.

"Mo," I told her. "It's Mo, mom."

"Mo." She repeated it thoughtfully. "I once had a friend by that name."

By the end, she'd had no idea who anyone was. Not even herself. Kind of like Vanessa.

I drove through a red light. Reminded myself that, unlike my mother, at least Vanessa had hope. Dr. Vogel's tests might reveal what was wrong with her, and her memory might come back. Or her family might identify her—over fifty calls had come in so far, not counting the ones from that guy in Haiti.

Who was she? How come no one recognized her? Could she be so isolated that she had nobody—not a single friend or relation? Even illegals had a community, didn't they?

I drove along Vine Street, picturing her in the tiny pantry, staring with vacant eyes. Feeling myself getting lost in them.

I pulled up to my building, into my parking spot. Home.

I sat in the car, not moving. Watching the dark sky, the moon peeking between tree branches. My dashboard. The streetlights. The front door to my building.

Inside, my condo would be dark and empty.

Maybe I should get a cat.

My stomach growled, reminding me that I hadn't gone to the market, had nothing for dinner.

D'Angelo's voice popped into my head. "You need to get out and meet people, Mo."

Fine. So, I'd join the Y, take a spinning class.

"You need a guy," he said.

Right. I'd tried that. It hadn't worked out well.

"You gonna let your divorce ruin your whole life? Open up. Meet new people. Join the human race."

As if on cue, a Jeep pulled into the lot. A couple got out, carrying groceries. Laughing. Having a great time. Probably they'd cook up some pasta, cuddle up in front of the tube, make passionate love, fall asleep in each other's arms—

Good God, what was wrong with me? What did I care what these people did or didn't do? I got out of the car, went into my condo. Poured some wine into a glass that had been a wedding gift. Sat on the sofa my ex and I had picked out together. Imagined him stretched out, pleading for a foot rub.

I swallowed wine. Poured more. D' was right. I needed to take charge of my life. Make a plan. Get out there and meet people. Tomorrow, I'd join a gym. Get my hair cut. Call a girlfriend—Not necessarily Evie. I'd call Lindsay or Sharon. We'd go to a few bars. And tonight—this very night, I'd join that dating site.

Good.

I turned on the television. For once, the screen showed something other than the Grangers. About nine o'clock, with my wine bottle almost empty, I ordered a Greek salad from the pizza place. Then I sat at the computer and punched up my dating profile.

I put a check beside "Law Enforcement," and moved on to the next question. Income level. Really?

I trekked on, answering questions, reaching out through cyberspace to lonely strangers. It wasn't until around eleven, when I was lying in bed, that I thought again of Vanessa. Pictured her alone in her hospital room, unknown, neither missed nor recognized. Falling asleep, I assured myself that she and I were not alike. I had intact memories, a career, friends. She and I had nothing in common, apart from being women alone.

Chapter 18

First thing Wednesday, I called Dr. Vogel.

He reported that his patient seemed to be slowly emerging from her confused state. That, although he hadn't yet identified a substance in her system, he was increasingly convinced that she'd been drugged and suspected he knew which drug it might be. Something with a long name that I didn't retain since he was just theorizing. He believed that with time, the drugs would wear off, and she would be clearer. She wasn't conversational yet, but he thought she would be soon. And meantime, he'd given her a blank book in which to write. So far, she'd written only one word: Peur. The French word for fear.

Fear.

What was she afraid of? Being murdered like the Grangers? Being found by their killer? Being caught? What had frightened her so terribly that she'd retreated into herself to hide?

D'Angelo was off testifying in court for another case, so I was alone, thinking about fear as I drove out to Bryn Mawr to talk to Susan Richards, J. Steven's widow.

Susan was petite, around fifty. Her hair was styled short, colored chestnut to hide the gray. Her eyebrows were defined and dark, dramatic over gray eyes. She wore no makeup.

We sat in her Main Line living room, surrounded by abstract oil paintings. Her sweater was the same dark green as the floral-patterned sofa. We sipped tea from rose patterned porcelain cups.

"Dixon Granger murdered my husband," she said it flatly, without venom.

Her fingers were slender, nails filed square, painted translucent cream. She still wore her elaborate diamond ring set.

"J was in the process of dissolving the law firm. Dixon was furious that J was going to take his clients with him. Fortunately for Dixon, J was killed before he could do so." She took a demure sip. Looked at me without emotion.

"So, you believe your husband was killed to prevent him from dissolving the partnership."

She put her teacup down. Lifted the teapot, poured a refill. Took so much time before replying that I almost repeated myself. Her perfume was floral, heavy. Made my nose itch.

"No, Detective." She abandoned the tea and folded her hands on her lap. Met my eyes with hers. "I've already told the police all of this. But I'll go over it a hundred times if it helps. J's desire to leave the law firm had little to do with his murder. Granger killed him for other reasons."

She took a moment, couple of deep breaths.

I waited.

She leaned forward, as if confiding. Looked around as if someone might hear. "In the months before his death," she lowered her voice, "my husband told me several times that he wanted nothing more to do with Dixon Granger or his wife. He was finished with them. J wouldn't tell me why, only that he'd found out something about Dixon that he couldn't tolerate. Something too heinous to tell even me."

Heinous?

Susan swallowed. Took another breath. "I pressed him but he absolutely would not talk about it. I assumed that Dixon had gotten involved in something illegal that could contaminate my husband and the firm. Maybe he'd bribed judges or politicians. Or smuggled drugs or weapons. Stolen art or artifacts. After all, Dixon handled many international cases, and he and his wife were always traveling abroad, especially to the Caribbean where, I understand, there's a lot of smuggling and drug activity. I never did find out for sure what it was. But a month after he found out about whatever it was and broke ties with Dixon, J was dead."

I let that thought linger, placed my cup on the tray. Hadn't heard about this estrangement before. "Mrs. Richards, did you mention this to the detectives investigating your husband's death?"

She nodded. "Of course. I told them I thought Dixon Granger was behind J's death. But I suppose they assumed that Dixon was above suspicion. He was—Well, he was Dixon Granger."

I nodded. Thanked her. Turned down a second cup of tea. Asked her if she knew anything about Sylvia Blake's death.

She looked away, stiffened. "Of course not. Why would I?"

I didn't say anything, let my question hover.

"I don't think there's any relationship between their murders, detective. Sylvia Blake had her own set of enemies."

I asked her to explain. Susan shifted her position, rearranged her legs. "I shouldn't really say. It's only gossip. But Sylvia—She was said to be something of a manipulative whore. Sleeping with married men, even the husbands of her so-called friends. She wasn't particularly discreet about it either."

I swallowed, thought I recognized the bristle of a wounded spouse. Recalled Lance Granger sharing a similar view of Sylvia. "Do you know who these married men were?"

Her mouth opened, then closed. Her hands clasped each other. "No. Of course not."

Bull. She knew. "Even rumors?"

"I don't have specific names. Well, except for Dixon. Everyone knew about that."

"Sylvia Blake was having an affair with Dixon Granger?"

"Of course. For years, off and on."

Wow. "But I understood that Judith Granger and Sylvia Blake were close friends."

Susan's mouth twisted into a strained smile. She tilted her head. "Yes."

"Did Mrs. Granger know about the affair?"

"I can only assume so." Her hand went to her throat. "But sometimes, wives of powerful men—Well, we see what we wish to. Denial is a wonderful mental tool." She cleared her throat. "Let's just say that lots of people wanted to kill Sylvia."

I wanted a list of names. Specific rumors. But Susan Richards claimed ignorance, would offer none.

"What about your own husband, Mrs. Richards?"

"Excuse me?" Her eyes were ice picks.

I knew how it felt to confront a husband's infidelity, so I worded my question carefully, "Did Sylvia have designs on him?"

"If she did, J. Steven would have none of it. He wasn't the kind."

Did her eyes widen? Did her voice crack a bit? I wasn't sure. But her animosity for Sylvia was too heated to be fueled by gossip alone. My question had hit a nerve.

I thanked her for her time, said the usual bit about contacting me if she thought of anything else. Asked if the Grangers had had a live-in maid. Susan Richards had no idea, and she didn't recognize the photo of Vanessa.

She walked me to the door. "I don't know who killed the Grangers, Detective," she said. "But I am convinced that Dixon was so desperate to silence J. Steven that he killed him. If you find out what the atrocious secret my husband knew," she nodded at a huge painting in the foyer, "I'll bet you that Jackson Pollock that it'll take you straight to the Grangers' murderer."

Chapter 19

At noon, D'Angelo and I met at Johnny Rockets for a burger. Sat at a booth near the window. Ordered without looking at menus. He was pissed off about court, saying what he wished would happen to the defense attorney.

"Jerk-off can't make a case, so he tries to discredit the investigating officers, specifically, yours truly." He went on, repeating the questions and answers. Mocking the attorney. "Asshole tried to make me look incompetent."

"Probably backfired," I assured him.

"You think?"

I didn't have a clue. But the court session was over. And there was nothing either of us could do about how D' had come across. "You did your job. You conducted a clean and thorough investigation. If the lawyer went after you instead of the evidence, it just shows how desperate he is."

D'Angelo chomped on a French fry, considering what I'd said. "Lawyers," he muttered. "Whatever you say, they twist it." He expounded about the ethics of that.

I looked around. The booth behind ours was empty. The counter only about half full. Nobody was near enough to hear us. When D' quieted down enough to listen, I told him about my visit with Susan Richards.

"If she was right about Granger having some dark terrible secret, that secret might be what got him killed." I took a sip of my milkshake. It was too thick to pull through the straw. Needed to sit awhile and melt.

He shook his head, talked with his mouth full of cheeseburger. "So, you're saying someone offed the Grangers because of the same secret that Richards found out about?"

"Maybe. If it was so appalling that it caused J. Steven to dissolve the law firm, and so dangerous to Granger that he'd kill J. Steven to keep him quiet, it might be lethal enough to get the Grangers killed."

"And Sylvia Blake?"

I wiped ketchup off my mouth. Chewed. Thought. Swallowed. "If Sylvia Blake was sleeping with Granger or Richards, there might have been pillow talk. Maybe she found out about the secret, too."

"So, your theory is that anybody and everybody who knew about this alleged secret got whacked?" He sounded as if the idea were preposterous.

"Maybe. Why not? Depends what the secret was."

"If there even was a secret. Because maybe there wasn't. Maybe Susan Richards was just blowing hot air."

What? "Why would she do that?" My fingers were greasy. So was my napkin. I reached for another from the container. About a dozen popped out, and spewed across the table.

"Okay. Good question." D'Angelo pushed the extra napkins aside. "Here's another theory. Someone killed Sylvia for banging her husband. Then that same someone killed her husband for banging Sylvia. Maybe those two deaths have nothing to do with the Grangers' murders, but the killer is using the Grangers' murders as a way to divert attention from herself."

I tried to picture it: Susan Richards killing people. Susan Richards, with her demure posture, her smooth hands folded primly on her lap. Could those soft skinned, delicate hands have plunged knives into flesh, slitting throats, spilling blood, ending lives? Was Susan Richards passionate enough to commit murder?

I wasn't sure. But I'd learned that, when pushed far enough, even the gentlest of people could kill. And I knew the rage of discovering a cheating spouse. Maybe D'Angelo was right, and Susan Richards had killed her husband and his lover. Maybe those two murders had nothing to do with the Grangers.

"You might be right." I played with a pickle slice. "But we can't ignore what Mrs. Richards said. We have to look at the possibility that Granger had a secret, and that it connects the cases." My milkshake had melted enough to drink. I picked up the glass, sucked on the straw.

D'Angelo scoffed. "You'll have us running in circles, Mo. I don't see what any of this has to do with the suspect we already have."

"So, Vanessa's our suspect now?" I put the glass down, reached for the check. "You're ahead of yourself again, D'."

He put his hands up, tried to make an innocent face. Innocent didn't work on D'Angelo's features, made him look surprised, as if his lunch was about to come back up. My phone beeped. I gave D'Angelo the bill and some cash. He paid while I took the call. It was Dr. Vogel. He had news.

Chapter 20

In the last few hours, his patient had made incredible progress. She still wasn't talking much, but she'd been writing in her notebook. Drawing more than writing. Vogel said we could come by if we wished, but so far the images she'd sketched were vague outlines of people. Still, it was exciting. She was emerging from her silence, obeying nurses, even eating on her own. A day ago, he would never have predicted that she'd have come so far. He was eager to see what would appear on the pages.

While Vogel talked, D'Angelo and I left the restaurant, stood on the corner of 5th and South, surrounded by traffic and swarming pedestrians. D' was antsy, wanting to walk. I covered my free ear, straining to hear Dr. Vogel on my cell while chasing D' up the street.

"Has she said anything?" I asked.

It was noisy. I thought Vogel said, "Yes."

"What was it?" Why was he making me ask? "What did she say?"

"I just told you," he sounded impatient. "She said, 'death.'"

Oh. I'd misheard. "Death?" I looked at D'Angelo, who was three steps ahead. "Was she talking about the murders?"

"We can't be sure. You see, from time to time, I've been asking her questions. For example, I ask if she knows where she is. I ask her name. She doesn't reply. But earlier, I asked if she remembered what had happened at the Grangers' house. She was quiet for a while, so I thought that, as usual, she wasn't going to answer. Then, very distinctly, she said, 'Death.'"

Death.

Correct answer. But what did it mean? Had she seen the murders? Heard them? Committed them?

THE WOMAN IN THE CUPBOARD 61

I thanked Dr. Vogel for calling and told him we'd like to come by to see the notebook. He suggested that we wait until she wrote something of substance.

I began to say that what seemed irrelevant to him might be significant to us, but he interrupted. "I don't want her to feel pressured, Detective. She's fragile."

I explained that she wouldn't need to know we were there. We could look at her notebook while she was out of the room. When he hedged, I insisted, told him we were on our way.

D'Angelo by now was half a block ahead of me. I hurried to catch up, dashing around pedestrians, a parking kiosk, a light post, a bike rack, and a newspaper stand. I slowed and did a double take, recognizing the face on the front page. Days after the murders, the Grangers and Vanessa the mystery woman were still a top story.

My phone rang again. It was Reynolds.

"More calls have come in. But I thought you'd want to know about one, Mo," he said. "Remember Kenny Wadd?"

"Who?"

"The guy from Haiti."

Oh, right. The one who claimed that Vanessa was his dead fiancée. "What about him?" I hurried to catch up with D'Angelo. What was his hurry? Why couldn't he slow down and wait for me?

"He called again. Insisted on talking to you."

The guy was awfully persistent. "He's a wacko, Reynolds. Be nice but get rid of him."

"Believe me, I've tried. Like about a dozen times. But he won't give up. He says he needs to talk to the detective in charge."

Fine. I'd have to get rid of the guy myself. "Forward his next call to me. I'll talk to him."

I caught up to D', grabbed his arm, pulled him to slow him down.

"Might not be necessary," Reynolds said. "The guy says he's flying into Philadelphia."

"What?"

"Apparently, he's coming to the Roundhouse to see you tomorrow. I told him I didn't know your schedule, but he said if you're not in, he'll wait."

Wait, the guy was coming all the way from Haiti? To talk about his long dead fiancée? The world was full of nut jobs.

Including my partner. D' had hurried ahead again. I rushed after him, trying to catch up.

Chapter 21

She's been told to write, and so she is writing.

Her hand is stiff holding the pen, as if unaccustomed to this type of task. She watches it pass along the line on the paper, slowly forming letters, leaving trails of ink.

She sits for a time between sentences, searching but finding no words for what she wants to say. If there are words, she has forgotten them.

A lot must have been lost. She tries to see beyond her blankness to remember a time before, but images appear only briefly then shrivel as in fire. As fast as they come, they are gone.

She spends time in gaps. She watches the rough grout lines between the tiles until they widen and grow, and she wanders in their vast dark pathways where no one else can enter.

She thinks she's been in this green-walled place for several days. Maybe longer, maybe not so long. There is no way to be sure. She is aware only of moments. The man Dr. Vogel tells her what she must do: She must eat. She must bathe. She must write down her thoughts. And so, she pays attention to meals being brought into the room, food being swallowed. Warm water flowing over her, towels wrapping around her. Her hand holding the pen, writing words. There is no order of what happens. No first and second and third. She cannot even be sure that she hasn't imagined this man's voice, or that any of these moments has occurred.

But the voice of the man Dr. Vogel has told her that he is the one in charge of her. He has told her to write down what she remembers. She holds the pen over the paper and looks at the tiles on the floor. She wanders the gaps, searching for words that come in small clumps. Until one morning, when they come in spurts, and she hurries to write before she forgets what she has to say, because she doesn't know where her clarity has come from or how long it will last.

And so, she begins. *Dr. Vogel*, she writes. *When you read it, I doubt you will believe what I write here. But although you will scoff, I must begin by explaining the only truth of which I am certain, which is this: I am no longer a living person. I was in fact murdered. Maybe it happened just days ago. Or maybe years.*

And so, as I write, it is as if I am writing about someone else. A person who was but is no longer. Even now, in this green room, I wait for commands from my bokor. Maybe you don't know what a bokor is? The bokor is the one who commands my soul, the one I must obey. But the people to whom my bokor entrusted me are no more, and you, Dr. Vogel, have told me you are now in charge. And so, I must obey you until the bokor sends new instructions.

You tell me to write down my thoughts, even though they are unclear. I have only images. Fleeting, like flickers of light. A child in the arms of loving parents. A child among sisters and brothers. A child with a name. At times I see bright sun on white flowing dresses, skirts twirling in the heat. Earlier, as clearly as in a photograph, I saw a small village school, children in their seats. A teacher holding a book. As I wrote those last words, an image came to mind of a stark white church, voices singing on Sunday morning. Oh, and now I remember something else: A boy. And a name. The name is Kenny.

She has to stop after writing the name. Her hand aches from holding the pen so tightly. Her head throbs from recalling so much. She sits motionless with her eyes closed, recovering. The name Kenny has come at her unexpectedly like a gust of hot wind. It sears her chest, saps her strength. Kenny. She whispers the name again and again, and it gives her both peace and terrible, inconsolable pain. No, not pain. The feeling is worse than pain. Kenny. Kenny. She stops repeating it and, after a rest, picks up the pen and, as Dr. Vogel has instructed, begins again.

Kenny. I shudder at this name. It is the sound of the ground opening under me so that I am falling into a dark hole, swallowed by the earth. About to be buried. It is the name on my tongue as, looking up from the hole, I see a woman standing at the edge, looking down at me. She is small and thin with spidery fingers and a white coating glowing on one eye. Is she blind? Can she see me? Kenny. I breathe the name. The woman lifts her hand, and it is trembling.

Or no. Her hand is steady. The hand that is trembling is not hers, but mine.

Chapter 22

Our meeting with Dr. Vogel wasn't really a meeting. He shoved a file at me, said he had a meeting to attend and had to run. "These are copies." He was abrupt. "I could have faxed them and saved you the trip."

"We were hoping to talk."

He glanced at his watch. "I updated you on the phone. There's nothing else significant, just what's in there."

I opened the file, glanced down, saw the first line. "I was told to write, and so I am writing."

"What she's written is pretty strange. But she's clearly surfacing. Bits and pieces of memory are coming back." He backed away.

"Anything in there about the murders?" D' asked.

"Not directly. Read it. She's not entirely coherent. But nothing in those pages either supports or refutes that she has knowledge of what happened."

Fine. I asked if he'd gotten more test results. He said, tersely, that if he had, we'd have been told. And then he hurried away. D' pushed the elevator button and in a few seconds, we were back downstairs.

In the car, D' got a phone call. While he talked, I looked at the pages, began to read. Saw a line that said, "I am no longer a living person." Swallowed. Reread it.

"D', you gotta see this—She mentions the name 'Kenny.' That's the name of the guy from Haiti."

"Yeah?" He shoved his phone into his pocket as he wove through traffic.

I scanned the pages. "She writes about being buried. D'—This is nuts. I think she's describing her own funeral. And he said she was dead."

"Wait, her what?" D' swerved, looking at me. "Shit, Mo. Her funeral? That's too weird—That's exactly what Teresa dreamed about—A young girl getting buried."

I wasn't interested in Teresa's dreams. I read on. "Listen to this, D'. 'I am no longer a living person. I was in fact murdered.'" Despite their absurdity, the words sent a tickle rippling up my neck.

D' grinned and let out a whistle. "She was murdered? So, she's not just any normal walking dead person?"

He wasn't taking her claim the slightest bit seriously. "You got to read this for yourself." I stared at the page.

"Come on, Mo. Clearly, she's trying to get off a murder charge, setting things up to claim mental illness." He dismissed the writing and went on about Teresa's dreams, her amazing clairvoyance all the way back to the Roundhouse.

I was glad to get to my desk, to have a chance to organize my notes and thoughts, but Sgt. Rodriguez was waiting for us.

"There's someone here to see you, detectives."

Who? I followed his gaze. Saw a slender middle-aged woman draped in layers of purple fabric, seated beside the water cooler. When she saw us looking at her, she stood and hurried our way, a mass of flowing purple.

Chapter 23

"She says she's a friend of the Grangers," Rodriguez began to fill us in, but the woman was already upon us, swooping like a falcon.

"Detective D'Angelo?" she eyed D'. "I'm Alexandra Lambert," she extended a hand decorated with three large gem stone rings. Bracelets jingled when she moved her arm.

D' introduced me, and we shook. Her grip was confident. Powerful but bony. With my eyes closed, except for the cloud of Chanel #5, I'd have guessed the hand belonged to an old man, a judge or senator.

We went to my desk.

"How can we help you?" I offered her a seat.

The woman didn't sit. She looked around the open office, purple lips frowning at the detectives at their desks. "Can we talk privately?"

D'Angelo shot me an "uh oh" look. "Let's step into an interrogation room." He shoved his hands into his pockets, already jangling coins.

The table and chairs were bolted to the floor. The walls were the color of old dill pickles. Alexandra Lambert seemed oblivious, swept in with her skirts flowing, and took a seat.

"Sgt. Rodriguez says you said you had information about the Grangers." D'Angelo began.

"Yes." She folded her hands. Her knuckles were large, the skin veined and dotted with liver spots. "They were dear friends." She paused, took a kerchief from her purse. Dabbed her heavily mascaraed and purple shadowed eyes. When she took the cloth away, it was stained with flesh-toned foundation, no tears.

I glanced at D. Was she for real?

"Can we get you something to drink, Mrs. Lambert? Coffee? A soda?"

THE WOMAN IN THE CUPBOARD 69

She shook her head. "No. Sorry to be so emotional. You see I'm stunned by this whole affair. Simply can't absorb it." She sniffed, took a breath. "I was away. But I saw the news—even out of the country, cable stations carry everything. I came back as soon as I heard."

"Where were you?" I wasn't sure why I asked.

"Oh. Just the Caribbean."

Just?

"In fact," she smiled briefly, "that's where I first met the Grangers. Nine or ten years ago, in Haiti. The trip when I hired Kadia and they hired Ja Vala."

Ja Vala? Wait. I heard that name before. I bit my lip, thinking, and remembered. The phone call from Haiti, the guy claiming Vanessa was his dead fiancee. I'd have to check my notes, but I was sure he'd used that name. "Excuse me." She'd gone on talking, but I interrupted. "Who did you say the Grangers hired?"

She looked from D to me. "Ja Vala. Their maid."

So, Vanessa's real name was Ja Vala, the same as the dead Haitian woman's?

D'Angelo's eyes were popping. "So, you know their maid?"

"Of course, I know her." Mrs. Lambert straightened her back, leaned forward. "You can't imagine how upsetting it was to see her picture on the news, poor darling. The news said she hasn't spoken since the murders. Well, who could expect her to? She must be in terrible shock. She loved them, and they loved her like family. Such a tragedy. Tell me, where is she? Is she all right? I'm terribly concerned about her."

D and I looked at each other. His look said he was passing the questions to me.

"Ja Vala." I repeated it. "You're certain that that's her name?"

"Of course, I'm certain," she nodded. "It's Haitian. Beautiful, isn't it? Ja means 'fiery,' and Vala means 'chosen.' Her last name is

French. Boudin. So musical. Ja Vala Boudin." She said it slowly with a lilt.

D'Angelo was writing it all down.

"Wait, you mean you don't even know her name?" Alexandra Lambert sounded appalled.

"She hasn't talked much," I said.

"But surely someone else has told you."

I didn't answer, didn't offer information about what others had or hadn't told us. "What was it you came to tell us, Mrs. Lambert?"

"Well actually, I came out of concern for dear Ja Vala. Over the years, with darling Kadia coming from the same country, we've become very close. So, of course, I want to visit her and let her know she's not alone. Make sure she's okay."

D'Angelo uncrossed his legs, leaned back in his chair. "Sorry, ma'am. She can't have visitors."

"You're joking." Her hands folded on the table. Her nails wore purple polish.

"No, Ma'am."

"But that's absurd. No visitors? For goodness sakes why not?" Now a hand went to her throat, bracelets jangling.

"She's hospitalized, Mrs. Lambert."

"Hospitalized? Is she hurt?"

"That's confidential, ma'am."

"Why? That's absurd. What hospital is she in?"

"That's confidential as well."

"Confidential?" The hand left her throat. Her eyebrows shot up. "Does she have a lawyer? Certainly, her lawyer must know where she is."

"She isn't ready for a lawyer—"

"What do you mean 'not ready?' The poor child has rights. The police can't keep her hidden, locked away from people who care about her—"

"Actually, it was her doctor who decided she shouldn't have visitors, Ma'am."

"Why not? For God sakes, that's criminal. You're keeping her in isolation."

"No, Ma'am. She's under a doctor's care and being treated by excellent professionals." D'Angelo crossed his arms, kept his eyes locked with hers.

"Really?" she huffed. "Exactly who are these so-called professionals?"

"We're not at liberty to divulge their names, Ma'am."

"That's not acceptable. Tell me who her doctor is. I insist that I talk to him."

Neither of us said anything. We met her glares calmly, with steady eyes.

Finally, she looked away, took a breath. Began again more calmly. "Look, I can be of help. It will do Ja Vala good to see familiar faces and be visited by friends. She'll recover faster."

There was a moment of silence. Then D'Angelo stood, indicating that the meeting was over. "Thank you for coming in, Ms. Lambert. Leave us your contact information, and when Ja Vala's doctor says it's all right for her to have visitors, we'll call you."

She gripped her purse, blinking rapidly. "I don't believe this. Poor Ja Vala must be frightened, all alone after such a terrible loss. What right do you have to hold her?"

D'Angelo didn't speak. His hand slid back into his pocket, jingled coins.

"She's not been arrested, Ma'am," I said. "She's in medical care. Surely, as her friend, you can understand that—"

"What I understand is that Ja Vala's being ill-treated. Trust me, there will be repercussions—"

"Mrs. Lambert, can you think of anything that would help our investigation?" I changed the subject. "Anyone who might have wanted to hurt the Grangers?"

She raised her chin, looked me up and down, as if offended. "Certainly not."

I stood, thanked her for coming in.

D'Angelo took her contact information. As I walked her to the elevator, she moved close, whispering as if we were friends. "Can you at least tell me where to send her a package?"

Really? I stiffened, moved away. "Send it here. When she's ready, we'll deliver it for you."

She huffed.

"It was a pleasure to meet you, Mrs. Lambert. If you think of anything useful, let us know."

We stood in awkward silence until the elevator arrived. She got in and, until the doors closed, glared at me with heavily mascaraed but blazing eyes.

Like Ja, I thought. The word for fiery.

Chapter 24

D'Angelo was already on the computer, looking for information on Ja Vala Boudin from Haiti.

"No arrest record," he reported. "No driver's license either. No filing for permanent residency. No work visa." He stared at the screen, frowning.

I sat, rolled my chair over to him. "What did you think of her?"

He faced me, smirked. "My gut tells me Alexandra Lambert likes purple."

Indeed.

He went on. "Something about her was off. The whole bit about how close she is to Ja Vala? How she could help the doctors? Way too pushy."

I agreed. "Think she knows something about the murders? That would explain why she's so desperate to get to Ja Vala."

"Could be. Let's check her out. First, I'm getting background on Ja Vala Boudin. At least we finally have her name."

"We don't know it's her yet. Not for sure." I was sticking with Vanessa until we had proof.

D' grumbled, typed computer keys.

I picked up the paper Alexandra Lambert had filled out, noted the address. A swank condo in center city. I pictured her again. The heavy makeup, the extravagant sweeping fabric, the abundance of jewelry, heavy perfume. Quite a contrast to the understated style of the Grangers. Not that friends had to dress alike. Still.

I got to work helping D' find information on Ja Vala. Maybe she had relatives in Haiti. I picked up the phone and called the Haitian embassy in Washington D.C.

Probably every country has red tape. It took an eternity to reach a person with the authority and knowledge to answer my questions. After that, I had to fax official police requests for information regarding a Haitian citizen. I lacked Ja Vala's birth date and town of origin, parents' names. All I had was her name, a rough guess at her age, and the approximate year of her entry into the U.S.

Given the layers of bureaucracy I'd had to go through to file my request for information, I expected it would be days before I heard back. Which is why I was surprised when someone from the embassy called back within half an hour.

The person calling had a beautiful, lyrical accent. His name was Emmanuel Blanc, and he worked as a consular assistant. He wanted to confirm that my request was for information on Ja Vala Boudin.

"Yes, that's correct," I said. His call was to confirm my calls? How many hoops would I have to jump through to get simple information?

"I'm asking you this only because it seems there must be a mistake," he explained. "We have records of a woman with that name. This woman would be twenty-seven years old now."

Twenty-seven? I pictured the strands of white in Ja Vala's hair. Maybe she was graying prematurely. Younger than she looked.

"Thank you. Sounds like you found her records." So why had he said there was a mistake?

"I'm afraid not," he said. "The woman you are inquiring about, known to you as Ja Vala Boudin—She is there living in Philadelphia, correct? She's in good health?"

"Yes." There was no reason to say more.

"But you see, Detective. That is the problem. Because the only record I have located for a person with that name is a death certificate."

I opened my mouth, didn't speak.

"Ms. Ja Vala Boudin died nine years ago at the age of eighteen in the town of Kenscoff. That is a small village in the hills, southeast of Port-au-Prince."

I don't remember responding. I don't think I moved. But I must have reacted somehow because D'Angelo looked up from his computer and said, "What? What happened?"

I was oddly cold. D'Angelo got up from his desk but seemed to shrink, as if I was seeing him from far away.

"...do for you, Detective Sterling?" Emmanuel Blanc had been talking, but I'd missed much of what he'd said. "Would you like a copy of the certificate?

A copy of what? Oh, the death certificate. Yes, definitely. "Please." I gave him the address for a hard copy and asked him to fax it in the meantime. I thanked him for his cooperation and efficiency. Said what I was supposed to say.

When I got off the phone, I sat still for a moment, remembering what Ja Vala had written. I picked up the papers Dr. Vogel had sent over and scanned them until I found what I was looking for. Her handwriting was careful, with large loops.

"I am no longer a living person. I was in fact murdered. Maybe days ago, or maybe years."

Obviously, I didn't believe in either zombies or ghosts, and the woman we'd been told was Ja Vala Boudin was clearly among the living. Still, it was eerie that official Haitian documents—as well as the man who'd phoned from Haiti, corroborated her claims that she was not. I stared at her handwriting, reread her words. Searched for an alternate, more reasonable meaning to the words, "I am no longer a living person."

Chapter 25

"I got it." D'Angelo raised his arms in triumph, delighted with himself, unshaken by news of the death certificate. "It's a scam."

"A scam."

"Obviously. The maid's an illegal who got here using a false identity. The real Ja Vala Boudin died about the same time this woman came to the U.S. using her name and no doubt her passport. Whoever brought her here matched up gender, approximate age, race—and poof. A new Ja Vala."

Of course. It was that simple. Scam artists had used the identities of the dead to get false papers. Except that there hadn't been papers. "They don't have records of a passport for her," I said. "The only document they could find was the death certificate."

D'Angelo frowned. He hadn't found any records on her either. "So, they got her a false passport. They probably have a ton of them." He fidgeted. Stood. Took a sip from a Stryofoam cup. Grimaced and tossed it into the trash.

"Hold on," I said. "Alexandra Lambert said that the Grangers brought the maid here. Maybe that's what J. Steven found out about—that Granger had smuggled an illegal into the U.S."

D'Angelo shook his head. "I don't know. I don't think he'd dissolve his law firm just because Granger hired an illegal maid."

We were quiet for a moment. My hands were cold.

"Wait," D'Angelo raised his pointer finger. "The purple manatee said she met the Grangers in Haiti, right?" He opened his notebook, rifled through a few pages.

Manatee? I'd thought she was more like a stingray. Either way, he was right. She'd said she'd been with them when they'd hired Ja Vala. And she'd hired a maid at the same time.

So, she would probably know something about Ja Vala's background and identity. And how the Grangers had hired her.

THE WOMAN IN THE CUPBOARD

We needed to ask Alexandra Lambert a lot more questions. D'Angelo reached for the paper with her contact information. He picked up his phone, punched in her number.

The woman who answered the phone said D'Angelo had the wrong number. He identified himself as the police, asked again for Alexandra Lambert. The woman said she didn't care who he was, she wasn't Alexandra Lambert, didn't know anyone by that name. "You got the wrong number." She hung up.

D'Angelo got off the phone, looked at the paper. Had he read a digit wrong? Punched in the wrong number? He held it out for me to see. "Is that a three or a five? A seven or a one?" He tried again. Several times. He even tried reversing some of the digits, in case the order was mixed up.

No Alexandra Lambert.

He looked up her driver's license information.

Apparently, Mrs. Lambert didn't drive.

Or own a car. Or pay city taxes. He was calling someone else when I said, "Why don't we just pop over to her building?" It was just a few miles to Rittenhouse Square.

D'Angelo put his phone down, stood up. He'd been sitting too long, was ready to go. "I've got a bad feeling about this."

So, did I. The woman had given us a fake name. I hustled to keep up with him on the way to the elevator.

"Whoever she is, she's got to be part of the scam. She gave us the name of a dead woman for the maid. Probably she got 'Alexandra Lambert' the same way—from the obits or some gravestone."

Whoever she was, she wasn't who she claimed to be. And her motivation was clear: She was looking for the Grangers' maid.

Chapter 26

A concierge was posted at a desk inside the building. He wasn't familiar with the name, but looked it up in the building directory. Big surprise: no Alexandra Lambert.

"No, I don't have her," he said. "She could be a recent sublet, or a new resident they haven't added yet. Even a guest."

Except that she'd implied that she'd lived there for a while.

"How about a domestic worker named Kadia?"

He rubbed his forehead, shook his head, no.

Okay. "Anyone named Alexandra with a different last name?" Maybe she was divorced, using her maiden name.

The concierge opened his mouth, probably about to say that the list didn't identify people by first names. But D'Angelo leaned his bulk onto the desk, and the guard reconsidered. "This'll take a minute or two."

D' backed off, folded his arms. He was fuming, mad at himself for not spotting a liar.

"She's not here," I said.

"Of course she's not," he snapped.

"You think she even knew the Grangers?"

"No idea."

"She could be part of your scam. A smuggler, supplying illegal labor."

"Who knows?" He wasn't in the mood to speculate. Not in the mood to talk. He stood at the window, tapping his foot, glaring at forsythia blooming in the park.

The concierge finished his search. "I'm sorry, Detectives. I don't have an Alexandra as a resident. The closest I have is Alex Sturman on eight, but he's a gentleman."

I thanked him as D'Angelo snorted, deliberately quickening his pace. I jogged to keep up.

78

"You won't accomplish anything by being cranky," I scolded him.

"I'm not cranky," he snapped.

"Yes, you are. And that's distracting you from the case."

He stopped without warning, his eyes bright. He was smiling.

"What?"

"We don't need to find her," he said. "She'll be back. She has to come back."

She did?

"She's looking for the maid." He started walking again.

It took a moment for me to grasp what he meant. Whoever she was, the woman posing as Alexandra Lambert had been desperate to find out about Ja Vala's condition, her location. We'd given her nothing, and we were her only links.

D'Angelo was right. We didn't have to chase the woman. We had what she wanted, so she'd be back. We could sit back and wait for her to come to us.

Chapter 27

Dr. Vogel, as I write to you in this book, I can say that my mind is getting clearer as if a mist is lifting, the sun drying it up. Today, early, I awoke and knew it was morning. I looked out the window and saw the glow of the sun low in the sky, a golden hue spilling over the horizon. And I remembered pieces of time. Chunks of a life.

    She sits at the table, writing quickly trying to grab thoughts and put them into words while they are still clear. The haze has been lifting, but she doesn't trust her clarity, suspects that the haze might return, again cloaking her memories in mist. But for now, memories burst to life in tangled clusters that need sorting. Only one stands apart. A man. At first, she sees him from afar, his stature and frame. But the distance disappears, and he is only inches away. She takes in his comforting eyes, his breath on her skin, his hand closed around hers. Love for him swells within her, and her breath quickens. Her soul is linked to his. Their wedding is being planned with joy.

    Then doubt pours over her. Who is this man? Is he even real? Is she writing what her mind recalls or merely what she has longed for?

    She stops writing for a while, questioning herself but begins again when another memory appears so vividly that she must write it down to capture it. Her mother, cooking a big feast. Meat is roasting, and an odor arises. Burning fat? She is not sure what it is. But she breathes it in, allowing the aroma to transport her through time. As in a dream, she glimpses a girl, hips swaying as she walks alone. Who is this girl, she wonders. How does she know her? A flicker of fear rises and she sees Josias—The name comes to her, she doesn't know from where, but she is sure of it without hesitation or doubt. Josias. He is well known to her but when she sees him, the sky darkens, cold with revulsion. Why? She tenses as she watches him approach the girl. He is smiling with snakelike eyes as he moves for the girl, but she refuses him. Does she laugh as she pushes him away, thinking he is only playing? Is she afraid when he becomes angry, reaching for her again? Does she panic when he paws at her breasts, presses his lips onto hers, thrusts his tongue into her mouth? The girl bites him hard, and he recoils, then shoves her to the ground, comes at her now full force, but while he is on top of her, she grabs a rock, swings it with all her strength at his skull. She misses and instead slams its jagged edge into his eye. The eye is crushed. Blood spurts from the socket.

In the green room at the table, Dr. Vogel's patient clutches the pen and races to write down the drama as it unfolds. She tells Dr. Vogel how Josias howls, cursing the girl as he stumbles away. How the girl lies on the ground, herself bleeding and her clothing torn, clutching the rock until finally, she sits up, alone, slumping like a beaten dog.

She stops writing, sickened by the roiling, dense smell of the girl's fear.

Her heart is racing. To calm herself, she focuses on the present moment, her surroundings. The neatly made bed and nightstand, the chairs by the window. The forsythia blooming outside. The quiet. She is safe. Josias is nowhere near, and the memory is from long ago. Even so, even knowing she is safe, she can't free herself from the fear. She keeps replaying the memory, Josias' grabbing arms and probing mouth. The weight of the rock in her hand, the hefting of it, the swinging. She sees him reel, hears him howl, and for a moment—no, less than a moment, she sees a flicker of metal—a knife protrudes from his savaged eye. A knife? No, it vanishes so quickly she doubts she has seen it.

Her hand is aching and cramped from writing. And the air is dense with the smell of food. Before she closes her notebook, she jots a final note. *Dr. Vogel. You tell me I must try to remember the past and write down what I recall. But in truth the more I remember, the less I want to. What is the reason for bringing back awareness of events that cannot be changed? Is it possible to stop these memories? I fear no good will come of reviving them and it would be best to leave them abandoned and lost.*

Chapter 28

It was late afternoon when we called Dr. Vogel to say we were coming back to the hospital to talk. He wasn't thrilled but said he'd be ready for us. On the way, my mind wandered from Alexandra Lambert and who she might be, to Ja Vala and who she might be. To the man who claimed to have been engaged to Ja Vala. To all of their various possible connections to the murders. And something else.

Even in the midst of a complicated homicide investigation, even though I knew it was embarrassingly inappropriate, I thought about the dating site. I didn't dwell on it—It simply crossed my mind. Briefly. But I wondered if anyone had viewed my profile. If anyone had responded. What I would do if someone had.

At the hospital parking lot entrance, D'Angelo took a ticket from the machine at the gate and cursed at someone blocking the lane. "Move it," he shouted. "Look at this asshole. He's waiting for somebody to come out of a spot. There are a hundred empty spaces up ahead, but he wants the one right by the exit. Doesn't want to walk ten extra steps. What's wrong with people?"

He went on like that, squeezing his car around the offending road blocker, exchanging curses and dirty looks. "I ought to get out and show that guy my badge. Ought to take him in for obstructing a police investigation."

"Go get him, Big Guy," I said. I pushed the dating site out of my mind. No sense thinking about it. Probably no one had responded anyhow.

"I'm not kidding," D' bristled. "Waiting for a guy like him to move can make the difference between life and death."

I didn't engage. Gazed out the window at the rear ends of parked cars. Definitely and deliberately not thinking about the dating site.

"I got a line of cars behind me. He's jamming us all up."

I glanced at the rearview mirror. Sure enough, cars were backed up to get into the lot. And the driver of the car behind us was a woman with big hair, dressed in purple.

Alexandra Lambert.

What? I took a double take, twisting to get a better look just as D'Angelo made a U turn, moving into the adjacent parking lane.

"D'—Stop!" I struggled with my seatbelt, trying to keep sight of Alexandra Lambert's car.

But D' didn't stop. Didn't even slow. "There's a spot right here." He kept moving, screeched into it.

"Damn!" I craned my neck to look for the car. It had been dark blue. Or maybe gray. And it was an Audi. I remembered the logo. But where was it? It couldn't have gone far.

"Mo? What're you doing?" D'Angelo turned off the engine, finally noticed I was facing backwards.

"Alexandra Lambert—She was right behind us." I jumped out of the car, looking for her.

"What?" D'Angelo slammed his door. "No effing way. You're sure?"

Of course I was. Mostly.

"She couldn't have been. I always watch behind me. I'd have seen her."

True. D'Angelo would have seen her. Except that D'Angelo had been obsessing on the lane-blocker.

"Just in case," he said, "did you get the plates?"

No. I hadn't had a chance.

"Great."

"Well I might have if you'd stopped when I told you to."

"How was I supposed to know why you wanted me to stop? Why didn't you tell me? I thought it was about the parking spot."

I didn't bother to argue. Looked around the lot, didn't see anyone who looked like Alexandra Lambert, or her gray or blue

Audi. Maybe I'd just seen someone who'd resembled Alexandra Lambert. Maybe a doctor or some lady visiting her new grandbaby.

Probably that was it. Because even though D'Angelo and I walked up and down the lanes of the lot, we saw no dark blue or gray Audi. No trace of anyone who even vaguely resembled Alexandra Lambert.

Not even anyone wearing purple.

Chapter 29

"Come in. I have more pages for you." Dr. Vogel ushered us into his office, talked to himself as he rustled through stacks of papers on his desk, located a file and handed it to D'Angelo. "These are the new pages. You'll see, Detectives. Our patient is making great progress."

"She talking?" D leaned against the door frame.

"Not much. But she's writing. In fact, although they aren't to be taken as literally, her passages are quite vivid. Also, the level of her writing indicates that she's had a decent education. She knows English well, and grammar. She's articulate. So we're gradually gathering information about her. As you'll see when you read the copies from her notebook, images and memories are coming to her much more rapidly than I'd anticipated. If her progress continues, you might be able to question her fairly soon."

D'Angelo opened the file, thumbed through the pages.

"Do you still think she was drugged?" I asked.

Dr. Vogel's head bobbed. "I'm more convinced than ever. We haven't identified the drug yet. She's tested negative to all the standard ones, but we're still screening for less common substances. Whatever the substance was, though, she's not being exposed to it any more. Her body is becoming free of it, and her mind is clearing. She's resurfacing." He pressed his hands together, clearly pleased.

"So. You have her writings. What else can I do for you?"

"We want to see her," I said.

His eyes darted away. "Detective, she's just beginning to make progress. I don't want to—"

"We don't want to question her." I glanced at D'Angelo. His eyes told me not to back down. "We've run across some information, and we'd like to see if she reacts to it."

"What kind of information?"

"A name. A place."

"What name? What have you learned, Detective?" Vogel sat behind his desk, a position of authority. "I'm her psychiatrist. How can I be expected to treat her if I'm not kept informed of whatever information—"

"We haven't verified the information yet. We want to see how she reacts to it, if she reacts at all. But we need to find out. It'll take just a minute."

He leaned forward, folded his hands. Spoke slowly. "If the patient has suppressed this name for psychological reasons, then hearing it might set her back. And that might delay or even prevent her recovery."

D'Angelo fidgeted. "No disrespect, Doc," his words were clipped. "But we need to run the name by this woman. At least two people have been killed, and she is at the very least a witness. We need to find out who she is."

"So, this name—You believe it's hers? You've learned her identity?"

D'Angelo was poker faced. He looked at me, letting me know the answer was my call.

"Maybe." He was her doctor, he deserved to know.

"Maybe? And when did you plan to share this with me? Are we or are we not working together, detectives?"

I took a breath. "No offense, doctor. We're telling you everything we can. And we'd like to see her now."

Vogel studied his hands for a moment. When he stood, his face was bright red, and he didn't look at either of us. "Fine. But only one of you," he said. "Follow me."

Chapter 30

She was in a small sitting room beside a window and a philodendron. She wore a pair of rose-colored hospital gowns, one over the other for modesty. Sunlight made her hair sparkle, her skin glow.

She didn't look up when I came in.

"Hi," I spoke softly. I didn't want to startle her.

Still no response.

I walked across the room, took a seat on a loveseat near hers. Her face registered no awareness of my presence. Her eyes didn't flicker, her body didn't move.

"I don't know if you remember me," I spoke softly. "I'm Mo Sterling. I'm a police detective."

"Yes." Her voice was small. She didn't move. Not even an eyelid twitch.

"You're looking well." I waited a moment, letting her get used to me. "Ja Vala."

Her eyes widened, or I thought they did, but only slightly, and only for a nanosecond.

"Is that your name?"

No answer.

"What about Kenscott. In Haiti." I paused. "Is that where you come from?"

Nothing. She didn't move. Didn't even seem to breathe. I waited.

"Ja Vala. It's a beautiful name." I said it again. "Ja Vala Boudin. That's you, isn't it?"

She didn't move. But her eyes changed. The pupils seemed altered. More constricted. Maybe they were reacting to the light beaming from outside. Or to withdrawal from some drug. But at the time, I was sure that the change in her eyes was caused by fear.

Chapter 31

Ja Vala. The patient repeats the name to herself. It is not her name, cannot be, although it is familiar to her. She recalls a person called Ja Vala. She was graceful and tall, and her laughter rippled like sunlight on water. She tries to picture Ja Vala, but the image, like ripples, floats away.

Where are the Grangers? They have to come and tell her what to do, but then she remembers that the Grangers are no more. Her bokor is not there, either. Dr. Vogel is now in charge. Dr. Vogel now tells her what to do. But it is difficult to perform the task he has assigned. She has done her best, writing down her thoughts, but only a few if the thoughts stay with her long enough to become words. Many images flicker and as her mind reaches for them, they are gone. Mostly, the images are of people. When they appear, she wonders if these people are dead, too. Why else would they dart just beyond her grasp? Maybe they intend to taunt her. Maybe it's a game to them.

Or maybe they have no choice, are unable to remain.

She sits, listens, waits for voices to become clearer, features more defined. Finally, a clear memory emerges: A man.

Kenny.

His name pierces her heart.

Kenny. His stride is light, and his arms swing loose and lighthearted until, alongside the road, he sees a young woman lying dead on the ground. Kenny stops in disbelief. He howls, sinks to his knees, reaches out, cradles her. This image of the man Kenny holding the dead woman freezes in her mind, and then, in a heartbeat, it is gone.

It is replaced by a menacing shadow. Recalling this presence, she shivers, even now.

Josias.

He has but one eye, and he uses it to curse the dead woman. But now, it is not Josias—it's a woman, a familiar presence, someone of power. A knife handle protrudes from one of her eyes. And—her face—skin is missing, and blood covers her. What's happened to her? A hand tugs at the knife, pulling and twisting it out of her, and finally she lies back, covered by a warm blanket. Maybe the fleece is cherry colored, but, no, the the color spills from her wounds, spreading, creating a terrible stain.

Chapter 32

Dr. Vogel was tugging at his mustache, fuming in the hallway. "I told you she wasn't ready yet."

"Get anything?" D'Angelo asked.

"No, she didn't 'get anything,'" Vogel scolded. "You saw for yourself."

He had?

"We were watching through the one-way." D' pointed to a small observation room adjoining the room I'd just left.

"She recognized the name," I said. "Her eyes flickered."

"Her eyes flickered?" Vogel crossed his arms. "Well. That's hardly a valid or reliable confirmation—"

"I know, Doctor. I'm not saying that it is." I cut him off, didn't want to discuss anything further until D'Angelo and I were alone.

"My point, Detective, is that the patient's response to your questions might be misleading. Her writings so far indicate that she's in a highly emotional, suggestible, and fearful state. Whatever reaction you observed might, or might not, mean what you think it does."

I glanced at D'Angelo, my look telling him not to say anything. We thanked Vogel, promised to be in touch, reminded him to keep us updated, and, as he sputtered, headed for the door.

"So. Think she's Ja Vala?" D' kept his voice low even as we started for the parking lot.

"If she isn't," I said, "then she at least knows who Ja Vala is or was."

"My gut says—" D'Angelo didn't finish. He bent over and barreled into me like a linebacker, sending me flying onto asphalt. I was still in the air when I heard the shots.

I went down hard, the impact reverberating through my bones, my skull. Light flashed, red and orange. For a few seconds, I couldn't hear, couldn't move.

When I finally looked up, D' was crouched, his weapon raised. I recognized the grimness of his eyes, the set of his jaw. He'd just shot somebody.

Chapter 33

The body was female, dark-skinned, about twenty-five, wearing a hoodie and jeans. No identification.

D'Angelo had seen her aiming just before she'd fired. He'd knocked me down, pulled out his weapon and shot. Saved my life.

Not for the first time.

We worked into the night dealing with the shooting. Filing reports, answering questions. Did we know the shooter? Or why she would shoot either of us? Or how she'd known we were at the hospital? How many shots had been fired? Had she been aiming at me? At D'Angelo? At someone else altogether? Had I seen her? When he'd first seen her, had her gun already been raised?

Endless questions.

D'Angelo was assigned to office duties pending investigation of the shooting. "Don't sweat it," our captain, McDermott assured him. "If that shoot wasn't justifiable, nothing is. It was self-defense, pure and simple. You'll be cleared for duty in no time."

D'Angelo had been through the process before, wasn't fazed. He accepted the customary post-shooting support of our fellow detectives, including the reminiscing, the razzing, the gifting of a bottle of good Scotch. I complained about how hard he'd shoved me, about the scrapes and emerging bruises on my arm and hip, about D' getting all the attention.

It was almost nine p.m. before I got back to my desk. D'Angelo had gone home. My body ached, exhausted, and images kept repeating in my mind. D'Angelo and I were leaving the hospital, talking. And then, whoosh. I lost my breath, saw a blur. Slammed against the ground. And then the scenario started over again.

Okay, fine. I was shaken up. My nerves would take a while to settle down. The replays would recur for a while—they always did after unanticipated violence. Especially when there was a death.

I pictured the dead woman. Who was she? Her eyes had been dazed, as if she hadn't understood what had happened to her. Her face had been young. Dark. Pretty.

Not unlike the face of the woman we'd been visiting in the hospital.

And with that thought, the obvious crystallized in my mind: The shooting had been about Vanessa, the woman who might be Ja Vala. Why else would it have happened at the hospital, right after our visit?

And right after I'd seen Alexandra Lambert driving her dark Audi behind us.

I sat up, put a hand on my forehead, finally digesting what had happened. Alexandra Lambert had wanted to know where the Grangers' maid, Ja Vala, was being treated. She'd clearly tailed us, watching us go to Hahnemann Hospital. Assumed that the maid was there. And sent the shooter to wait for us there. My head hurt, my eyes burned.

Who was Alexandra Lambert? Why was she so desperate to find the maid Ja Vala that she would follow us on the chance that we'd lead her to her? And once she'd found out where Ja Vala was being treated, why would she send someone to kill us?

I rubbed my eyes, tried to untangle my thoughts. Couldn't. But I was certain that whoever the shooter was, she had connections to Alexandra Lambert, the Grangers, and their maid.

I needed to go home, get some sleep. Sat at my desk, reliving the shooting, not moving. Wasting time. The file Dr. Vogel had given us sat on my desk. Maybe the maid's writing would tell me something useful. I opened the file, began reading. Dr. Vogel was right about her mastery of English, the vividness of her descriptions. I wondered how much of what she'd written was accurate. Had she actually been attacked, taken out her attacker's eye?

And what about the other eye she'd written about—The one with the knife protruding from it? She'd pretty accurately described Judith Granger's wound. Which indicated that Vanessa was beginning to remember what had happened in the Grangers' house. Maybe tomorrow, she'd recall even more. Like her name.

I closed that file, leafed through another full of news clippings about the Granger murders. Vanessa's face had appeared in article after article. Even if she was here illegally, how was it that no one other than Alexandra Lambert—not a single neighbor, relative, delivery person, or friend had known who this woman was? Had she never walked in the park? Run an errand? Spent a day off with a pal? Answered the phone or the door? Had she been known by absolutely no one?

I rubbed my temples. Saw the dead woman lying in the parking lot, her gun beside her, her eyes dazed. Why had she been there? What would she have accomplished by killing us? Because even if D'Angelo and I had both been killed, the investigation into the Grangers' murders would have continued—In fact, it would have been amplified. So, the shooting made no sense.

Unless there was something only he and I knew.

Like what?

I sat back, closed my eyes. My thoughts were muddled. I needed a break. Looked around at a row of empty desks. Checked the time. Wow, already after ten. I wondered how D'Angelo was doing. Imagined him at dinner with his family, the smell of roasting pot roast. My stomach gurgled. I realized I hadn't eaten all day.

Didn't feel hungry.

Needed to leave. But I dawdled, felt shaky. Didn't trust my legs to carry me. Again, as if from a distance, I saw us stepping out of the hospital.

"Think she's Ja Vala?" I heard myself ask.

Again, D' began to answer. Stopped. Shoved me. I flew, and colors flashed in my head, electric like lightning.

I needed to stop replaying the shooting. If I didn't get it together, I'd have to see the department shrink. I took a breath, sat tall. Started to stand, but my eyes filled and I smeared tears across my face. I was crying? Now? Hours after the shooting?

Don't resist, I heard D'Angelo scold. You have to let the emotions play—otherwise everything will fester inside you and you'll get cancer. I smiled at the warning. But still, I didn't feel ready to trust my legs. It wasn't just the shock of the shooting that tore at me. It was something deeper, roiling under my ribs. Guilt? Shame? Whatever name I hung on it, it was there, clinging to my bones. The sickening awareness that I'd messed up.

I should have seen the shooter. I hadn't even tried to protect my partner and myself. I'd failed to be alert, had let myself be distracted. Had let D' down. Could have cost him his life.

I blew my nose, blinked away more tears. I was made of cold stone logic when it came to confronting victims and murderers. But apparently, I sucked when it came to reacting on the spot. I was loser, a liability. D'Angelo's voice interrupted, telling me to get over it. Promising that I'd get the next one. Assuring me that nobody can see everything all the time. Scolding me to lighten up. Again, I pictured him at home, stuffing himself with Teresa's special meatloaf drenched in her homemade sweet tomato sauce. D'Angelo would be fine, cleared for duty in no time. And we were both alive.

Even so, my hands were unsteady as I put the files in the drawer. And my legs were wobbly when I managed to stand. My body refused to pretend that all was well. What would have happened if D'Angelo had been looking the other way? Would I have gone down in the middle of a sentence, a syllable? And afterwards, would my eyes have looked like the shooter's, dazed, as if they didn't understand?

Chapter 34

Josias. The thought of him makes her blood freeze. Remembering him makes her skin draw into itself, attempting to hide. She sees him by the road near his shiny motorbike. Josias is small and ugly—his eyes are shifty, narrow like a lizard's. Yet he knows that no one dare oppose him, as his mother is Madame Armistead. Only because of his mother, Josias has power. And so, when he surprises the woman as she walks home—Wait, no. She is not a woman, really. She is only on the brink of womanhood. When he sees her walking without a care, humming a song, her body glowing with love for the young man Kenny Wadd, Josias is aroused. He is drawn to her simply because she is not his. And because he knows that she belongs to another. He moves for her without pretext, without shame. He pulls her off the road—his hands paw at her breasts. He is Josias, the son of Madame Armistead, so he can't believe that she resists him. That she scratches him and strikes him with a jagged rock. That her blows are so hard and insistent that they crush bones on his face, smash a reptile eye. That blood pours over him. He blinks at her through the torrent, cursing her. Promising that she will pay for what she has done. That his family will see to it. That she will regret her rashness forever.

Writing this account, the patient feels her mouth go dry. She sees Josias tottering to his feet, holding his shattered and bloodied face. She hears his curses and she trembles.

She is almost relieved when sometime in the night, a nurse comes in. The interruption allows her to stop writing, to escape from Josias and his rage.

The nurse is new, someone she has not seen before. She smells heavily of perfume and her lips are coated shiny and dark, her eyelids painted with purple shadow. She leans close, says that the bokor sent her with new medication.

"You have already gone too long without it," the nurse whispers. "If you don't take it immediately, decay will begin."

The patient is uncertain. The bokor told her to obey only the Grangers, and the Grangers are no more. So, she has been obeying Dr. Vogel, and he has given her no intruction about obeying this nurse. But if this stranger is a nurse, she must work for Dr. Vogel, not for the bokor. So how would the nurse have the bokor's medication? Unless—and the idea frightens her—do the bokor and Dr. Vogel work together? How else can the nurse know the bokor? Does she really have the medication? Why hasn't Dr. Vogel himself given it to her?

"There's no time left," the nurse repeats. "If you don't start your meds immediately, it will be too late to prevent your decomposition. Maybe it's already too late."

The patient puts down the pen she's been holding and examines the skin on her hands. Oh mondieu, the nurse is right. The skin is dry and flaky. The dreaded process has begun. But maybe if she takes the medicine, it can be stemmed. Her fingers tremble as she closes her notebook and turns to the nurse.

Chapter 35

When I left the office, I didn't know where to go. I didn't want to go home, wasn't ready for the silence. But I also didn't want to chitchat, so calling Evie or another friend and asking her to meet me wouldn't work. Fact was I didn't want to be anywhere, not by myself or with anyone else. I drove around for a while, finally decided it would be best to be around people and noise and ended up in Old City, a place called Khyber Pass.

I sat at the bar, ordered a beer and a sandwich. The place was busy but not packed, and the music wasn't overwhelming. I looked around at a smattering of clients. Couples touching. Booths seating groups of pals. I didn't know anyone, and no one knew me. A single woman was perched across the bar from me, talking to the bartender. They seemed familiar, comfortable. Probably she was a regular. Off and on, she bantered with a guy sitting a few seats away from her, laughing easily, baring shiny teeth. What was it like to be her? What did she do? Work in an ad agency? A law firm? I wondered. In the dim light, she flipped long wavy hair off her face, flashed perfect nails. Maybe she was in marketing. Bingo—That was it. Pharmaceuticals. If she wasn't, she should be. She looked exactly like a sales rep.

I swallowed beer, stared at the glow of the bottles against the wall. Felt like an outsider, a misfit. My days weren't spent with clients closing deals or figuring out a monthly sales quota. No, I spent my time studying homicides, interviewing suspected killers, getting shot at. Having my partner kill people to save my ass.

My sandwich came, and I attacked it. Savored the tang of the sauce. Tried to turn off my thoughts. But in the corner of my mind, a purple driver whose name wasn't Alexandra Lambert idled her Audi, and, bam. Once again, I flew through the air. Slammed onto asphalt.

D'Angelo had really thrown me. My bruises throbbed.

I swallowed more beer. Ordered extra fries. Watched people come and go. A guy sitting two stools away smiled in my direction. I nodded at him and diverted my eyes. What was wrong with me? He was being friendly, inviting conversation. And he wasn't bad looking. Talk to him, I told myself. Make a friend. But what should I say? The fact was I had no game, no witty pickup lines. Okay, so I didn't have to talk. But I had to at least be a grown up and smile at him. Fine, I'd do it. I gathered my nerve, sat up tall, took a breath, turned to him, and beamed a warm inviting smile.

Directly at his back. The guy had shifted his position, was facing the other way. I sat smiling stupidly at the back of his shirt.

My face got hot, but it was dark in the bar and besides, no one was watching me. I was a stranger, a woman alone with a beer and pulled pork. I ordered a refill, considering that, if not for D', there'd be none of this. No pulled pork. No beer. No messed-up bar interactions. No Mo. At least D' hadn't been shot for his trouble. Not like the last time he'd saved my ass. I could still feel the rain, the weapon in my hand. Could smell the wet ground, the wet dumpster. I heard a squish and spun around, heard two shots. A dead man with a .45 lay in a puddle behind me and, across the lot, D' slumped in the mud, not moving. I'd thought he was dead.

He'd saved me, almost got killed for it. Today, he'd done it again. Bang. Bang.

Why hadn't I seen the shooter? Why did I keep messing up, relying on D' to save my ass? And why did he put up with it? Didn't he get what a fake I was, pretending to be tough, acting as if I could hold my own like the big boys? The truth was I kept missing things, endangering him, letting him down. If D' hadn't had my back, I'd have been on a slab. I lifted my new beer. Silently toasted D', the big gallant galoot. I wished he was there with me so I could clink his glass and thank him to his face. Better though, that he wasn't, that he didn't find out what a sorry mess I was. I finished my fries, downed my beer. The bottles behind the bar gleamed and swayed. I settled up, headed out of the bar while I could still walk.

Chapter 36

The stranger is dressed as a nurse but is not a nurse. She does not work for Dr. Vogel. Her eyes pierce, veiled by painted lashes, and her darkened nails ache to tear flesh.

"You know why I have come," she says.

The nurse who isn't a nurse says that Madame Armistead has sent her.

Madame Armistead. The patient stiffens at the name.

Probably Madame Armistead has sent this nurse to punish her yet again. Her flesh tightens, anticipating larva, maggots, flies. The stranger impersonating a nurse notices her discomfort and seems pleased. She orders her to tell her what happened to the Grangers.

"They died." She doesn't know what else to say.

"Did you resist them?" she asks.

Resist? The question puzzles her. How could she resist? She could do only what they told her to do. It would have been impossible even to imagine disobeying them. She answers, no. Not ever.

"Then how did they die?"

She explains what she remembers about the Grangers, what they'd wanted of her. How they'd fought each other. What each of them had done and ordered her to do. But she tells Madame Armistead's nurse that she is not sure how they died.

The nurse listens, watching the patient like a judge. Like St. Peter, deciding whether to open the heavenly gates or cast her down to hell. Finally, she frowns. "I am an associate of your bokor. She trusts me to decide what to do. If I put you under, we might be able to recover your body in time to start you fresh in a new position."

The patient's eyes do not flinch. She doesn't shudder as she pictures the process. Her arm sliced open, powder rubbed into the wound. A wooden casket. The smell of cold clay.

The nurse continues. "But the police have been talking to you, and they would be suspicious if you were to die suddenly from unknown causes. They'd order an autopsy, which would take time and destroy your body. You would be rendered worthless."

The patient's hand rises unbidden to her throat. She sees herself on a stainless-steel table, torso sliced open, organs laid bare.

For a moment the nurse is silent. "Enough. I have to decide." Her violet eyes rest on the patient, studying her. Then she reaches into her satchel, takes out a packet. "Okay. I believe you that you have obeyed your bokor and followed the Grangers' direction to the end. I don't know who killed them, but I'm satisfied it couldn't have been you. So instead of putting you down and creating a stir, I'm simply going to preserve you for now. Madame Armistead sees value in you—she will approve."

She opens the packet and takes out a handful of small envelopes. "Our first and most important job," she smiles, "is to keep you from decomposing." The smile reveals a lipstick smudge on her canine tooth. It resembles a smear of blood.

The patient examines her hands. Is her ring finger decaying below the nail? The knuckles also look thin and dry. Has the process started already? Can it be reversed? The woman pours powder into a water glass and tells her to drink it, watches as she does. The nurse instructs her to listen carefully to her instructions and insists that she follow them exactly for, if she does not, the bokor will show no mercy—Not for her, and not for those at home who've mourned her loss.

Chapter 37

D'Angelo was already at his desk when I came in the next morning. My head hammered, but merciful coffee and a jelly donut were waiting on my desk.

I thanked him, asked how he was.

"Couldn't sleep," he bounced his knee. "I'm already stir crazy. I got to get off desk duty."

I took a bite of donut, changed the subject to distract him. "So. Teresa have more dreams last night?"

"No, she wasn't asleep long enough to have any dreams." He rubbed his eyes. "One thing about my bride, she doesn't do things halfway. If she's happy, she's entirely happy. But if she's not, well. Watch out."

"What's she not happy about?" I asked without thinking. I knew the answer before he said it.

"What do you think? The shooting. She acts like it was my fault. She blames me because someone tried to take a shot at us."

"She loves you, D'. She worries." My face reddened. Teresa must blame me.

"If she loves me so much, why doesn't she let me sleep?" His knee bounced rapidly and he cracked his knuckles. "No way I can sit at a desk all day."

I didn't know what to say. It was my fault he was on desk duty. I bit my lip, ashamed. Took a sip of coffee.

"So, have you seen these?" He handed me a pile of newspapers. "And how about the news last night? Six, ten and eleven—We were the big story on every channel."

Or rather, he was. I scanned the articles. The news media had hailed D'Angelo for his "heroic quick response" to what was assumed to be yet another act of random violence in a public place by a person with an unknown motive. A nurse was quoted as saying, "If not for that detective, who knows what would have happened? The shooter could have come into the hospital, and who knows how many casualties we'd have had?"

D'Angelo was pictured in the *Inquirer*, and the shooter's face was plastered there and in the *Daily News*. Apparently, she'd been featured on local television, too, and the public was asked for any information they might have about her identity. The incident wasn't linked to the Grangers' murders, as no one from the press knew that their maid was being treated in that hospital. Still, the *Daily News* ran a sidebar with the photos of the two mystery women, side by side. The editor might have found it interesting that two unknown women of similar age and appearance had been connected to local acts of violence within a few days.

"Good for you, D'. You're famous," I gave him back the papers, licked jelly off my lips. I'd looked, but seen no mention of my name anywhere. A relief.

"Yeah, unlike my wife, the press effing loves me, Mo. I prevented a massacre. But the department? That's another story. I'm off the street, stuck like a rookie here with paperwork."

"It's protocol, D," I told him. "They're just following procedure."

"Captain said they'd speed things along, given the pressure to get the Grangers' case solved. Meantime, you might have to work with Colby."

What? "Seriously?" Colby was the runt of the department. Plus, he had a nasal twang that got on my nerves. The guy needed to get his adenoids out. Should have done it like twenty years ago.

"I'm begging you. Tell the captain you need me, that I'm essential to the investigation—"

"Wait, so that's why you got me a jelly donut? A bribe?"

He snorted. My phone rang.

The caller had an island accent. Musical, like Vanessa's.

"Ah, Detective Mo Sterling. Finally. It has taken me much effort to contact you. I hope to meet with you to discuss important matters. I have come all the way from Haiti."

I shot a glance at D'Angelo, made eye contact. He rolled his chair over.

"Can I have your name, sir?"

"I am Kenny Wadd." He took a breath. "First, let me explain why I have come. In Haiti, I regularly watch a variety of news programs on the internet. And on the news, I have seen photographs of a woman connected to a murder case here in your city. I called several times to speak with you about her, but I was unable to reach you."

"Mr. Wadd, where are you now?"

"I am nearby in a Holiday Inn. Detective, please tell me. How is this woman? I understand that she is in a hospital. Is she unwell? Can you tell me her condition?"

I hesitated. Who was this guy? Why did he want to know details about the maid? "All I can tell you is that she is safe. Mr. Wadd—"

"She is safe? Thank God. Okay then, Detective Mo Sterling, let me continue. I live in a small town where every person knows each other and hears about what's going on. You yourself called my town to request records of a woman, Ja Vala Boudin. This fact was told to me by my uncle who works in the town hall."

I motioned D'Angelo to pick up the extension. "Yes, Mr. Wadd. What do you know about Ja Vala Boudin?"

"She is the reason I am here. Ja Vala Boudin, the woman whose records you requested, was my intended wife. We were to be married." He stopped, cleared his throat.

"I'm sorry. I understand that she died." My eyes met D'Angelo's.

"Yes, sadly. I was devastated. But with time, I recovered and in fact have married someone else, La'a. She is a good wife, and we have two small sons. Nevertheless, I have remained close to the family of Ja Vala. We are still like family despite the years that have passed."

D' was getting antsy, drumming his fingers on the desktop.

"I'm glad for you, Mr. Wadd. But I don't understand. Ja Vala Boudin died years ago. So, what exactly is the purpose of your call?"

"Okay, let me continue. Ja Vala's family are fine people. Educated people. Like me, they watch international news programs on the internet."

"Okay." And?"

D'Angelo rolled his eyes.

"They are why I've come. Because Ja Vala's family beseeched me to, Detective Sterling. Like me, they have seen the photographs on the internet. And they are convinced, absolutely, that they know why you requested information about their daughter. It is because the photographs in the news were of Ja Vala."

I looked at D'. He held the extension away from his ear, shook his head.

The man went on. "Of course, I've told them many times that they are mistaken. It is impossible, in fact, as we buried our beloved Ja Vala years ago. Nevertheless, they remain adamant, and as they are infirm and unable to travel, I have come as their agent to see the woman in the photograph and to ascertain whether or not she is indeed Ja Vala."

D'Angelo's finger made a cuckoo motion around his ear.

"Mr. Wadd, let me ask you this: If Ja Vala Boudin has been dead and buried for years, how can she possibly be the woman in the photos? Obviously, she can't be. The woman must just resemble her."

"Yes, indeed that is undoubtedly the case. I am of the same opinion. But unfortunately, her family is not. They are relentless, and no matter how I've tried to reason with them, they have insisted that the woman is Ja Vala. After all this time, their hearts remain broken from her early and unexpected death. They sent me to see the woman for myself."

What? I took a breath. "Well, Mr. Wadd, since you're here in town, I certainly hope you'll enjoy Philadelphia. But I'm afraid that Ja Vala's parents will be disappointed. The woman here is probably an identity thief, living under the alias of a dead person."

Kenny Wadd was silent for a moment. "Yes, I understand. But just to be thorough, what if I show you a photo of Ja Vala with her family? You can see the resemblance for yourself. And you can show it to the woman to see if she recognizes them."

I saw no reason to say no.

"And if you agree it's the same woman, I can go see her."

"Hold on." I ran a hand through my hair. "Ja Vala Boudin is dead, right?"

"Tragically, yes. I kissed her goodbye in her coffin."

The man was wasting my time. "You saw her in her coffin."

"Yes."

"You kissed her corpse."

"Yes. I did."

"So then, with all due respect, how can you possibly imagine that she's the living breathing woman in the news photos?" I stopped myself from calling him a whack job and slamming the phone down.

Kenny Wadd didn't hesitate. "Yes, I see your point. But let's go according to plan. I'll deliver the photographs. You can look at them, and then we can talk."

There was no point in continuing the conversation. Instead of having him come in, I gave him an email address, took his contact information, and turned around to talk with D'Angelo about the call.

Except that D'Angelo was gone.

Chuck Colby was sitting at his desk, reading a magazine.

Chapter 38

"Captain called him in," he told me. "Poor sucker. Word is they're going to push him to take a package."

What? "Who says?" Colby had to be exaggerating. Causing drama. Nobody was going to pressure D'Angelo to retire early.

"It's his third kill in less than three years. Department frowns on high numbers—"

"Who'd you hear this from?"

Colby squirmed, looked away. "Nobody. Everybody. It's talk."

"So, talk is that D' should have stood there and let us get shot?" I rubbed my elbow where it was sore from hitting the pavement. "Listen, Colby. D'Angelo should get a medal. Anybody says anything else about him, you tell me."

"What're you so steamed about, Mo? I'm just saying what I heard." He looked down at the desk, cleared his throat, shuffled papers. "Anyway. I'm filling in. They briefed me, but it'll take me a while to catch up."

Damn. Everybody knew how close D' and I were. D'Angelo hadn't been gone ten minutes and already I felt off balance. I looked at the clock. Only ten after nine. Colby was already frazzling my nerves.

"You seen these yet?" Colby pointed to a report.

That would depend on what "these" were.

"Lab reports on D's vic."

I grabbed the paper from his hands. Scanned it. Saw that the standard drug tests were negative. No alcohol either. Who was she? Why had she tried to shoot us?

Colby asked if I wanted anything, left to get coffee.

I slumped into my desk chair, shaken up about D'Angelo. What if the rumors were true and he was being pushed out? What if he wasn't coming back?

I couldn't imagine it. Didn't want to. I stared at the toxicology report, letting the words slide out of focus. Missing D'. When I finally looked up, Colby was back at his desk, eating a soft pretzel. It was twenty after nine. And my computer screen announced new incoming mail.

Chapter 39

One was a formal shot, a family posing for a portrait. Parents surrounded by kids, one who looked like the woman I'd found in the Granger's pantry, only younger.

The other was a close up of a couple. A young man, his arm around that same young woman. Kenny Wadd and Ja Vala Boudin held their heads together, tilted at the same angle. They beamed the same smile, glowed the same light.

No question, Ja Vala Boudin strongly resembled Vanessa.

I called Dr. Vogel, left a message that I was on my way. Called Kenny Wadd, arranged for him to come in that afternoon. Grabbed the car keys.

"Where are we going?" Colby hopped to his feet, ready to go.

I didn't want to take Colby with me, felt like my kid brother was tagging along. Didn't have the patience to get him up to speed on the Granger case. I wanted D', his bulky frame, his short attention span, even his obsession with his wife's dreams.

"So, we're going to see the maid?" Colby asked. He kept asking questions, making me repeat things.

"She's beginning to be lucid. Maybe she'll recognize the people in the photos."

"The photos from Haiti."

"Yes."

"The ones from that guy Wadd—is that really his name?" Colby snickered. "Wadd?"

"Yes. He sent them. He thinks the Granger's maid is his old girlfriend, Ja Vala Boudin."

"Even though we have her death certificate."

"Yup. And even though Kenny Wadd himself was at her funeral."

"So maybe the maid just looks like the dead girl. Maybe they're sisters." Colby studied the photos I'd printed out. "Maybe she's just a look alike. I mean everybody's got a double somewhere, right? That's what they say. What's that word? Doppelgänger? Maybe that's what this woman is, the dead girl's doppelgänger." He went on talking.

I tried to tune him out. I missed D'Angelo. Wanted to show D' these photos, hear what he'd have to say.

Was he really going to have to retire? Was he angry about it? Depressed? Was he going to fight it?

Would I have to work with Colby from now on?

Mercifully, by the time we got to the hospital, Colby had stopped talking. But he began again on the way to Dr. Vogel's office. "I'm just here as back up, Mo. You're in charge. Just let me know what you want. It's going to take some time for me—"

"Detective Sterling, I was just about to call you," Dr. Vogel burst out of his office, grabbed my arm. "Something's happened, I don't know what." He was flushed, blinking rapidly. He took no notice of Colby, just pulled me down the hallway to the observation room. "She was doing so well. The drug was wearing off, I was sure of it. But this morning, all of a sudden, for no apparent reason, she's had a setback. I can't figure out what happened, but she's faded again."

"Faded?"

"Slipped back into semi-catatonia. Over the last few days, her writing has become coherent but this morning, it's back to meaningless. Even last night, her demeanor was responsive. She was conversing, beginning to interact. But now, she's silent again. Unresponsive."

How could she have changed overnight? "Could it be her medications?"

"No, no. I've carefully monitored everything she's ingested. Nothing she's taken could have affected her this way."

"Could she be sick? Does she have a fever?"

He shook his head, no. "Her vitals are normal." He stared through the window to the adjoining room. Vanessa sat motionless, expressionless in her customary easy chair. Colby stepped to the window, observing her.

I thought for a moment. "Has she had outside contact?"

"Of course not. She has no visitors. Only you and your partner." He took a double take at Colby, finally noticing that he wasn't D'Angelo. "Who's this?"

I introduced him to Colby.

Vogel lifted his chin, quickly looked him over, turned back to me. "We're back to square one, Detective—But the question is why? What's caused her to regress?" He crossed his arms, stroked his mustache. Shook his head. "Even though we haven't identified them, I was positively certain that she'd been kept on drugs. I expected that, as they cleared out of her system, she'd recovered from their effects. Now though, it seems I was wrong. I'll have to reassess, revisit other possibilities. But I was so sure." He stared through the one-way window, studying the patient as if she were a puzzle he was stumped on.

Colby stood silent, watching the woman. He opened the file and took out the photographs, held them up, comparing the faces.

"Colby," I said, "show those to Dr. Vogel. See what he thinks. Do you recognize the woman in the photos?"

He took the pictures from Colby, looked them over. "My God," his eyes widened. "Yes. They certainly look like her." He looked at the photos, then the woman. Back at the photos. Again, at the woman. "What are these?" He turned to me, sputtering. "You've found out who she is?"

I glanced at Colby. He was still staring through the glass.

"Nothing's certain yet."

"Where did you get these?" Vogel held them in the air, as if about to swing them at me.

"I mentioned this to you, Dr. Vogel. A man from Haiti recognized her photos in the news. He called claiming to know her. I wasn't sure, given the number of years since he'd seen her—"

"You didn't tell me someone confirmed her identity."

"Because nothing's confirmed." I told him about the possibility of identity theft, that criminals might be stealing dead people's information for illegal immigration purposes.

Dr. Vogel crossed his arms, turned away. "So, what do you propose to do?"

I explained. He scowled. "In her present state, I'm not sure it would do any good."

"Look," I insisted. "The photos might jar her memory. If they don't, nothing's lost."

He watched her through the window. Folded his hands behind his back. Took a breath.

"Get with it, Doc." Colby frowned. "Cooperate. This is a homicide investigation."

I shot Colby a look. What happened to him just being back up, letting me do the talking? But he didn't notice my glower—his eyes were on Dr. Vogel.

Dr. Vogel didn't say anything. He handed the photos back to Colby and stepped back, his silence speaking for him.

Chapter 40

When I came into the room, the woman didn't look up. She didn't move at all, even when I sat opposite her beside the window.

"How are you, Ja Vala?" I said.

She didn't react to the name, held her face toward the window like the potted plant beside her.

"Remember me? Detective Sterling."

Not a stir.

"I thought you'd be interested that someone contacted me about you. Someone from your hometown. Kenscoff."

Nothing.

"He says you are Ja Vala Boudin. And he sent some pictures. I'm going to show them to you." I waited a beat. Then, slowly, I picked up the photo of her family and held it directly in the line of her vision, about eighteen inches away.

I watched her eyes. They looked unfocused, as if staring beyond the picture, or through it.

"Do you recognize these people? Is this you?" I pointed to the young Ja Vala.

Her eyes registered nothing. Her gaze didn't waver. Her body didn't move.

Dr. Vogel had been right. The woman had sunk into herself again.

I switched photos. Held up the one of Ja Vala with her boyfriend. "Do you recognize this couple?" I studied her face. "The man's name is Kenny Wadd."

Did her eyelid twitch when I said his name? Did her breath quicken, her back stiffen? Her gaze flicker? I wasn't sure. The reactions were tiny, almost imperceptible.

Possibly I imagined them.

"Kenny Wadd." I said his name again. "That's the man who called. He said he and Ja Vala were in love. They'd planned to marry." I paused, waited.

Only her chest moved, taking in air. Letting it out.

"Kenny Wadd also said that Ja Vala died nine years ago."

Her eyes were empty. Without the faintest spark. Was she even hearing me?

"But her family doesn't believe she's dead. See, they believe she was kidnapped, and they've never stopped searching for her."

I paused again. Put the photos away and leaned forward, lowering my voice. "Tell me. Is he right? Are you Ja Vala Boudin?"

I waited. After a moment, her mouth opened slightly, but she didn't speak.

"Because if you are, Kenny Wadd wants to see you." I paused. "Would you like him to visit?"

Her mouth remained open. She didn't make a sound. Didn't move.

I put the photos on the end table between us. "I'll leave these with you. Maybe they'll stir your memory."

I stood to leave, but paused, crouching beside her. "What happened to you?" I whispered. "Why have you stopped communicating? Did someone drug you? Or threaten you? If you don't want to say anything out loud, that's okay. Blink twice if someone has bothered you, once if not."

I waited, but she didn't blink at all.

Finally, I stood to go. At the door, I stopped and looked back. In the sunlight from the window, I saw something glisten on her cheek. I was sure it was a tear.

Chapter 41

A woman's voice comes to her. The patient wants to say that she can hear her, but her lips won't open. Her body has separated from her, is not subject to her commands. This state is not new to her. Her mind is still clear enough to understand that Madame Armistead has taken charge again, has sent a representative, an imposter nurse to tell her what she must do. The powders brought by the imposter nurse have aborted her decay but have also begun to muddle her thoughts. The powders bring with them the fog that enveloped her for so long. She can see that fog ahead, hanging thick and dark on the horizon, rolling toward her, promising to swallow her so that she will again disappear, becoming part of it. Even so, she must take the powders. Madame Armistead has sent them because only the powders can keep her intact. Certainly, having a muddled mind is preferable to having a rotted body.

And yet, despite the dose of powders, she is still alert enough to hear a woman's voice calling her by name. Ja Vala, it says. It tells her about a photograph. She doesn't see this photograph, but the image of a man emerges as if from a cloud. His smile is wide and dazzling. He leans close, and his lips settle softly on hers; his strong hand grips her own. As if from afar, she sees him walk with her, taking her to her father's home.

The voice says this man's name: Kenny Wadd.

Kenny Wadd.

Thunder claps, and waves crash over her, drawing her deep into darkness where she can neither fight nor breathe. She is lost, falling. Where is the imposter nurse, the agent of Madame Armistead? Why doesn't she save her, tell her what to do? From the depths, she hears low voices asking, "What has happened to her?" and "When did this start?" They discuss a woman who is not responding, who will not eat or drink. A woman who seems to have slipped away.

The air stirs. She feels people moving around her. Someone picks up her wrist and presses it, someone wraps a cuff around her arm and tightens it. Someone shines a light into her eyes.

They treat her as if she's alive.

She waits. Listens. Hears no voices. Her mind keeps repeating the name, Kenny Wadd. She stops resisting, surrenders to the sound, the name. And despite the powders and the darkness, she sees Kenny Wadd, clearly as if he were beside her. He is walking her home, kissing her with gentle promises. But in the shadows, another man is watching and, when Kenny Wadd has gone, Josias comes at her like a rabid dog. She runs, screaming for Kenny Wadd, but Josias with his one remaining eye covers her mouth. She kicks and fights, but he has a knife and holds it against her ribs. He is determined, and the knife is sharp, glistening in the light of the moon. And then they are inside her house, where her parents are sleeping. Josias' fist presses her throat so she cannot make a sound. When he finishes with her, a woman arrives. Together they slice her arm open and rub powders into the wound.

She tries to get up but her she can't breathe. Can't move. Can only lie in her bed, dying.

After a while, she hears her mother wail.

Chapter 42

This time, leaving the hospital, I was vigilant. I kept a hand on my weapon, scanned the parking lot. But no one was lurking there to ambush us.

In the car, Colby talked, mostly about the case. "You got to admit," he said, "whoever she is, she's hot."

Hot?

"She could be a model."

I supposed she could.

He went on about how it was hard to believe she was just a maid, looking the way she did.

I only half-listened. I was thinking about the name, Ja Vala Boudin. Alexandra Lambert, whoever she was, had used that name for the maid. And she'd said that the Grangers had hired Ja Vala in Haiti. Which meant that the maid had already been using the dead woman's name before she'd worked for the Grangers. Which meant...what?

Colby was still talking. "So maybe the wife found out the husband was having an affair with the maid and took out a hit on him. And the hit went wrong. Anybody thought of that?"

I forced a smile, tried to be encouraging. "No," I said. "Interesting theory. But actually, Colby, I need you to be quiet for a few."

"Yeah? Got a headache?"

I formed another smile. "No. I just need to think."

"Oh, okay." He was quiet for about three seconds. "But you know what? I find that when I'm confused, it helps to talk things out." And he proceeded to do exactly that, which apparently meant recapping everything he'd just said. I gave up, stopped thinking about the case and continued to miss D'Angelo. Appreciating him, his instincts, his savvy. Again, I saw the flash of white. D' with his gun drawn. The woman dead on the street.

I kept my eyes on the road, didn't look to my right. Didn't want to see Colby instead of D'. And when we got back to the Roundhouse, I walked fast, keeping ahead of him. In the elevator, he talked all the way up. But when the doors opened at our floor, Colby was immediately drowned out by clamor. A crowd was gathered around D'Angelo's desk.

"Condolences, Mo," one of them called—probably Rodriguez. "The big dude's back."

"No way. Already?" Colby looked stricken.

"Cleared." D' stood, opened his arms to me, grinning. "I may even get a commendation."

I flew into his hug, basking there while the gang of detectives hooted, told us to get a room.

"What happened?" I asked.

He released me but hung onto an arm. "No idea. Deputy Commissioner might have rushed things along, and sanity prevailed. All I know is I got official word that the investigation had been completed, and I was to return to active duty post haste."

"Let's move across the street." Rodriguez looked at his watch. "It's lunchtime. Which means happy hour."

It wasn't yet noon.

"No drinking on duty," D' said.

"Just one round, D'Angelo." Reynolds grabbed his jacket.

"It's a special occasion," someone else said.

"Start your engines, gentlemen. D'Angelo's treating!"

"Hell I am," D' protested. "Unlike you assholes, I got work to do." But a band of detectives yanked him from his desk and escorted him to the elevators.

"Mo. Come on!" D' called.

"Yeah, Mo," Rodriguez hollered. "It's a party for your better half."

I hesitated, didn't want to be a party pooper. "I'll catch up with you," I waved, watched them swarm away, jam themselves into the elevator.

When the elevator doors closed, the office was silent.

Until Colby started to talk. "Well. I guess I'll head over and join them. You coming?"

"I don't know."

We faced each other. Why was the moment so awkward? We'd worked together for what? Three hours?

Colby put a hand in his pocket. "Tell you the truth, Mo. I was looking forward to working with you." He was pouting. Was his chin wobbling? "I mean, I'm glad for D'Angelo. He deserves to be back. It's just—I haven't ever worked such a high-profile case. And I was excited to work with someone as experienced as you."

Really? Experienced? Did that translate to old? How old was Colby? Twenty-seven or eight? Young for a detective. And only a few years younger than I was. Okay, seven or eight. He was dapper, almost pretty. I felt my cheeks heat up.

"Don't sweat it, Colby. In homicide, there's always a next time. Besides, like you said, it's hard to pick up a case in the middle. Next time, you'll be in it from the beginning." I didn't know what else to say.

He nodded. I sat at my desk, took out my case files.

"What's the deal, Mo?" He planted his butt on my desktop right beside the file. "You and D'? You're like the Bobbsey twins."

"So?"

"So, he just got reinstated. And you're not over there congratulating—"

"Colby, back off." I sounded harsher than I intended. "I've got stuff to do first." I opened the file, leafed through some pages. My decisions were none of Colby's business. Truth was, I didn't know exactly why I was hanging back. I could go for one beer, be part of the gang. The case could wait a few minutes.

Colby didn't move.

I looked up at him. "You're on my desk."

He nodded, didn't move. For once, he was silent, watching me fiddle with papers. Finally, he said, "Don't be so hard on yourself, Mo."

What?

"Stuff happens. Don't blame yourself."

Blame myself?

"Nobody can see everything every second."

Okay.

"So you weren't on your guard after seeing a protected witness. So what? It still wasn't your fault someone tried to kill you."

My eyeballs bulged.

He went on about the shooting. The more he assured me that it wasn't my fault, the clearer it became that he and lots of others had decided that it was. I closed my eyes, felt myself fly onto concrete, hearing shots.

Colby continued his pep talk. I saw the dead woman's eyes. Who was she? Why had she wanted to kill two detectives?

Maybe she hadn't. Maybe she was a random shooter, aiming at anyone within range.

I thought back, pictured leaving the hospital. Other people had been in the area, but she hadn't fired at them. No, the shooting hadn't been random. It was connected to the Grangers and their maid. And Alexandra Lambert, whoever she was, must have orchestrated it.

But I still didn't understand why. Even if we'd been killed, our deaths wouldn't stop the investigation.

I ran a hand through my hair, rubbed my temples. Recalled Alexandra Lambert's visit, her purple ensemble. Her false identity.

And a thought crossed my mind: She'd insisted that we go into an interrogation room. Isolated. So D' and I were the only people who'd spent any time with her. The other guys would remember her gawdy outfit, but we were the only ones who would recognize her. Maybe that was her motive—If D' and I were dead, no one could identify her.

Did that make sense? Would a woman want to kill cops just because they'd seen her face? Why would she need to be unrecognizable—Was she some bigtime international drug dealer or assassin? And what was her connection to the Grangers?

"So, I'll save you a barstool, okay?"

Colby eased off my desk, and I realized he'd been talking for a while. I nodded and smiled at him, gave him a wave. "See you in a few." And I sat still, shoulders tight, staring at the pages in front of me. Before long, I heard the elevator doors open and close.

Chapter 43

Kenny Wadd answered his phone on the first ring.

Before I could speak, he asked about Ja Vala. "Did you show her the photographs, detective?"

I told him that I had and that the woman had shown no reaction.

"Not even when you told her that I personally had given them to you? She had no reaction at all?"

To be fair, she hadn't reacted to anything. "Mr. Wadd, the woman's condition has changed dramatically in the last few hours. I shouldn't tell you this because it's not public knowledge, but she's not communicating."

I heard him draw a breath. "What do you mean exactly, Detective Sterling? Are you saying she's in a coma?"

"No, no. She's conscious. But her mental state—"

"Of course her mental state is not good. It's the poison—They are poisoning her." His tone was frantic.

"No, Mr. Wadd," I tried to calm him. "There is tight security around her. No one is poisoning her."

More deep breaths. "I must see Ja Vala. It is essential."

"Sorry. Besides, I doubt this woman is your Ja Vala. As we discussed, she's most likely an illegal immigrant using a stolen identity."

Kenny Wadd was silent for a moment. "I see that there is no alternative, detective. I must meet with you face to face. There is much to explain."

"I'm afraid I have a full day—"

"What I have to say will change everything." He sounded determined. "Give me one half hour of your time."

I looked at the clock.

"Please, detective."

THE WOMAN IN THE CUPBOARD

Oh, what the hell. The man had come all the way from Haiti. What was the harm in seeing him for half an hour? I told him that my partner and I would squeeze him in at the end of the day. For half an hour.

After the call ended, his voice resonated in my head. "They are poisoning her." Damn. Why hadn't I asked him to explain that? What made him so sure that she was being poisoned? And who had he meant by "they"?

Chapter 44

I glanced at the elevator. Figured I ought to join the guys across the street. But I didn't. If Colby was right, they'd been blaming me for D's suspension. Judging me. I wasn't ready to walk into the fray. Besides, I had to put together pieces of the case.

Haiti, for one. According to Susan Richards, she and her husband had spent time there with the Grangers. Alexandra Lambert had also claimed to be with them there when the Grangers hired their maid.

Their maid had used the identity of Ja Vala Boudin, a dead Haitian woman.

The dead Ja Vala's photographs highly resembled the living, breathing woman in the hospital.

So what did all of that mean?

Maybe the mysterious Alexandra Lambert was a broker? A trafficker who arranged false identities for illegal international workers?

Except that there were no papers—false or otherwise for Ja Vala Boudin. No passport or work permits. Nothing.

I couldn't make sense of anything. I closed my eyes for a moment. And remembered something Susan Richards had said. I sifted through my file, found my notes on her interview. Mrs. Richards had said that her husband had been dissolving his partnership with Dixon Granger, that J. Steven had wanted no part of something Granger had become involved in. That "something" might just involve identity theft and smuggling illegals into the country. And drugging them into compliance—And maybe Granger and Alexandra Lambert had been partners in this enterprise. And maybe their partnership was the reason for the murders.

Bingo. I had to talk to D'Angelo, tell him my theory.

But I pictured his reaction: Dixon Granger? Are you kidding? He was one of the city's most prominent citizens. You have no evidence, but you're accusing him of human trafficking?

He was right. It seemed impossible. And yet, it explained almost everything.

I made a to-do list. D' and I had to talk to Susan Richards again. She'd probably known more than she'd told us.

And we had to go back to the Granger crime scene. The Grangers might have kept personal diaries or travel papers, records that indicated exactly where in Haiti they'd traveled, who they'd dealt with there, what they'd paid for.

What else? Check on Sylvia Blake. Had she gone on any of the Haiti trips?

And Kenny Wadd. We had to look into him, his background. Find out if he really was who he claimed to be. Maybe his story was fabricated. He could be working for the traffickers.

I stuck the list into the folder, ready to leave. Realized as I stood that I'd left something off the list. Of course I had. I didn't want to think about the shooter who'd almost killed us. But we needed to find out who she was. Whether she had any connection to the Grangers or their maid.

Fine. I sat again and added her to the list. Then I closed my eyes again. My head ached. I pictured the guys at the bar across the street, celebrating D'Angelo's reinstatement. Raising their glasses, toasting him. I'd pop in, be supportive. Join in the merriment.

I hurried out of the building, crossed the street. I was about to open the door when it swung out, knocking into me. Reynolds and Colby were leaving. I was too late. The party was over. D' and the others had already gone.

Chapter 45

Words swirl, air moves around her. A distant light fades and she smells spices. A chunk is pushed into her mouth. She chews, swallows. Complies. She waits for silence and stillness. Because when she is alone, she must act.

Madame Armistead's directions were very clear. The woman who brought them warned that she must follow them closely, exactly, must take the packets of powder that are taped to the bottoms of the dresser drawers. Or decompose. Madame has sent enough for one week only, but she has promised to send more if she follows the directions.

Meantime, she must not repeat to anyone what the woman has said. Must memorize the directions exactly.

More moist food is shoved into her mouth. And more. Until finally, dishes clatter. Voices move away. She listens and hears no one. Looks through the mist of her mind and sees no one.

She recalls the directions, repeats them in her head as a song: Hide the powder, so no one can see. Two doses each day, in water or tea.

The rhyme helps her remember what the imposter nurse has warned: if anyone finds out about the medicine, they will take it away, and without it, in a matter of days—maybe of hours, irreversible decay will begin. The powder would make her feel foggy, but Madame Armistead's fake nurse told her that was unimportant. Being foggy was far better than decomposing.

She repeats this fact in her head. Being foggy is far better than decomposing.

When she is certain no one is nearby, she moves silently, sliding open the dresser drawer. Removing one small envelope from those that are taped underneath. Pouring the contents into her water glass. Drinking it all. Tearing the envelope to pieces and tossing them into the trashcan with a page of writing paper, so not a trace of envelope will be noticed.

She sits on the bed, reciting the rhyme so she will not forget them. The words are like a beam from a lighthouse, guiding her through mist. She must obey, must hide the powders so no one can see. Two doses each day, mixed in water or tea.

She closes her eyes, runs her hands over her body. Feels her lips, nose, breasts, feet. So far, the powder is working. Her skin remains intact.

Chapter 46

I grabbed a hoagie and ate at my desk, waited for D'Angelo. When he came in half an hour later, his eyes were shining.

"I was hoping you'd join us."

"Somebody has to work." I stood, hugged him. "I'm glad you're back."

He rolled his chair over to my desk. "What did I miss?"

I filled him in. Told him about Kenny Wadd's call, our upcoming meeting with him. The maid's regression, her lack of reaction to hearing the name Kenny Wadd and even to seeing his photos. D' picked up the pictures. Squinted at them.

"I don't know. This one's younger and happier. But my money says they're the same person." He tossed the pictures back onto my desk, frowning. "But when she saw these, she had no reaction? Nothing?"

"She didn't make a sound, and her pupils didn't dilate."

"You watched her pupils?"

"Well, it was hard with her eyes so dark. But yeah. If a person's interested in something they're looking at, their pupils dilate. Everybody knows that."

D'Angelo snorted. "So you're saying the photos didn't interest her?"

"Or maybe a drug controlled her pupils." I swallowed the last of my hoagie, recalling her blank face. And the tear I'd seen on her cheek. "I think she recognized everybody in the shots, but wasn't willing to say so."

"Wasn't willing? Or wasn't able?"

Able? "Either way." But why had she cried? Had the pictures made her sad? Frustrated? Angry? Frightened?

"What about Vogel?" D' asked. "He still thinks she was drugged?"

"Yes, but he can't figure out how the drugs are getting to her. And lab tests haven't found anything. So he can't be sure." I opened the file, replaced the photos.

D' leaned closer, lowered his voice. "And Colby?"

Colby? "What about him?"

"How was it, working with him?"

I smiled, met his eyes. "Nobody's as good as you, D.'"

He grinned and leaned back, satisfied. "So, you missed me."

"A little." A lot.

"So." He stood, moved his chair back to his desk. "What now?"

I tossed him the car keys. "J. Steven Richards' widow."

"Again?"

While we waited for the elevator, he put his hand in his pocket, jingling his change.

Chapter 47

Susan Richards was in her exercise room. "Sorry," she panted on her treadmill. "I'm on a strict regimen. The doctor says physical activity will help my depression."

Depression? Susan wore lululemon athletic apparel, perfect makeup, a fresh manicure, brand new Addidas. She looked like a model for some sportswear magazine. I glanced at D'. His lips were pursed, his hands pressed together. He made no comment, just watched.

"We have just a few questions, Mrs. Richards." I stood in front of her so I could see her face.

"Shoot," she huffed.

"When we talked before, you said your husband had issues with Dixon Granger."

"That's why he was dissolving the partnership." She raised a hand, smeared sweat across her forehead.

"You indicated it had to do with something in Haiti."

"I did?"

"Yes." I looked at my notes, read the quote. "You said you thought 'that Dixon had gotten involved in something so illegal that it could contaminate my husband and the firm.' Should I go on?"

She shook her head. "I said what I said. But I have no idea what was bothering J. Steven. He never said." She kept jogging.

"What about the secretary?"

"Sylvia? What about her?"

"Do you think she was murdered because of her relationship with Mr. Granger?"

"How would I know?" She looked from me to D', back to me.

"Do you think Judith Granger found out about the affair and killed Sylvia out of jealousy?"

Susie lifted a towel, dabbed her forehead. "You're joking, right?" She tossed the towel aside. "Look, I'm sure Sylvia wasn't Dixon's first or only affair. That aside, yes, Judith had quite a temper. But if she wanted to kill someone over Dixon having an affair, it wouldn't have been the woman. It would have been Dixon. The two of them were like angry cats. They fought constantly." She chuckled. "What am I laughing about? They're all dead." She grabbed the towel again, wiped her face, slowed her steps to a slow trot, then a walk. Her mascara was smudged.

"Personally," she squinted into the distance, "At the time, I thought it was Dixon who killed Sylvia Blake."

Really? "Why would you think that?"

Susie smirked. "It seemed obvious. They were having an affair, and Sylvia was out for Sylvia. Very ambitious. She had access to Dixon's confidential information. So, it occurred to me that, if it suited her, she might have been blackmailing him."

Blackmailing him? About what? Their affair?

"You think Sylvia knew about the issue that drove your husband to dissolve the partnership?" D'Angelo asked. "That's what she'd blackmail him about?"

Susan backed off the treadmill, hung the towel around her neck. "Maybe. Maybe not. Dixon had lots of secrets, not just that. All I know for sure is that Sylvia and Dixon had something going. And now both of them, and Dixon's wife, and my husband are dead." She bit her lip. Smoothed her hair. Cleared her throat. Looked at me, then D'. "Oh my." Her eyes widened. "Forgive me, I've been rude. I've given it up, but would either of you care for coffee?"

Neither of us did. As we walked to the door, she thanked us for coming by, said it was nice to have people over. "Without J. Steven, I don't have much of a social life any more. You'd be surprised how quickly people forget about you when you're not part of a couple."

She curled her lips, looked away, and closed the heavy mahogany door.

Chapter 48

D'Angelo turned onto the main road. "So? Think Granger killed his secretary?"

I wasn't sure. "I think Susan Richards wasn't a fan of Dixon Granger." She'd called him a philanderer involved in whoknowswhat—Drug dealing or smuggling or bribery or trafficking. Maybe murder?

D' turned a corner. "I thought she was being honest with us."

"She probably believes everything she said."

He eyed me from the drive's seat. "But you don't?"

"Do you?"

"I did until you sounded doubtful." He let out a breath. "Now, I don't know."

"D." I needed to say it, wasn't sure how. Finally, just said it. "I'm glad you're back."

"I know." He glanced at me. "Me, too."

"And thank you." My face heated up.

"You're welcome."

"I mean for saving my life."

"I know. Don't thank me. We look after each other."

I didn't say anything. He'd been the only one doing the looking. I took a chocolate bar out of my bag, offered him a square.

"No. I'm off sweets for a while."

"Since when?"

He muttered.

I said I couldn't hear him. Repeated my question.

"Since I made a deal with God."

I looked at him, wondered if he was kidding. "A deal? What are you talking about?"

"You wouldn't understand, Mo. You're not religious."

"So what? This isn't about me. What deal did you make?"

He shook his head. "Never mind. Let's talk about our next interview."

"Tell me about the deal."

He glanced at me. "What are their names again? Katie and Ed?"

"Kaye and Ellis. What was the deal?"

He ignored me. Began whistling Ave Maria.

"Why can't you eat sweets? You give them up and you get what?"

No response. Just more whistling.

"Something about Teresa? Or your kids? Come on, D', tell me. You made a deal so you'd be healthy? Or get a raise? Is it about the job?"

He stopped whistling and looked at me.

Bingo—It was about the job. "Is it about this case? The shooting? Or wait—was it about your reinstatement?"

"Let it go, Mo." He wouldn't look at me, but his face turned scarlet.

So, I was right? It was about his reinstatement? I laughed, couldn't help it. "D', please tell me you're not serious."

"Mo, you're crossing a line. This isn't your business—"

"But for real? You promised God that if He got you reinstated, you wouldn't eat sweets—for how long?"

He turned a corner too fast—the car screeched. "If you must know, it's for a month. But it's not that simple."

It wasn't?

"I'm also making a charitable donation." He clamped his jaw shut and narrowed his eyes. I knew that look. It meant that I should back off. He was getting mad.

I tried to keep a straight face. "Okay. I'll stop." But I couldn't stop. "Except tell me this. Do you really seriously believe that the God of the entire universe, assuming He even exists, cares whether or not some schmo eats a piece of chocolate?"

D' didn't answer. He peered out the window, looking at addresses. Finally pulled up to the curb. "It's that one," he nodded to a red brick duplex.

I undid my seatbelt, picked up my notebook, reached to open the door.

"It's not about a piece of chocolate, Mo. It's about personal sacrifice by little schmos. And the expression of faith and atonement. I don't expect you to understand. But maybe, given that the deal I made includes you and your safety, you can at least pretend to show some respect?"

Before I could reply, he was out of the car. The door slammed behind him. I sat for a moment, turning scarlet, and then I got out, hurrying to catch up.

Chapter 49

I caught up with him at the door. "Sorry." I rang the doorbell.

He glanced at me, looked back at the door. Still peeved.

"Your God deal really involved me?"

"Why wouldn't it?"

I opened my mouth to reply but hesitated, not sure what to say. And before I could decide, the door opened. A striking dark-eyed woman greeted us, her pure white hair tied into a chignon.

"Detective Sterling?" She held her hands together at her waist.

"Yes," I flashed my ID, introduced D'Angelo.

She lifted her reading glasses to check the ID before inviting us inside. Her husband was reading in the living room, his feet on an ottoman.

"These are the detectives, dear," the woman spoke slowly, introduced us by name, told us that he was Ellis and that we should call her Kaye. Ellis stood to shake our hands. Kaye offered us hot drinks.

"I have a fresh pot of coffee." She worried her hands, looked toward the kitchen. Seemed uneasy.

I said, "No thanks," just as D'Angelo said, "That would be great. With a little milk."

"Sugar?" she asked.

D' looked at me when he said, "No, thanks."

Mrs. Blake rushed off, skirt swishing like a housewife from another era, the mom in a Fifties television show.

D' and I sat, he on the wingback opposite Ellis Blake, I on the sofa. The room smelled of sweet smoke, a pipe rested on an ashtray beside Ellis' chair.

"Kaye says you want to talk about Sylvia," Ellis kept his voice low, confidential. "Does that mean there's news about her case?"

"Nothing definite," D' leaned forward, matching Ellis' tone. Talking man to man. "But we have a few more questions."

"Maybe I can answer them now, so you won't have to bother Kaye." Ellis picked up his pipe, held onto it. "Losing Sylvia was—still is very hard on her. On me, too, but even more on Kaye. Sylvia was our only child. She was beautiful, bright. Successful." His eyes drifted to the mantelpiece. It was covered with photos of Sylvia, a small shrine. "Do you have children, Detective?"

D' nodded. "Yes, a few."

Ellis looked at me. I shook my head.

"Well, you will someday, and then you'll understand. Once you're a parent, your life isn't about you anymore. Your child is your priority. Her future is your main concern. When that future gets cut off prematurely...Well, it's difficult to find a reason to go on."

For a nanosecond, I met D's eyes. They were level and calm, assuring me that he didn't think Ellis was suicidal.

"Sorry. It's not as dire as it sounds. We are in the process of redefining our lives. It's not easy. But you haven't come here to listen to me go on. It's a bad habit left over from my teaching years." He set his pipe aside, relaxed his hand.

"You were a teacher?" I finally entered the conversation.

"English Professor. University of Delaware. My wife was a professor, too. Mathematics."

"Not tenured like you were, though." Mrs. Blake glided into the room, carrying a tray of coffee and cookies. "I brought an extra cup in case you change your mind." She smiled at me. Her lipstick was bright red. Had she reapplied it while getting coffee?

The next moments were occupied by the pouring of coffee, the passing around of cookies. Questions about the heat of the beverage.

"The ginger snaps are sugar free, Detective," she held the plate out to D'. "They're store bought, not like the others. But I put them out because you said you can't have sugar."

D'Angelo thanked her but passed the plate over to me without taking a cookie. Mrs. Blake watched me expectantly, her smile stiff, eyes strained. It seemed rude not to take something, so I helped myself to an oatmeal cookie, waited to bite into it until she sat down. Told her it was delicious.

D' drank his coffee, asked Ellis what he'd been reading when we'd come in.

Ellis answered with too much enthusiasm. Said that he'd decided to reread the classics, now that he was retired. He held up the book. "This is Chaucer. It's like meeting an old friend—"

"Ellis, my God." Mrs. Blake's tone was sharp. "The detectives didn't come here to find out how you occupy your time."

Ellis closed his mouth, chastised, but said nothing. Sipped his coffee.

Mrs. Blake turned to me. "What is it that you want to talk about? We've already told investigators everything we know."

D's eyes indicated that I should take over, woman to woman.

"Mrs. Blake—"

"Please. Call me Kaye."

"Kaye." I smiled. "We don't want to intrude. But we know you want to assist the investigation in any way you can."

"Of course." She picked at a raw cuticle.

I looked from her to Ellis, back to her. "Good. So this line of questioning might seem sensitive, but—"

"Nothing about Sylvia is sensitive anymore. The dead don't have feelings." Her eyes flashed anger and pain. But she looked away and blinked, and when she turned back to me, her eyes were empty, revealing nothing.

Ellis put down his coffee cup, stared at the wall.

I set what was left of my cookie on a napkin, sat straight. "Okay. Then I'll just go ahead." I looked from one of them to the other. "As far as either of you know, was Sylvia involved with anyone?"

"Involved?" Kaye repeated.

"You mean was she seeing anyone?" Ellis asked. "No. She was between relationships. We already told that to the police."

"Are you sure she would have told you?"

"Absolutely."

"Of course. We discussed everything."

I nodded. "But what if the relationship was with someone she thought you wouldn't approve of."

"Wouldn't approve of?" Kaye raised her eyebrows. "Why wouldn't we?"

"We're a very liberal family, detective." Ellis sat straight. "We don't judge people by superficial qualities. If Sylvia cared for someone that would be enough for us."

I paused. "Even if that someone was married?"

Kaye blinked rapidly. "Impossible," she said. "Sylvia wouldn't waste her time on a dead-end affair. She was far too practical."

"Hold on, Kaye." Ellis leaned toward D'. "Why are you asking us about this? What have you found out? With whom do you think she was involved?"

"We don't know for sure that she was involved with anyone," D' said.

"But you suspect."

D' shrugged and turned to me, letting me continue. The three of them stared at me, waiting.

I took a breath, watched the Blakes. Did they already know what I was about to ask? "What do you know about Sylvia's relationship with Dixon Granger?"

Kaye opened her mouth, stumbling for words. "Dixon Granger? What? See, Ellis? I told you the murders are connected." Her hand went to her mouth.

"We're not sure of that, Ma'am. We're simply looking into their relationship."

"Well, if you're suggesting that they were romantically involved, I can assure you that they were not," Ellis said. He reached for his pipe again, picked up a pipe cleaner. "They were in business together. That was all."

"Business?" I asked. "You mean because she was his legal secretary."

He poked the cleaner into his pipe. "No, not just that. A while back, Sylvia asked my opinion about Granger. She wanted to know whether or not I thought he'd make a trustworthy business partner."

"When was this?"

"About a year ago. Some months before she—before her murder." He looked away, opened a bag of tobacco.

Kaye winced. "You're not going to smoke now, are you Ellis? We have guests."

"It's okay, ma'am," D' said. "We don't mind."

"Are you sure?" Kaye fretted.

"And what did you advise her?" I ignored Kaye, kept the conversation focused.

Ellis looked up from his tobacco. "Well. I pointed out that Granger was tremendously successful and that I doubted he'd achieved his vast success by being either particularly generous or kind. I advised her to have the terms of their relationship put into writing and then to ask an impartial lawyer to go over their contract to make sure Granger couldn't, for lack of better words, screw her over."

Kaye said nothing, folded her hands and watched her knuckles.

"What was the nature of the business?"

Ellis opened his mouth and held still, his pipe suspended in the air. "It was an international venture. Importing from the islands. Isn't that so, Kaye?"

Kaye looked at her hands. Her shoulders tensed. "Yes, from the Caribbean. But it doesn't matter because they were still negotiating when she died. The business never actually got off the ground."

"Wait, now," Ellis raised his pipe. "It was Haiti, wasn't it?"

I held my breath, glanced at D'.

"Yes," Ellis tilted his head. "I'm certain. It was Haiti. Some kind of import business. We have no details, though. We discussed the general idea of working with Granger, not the specifics." He stuffed tobacco into his pipe, packed it down.

I looked at my unfinished cookie. Tried to digest the news that Sylvia and Granger had been planning to do business in Haiti. The place where Ja Vala Boudin had lived. Where Kenny Wadd had come from. Where Alexandra Lambert claimed to have met the Grangers and their maid, and where the Grangers had traveled with the Richards just before J. Steven decided to break off his partnership with Dixon. Whatever business Sylvia and Granger had been planning in Haiti might link up all four murders.

D' cleared his throat. I didn't have to look at him to sense his restlessness. He was antsy, ready to go. So was I, actually. We stood, thanked the Blakes for their time, said we'd be in touch if we found out anything more about their daughter's case.

Ellis stood to say goodbye, lighter and pipe in hand. He wished us luck with our investigation. Kaye rose to walk us out.

At the door, she put a hand on D's arm. "Believe me, it wasn't an affair, detective." She narrowed her eyes. "Sylvia was a beauty, and she was smart. She could have had any man she wanted. Why would she have wasted her time with a married man? Especially a predator like Dixon Granger? She wouldn't. And if she had had a foolish fling with him, I'd have known about it. Sylvia and I had no secrets. Plain and simple, theirs was a professional relationship. Nothing more."

D' and I thanked her for her candor. When we pulled away from the curb, Kaye Blake was at the window, watching our car.

Chapter 50

D'Angelo was silent.

"Haiti again," I said. "An import business?"

D' didn't answer. His forehead was damp, his eyes glassy. "Look in the glove box. Get me a pack of peanuts, would you?"

Really? He was allowed to eat peanuts, but not cookies or donuts? I opened the glove box. Found his stash. Took out a bag of peanuts and opened it. Handed it to him.

"Thanks." He popped a few into his mouth.

"If you're hungry, I'm in. We can stop—"

"No, I'm okay. Just a little light-headed. Probably hypoglycemic."

Seriously? Hypoglycemic? "Dammit, D'. You need sugar." I dove into the glove box, retrieved a chocolate bar. Tore the wrapper off.

"No, I'll be fine. These'll do."

"Peanuts are protein, you need sugar."

"I said I'll be fine."

"How about you pull over? I should drive."

"Mo. Leave it alone." His jaw tightened.

"When was your last physical? You could be diabetic."

"I'm not diabetic. I'm off sweets." He held the bag up to his mouth, dropped more peanuts into it.

I watched him, hoping he was really all right. Not sure what to do. "D'—"

"Leave it alone, Mo."

"Are you going to pass out and smash the car?"

"Cut it out, Mo. I was a little dizzy. I'm fine." He waited a beat. "So, what do you think?"

"I think you should see your doctor."

He smirked. "About Sylvia Blake. Was her thing with Granger just business?"

"I don't know. Susan Richards was pretty adamant that Sylvia and Granger were doing the happy dance."

He plowed through a yellow light just as it turned red. "And she seemed credible. My opinion? Mama Blake was protesting way too much."

"You think she knew Sylvia was seeing Granger?"

"I do. Otherwise, why would she be so insistent that Sylvia wasn't?"

"But Sylvia and Granger are both dead. Why would Sylvia's mother try to hide their affair?"

D' snorted. "No idea. But she sure was determined to."

"And what about the import business? From Haiti? Everything seems to spring from there."

"Okay, I give up." D' swerved into a parking space outside a food court on Walnut Street. "I can't think. My mind doesn't work without sugar. Maybe I'm allowed to have orange juice."

I followed D' into a food court near U of Penn and stopped, surrounded by booths offering pizza, burgers, Chinese, deli, fried chicken, salads, frozen yogurt. I stood still, unsure where to go, which line to hook onto. The court, like the Granger case, offered too many choices.

Chapter 51

I got wings. Yummy, but messy, made my fingers greasy and sticky. D' got a couple of egg rolls and a large coke, not diet.

He opened a mustard pack. "The Chief apologized for my suspension—That's a first, isn't it?"

It was, as far as I knew.

"He told me I should get a medal. A commendation. He called me a hero. How about that?"

"He's right." I swallowed chicken. Told him I was sorry.

His mouth was full. "What for?"

"I should have seen the shooter." I picked up a napkin, rubbed grease off my fingers. "Sorry, I screwed up."

He looked down. "Don't keep going there, Mo."

Really?

"You have nothing to be sorry about."

I hoped he meant it. Crumpled my napkin, put it down. "Anyway, she's dead, so we can't question her. Or identify her. But whoever she was, Alexandra Lambert sent her."

"Whoever Alexandra Lambert is."

We sat silent for a moment, thinking. I started making a map in my head, placing each part of the case in a different quadrant. "I need a piece of paper."

He looked at his tray, pulled off the paper placemat. Smeared away a droplet of soda. Turned it over and pushed it across the table.

Fine. It would do. I took a pen from my bag. "First, we have the Grangers." I drew a circle in the middle of the paper, labeled it DG and JG.

"And along with them, we have a maid who has no apparent affect or memory, and whose identity might belong to a dead woman." I drew a box, adjacent to the Grangers, wrote, "Vanessa," and in parentheses, added, "Ja Vala?"

D' looked at my drawing. "She might have been trafficked under a stolen identity. How are you going to draw that?"

"Hold on." I drew another circle, connected with a line to the Grangers' circle. Wrote "J. Steven" inside. "J. Steven's wife says Dixon Granger was involved in something horrible and illegal. Maybe human trafficking—that would explain the maid. But whatever it was, it coincides with what Sylvia Blake's parents said, that she was involved in an import business with Dixon." I drew a third circle, connected it to the Granger's circle. Labeled it Sylvia.

D' nodded. "I think you have something here, Mo. But you haven't shown our dead shooter or Alexandra Lambert."

Right. I added another circle, wrote "shooter" in it. Drew a line to a box with "A.L." inside.

"But—assuming we're right, and Alexandra Lambert sent the shooter, what does that have to do with the rest of this?"

I wasn't sure. I looked at the drawing. Realized that connection lines were missing. "Haiti," I said. "They've all been to or come from Haiti." I added dotted lines, connecting Alexandra Lambert, the Grangers, J. Steven, Sylvia, and the maid.

"Want to bet our shooter is Haitian?" D' said. "Because it's looking more and more like we've bumped into a human trafficking ring."

"What about Vanessa's state of mind, though? How come she's so out of it?"

"Drugs. Maybe they drug their imports so they won't escape. Maybe they deal both drugs and humans."

"But Dr. Vogel hasn't identified a drug."

"It's been only a few days, Mo. Testing takes time. Some drugs are never identified. They don't all show up in the screenings, and there are so many to test for."

I picked up my soda, drained the can. Looked back at the drawing. "Okay, so J. Steven wanted no part of Granger because

Granger and Sylvia were getting into the human trafficking business. They were using the names of dead people to conceal the identities of their kidnapped victims and drugging them to keep them from escaping or exposing their captivity."

"And Alexandra Lambert?"

I chewed my lip. "Maybe she's another business partner?"

"Maybe." D' scowled. "But who killed everyone? Lambert? Because except for the maid, she's the last one alive."

Except for the maid. Vanessa. I thought of her bloody clothes in the Grangers' machine. The murder weapons in the dishwasher. Could the evidence have been planted? Had Alexandra Lambert killed the Grangers and tried to frame their maid?

I leaned my elbow on the table, stared at the drawing. What motive would Alexandra Lambert have to kill all these people? J. Steven, for example. He wasn't part of the business, but he knew about it and might expose it. She might have killed him to keep him quiet. Sylvia and Dixon were supposedly partners. Was Lambert a third partner? If so, she might have killed them because of a business issue—money or power. Maybe she was jealous of Sylvia's affair with Dixon? And Judith? She might simply have been unlucky, killed just because she was there.

It fit. If Lambert was a third partner.

"D'," I began.

"Wait," he put a hand up.

"What if Lambert wasn't their partner?" I began.

"What if she was their competitor?" D' finished my sentence, slapped his hands on the table, and stood to go. "That would be motive."

I picked up the drawing, stuck it into my bag. We plopped our trays onto the stack by the trash, and headed back to car. Nothing was sure, but now at least we had a theory.

Chapter 52

The aide feeds her soft food without flavor. This is the round brown aide called Kylie, the one who speaks in cheery singsong as if to a child. When she swallows, Kylie says she is doing a good job. Kylie praises her for chewing, for opening her mouth. For sipping juice or tea upon command. "Very good!" Kylie says, as if by parting her jaws, her patient has accomplished a deed of impressive skill. As Kylie feeds her like a child, the patient thinks about her unborn children. And the man Kenny Wadd.

"How many shall we have?" She is wrapped in his arms as he asks. She laughs and tells him that God will decide the number.

"But God won't make them for us. That we will have to do ourselves." He nudges her face with his cheek. She tingles from the scratch of his stubble, the softness of his lips, and she shoves him playfully away.

"How about five?" he says.

"Five?" She holds her belly.

"Not five? Okay, then six." He kisses her neck.

"How about we try for one and see what happens."

Kenny Wadd remarks that he would like to have a big family. Lots of playful children running around. Lots of faces at dinner.

Lots of mouths to feed, she replies. She says a big family will be a lot of work.

He says it will be more joy than work.

She looks at his soulful eyes and smiles.

The aide Kylie tells her it's good to see her smiling, tells her again that she is doing a good job. The mushy food has all been swallowed. Kylie urges her to take some milk, and she complies.

Finally, Kylie picks up the tray and says that Dr. Vogel will be in soon. The patient waits until she is gone and goes to the dresser. She must move as she has been told, quickly remove a packet from under the drawer, empty the powder into a water glass. Drink it before the man Dr. Vogel appears.

Her fingers yank the packet from the wood. But in her haste, she pulls too hard, and the tape rips off a corner of the envelope. Some of the powder leaks out into the drawer below. Do not panic, she tells herself. Take what powder is left and mix it into the water. Or maybe she should take a different packet, so the amount will be correct. She looks at the spilled powder. Maybe she can scrape it up.

She looks at the door. Any moment, Dr. Vogel will be there. She must hurry. She pours the remaining powder into the water glass, uses the envelope to scrape up what has spilled into the drawer, but can't get it all. Some of the powder has spilled onto a stack of washcloths. She picks the top one up and shakes it over the water. A tiny cloud of powder falls into the glass. She glances at the door. Was that a footstep? Is the handle turning?

She hears the voice of Madame Armistead's agent insisting that she follow directions exactly. She lifts the glass to drink but, at the last moment, hears the name Ja Vala and recalls the hands of Madame Armistead and her son Josias. The deep cut they made on her arm, the powders they rubbed into the wound. Did the man Dixon Granger and his wife Judith add those same powders to her food? That would explain why she has not decayed. She tries to look into the past, to remember, but sees only fog. These powders. Each dose makes her mind less clear. Soon, they will bring back the haze from which she has just begun to emerge.

She holds the glass away from her mouth and studies her hands. The cuticles have already become dry and broken, the skin on her arms dry and flaky. She imagines her body dotted with rotted patches, reeking of death.

The handle of the door turns, and Dr. Vogel steps into the room.

Before he can say hello, she gulps down the contents of the glass. Maybe the amount she swallows will be enough to protect her body, and because of what she has spilled, not quite enough to smother her mind.

Chapter 53

On our way back to the Roundhouse, we had to drive past the hospital. D' wanted to stop and see Vanessa, see if our theory would cause a reaction. I told him it would be useless. She hadn't reacted to the photos;, why would she to the mention of human trafficking?

"Well, Vogel might have some thoughts," D' insisted.

I called Dr. Vogel to let him know we were on the way.

"No use coming by," he said. "The patient has continued to regress."

He said she was worse than she'd been even the day before. Completely non-verbal, not writing anything. Not responding. She ate only if someone fed her, and performed hygiene and toilet tasks only if someone guided her.

"She is awake, docile. She obeys if asked to open her mouth or to make a fist for a blood test. But whatever progress she was making seems to have halted. In fact, it's reversed." Dr. Vogel's voice was thin, distraught.

"What do you think caused the change?"

D' looked at me. "What change?"

I pointed to the road, reminded him to watch it.

"Detective, I wish I could tell you." Dr. Vogel let out a sigh. "Her tests have been normal. Even her brain scans. We've found no physical cause for her behavior. It's possible that she suffers from a dissociative disorder in which she vacillates between interactive and withdrawn states. If I didn't know it was impossible, I'd still suspect that she's been drugged."

"And it's impossible because?"

"Because, as I've told you, she has no access to drugs. She never leaves and has no visitors. She's closely monitored day and night." He went on, reviewing his unit's security procedures. The locked and secured unit. The security guards. Etcetera.

I leaned back against the headrest, stymied. Saw a dark-skinned woman lurking the hospital parking lot, aiming a gun at me and D'. If she'd been sent by Alexandra Lambert, then Alexandra Lambert knew where the maid was being treated. Could she have somehow gotten drugs to Vanessa?

Of course, she'd first have to penetrate Vogel's security measures. And even if she could, why would she simply drug the maid? If she wanted to keep her quiet about the trafficking business, why not just kill her?

I closed my eyes. Maybe Alexandra Lambert had good reason not to kill her—If she killed her, the maid couldn't take the fall for the murders. Alive but unable to speak coherently or defend herself, she'd be blamed for killing the Grangers and, whether or not she was convicted, the case would be resolved. Leaving Alexandra Lambert, whoever she was, to continue whatever she was up to.

D' was asking me questions. Vogel was still talking.

"Mo? Hello? What's going on?" D' swerved around a construction vehicle.

I asked Dr. Vogel to hang on. "Head back to the Roundhouse," I told D'. "We're not going to the hospital."

"Why not?"

I waved my hand, pointed back toward the Roundhouse.

"Detective?" Dr. Vogel snapped, impatient. "Are you there?"

"Yes, sorry. I'm in traffic." It was the first excuse that came to mind.

D' rolled his eyes, made a turn.

"So, that remains the most likely drug. I mentioned it to you earlier as it could explain her passivity and compliance as well as her clouded memory and thoughts."

Wait, what? "Sorry, doctor. Can you repeat that?"

"Again? Why? I just explained it."

"I want to make sure I understand."

"Scopolamine." His tone was snippy. "What else do you need me to repeat?"

How about all of it? "Tell me again."

He sighed. "From the beginning?"

"Please."

He cleared his throat, annoyed. "It's made from the Borrachero tree and it's known by many names: Hyoscine, burundanga, scopoderm, Jimson weed, Devil's breath."

Devil's breath?

"But like I said, I'd ruled out drugs like scopolamine because there's no way she'd have access to them."

"Just tell me why it's interesting."

"Well, for one thing scopolamine can be given transderm—through the skin or by ingesting. It's tasteless and odorless in powder form, so it can be given without a person's knowledge."

"So she might not know she's taken it?" I sat straight. "And what if she has? What happens?"

D' scowled at me. "What?"

"It causes compliance, or weakening of the conscious will. And, at certain dosages, it effectively prevents the brain from recording events that occur during intoxication, so it can cause complete or intermittent amnesia."

I grabbed D's arm. "Oh my God—That's got to be it. You've found it!"

"Found what?" D' pressed. "What happened?"

I shook my head, mouthed, "Wait."

"Once again, detective: I don't think I've found anything. Because, even though scopolamine might cause a condition like my patient's, there's no way my patient could have taken or been given it."

"But what if she somehow—"

"It's not possible. She hasn't."

I persisted. "But what if she has—"

"If she has, which she hasn't, then yes." Vogel's tone rose, irritated. "That was my reason for mentioning to you. At first, I didn't consider it because it's not typically accessible. But having ruled out the more common drugs, it occurred to me that scopolamine could explain her condition, depending on the dosage, frequency and purity of the drug."

He went on, saying he shouldn't even have mentioned the drug since it couldn't be an explanation.

"Have you tested her for it?" I interrupted.

"Tested her for what?" D' asked.

I shot him a be-quiet-or-else look.

"Naturally. I ordered the test. But, as I've said, the test is a formality. Clearlythe drug is not available to her." He sounded miffed, as if I'd insulted him. "I'll let you know when I have the results. Should take three or four days."

Before I could reply, he hung up.

Chapter 54

When we walked into the office, D' and I were still talking about scopolamine. D' agreed with Dr. Vogel that the test was probably a waste of time and money, since the patient was in a locked and tightly controlled environment, that her caretakers would know if she'd taken the drug.

I'd argued that there was always a way to penetrate security. That, for all we knew, the drug was being given to her through her skin. In her bath powder or mouth wash. That Alexandra Lambert knew where she was, might have bribed a nurse.

D' scoffed, but finally agreed that the test was a good idea so that we'd be able "to rule it out."

I sat at my desk, bothered. A bunch of the guys wandered over to D's desk. Reynolds, Graham, Rodriguez. Colby. I heard their voices, low and conspiratorial. Then an eruption of laughter.

"Batshit crazy," someone said.

Someone else had a follow-up story. More hushed voices. More laughter.

I opened my file, made a note about the drug test. Decided to take a break and join the group. I stood and turned without looking, bumping into someone head on.

"Oops—Excuse me." I tried to regain my balance.

"My apologies." He took my arm to steady me.

He was about six feet tall, broad-shouldered, wearing a dark suit with a white open-necked shirt. His skin was dark and smooth, eyes dark and shining. Smile dazzling. Even when his smile faded, his face seemed to glow.

A uniformed officer named Wilkins stood by his side. "Detective," he said, "the sergeant called, and Sgt. Rodriguez said to bring him on up. He says he's got an appointment with you about the Granger case."

"Thank you, officer."

"Detective Sterling?" The man released my arm.

My face burned red. I cleared my throat, offered him a seat beside my desk, noting that the band of detectives were all watching us. D' shot me a look asking whether he should join us.

But I was fine. When my visitor spoke again, I recognized his voice, his musical accent. And as I took a seat, even before we talked, an inexplicable sense of loss washed over me, and my eyes filled with tears.

Chapter 55

I felt foolish, confused. Blinked the tears away, blew my nose. Took a breath. Pulled myself together. Asked Kenny Wadd if he'd like coffee or a cold drink. He declined, thanked me, said he wasn't thirsty.

"Thank you for seeing me, Detective Sterling." His eyes glowed.

"Of course."

He continued, expressed gratitude for the chance to speak with me. He kept his voice low, and looked around as if to make sure no one was listening.

D' was, of course. He'd banished the others and sat a few yards away, staring at his computer, pretending to be working on something. Straining his ears.

"I must explain to you," Kenny Wadd held his hands together, "the reasons I have come." He looked at D'Angelo. Turned toward Colby and Reynolds who were standing near a partition. "Would it be—Is there a more private place to speak?"

I tossed a look at D', indicating that he should listen in. "Is it okay if my partner joins us?"

"I would prefer to speak to you alone."

I nodded. Stood. Led him to an interrogation room. D' would watch through the one-way mirror, listen through the speaker.

We sat at the table. Kenny Wadd folded his hands. His fingers were long and solid. Strong. His eyes gleamed, seeming to smile even though his face remained somber.

"As I have said, I am here at the insistence of the family of Ja Vala Boudin." He glanced down, took a breath. "I can remain here only a short time. You see, my absence at home must not be noticed."

I didn't ask why.

"The Boudin family, as I mentioned on the telephone, is convinced that their daughter and sister Ja Vala is the woman whose face was in the news."

"But Mr. Wadd, as we discussed, that is not possible—"

"I need to know if she is well." He looked at me. "The family is very worried."

"Mr. Wadd," I said, "as you know, Ja Vala Boudin is not at all well. She's dead for a number of years. I have a copy of her death certificate—"

"Yes, detective. I am aware of that. As I have told you, I was at the funeral. But the family and I have also seen the news photographs and believe that remarkably, Ja Vala may be alive. What did you think when you saw the photos I sent?"

I wasn't sure. "The women resemble each other."

He tilted his head. "Resemble? Is that all?"

I shrugged, recalled that Vogel had been sure that the woman in the photo had been his patient.

"Because the family are convinced it is more than a resemblance. They think the woman is Ja Vala." His eyes pulled at me.

I shook my head, asked how that could be possible. "Mr. Wadd, you've said you personally saw Ja Vala's dead body."

"Yes." Kenny Wadd folded his hands, leaned forward and looked into my eyes. I forced myself not to look away, to meet his gaze. But his gaze swallowed me. I felt unbalanced. My breath quickened, face flushed.

Finally, he lowered his eyes. "I was once in love with Ja Vala." His voice was soft. "That is why her family believes that I, more than anyone else, will know whether or not she is actually the woman from the news. I have explained to them that years have passed. I am no longer the man who loved their Ja Vala. I am the husband of another woman. The father of two boys. For me, Ja Vala is a memory belonging to the past."

He looked at me as if for confirmation. I didn't say anything, didn't move.

"Still, when I saw the photograph in the news, it stirred that memory. And so, I had to come. For the sake of what once was."

I let out a breath. "Sorry," I said. "I still don't get it. You yourself saw Ja Vala's body. How can you imagine that the woman is not dead?"

He looked at me with urgent eyes. "Detective Sterling, I don't expect you to understand." He lowered his voice. "But it is possible that she was dead, but is dead no longer."

Dead no longer? Right. I sat back and crossed my arms, watching him. If not for his grim expression, I'd have assumed he was making a bad zombie joke. After all, he was from Haiti, zombie central. And zombies were all the rage lately—In television shows, movies. Comic books. Had he taken these stories seriously? Did he honestly believe that Ja Vala was a zombie? I glanced at the one-way mirror, imagined D' chortling on the other side, making cracks.

And then I recalled what the maid had said. Something that had chilled me, something like, "I am not alive."

"I know it sounds impossible," Kenny Wadd continued. "But please listen and try to keep an open mind."

He waited until I agreed. Then, again, he met my eyes. "There is a woman here in Philadelphia. She is a mambo, which is a leader of the voudou religion. She knows things I do not. She can explain how Ja Vala might have been revived—"

"Mr. Wadd. Seriously—"

"Listen to me. After the funeral, Ja Vala might have been brought back to life, kidnapped, and sold or enslaved."

I blinked at him. "In other words, you think she's a zombie." There, I said it.

His jaw dropped, indignant. "Do not insult me, detective. A zombie? A walking dead person who eats brains? Pardon me detective, but I am here to discuss the fate of a woman I once loved. I am not a fool." His nostrils flared.

THE WOMAN IN THE CUPBOARD

Again, I glanced at the mirror, letting D'Angelo know I thought that Kenny Wadd, if not a fool, was a certifiable nutcase. "A dead person brought back to life? If that's not a zombie, then what is it?"

His eyes burned mine. "A revenant."

"A revenant."

"Yes. Her family believes Ja Vala was made into one, and we know who might have done it. The woman I mentiones before. She is in Philadelphia—A mambo—"

"Mr. Wadd, I have no idea what you're talking about."

"Revenant?" He saw my blank expression. "You are unfamiliar with this term?"

"Completely." I had a feeling it meant zombie. "And, honestly, I have a meeting to—"

"Give me a minute, detective. Let me explain." His eyes grabbed mine, held them.

I looked away, checked my watch. "Five minutes," I said.

Chapter 56

Apparently, revenants were people who were given a toxin that paralyzed them and caused their hearts to all but stop, so that they seemed dead. Kenny Wadd said that only a small number of people knew the precise secrets of the process or how to reverse it. But for revenants, the process was reversed. Victims were revived and controlled with drugs that deprived them of memory and independent wills.

Drugs that sounded eerily like scopolamine. I considered the possibility: Could this man be right? Was Ja Vala actually a revenant? I crossed my legs, shook my head. What was I thinking? His intense gaze, soft rhythmic speech must be hypnotizing me. "Mr. Wadd. Even if this process were possible, those toxins and drugs—How would Ja Vala have gotten them into her system?"

Kenny Wadd sighed. "It's complicated. In Haiti, there are some voudou leaders—mambos who practice black arts. Evil mambos called bokors. The bokor mixes secret combinations of roots and barks and so forth to create the substances—"

"So, the drugs come from natural sources?" Hadn't Dr. Vogel said scopolamine came from some kind of tree? And what else had he called it? Devil's breath? I pictured an old hag at a steaming cauldron.

"Yes. All-natural sources. Some are well known, especially the toxin that mimics death."

"So we can have Ja Vala tested for it?"

"No, Detective. That toxin was used to imitate her death, and that happened years ago, but the substances used to control her might still be in her blood."

"You know what they are?"

"No, but the mambo might."

Mambo. Sounded like tango and samba. I heard steel drums. "Have you heard of scopolamine?"

He blinked rapidly. Shook his head. "Should I?"

I didn't answer, moved ahead. "So, to be clear. You think Ja Vala Boudin, by the use of toxins and drugs, was made into a revenant by an evil mambo called a bokor." I felt D'Angelo rolling his eyes.

"Her family believes this, yes, exactly."

"Okay." As bizarre as it sounded, everything Kenny Wadd said could have explained the maid's behavior, even her catatonic state. "Why would anyone do that, Mr. Wadd? Why take away your fiancée?"

"There are reasons." His eyes asked if we could skip them.

"Such as?"

"Is it important?"

I watched his eyes, waited for him to continue.

He let out a breath, sat back. "As you know, Ja Vala was in love with me. But another man, the son of a powerful family in our community, also pursued her. She rejected him, but he persisted." Kenny Wadd looked at the ceiling. Licked his lips. His hands tightened. "He tried to force himself on her but Ja Vala fought. In the struggle, she took out this man's eye. His family vowed vengeance and, not a week later, Ja Vala was dead."

I folded my hands. "Okay. I see why you suspect this guy and his family of killing her. But not why you think she came back to life."

Kenny Wadd spoke so softly that I had to lean forward to hear him. He smelled spicy. And musky. His voice was melodious, rhythmic. It lulled me, painting images of heat and duplicity, passion and darkness. Of a bokor who had methods, secrets. Mysterious potions and powders. Toxins and antidotes. Who could make the dead rise and obey her. Who kept a private collection of revenants. And who, when her son was disfigured by a haughty young woman, took revenge.

"By killing Ja Vala."

"For the bokor, killing was not enough."

Not enough? I looked at the one-way mirror. Chewed the inside of my cheek. Needed a break.

Kenny Wadd pressed his hands together. "The young man and his bokor mother—Ja Vala's family believe that they made her into a revenant. Instead of letting her die, they took possession of her soul."

Took her soul? Was I really hearing this in an interrogation room as part of a murder investigation? The inside of my cheek was raw from gnawing. I took a breath. Another. For a moment, God help me, I believed him. Everything he said made sense, except that none of it did. I'd fallen under the spell of his charm, intoxicating scent, sculpted muscles and glowing-eyes, buying into his far fetched, outlandish ideas. No. I was a cop. I would not be seduced by tales of islands, passion, and voudou witch doctors. I took a breath, looked away. Told myself that Kenny Wadd was off his rocker. Out of his tree. Bananas. Nuts.

I flashed another look at the mirror, and, mostly for my own sake, again signaled D' that the man in interrogation was a fruitcake.

Kenny Wadd must have noticed the gesture. "I know that what I've said is difficult for you to accept."

No argument. I cleared my throat. Wanted to get free of him. "Yes. It is. But thank you for coming in, Mr. Wadd. We know where to contact you—"

"Detective, what I tell you is positively accurate. If you will come with me to see Madam Yveny—"

"Who?"

"The mambo I mentioned. She is from my village but lives here now. In this city. She can explain about revenants."

I glanced at the clock, then the door. I didn't have time for superstitions and nonsense. I had cases to solve. Evidence to review.

And it was the end of the day. I was tired. Needed to get home, to log onto my dating site.

What the hell. I looked at Kenny Wadd, his gentle compelling eyes. "Fine," I said. "What exactly do you want to do?"

Chapter 57

The mambo called Madame Yveny had come from his village, but now lived in West Philadelphia. Come with me, he said. Visit her. Hear her explain. This woman knew processes he had heard about but didn't know about in detail. She would convince me. His words flowed, a soft, steady pulse. He'd promised Ja Vala's family that he would find out if she'd been revived from her grave and, if she had, that he would bring her home. His eyes pleaded, pulled at me.

When he stopped talking, I sat for a moment, reorienting myself. Had I really been listening to this nonsense? Did people actually believe such things? I shook my head, freeing myself from his influence, deciding not to sugarcoat my response. "Look, Mr. Wadd. I'm sorry your fiancée was killed. But people simply don't hop out of their graves and return from the dead, even with magic potions." I almost wavered, watching his eyes. "I wish you well. But I can't help you. Have a good trip home." I started to stand.

"Please, detective." He put a hand on my arm. His voice pulled at me. "Come with me to Madame Yveny—"

"Nobody comes back from the dead." Why was I repeating myself? Why was I even engaging in conversation?

"But what if they sometimes do?"

Really? "They don't."

He looked at me, silent. His gaze seared my skin.

I turned away again.

Kenny Wadd reached into his pocket, pulled out an envelope and set it on my desk. "Maybe you can run some tests. Maybe then you will be convinced."

"What's this?"

"It's from Ja Vala's hairbrush. All these years later, her mother still keeps her things. She retrieved some strands of her hair."

What?

THE WOMAN IN THE CUPBOARD

"Maybe you can do a test. See if the hairs match the woman's from the news. Detective, you are their only hope. After seeing the photograph, the family wanted to have her grave exhumed to prove that she is not buried there, but the court requires them to show cause, and the picture was not enough—"

"And if the hair matches, they'll have cause."

"Exactly." He looked around the interrogation room. Looked into the mirror as if he could see through it. Stared down whoever was on the opposite side. "Detective, by coming to you I have risked my life and endangered my family. The powerful people I have mentioned do not wish to have their secrets exposed. But I have done this because it is the right thing. I once loved Ja Vala. Please. Help us learn the truth." He slid the envelope toward me.

I looked from the envelope to him, back to the envelope, trying to put Kenny Wadd's claims together with the theory D' and I had come up with. What if somehow, Ja Vala Boudin hadn't died? What if she'd been not dead but only drugged when her body was seen at her funeral? What if she'd become a victim of human trafficking, a slave bought by the Grangers?

It was possible.

And testing the hair would finally show whether the woman in the hospital was or was not Ja Vala Boudin.

I picked up the envelope. "I'll send this to the lab."

"How long will it take?" Kenny Wadd pressed. He looked over his shoulder, back to me. "I am only able to stay a short time. Can the test be rushed?"

"I'll let you know as soon as results come in."

He frowned. Sat straight. Watched the envelope.

"I know how to contact you." I expected him to leave.

But Kenny Wadd made no move to go. "When can we go?"

Go?

"To see Madame Yveny."

Who? Oh, the woman from his village.

"It is critical that you speak to her. As a mambo, Madame Yveny knows voudou practices. And since she comes from my village, she knows the bokor I've told you about. Ja Vala's family has already been in touch with her to ask for her guidance. They have offered to retain her as a go-between to redeem Ja Vala."

Redeem her? As in buy her back from her supposed traffickers? Or from the Grangers, who'd supposedly purchased her? "Hold on, Mr. Wadd. You're saying they've paid—"

"Let me be clear, detective. The family believes Ja Vala is alive and are determined to free her. They hope the police will help. But they will do whatever is necessary, even at their own risk, to get her back. Madame Yveny's help and guidance is essential to them."

I looked at the window, wondered what D'Angelo was thinking. Whoever she was, this Madame Yveny had accepted money from Ja Vala's family, agreeing to help them "redeem" Ja Vala. Which probably mean she was ripping them off. Another scam.

"Call her," I told Kenny Wadd. "Set up an appointment for tomorrow morning."

For the first time since he'd arrived, Kenny Wadd beamed a smile. His face opened like the sun, and he reached his hands out to shake mine, thanking me warmly. My hand tingled, lost in his grasp, and for a long moment I felt off balance, as if my decision, my judgment were not entirely my own.

Chapter 58

D'Angelo rode his chair over to my desk the moment Kenny Wadd stepped into the elevator. "Wow."

"What he says is crazy, but when he says it, it makes sense."

D' grinned. "He had you from hello. I saw you gawking."

Gawking? No way. "I was stunned by what he was saying, that's all."

D' frowned. "So. Think he's right that the maid's a zombie?"

"Not a zombie," I corrected. "A revenant."

"Whatever. Do you?"

I didn't, did I? "Of course not." Still, the maid did look very much like Ja Vala. And had cried at the mention of Kenny Wadd's name.

And her family was convinced.

But a revenant? Absurd. Beyond belief. More likely, the woman wasn't Ja Vala but was simply a victim of trafficking. There were what—50,000 victims a year just in the U.S.? Vanessa might well be one of them.

"Why?" I asked. "Do you?"

D' bit his lip. "I hope not. Because regular traffickers are boy scouts by comparison to the guys he was talking about. Traffickers don't bury people alive. Or drug people into subservience—"

"So you believed him?" I wanted D' to say no, that he thought the guy was a lunatic.

But D' had no trace of a smile, and his eyes didn't twinkle. "All I know is that I don't know."

Well, of course he'd say that. D' was open to the supernatural and paranormal. He made personal deals with God. He believed his wife's dreams were signs of the future. "D', Kenny Wadd's story is like some grade B horror movie. Gravediggers in the night. Mysterious potions. The dead coming back." And yet, I'd agreed to meet his mambo.

"So why'd you agree to see that mambo?"

"Because she's scamming Ja Vala's family. And you're going with me."

One of his eyebrows rose. He bit his lip again. "I am?"

"Of course you are." What? Was he scared? I didn't tease him, told him we needed a hair sample from the maid for DNA testing, asked what he thought about letting Kenny Wadd visit her.

"Not a bad idea." D' said. "Maybe they'll recognize each other, fall into each other's arms, and live happily ever after."

"He's married with kids."

D' nodded. "Fine. Unhappily ever after. At least we'd find out who she is." He watched me, frowned. "Okay, Mo. What's the matter?"

"How can you ask that? We have four murders plus Alexandra Lambert and her dead shooter, plus a catatonic maid, plus possible identity theft of Ja Vala Boudin by human traffickers. Now we've got revenants and voudou priestesses."

"You forgot the partridge in a pear tree."

"And we've got a possible con game with scammers collecting from grieving families, convincing them that the loved ones they've laid to rest aren't really dead and can be ransomed back."

D'Angelo put a hand up. "Who knows? Maybe they can be."

"You need more sugar. Your brain's shutting down." I labeled an evidence bag for the lab for the DNA comparison, thought of the hope in Kenny Wadd's face as he was leaving.

"You need to be open minded, Mo. And by the way, if our maid was trafficked, this is a case for the feds."

He was right. Human trafficking was beyond our jurisdiction. "So, let's send this hair to the lab, find out what we've got. And meantime let's talk to the mambo."

"Fine." D' leaned back, folded his hands behind his head. Narrowed his eyes. "Bet you twenty bucks the hairs match."

Chapter 59

The powder fills her head with fog but she struggles to resist it. The man Dr. Vogel tells her that she has changed. He shines a light into her eyes and his voice is stern. Says that he knows she has taken a substance. He asks, "What have you taken? Where did you get it?" His eyes pierce like beaks of small, angry birds. "I need to know," he insists. "I can't help you unless you tell me." His breath bursts onto her face, warm, smelling sweet like lunchmeat. She wonders if he ate it on white bread or wheat. A roll? A memory arises. A picnic beside a stream. A boy bringing honeyed rolls, cheese, thick slices of ham. And promises.

Someone fat wearing a smock the color of daffodils joins Dr. Vogel. He tells her to look in the closet, the cabinet, the nightstand, the bed. "It must be here, somewhere in the room," he says.

"I've already looked and so has Lorraine." She puts a hand on her hip.

"Look again." He snaps. His eyes do not leave his patient. "I want security and staff watching her door day and night. No one—not a janitor, not a nurse—Not even a cop can be admitted here without my permission."

His voice slashes through the mist, but the patient sits very still, not reacting, not making a sound or a movement. She must not reveal where Madame Armistead's powder is hidden, must not look at the nightstand drawers. Must not even think of them. Her eyes remain focused on the green wall, because if Dr. Vogel finds the powder, he will take it from her. And if he takes it from her, she will decompose.

She pictures herself rotting. Would her flesh dry up and crumble? Melt like ice cream left out of the freezer? She wants to check the flesh on her hands, but she stares at the green wall.

Dr. Vogel asks if she can hear him. If she remembers who he is.

She sits with her eyes aimed at the wall. She does not move.

He tells her that he thinks she can hear him and urges her to respond. "You are in a serious situation." His voice feigns softness, but glistens like a razor. "Do you know why you are here?"

She tries to remember. She recalls a policewoman visiting. The policewoman's legs are long and slender, and her breasts are ample. But she crops her hair bluntly as if telling men to overlook her. The policewoman came to see her, so, the patient reasons, maybe she has been arrested. Has she acted illegally?

"I'm going to be blunt, my dear. If you understand what you're facing, you'll understand that it's in your interest to work with me." He puts his head squarely in front of his patient, his nose inches from hers. "Do you remember the Grangers? Judith and Dixon?"

Dr. Vogel says the names again, and she recalls two tall and elegant forms. Clothing swishing past, a lingering scent of Chanel. A sparkling chandelier. A clinking of ice cubes. Voices rising in anger, exchanging venom.

Shoes clacking on marble floors. Doors slamming.

A scream.

A white room—maybe a kitchen? A laundry? Dark stains on the floor.

"The Grangers were murdered." He watches her skin, studies it to see if it flinches or twitches. "Stabbed in their home."

She doesn't twitch or flinch. He watches. Does he see her skin begin to slacken, preparing to decay?

"Your blood-stained uniform was found in their washing machine."

Her what?

"And the police found you in the Grangers home, alone with their bodies."

She tries to process his words. Alone with their bodies. A bloody uniform. What is Dr. Vogel trying to say?

"You are suspected of killing them." He leans back, fondles his mustache. His eyes are like sharp claws.

The green wall flashes, reveals a smeared crimson trail that leads to a satin slipper. Beyond the slipper, the trail continues to its mate and the foot that's wearing it. The patient's heart braces in anticipation. She sees the woman on the floor, a knife plunged into her eye. She skips a breath as the woman's eye becomes Josias', the knife a rock, and she breathes again only when both images vanish into a flat expanse of green.

"That's right. You're suspected of a double murder. You behave as if you don't understand me. But just a day ago, you were coherent. And even if you've started taking the drug again, I believe your system is still clear enough that you can indeed understand me. So, consider this. Your best—No. Your only chance of having any future at all is by working with me to show that you've been acting under the influence of a drug. But first, you must stop taking it. Let it wear off and clear your system. Then talk to me." He waited, probing her eyes with his daggers. "That is your only hope."

Hope? She thinks about the word. She sees a man carrying flowers and a wide shining smile. Hope. She repeats it in her mind. Hope, hope, hope, hope, hope, hope. After a while, it stops sounding like a word, becomes just a long irritating noise, devoid of meaning.

The green of the wall swells like a balloon, like a bubble. It stretches so wide she fears it will burst. But it doesn't. It sits full and bulbous, stretching to its limit, long after Dr. Vogel leaves the room.

Chapter 60

Friday morning, I was edgy. And not just about the case. The night before, I'd found twenty-two responses to my profile. Hotjohn was thirty-eight and supposedly a one-hundred percent mutual match. Wanderlust Philly was thirty-six, and a ninety-seven percent match. I'd also been paired with Sincere2610, Freshstart31, Laidbackrocky, and Magikman. For about ten minutes, I'd stared at my computer screen, frozen. The faces of twenty-two strangers stared back at me, some smiling. One guy was flexing. Several had facial hair. Were the photos real? Were the guys who they claimed to be? Oh God. Signing up had been a mistake. Ignore these, I told myself. Push 'delete' and forget about the whole thing. Instead, I walked away from the computer, got a glass of wine and called Evie.

"Just pick one and answer him." She made it sound simple. "You've got nothing to lose."

I had plenty to lose.

"Like what?"

Like, for example, my life. "Evie, these guys could be anybody. Predators. Serial killers."

"Stop, Mo. You've been a cop too long. All you see is the dark side."

Was there any other? "You should see these pictures, Evie. Why would guys who look like underwear models need a dating website?"

"Same reasons you do. It's hard to meet quality people. They're busy. And lonely."

We'd gone on like that for almost an hour. Before we'd hung up, Evie made me promise to answer at least two of the guys. But I hadn't. I'd sat at my laptop, finger poised to push the respond button. And stopped.

Coming into work in the morning, I was still wondering what had stopped me. My instincts? Some intangible sense telling me those two guys weren't right?

Or me. Maybe I was the one who wasn't right.

D'Angelo stumbled in a few minutes after me, bearing coffee and a box of donuts, even though his deal with God meant he couldn't eat any. He sank into his desk chair.

"Bad night?" He looked worse than I felt.

"You have no idea."

I picked up a glazed. Thought about Hotjohn.

"Teresa had another dream. This time, it was about an empty house. She was all alone in it."

"If she was there, how was it empty?"

He ignored me. "She thinks it's a sign that I'm about to die. She's decided I better retire now before somebody kills me." He picked up his coffee, stared at the donuts.

What? Retire? No way. I remembered what Colby had said, that the brass wanted D' to take a package. Needed to quash the idea before it took hold. "You're not retiring, D'. Teresa's still upset about the shooting. She'll have another dream tomorrow and forget all about this one. Let it go."

He sighed, watched me lick icing off my finger. "Okay. You're probably right. Still, what if she's right? Teresa has a gift—"

"Nothing's going to happen to you, D'."

He watched my donut.

"Forget it, D'. Get your mind back to our case." I was talking to myself as much as to him, dismissing Hotjohn. "We're supposed to go see Kenny Wadd this morning."

He checked the clock. "He's late, isn't he?"

He was.

A few minutes later, the call came in. D' took it, turned pale as he listened. When he hung up, he said, "Kenny Wadd isn't coming in."

He'd been knifed in an alley behind his hotel.

We dashed to the car. D' put the siren on and sped to Hahnemann Hospital.

"Could be a coincidence." D' went through an intersection against the light. "After all, people get assaulted every day. He might have just been unlucky. It probably has nothing to do with the case."

"Yeah. And Santa Claus is probably real."

"This case sucks," D' growled.

I pictured Kenny Wadd, his gleaming eyes. Wondered if he was still alive.

D' swerved around a bus, cursed the driver for not pulling far enough over.

I clung to my armrest, swaying around corners and hunkering down through intersections all the way to the emergency entrance.

When we finally reached him, Kenny Wadd was indeed alive and, although he was groaning, didn't seem gravely injured. His only wounds were a bump on his head and a serious slash on his arm that would require a number of stitches. Even so, the EMT who'd brought him in said that Kenny Wadd had been raving when they'd brought him in, convinced that he would not survive. His heart rate had been erratic, his blood pressure low.

"Mr. Wadd," I stepped over to his bed. "What happened?"

His eyes swam in their sockets. "Poison," he breathed. "They put. Poison. My arm. Puff fish."

Puff fish? What? "Who? Did you see who cut you?"

"Two men." His eyes closed. "Poisoned me. Just like Ja Vala." He was winded, panting.

Like Ja Vala? "What did they look like?"

He let out a breath. "Haitians. Tried to take me. Because I found. Ja Vala."

"Detective," a doctor edged me away. "Are you finished? You need to step out so we can treat him."

"He's identifying his attackers—"

"But his treatment comes first." He nudged me out of the cubicle, pulled the curtain closed.

When I stepped out, D' was talking to the EMTs. They backtracked for my sake, reviewing what they'd already said. Apparently, Kenny Wadd had told them that two men had attacked him behind the Holiday Inn. He'd broken away and made it into the hotel lobby. When they'd arrived, Kenny Wadd had told them that his attackers had cut his arm and tried to rub poison into his wound. He'd managed to escape before they could finish with him.

"Maybe this will make sense to you," said the EMT with 'Bob' on his nametag. "He told us to tell the police that he'd been attacked because of—a weird name—Valaja?"

"Vajala," Ned, the other EMT said.

"Ja Vala." I glanced at D'Angelo. "What did he say about Ja Vala?"

"He said the men who assaulted him tried to give him the same poison as—Is Lajava a male or a female?"

"Female." What difference did it make?

"Okay. So he said his attackers tried to do to him the same thing they'd done to her."

"I don't know, Bob," the second EMT scratched his shoulder. "I think he said this Va—What is it again? Ja Vala? I thought he said it was her fault he got attacked."

Bob nodded. "Yeah. But he also said she was given the same poison. Tetrodotoxin."

"When did he say that? I didn't hear him mention tetrodotoxin."

"Because he didn't, Ned. He called it puffer fish."

Puffer fish? Kenny Wadd had tried to tell me that, too. What was a puffer fish? I looked at D'. He raised his eyebrows and shrugged.

"Puffer fish?" D' asked.

"Yeah. We first ran into it at a Japanese restaurant, remember, Ned?"

The other EMT nodded, wincing. "That was bad."

"A guy ate soup made from puffer fish. Nearly died."

"No—He did die," Ned corrected.

"He did? Damn." Bob stepped back, leaned on a gurney. "It's nasty stuff, puffer fish toxin. Shuts down your body, little by little. I don't know why anyone risks eating it."

"It's like dietary Russian roulette." Ned stared at the floor. "But they call it a delicacy."

"So, people eat poisonous fish?" I asked.

Bob nodded. "Most of the time, the chef gets all the poison cleaned out. Sometimes not."

D' looked at me, silently saying he'd never eat Japanese food again.

"It's fine. Just don't order puffer fish," I answered.

"Good idea," Bob said.

"But Kenny Wadd didn't eat it," I said.

"Right," Bob pushed the gurney against the wall, making room for a passing wheel chair. "There was powder on his shirt. He said his attackers tried to rub the toxin into his wound. And I'll tell you what: If that powder was really puffer fish toxin and they'd got it into his bloodstream, the guy would have been in trouble."

"Tetrodotoxin. That's the scientific name for it," Ned said.

"Where's his shirt now?" I asked at the same time that D' asked, "Anyone collect the powder?"

They both shrugged. "You'll have to ask the docs," Ned said.

Bob shook his head. "But I doubt it was tetrodotoxin. Because if it was and they got it into his wound, he'd probably be dead now. Puffer fish are one of the most poisonous creatures in the world—"

"Which is why it's so crazy that people eat them," Ned said. "But they love them in Japan and Korea."

D' looked at me. His eyes said that we should find the shirt. And involve the feds. I shook my head. His eyes persisted, reminding me that an organized effort was being made to kill or drug everyone connected to the Grangers' murders. That we weren't dealing with typical street drugs. First scopolamine? Now puffer fish toxin? And the crimes seemed to cross borders, involving international trafficking. I shook my head again. No feds. Not yet.

Curtains opened and a gurney burst out. Kenny Wadd was being wheeled away. He was wearing a hospital gown. I rushed to catch up with the doctor as he left the cubicle. "Where's the patient going?"

"He's being admitted." He tried to pass me, in a hurry.

"Doctor, hold up. We need to be informed of his condition." D'Angelo blocked his way, flashed his badge. He towered over the guy, whose eyes darted from D' to me to the EMT's.

"I don't have much to tell you. The patient's confused, probably a result of his concussion. We're going to keep an eye on him."

"What about puffer fish toxin?" I asked.

The doctor smirked. "Yes. He insists his assailants tried to poison him with tetrodotoxin. I don't know where he got the idea. He exhibits none of the symptoms."

"Was there powder on his clothing?"

"I didn't see any. His shirt was torn and bloody, so we probably tossed it." He called to an orderly, asked if he knew where the bagged waste had been taken.

The orderly wasn't sure. He said he'd check when he had a minute. Never mind. The shirt would have been contaminated by other items, would no longer be of use. Colby could go check the crime scene, see if any powder had spilled there.

I watched the curtains surrounding the space where Kenny Wadd had lain. Recalled his deep melodic voice, his fiery eyes. "So, he'll be okay?"

"Should be." The doctor spoke quickly, still in a hurry. And since he seemed to have nothing helpful to tell us, we let him hurry off, leaving us stymied beside an empty cubicle.

Chapter 61

A catastrophe has occurred. The patient doesn't know what to do. She has created a terrible mess and fears she will pay dearly for it. Even now, on her knees, reaching into the bowel of the empty nightstand, she tries to rectify her clumsiness, pinching tiny clumps of powder, dropping them into the envelope. If only the false nurse would appear with more doses, she would not be so concerned. But the nurse has said it would be days before her return. And she was stern with her warning about her instructions. "Remember, we have killed you once. We can do it again."

The patient doesn't know which is worse: fear of being killed again or fear of decaying while alive.

How has it happened that another envelope has torn and more powder has spilled? Did the packet catch on the edge of a drawer? Did she accidentally rip an envelope while removing it? All she knows is that another packet has ripped and is nearly empty. She holds it in her hands, pleading for it to heal itself. For the powder to hop back inside. She watches the door, listens for visitors. Then she removes the drawer, turns it over, examines the remaining envelopes. Finds to her horror that all four have been similarly damaged. That much of the powder has spilled.

She pulls out the lower drawer and releases a sigh of relief. The envelopes taped there are undamaged. So, five doses are intact. But five are not. And the doses have been carefully measured. There is just enough of the powder, the nurse said. Just enough to prevent decay. But the patient has defied her, taking less than full doses so she can retain some awareness while monitoring her skin for signs of decay. But now, with so much powder gone, she is not sure if she has enough to prevent decomposition. The Grangers and the bokor made it clear: If she does not swallow enough powder, her body will resume the process of death.

THE WOMAN IN THE CUPBOARD

She watches the door. At any moment, a nurse or aide, even a security guard might look in. Dr. Vogel has them watching her closely. And anyone who comes in will see the nightstand drawers lying on the bed and the floor. The light coating of loose powder.

It has taken her some time, but she has formed a plan, splitting the remaining powder into equal parts, hoping that the amounts will be sufficient. She reaches into the hollow of the nightstand where the powder has fallen, scraping and pinching together what few grains she can. Adding them to that which she has divided among the envelopes. Finally, she takes what there is from an envelope, pours it into a glass of drinking water, and swallow it.

She tries to replace the remaining packets, but the tape is no longer sticky, will not re-adhere to the undersides of the nightstand drawers. She must hurry to conceal them. Her mind races, sifts through possible alternatives. This acuity frightens her because the powder that keeps her intact also dulls her mind. The clearer her thoughts, the closer her flesh is to rotting. But this fact is not relevant to the moment. She must focus on hiding the packets. She looks around the room. The windowsill offers no hiding place. Nor does the bed, as the maid will change the sheets and expose the mattress. What then? A pitcher of water. A stack of plastic cups. A face towel. A washcloth. A pair of slippers.

A tissue box.

She picks up the box and removes the tissues, gathers the packets and presses several of them inside, then she replaces the tissues. She takes another packet and places it high on top of the bathroom medicine cabinet. She has to stand on the toilet to reach it. She squeezes another into the metal of the bed frame. A few more slide into the toes of her spare socks. She has stashed them in several places. This way, even if Dr. Vogel finds some of the powder, he will not find it all.

She returns the drawers to the nightstand, tears the envelope she's emptied to tiny bits and flushes them down the toilet.

She wonders, with less powder, if this new clarity will become her normal state. And whether, when Dr. Vogel comes to see her, if he will know that she has changed.

She sits by the window. The door opens. A nurse comes to check her vital signs. Glancing down, the patient sees that her fingernails are crusted with powder. She thrusts her fingers into her mouth, licking the powder away before the nurse can notice. The nurse doesn't question the act. Maybe she is accustomed to unexplained behavior. The nurse guides the patient's hand out of her mouth to put the blood pressure cuff around her arm. The patient feels her mind becoming solid, like a swamp slowly drying out.

The nurse turns away to read the dial on the machine and make notes on the chart. While her back is turned, the patient notices syringes in her pocket. The kind doctors use to vaccinate children against measles or diptheria. She doesn't think about it, doesn't know why she's doing it, but neither does she hesitate. While the nurse is writing on the chart, the patient lifts a needle from her pocket and slides it into her gown.

The patient's touch is light. The nurse doesn't notice. If she discovers the loss later, she will assume she's dropped a needle somewhere, retrace her steps and look for it. But she will not find it. When she is gone, the patient digs a hole in her pillow and buries it deep in the fluff. Even if she looks in the room, the nurse will not see it there.

Chapter 62

No powder was found at the crime scene. No blood either. Turns out, the alley behind the hotel was hosed down each morning, so whatever might have been found had been washed away.

But the good news was that Kenny Wadd recovered quickly from his ordeal. His concussion required him to rest, but his heart rate and blood pressure normalized, and when D' and I walked into his room, we found him ready to leave, pulling off his covers, getting out of bed.

I stopped him. "Not so fast, Kenny." I hadn't intended to call him by his first name. It just happened. "You need to stay quiet." I put a hand on his shoulder, pushed him back onto his pillows. Pulled the blanket back up. Noted the muscles in his bare thighs.

His hand grasped my arm. "No, detective. Ja Vala is in grave danger." What was it about his eyes? Glints of gold? I couldn't look away. "I must go to her." His grip on my arm was surprisingly strong. I did nothing to remove it.

D' stepped over, glowering. "You need to let go of Detective Sterling's arm, son."

Kenny Wadd looked at D', released my arm. "Please. Take me to Ja Vala. They know I have come for her. They'll harm her."

"Who'll harm her? Who are you talking about?" D' asked.

"The people who've taken her. They attacked me because they know I've come for her. They're afraid I'll expose them." His gaze was intense, darted from D' to me. "And they'll inform the bokor—if they haven't already. We have to move quickly—" He started to get up again, and again, I pushed him back.

"Tell us what happened to you."

Kenny Wadd shook his head, his eyes pleading. "There isn't time. We have to get to Ja Vala."

"Ja Vala is safe," D' told him.

When he saw that we wouldn't move until he answered our questions, Kenny Wadd blurted out the facts that he'd told the EMTs: he'd been accosted and dragged into an alley. Slashed in the arm so that puffer fish poison could be rubbed into the open wound. But he'd broken away.

"How did you know it was puffer fish poison?"

Kenny Wadd hesitated. "Because they'd cut my arm. That's how they rub the poison into the blood. It's a practice of the bokor."

D' and I exchanged glances. D' was skeptical.

"You don't believe me? Look at Ja Vala's arm. I promise she'll have a scar there."

He was right. I'd already noticed the scar.

"Look. Madame Yveny, the mambo I told you about. She will explain it to you later. But now I beg you. Take me to Ja Vala. I am certain that she is the woman in the hospital. Ja Vala is alive. That is the only explanation for my attack. The people who took her tried to kill me so I would not expose what they've done."

D's glance asked what I thought. Mine answered, "Why not let him?" She was right there in the hospital. What harm could it do? And getting them together might answer some questions.

I called Dr. Vogel to arrange a visit, explaining who Kenny Wadd was, why he'd come from Haiti, what had happened to him.

"I don't think it's wise," he argued. "She's in an unstable emotional state."

"His visit might help her improve."

"But it might do her harm. Besides, it still isn't clear where her drugs are coming from. Every person with whom she has contact needs to be carefully screened."

I rolled my eyes, explained that the visitor wasn't carrying drugs, had no place to carry them—his clothes had been covered in blood, so he was wearing a pair of hospital gowns.

THE WOMAN IN THE CUPBOARD

Dr. Vogel squabbled but eventually agreed to prepare his patient for company, and D' and I led Kenny Wadd from his room to the hospital's psychiatric unit.

As we walked, Kenny Wadd's breathing quickened. As we entered the unit, he began chewing his lower lip, and, when D' told him to take a seat in the waiting area, he seemed not to hear.

"Kenny?" I pointed to the chairs. "Sit down."

When I said his name, Kenny looked at me as if surprised to see me there. Silently, he sat down, eyes forward, back straight, hands pressed flat against the well-defined muscles of his thighs. Nervous.

Chapter 63

While D'Angelo waited with Kenny Wadd, I located Dr. Vogel outside the observation room. He bristled as I approached.

"She's ready," he grumbled. "But I must repeat my reservations—"

"Thank you, doctor," I cut him off. "I understand." Flattery worked well with Vogel, so I slathered some compliments onto him, and I saw him relax. Then I asked what he knew about puffer fish toxin.

He raised an eyebrow. "It's stronger than cyanide. Kills by paralysis. Why?"

I repeated what Kenny Wadd had said, that people had tried to poison him with it. "He also said the paralysis caused by the toxin can be mistaken for death."

Dr. Vogel's eyes flashed. "Yes. I've read about cases where its effects have mimicked death." He looked away, into the observation room. "Exactly what are you suggesting, detective?"

"I'm just confirming what I've been told. Getting your opinion."

He opened his mouth, closed it. Turned to walk into the observation room.

"Dr. Vogel?" I had another question. About scopolamine, the drug he'd said could cause amnesia. "Would the amnesia it causes be total?"

"It might be. Or partial, depending on amount taken, the frequency, and so forth."

"So, a person might have spots of memory?"

"We've discussed this, detective. Yes, they might. But the big question, before we consider the effects of the drug, is whether the patient can be acquiring it. If she has no access to it, the properties of the substance are irrelevant."

He watched me closely for a moment, probably to make sure I understood.

"But you've tested her for it?"

He raised his chin. "I agreed to test her, did I not? The results are not yet in." Then he whirled around, entering the observation room, making sure his patient was positioned where he could watch her every move. When he was sure that the microphones were on and the patient comfortably seated, he called a nurse to bring in her visitor.

Chater 64

I stood behind Dr. Vogel, watching through the one-way mirror. Kenny Wadd stood at the door as if he'd forgotten how to walk, as if his legs didn't work. He watched the woman seated beside the window, his eyes reaching across the room, touching her face, her hair, her arms, her back.

The woman didn't move, didn't look up. Time passed.

Dr. Vogel fretted. "What's he doing? Why's he just standing there? This is a waste of my time."

D' stood beside me, squeezed my arm to stifle my response.

Finally, Kenny Wadd moved. He didn't walk across the room. He moved to the woman as if pulled by an invisible lasso. His gaze never left her. And when he came close enough to touch her, he sank, collapsing at her feet, shoulders convulsing.

Dr. Vogel got to his feet, but D' put a hand up, stopping him from interrupting. Oddly, Vogel didn't insist. He sat again without uttering a word.

The woman still hadn't moved. She didn't speak. Didn't look at the large, strong man sobbing against her knee.

Kenny Wadd took her hand, struggling to control himself. "Ja Vala," he said. He waited on his knees, holding her hand, looking up at her. "It is really you."

He got no response. Not a glimmer, not a sigh.

He replaced her hand on her lap. Knelt beside her, studying her, weeping. "What have they done to you, Ja Vala? I am so sorry." Finally, he smeared away his tears and managed a smile. "Well. I'm here now. Whatever has happened to you is finished and past. We've found you." His hand ran over her hair, gently, barely touching it. The hand moved to her face, her shoulders. Traced the shape of her body. "You are as beautiful as ever."

I felt lightheaded, took a deep breath.

Again, Vogel began to rise.

Again, D' stopped him.

"I need to intervene," Vogel said.

"She's fine." I said. "He's not hurting her."

"Not every hurt is physical," Vogel snapped.

My mouth was dry.

Kenny Wadd took his hands off Ja Vala. He got to his feet, backed away, and dried his eyes, recovering. He walked once around the periphery of the room before taking a seat beside her.

"Ja Vala." His voice was low, hard to hear. Almost a whisper. "Can you forgive me?" Tears flowed down his face, and he made no effort to stop them. "I believed you were dead. If I'd thought you might be alive, I never would have married. I would have searched the earth, fought for your return. You must believe that I would never have abandoned you."

Nothing from the woman. No sign that she heard.

"It is useless to say that I am sorry." Kenny Wadd swallowed. "I can't imagine what has been done to you, what you have suffered. But I promise no one else will hurt you. Your family is waiting to hear that I've found you. And as soon as is possible, we will bring you home."

He leaned over and pressed his lips onto her forehead. Watching the kiss, my own forehead burned. Once again, his hand rose, caressed her cheek, her head, her shoulders. I took a breath, shut my eyes, ran a hand roughly through my hair. Opened my eyes in time to see Kenny Wadd lifting his hand and plucking strands of hair from the woman's head.

Even then, she did not respond.

Chapter 64

An aide brings her into the sitting room, leads her to a chair near the window. She sits beside a plant, a philodendron. The aide whispers to a nurse. Their talk is rapid and tense. Why? Are they searching her room again, looking for the powder? The patient wonders if they will find it. She does not wonder long.

It is not the powder that they whisper about.

She knows who it is as soon as he steps inside the room. The spicy scent that emanates from Kenny Wadd's pores. The music of his steps. The swing of his bones. She freezes at his presence, unable to turn to look at him, unable to move her eyes. Unable even to breathe. Her throat clenches and her heart ricochets against her ribs. A large dark hole opens at her feet, swallows her slippers, her ankles, reminding her, inch by inch, that it owns her. But she ignores it: Kenny Wadd has come for her.

Kenny Wadd. The breeze is light and his arm encloses her shoulders as he walks her to her parents' house. They talk about their wedding, how they will dance up the hill to the church along with musicians, how everyone will sing throughout the mass. And afterwards, how they will serve a feast of conch, pork, goat, and not just beer but also champagne, and how they will celebrate with their guests through the night until sunrise. Kenny Wadd whispers in her ear, and his message tingles along her neck and spine, reminding her it is but a week until she will become his wife.

The tingle alters, becomes a shiver of warning. Kenny Wadd has come for her, but she dare not jump into his arms. She listens without giving a sign. If she as much as looks at him, the darkness that pulls at her legs will swoop, open its jaws, and swallow her whole.

Kenny Wadd kneels, weeping, touching her hands. She aches to comfort him, to say that he has no reason to cry anymore. That together they can defy the darkness. Escape it. Get home in time for their wedding, only a week away.

Kenny Wadd speaks softly. His voice is thick. His hands tighten around hers, and she notices a gold band on his finger. She doesn't understand. Is it a wedding ring? But how? Unless—Has she missed their ceremony? Or forgotten it? His voice chokes. She strains to listen to broken words.

She sees him again at sunset. They stand near the river. Their eyes connect. Their lips join. They are one.

Kenny Wadd says that, in his eyes, she is still beautiful. What does he mean? For a moment, she hears her mother weep, and the sound of dirt being shoveled onto a coffin. And in that same instant, the name Josiah flashes to mind with hard legs straddling her, hands grappling her throat. And when he has finished with her, a slash is made to her arm, and a smoky voice declares that she is now theirs. She knows the voice, the woman who owns it. Darkness tugs at her ankles. She stiffens and resists. Kenny Wadd is there, holding her hand. He has come to take her home.

Kenny Wadd says he is sorry.

Sorry? Her mouth is dry, throat closed. She cannot swallow. Kenny Wadd has come for her. Why is he sorry?

She finds out with just a few words. At first, she is sure that she has misheard. But he repeats that he is sorry and says again the impossible words that rip out her heart: Kenny Wadd has married someone else.

He is sorry? Kenny Wadd has married another woman, and he is sorry?

She sits very still even as her heart shatters. Does he see her falling, arms flailing, into nothingness? Has he seen the earth fall away?

She must have misheard.

But no, Kenny Wadd is crying, apologizing still.

She does not look at him. Does not shout or cry. Does not ask what woman he has married or why he has broken his promise. Does not let him know that his betrayal has finally killed whatever has been left of her.

With just a week before our wedding, Kenny Wadd has abandoned her for another. He explains that he'd thought she was dead, that he'd seen her body and attended her funeral.

He says that, even then, he could not marry another, not for years.

Years? Their wedding is planned for a week from today. How can Kenny Wadd say that he waited years? She is the same as she has always been.

But he has changed. Maybe time is only for the living.

She moves her eyes, looks at her hands. They show no decay.

Kenny Wadd goes on talking, but says only garbled, meaningless sounds. She watches the hungry darkness devour her legs, flicking its tongue at her thighs.

After a while, Kenny Wadd stands, scalds her forehead with his lips, and leaves.

Chapter 65

D'Angelo was convinced now that the woman in the hospital was Ja Vala Boudin. We'd dropped Kenny Wadd at the Holiday Inn so he could get fresh clothes before our meeting with his mambo friend. Then we'd gone back to the Roundhouse. D' sat on the side of my desk, watching me fill out paperwork for the lab.

"A guy can't fake that, Mo," he said. "Did you see him bawling?"

Of course, I'd seen it. And an hour afterwards, I couldn't stop seeing it. His visit had burned itself into my brain, replaying itself. Kenny Wadd first seeing the woman, falling to his knees, his face dissolving into tears. His gentleness with her, even when she didn't respond. His final tender kiss. I'd not only seen it—I'd felt it.

"It's her," D' insisted. "She's Ja Vala."

It seemed that way. I bagged the hair Kenny Wadd had plucked from her head, asked Colby to get it to the lab. "We still need definite proof."

"Well, when the hairs match—"

"Even that won't be enough. Remember, Kenny Wadd brought us the hair. We can't be sure that the woman he got it from was Ja Vala Boudin."

"Oh, come on, Mo."

But D' didn't argue. He knew I was right. There'd been no chain of custody for the hair sample.

"That's why I'm filing these requests." I pointed to the computer screen to show him what I'd been working on.

"You're requesting the exhumation?"

We'd talked about it. He'd agreed to it. Now he sounded surprised? "You yourself said it would be the only way we'll know for sure that Ja Vala Boudin is not buried in the grave marked for her."

"But that was before her boyfriend identified her."

He had, yes, identified her. Again, I saw Kenny Wadd's tears. The softness of his lips above her eyebrows. I scratched a tingle on my forehead, while I continued filling out the online forms. Recalled filling out other online forms. Magikwillie and HotJohn. My personal life had become absurd. A cartoon. I typed in Ja Vala's birth date. Her date of death.

D'Angelo sputtered, reminding me that Haiti was a foreign country, that they would have their own paperwork, procedures and laws, and that the process would take forever if it could ever actually be completed at all.

I kept typing, pictured Kenny Wadd's tears. "I know," I said. "But we have to try."

D' sighed. Nodded. Went back to his desk. Saw that an informal summary had come from the lab. Opened it.

Read it out loud.

It said that Judith Granger, J. Steven Richards and Sylvia Blake had been stabbed with, if not the same weapon, then one of the same dimensions and serration type. Each victim had wounds that were similar in direction, depth and angle. Indications were that the killer was right-handed, between five-foot-six and five-foot-ten. So, it was possible that the same perpetrator had killed all four victims.

Unlike the others, Dixon Granger had been killed with a single strong swipe of a substantially sturdy, sharp unserrated blade.

I pictured the woman who might be Ja Vala. She was five-foot-seven. Her height matched the suspect's. I closed my eyes, saw her sitting silent and unresponsive as Kenny Wadd professed his love and sorrow. The same unreadable demeanor she'd had when we'd found her in the Grangers' pantry. Could she have killed all four people? Was she physically strong enough? Cold-hearted enough? And what would her motive have been?

D'Angelo stood, put on his jacket, addressed my unspoken thoughts. "I can see Ja Vala offing her bosses," he said. "But the other two? What reason would she have to kill them? I don't buy it."

He stopped talking when my phone rang. It was Dr. Vogel. He had news.

Chapter 66

They'd found the drugs.

"She hid them all over the room, in small envelopes. Scopolamine, just like I thought. It was on top of the medicine cabinet, jammed into the bedframe. Inside her socks."

I put my hand over the mouthpiece, told D' the news.

"Yeah?" he sat down, rode his chair over to my desk. "If it was all over her room, why didn't they find it before?"

He was right. A routine search should have involved looking on top of the medicine cabinet and in the bed frame.

"Strange thing," Vogel answered D's question. "In our earlier searches, we looked in those same places and found nothing."

Really. "So, you think she's been moving the packets? Changing her hiding places?"

"Maybe," he said. "Unless she somehow got a new supply and stashed them in new places. But I don't know how, not with security so tight."

Unless someone inside the hospital was providing the drugs. "So how could she have gotten a new supply?"

"No idea," he said. "All I know is that it's not any of our people."

How could he be sure? "And yet she's had no visitors."

"Someone might have slipped in right after she got here, before the shooting. That's when we tightened security."

Except the shooting had occurred almost immediately after she'd been admitted. "But you've said before that she's had no visitors, right? And that security has always been tight."

"What are you suggesting, detective?"

I wasn't sure. But obviously someone had managed to bring drugs into the patient's room.

Vogel sounded miffed. "I thought you'd be pleased that we found the drugs. Now she can be weaned off the scopolamine and answer your questions."

I assured him that I was pleased, congratulated him on the find. Said I was eager to talk to her.

D' tapped my hand. "We got to go." He pointed to his watch. "Voudou time."

I told Dr. Vogel to keep us updated on how his patient was doing and said we'd be by to see her in the morning. When I ended the call, D' was already on his way to the elevator.

It was time for our meeting with Kenny Wadd and the mambo, Madame Yveny.

Chapter 67

The house was in West Philadelphia. Old, made of stone, closed in by wild foliage and overgrown bushes. Kenny Wadd had insisted on going separately in a cab. He was supposed to meet us there at four o'clock, but he wasn't out front. After a few minutes, we ventured up rickety steps to the front door on our own.

D'Angelo hadn't knocked yet when the door swung open, and Kenny Wadd welcomed us, ushered us inside. The foyer was unlit and for a moment, stepping in from the bright sun, I was blinded and stood still, overcome by smells of mildew, roasting meat, sweet rotting flowers.

"Madame Yveny is waiting in the living room." Kenny Wadd's breathing was rapid and short. Nervous?

"We thought you'd meet us outside."

"I arrived early." His voice wavered. "I was about to come out to meet you, but here you are."

D' harumphed. "Why did you come here before us?"

"Actually, I wanted to see how Madame Yveny was doing. She isn't accustomed to meeting with police."

My eyes adjusted to the dimness. Shapes defined themselves, became chairs and tables, lamps, lush plants. We followed Kenny Wadd through cut glass double doors into a sunlit room crowded with chairs. Over a dozen, all colors and sizes. Upholstered, wooden, wingback, reclining, folding. They filled the room, formed a semicircle around a fireplace, a well-worn rose-colored loveseat, and a table covered with white candles, water glasses, bundles of dried herbs and flowers, bottles of what looked like oil, a cluster of framed photographs. A shelf beside the window held books, decorative jars and canisters. The walls were mostly bare, except for a couple of icons, two pictures of saints, a crucifix. Doorways and windows were draped with sequined flags and beaded strings. Something acrid lingered in the air.

Kenny Wadd introduced us to someone unseen. A coarse voice repeated our names, but Madame Yveny remained out of sight until I stepped further into the room. Almost lost in the cushions of a large easy chair, she resembled a withered potato wrapped in madras fabric. Her face was in the shadows, but tight white curls peeked out of her red head-tie.

"Please sit down." Her voice was deep, leathery. "I can offer you tea and pound cake."

I glanced at D'Angelo. He loved pound cake, but thanked her and declined for us both. Moving gingerly, he planted himself on the edge of a folding chair as if he didn't intend to stay long. I sat beside him. Kenny Wadd took a seat opposite Madame Yveny.

"You have so many chairs," I remarked.

She nodded. "Yes, for my singing group. We gather to sing Haitian music and eat Haitian food."

Kenny Wadd cleared his throat. "In Haiti, Madame Yveny was a very popular mambo. She had quite a following."

A following?

"Yes. Including your own family, Kenny Wadd. They worshipped with me."

Kenny Wadd bit his lip, said nothing. The air hung heavy, thick with scents.

"When you arrived, I was reacquainting myself with Kenny Wadd," Madame Yveny raised a birdlike arm, indicating who Kenny Wadd was. "It has been some time since we last saw one another."

"Have you been here long?"

She chuckled. "Here? You mean in the world? Yes, forever."

"No, I meant—"

"I know what you meant. I left Haiti years ago. When you arrived, Kenny Wadd was giving me news of his family and others we both know." She turned to Kenny Wadd. "But you haven't yet talked about Madame Armistead. How is she?"

Kenny Wadd rubbed his palms on his pant legs. "I haven't seen her."

"But surely she knows you've come to see me."

He looked at her, then at the floor.

"You didn't tell her?" Madame Yveny frowned. "Kenny Wadd, was that wise? She is influential, with many followers. And your family members are well known to her."

I glanced at D'. He'd caught her tone, too. Was it a warning? Even a threat?

"Who's Madame Armistead?" I asked.

Kenny Wadd looked at me, said nothing.

"A mutual acquaintance," Madame Yveny said. "A religious leader in his community."

Kenny Wadd seemed rattled. "It was best not to tell her that I planned to see you."

Madame Yveny made a "tsk." Her skin was taut around her cheekbones, her eyes narrow, deeply set. Hard to see. "Best not to tell her? You know better than that."

Really? Why? What did this Madame Armistead have to do with Kenny Wadd's visit? Why should he report his travel plans to her? Unless—was Madame Armistead the powerful woman Kenny Wadd had talked about in the interrogation room—the one whose son had lost an eye? The woman he'd accused of poisoning Ja Vala?

"Normally, I would have told her. But I couldn't because, in fact, she's part of the reason we've come to see you." He lowered his voice and leaned forward. "Madame Yveny, I suspect Madame Armistead of being a bokor."

For a moment she said nothing. Then she cackled. "What? Madame Armistead? Kenny Wadd, whatever gave you such an idea?"

So, I was right. Madame Armistead was the suspected bokor whom Kenny Wadd suspected of making Ja Vala into a revenant.

What was I thinking? What were these words: bokor, mambo, revenant? What were we doing in this old lady's stuffy smelly living room? I looked at D'.

His knee was bouncing. He was on edge, ready to leave.

"Never mind." Kenny Wadd licked his lips, gestured at D' and me. "Forget what I said, Madame Yveny. The police are here to ask about Ja Vala Boudin."

Madame Yveny held up a gnarled finger. "No, wait. You accuse Madame Armistead of being a bokor?" She stared at Kenny Wadd. "This claim is very serious."

"Please. I shouldn't have said it. We are interested only in Ja Vala."

Madame Yveny said nothing for a moment. "Tell me the name again?"

He repeated it.

Madame Yveny looked at the ceiling, said the name over and over. Ja Vala Boudin. Ja Vala Boudin. It sounded musical, as if she were casting a spell.

"You remember her?" Kenny Wadd leaned forward, shoulders huge, eyes intense.

So far, neither D' nor I had said much of anything.

"She was a pretty one? Lithe? Yes. I remember how she seemed to dance as she walked." Madame Yveny shook her head. "I'd already moved here when it happened. But I remember hearing that she died, poor young thing." Another "tsk."

Kenny Wadd moved closer to her, spoke softly. "She and I were to be married."

"Of course. I remember now." More tsking. "I am sorry for you, Kenny Wadd."

"I hope you can tell the police what you know about her, Madame Yveny."

"What I know? About her death? I know nothing. I was here—"

"But do you remember what happened with Madame Armistead's son? How he forced himself on her—"

"Be careful not to spread lies, Kenny Wadd." She shook the bony finger.

"It's no secret, Madame Yveny. Ja Vala fought him off. That's how he lost his eye."

Madame Yveny's face was stony. "They were young. The young are passionate and foolish. These things happen—"

"But in this case, Josias and his family promised revenge, and a few days later, Ja Vala was dead—"

"It was a long time ago."

"Madame Yveny, please don't pretend you don't know. I know that Ja Vala is here. That she is alive."

Madame Yveny said nothing. She stared at Kenny Wadd, her mouth open as if he'd slapped her.

"Look at these photographs." I finally entered the conversation. I took out a picture of Dr. Vogel's patient, another of the young Ja Vala with Kenny Wadd. I handed them to Madame Yveny. "Can you identify these women?"

She reached over to the table, rifled through clumps of dried herbs, searching for a pair of reading glasses. Put them on, peered at each picture. Shook her head. "No. This is Ja Vala. But not the other one. These are two different women."

"How can you be certain?" D' asked.

"Because Ja Vala is dead. She'd be nothing but dust and bones now." She handed the photos back to me, sat back. Nobody spoke.

Then Kenny Wadd said, "Madam Yveny, I have seen her. She is alive."

Madame Yveny's gaze was sharp. "Impossible."

"Tell them," he said. "You were a mambo. You know what must have happened to Ja Vala. Tell them how it's done."

Madame Yveny gaped at Kenny Wadd.

"Tell them, Madame Yveny." He sat forward, urging her.

She scowled. "You're not suggesting that Ja Vala is a revenant?"

D's knee stopped bounding. We said nothing, made not a sound.

"I am. And that Madame Armistead is the bokor who made her one."

"And that's why the police are here?" She nodded toward us. "Do they believe you?" Her tone was sharp, scolding.

"I haven't told them anything," Kenny lied. "I brought them to you so you'd explain."

"Why would you even suggest this outrageous idea to them? It's only superstition. There's no substance to it."

I looked at D'. He was frowning, looked annoyed.

"Madame Yveny, please." Kenny Wadd begged. "I've come all this way."

"There's no such thing as a revenant." She glared at him.

"Well," I broke in, "how about you tell us anyway."

D' crossed his legs, folded his arms, distancing himself from the conversation.

Madame Yveny paused, eyeing Kenny Wadd. "If I speak about this, Madame Armistead will find out. She will not be pleased."

"How will she find out?"

"There will be consequences if she does."

"I'm not going to tell her. Are you?"

Their eyes met in a silent debate.

Finally, she sighed, relenting. She looked at me, then at D'Angelo, assessing us. "What do you know about voudou?"

Chapter 68

Voudou? Nothing really. Neither of us knew anything.

"Just that it's a religion," D' sounded noncommittal. "And it's practiced in the Caribbean—in Haiti."

I pictured dolls with pins in them, people dancing around fires at night, magic potions, sacrificed chickens and goats—Were these stereotypes? Did voudouists really do any of that?

Madame Yveny took a long deep breath, exhaled, brushed scrawny fingers over her chin as if deciding what to say.

Nobody made a sound. We waited, not moving. The air had become denser, the sweet and acrid smells heavier. Kenny Wadd hung his head, D'Angelo drummed his fingers on his elbows.

When she finally spoke, her words were hushed and fleeting. "Let me tell you then. Voudou is a blend of beliefs, a mix of African religions, mysticism, and Catholicism. You are right, detective, that it originated in Haiti when it was a French colony and the slaves were forced to convert to Catholicism, forbidden to practice their old rituals."

She paused, folded her hands. Looked at each of us, one by one. When she faced me, I saw that her left eye was clouded over, the iris hidden by a gray film. I shuddered. Her right eye aimed at me when she continued in a low slow voice. "Because of its roots, voudou retains many primitive aspects. One of these is what Kenny Wadd is referring to. It's the belief that certain priests—we call them mambos—use their knowledge for evil. These evil mambos are called bokors. The dark arts they practice allow them to steal people's souls."

"I'm sorry?" Unintended, my hand rose to my chest. I swallowed, told myself that no cold chill had just passed through me.

"A revenant," she continued, "is the bokor's victim. It is the person who's been robbed of his soul. The revenant has no will of his own and is completely owned by his bokor." She tsked and waved her hands. "But all of this, the whole idea is foolishness."

"No, it isn't," Kenny Wadd's voice was raw. "You know it isn't. That's why I brought them. Look at the photographs, Madam Yveny. Explain to them what's been done to Ja Vala—"

"I saw your photographs," Madame Yveny scoffed, "but only one of them was of Ja Vala. I don't know who the other one was. Ja Vala died years ago, Kenny Wadd. No bokor did anything to her. You can't honestly believe there is such a thing as a revenant. It's like the Bogeyman, an idea used to frighten people, to manipulate them. A scary story from long ago. But the rituals to create one? They are never performed—Believe me, I was a mambo for over thirty years. I would know."

"Tell them about the rituals." Kenny Wadd's tone had changed. He was no longer begging. He sat straight, glaring into Madame Yveny's eyes. "Even if they are never performed. Tell them what a bokor would do."

His tone was steel.

She looked away. "Bokors are not real. No one ever performs the dark arts."

"Tell them."

Madame Yveny's shoulders caved. She lowered her voice and spoke in a listless monotone as she explained that a certain toxin could supposedly be extracted from a fish and used to stop a person's heart from beating long enough to have him, or her, declared dead and then buried. If that person's body were dug up quickly and given an antidote, the heart could be started again. After that, the revenant could be controlled by a second substance that made him passive, obedient, and completely subject to the bokor's will. All of this was theoretical, though. The process involved rare substances and would be far too complicated for most mambos to attempt. And, even if it were attempted, it was all about chemistry, not magic. It didn't actually reverse death, much less allow for the actual stealing of any souls.

When she finished, I was silent. Madam Yveny's story exactly and precisely matched what had happened. Kenny Wadd had said his attackers had tried to poison him with puffer fish toxin, that Ja Vala had been mistaken for dead because of it. And the rare substances that made revenants passive and obedient—Those could be the very drug found in Ja Vala' room—Scopolamine.

Was Kenny Wadd right? Had Ja Vala been poisoned and drugged for all these years? I imagined her, unable to move or protest as she heard others pronounce her dead. Unable even to blink as they laid her inside a coffin, closed it. Buried it. Oh God. I shivered, hugged myself, looked at D'. He was talking to Madam Yveny, asking questions. I pictured lying alone inside a closed coffin, hearing splats of dirt landing on the lid.

I sat straight. Assured myself that the poisoned person would probably be unconscious, out cold until the antidote was given. Wouldn't be aware of the intervening moments. Still, my chest hurt. The air felt close, difficult to inhale.

D' asked Madame Yveny what toxin would be used in the procedure. She said he'd probably never heard of it. It was rare, extracted from a specific variety of puffer fish.

Just as Kenny Wadd had said. I looked at D' who looked at me, mouthing syllables. "Tea trade to duck skin?" I tilted my head. He mouthed it again. Finally, I got it: "Tetrodotoxin."

I nodded. Yes.

Kenny Wadd was on his feet. "Now do you see? Ja Vala was poisoned to make her appear dead. Then she was revived, drugged, and kept as a revenant slave for all these years. And because I've come for her, they tried to punish me by poisoning me, too."

THE WOMAN IN THE CUPBOARD

Madame Yveny argued that Kenny Wadd was talking nonsense. Revenants weren't real—they were superstition. And if they were real, no mambo would be evil enough to create one.

Kenny Wadd narrowed his eyes and answered that, yes, some people were evil enough: Josias and his bokor mother, Madame Armistead.

Madame Yveny sat bolt upright. Her good eye squinted at Kenny Wadd. "I will not allow that kind of talk. Remember that you still live in Madame Armistead's village, Kenny Wadd. As does your family." She watched him absorb this comment.

"She will know what I've said only if you tell her, Madame Yveny."

Madame Yveny smirked, shaking her head. "Madame Armistead has many ways of knowing things, Kenny Wadd. It's best not to oppose her."

"You could have. Not just opposed her, but destroyed her," Kenny Wadd simmered, staring at Madame Yveny. "Instead you left."

Madame Yveny put a hand over her left eye. "You know nothing about the circumstances of my leaving. I decided I could be of more use here. I remain on good terms with Madame Armistead and everyone else in Kennicott." Abruptly, she turned away and faced D'Angelo, apologizing for being a poor hostess. "You must ignore our banter," she said. "It's nonsense, based on old gossip." She clapped her hands together. "Betiane," she called, "bring us tea and pound cake."

Betiane? I looked around, saw no one but us.

D'Angelo didn't want to be anywhere close to pound cake. And his knee was bouncing. Soon, he'd be jingling his pocket change. "Thanks, no. Don't bother. We have to get—" he began.

But Kenny Wadd cut him off. "Detectives, I knew Ja Vala was the woman in the hospital the minute I saw her—"

"Kenny Wadd," Madame Yveny's voice boomed from her tiny body, "Enough."

But he continued. "And when the hairs I brought from Haiti match the ones I took at the hospital—"

"What hairs?" Madame Yveny's hands clutched the arms of her chair, and her single eyed gaze hit me like a slap.

"—you'll have scientific proof. Ja Vala never died. Madame Armistead made her a revenant."

"Kenny Wadd!" Madame Yveny growled. "It's not true. Revenants are stories like black cats and broken mirrors." She waved a hand, denying Kenny Wadd and his claims. Her gray eye looked swollen, threatened to pop its socket.

Kenny Wadd glanced at her but continued, "When those hairs match, you'll see, and then I'll take Ja Vala home with me."

D' put a hand on Kenny Wadd's shoulder, explaining that the woman in the hospital couldn't simply be released no matter what her name was, that she was a murder suspect. Kenny became frustrated, yelling at D'Angelo that Ja Vala had been through hell and couldn't be held responsible for anything she might have done while drugged and in captivity. D'Angelo reared up and yelled back that there were laws and procedures, and Kenny Wadd needed to back off.

I said nothing. I sat watching them. Studying Madame Yveny, her dried plants, shelves of canisters. The chairs facing the sofa. The room was set up like a classroom. She'd said it was arranged that way for her singing group. Maybe that was true. Or maybe she was still a voudou mambo? But if she was, why hadn't she said so? Was she ashamed of it? Hiding something?

A woman came in with a tray of tea and pound cake. She didn't speak, didn't make eye contact. Simply served tea. When she was finished, she stood still, waiting, until Madame Yveny told her to go back to the kitchen. Even then, she didn't respond, didn't even nod. She merely turned around and floated away.

Chapter 69

She lies in the dark, on the bed, her skin throbbing from the touch of Kenny Wadd's lips. She puts her hand on her forehead, trying to brush away his kiss. But her hand cannot erase the wound. She still smells it, sharp like charred flesh.

How long has it been since he last kissed her? How long since anyone has touched her with tenderness? She is not sure. But Kenny Wadd has been there, reminding her of what she has lost. If not for the burning of her skin, she would think his visit was a dream and not dwell on it. But the visit, along with the kiss he left on her skin, was real. He was there. She saw his tears.

Kenny Wadd. He says he has married another. So why has he come? What does he want? Does he hope to rescue her? To take her home? Does he not know what has happened, that she cannot exist without her bokor and the powders she provides? That her body is no longer alive? Or does he weep because he knows that he has found her too late?

She is wrestling with these thoughts when someone opens the door to her room. She closes her eyes and pretends to be sleeping. She does not move. The hallway light reveals a silhouette, a nurse. The nurse looks over her shoulder, closes the door, crosses the room. Turns the on the lamp beside the bed. The patient's eyes open, and she recognizes the false nurse who brought the powders. The nurse smiles and says that the bokor has sent more of the drug.

The bokor. The patient remembers the reflection of fire on her face, the vibrato in her voice. Other sounds—The ringing of her clochette, the rattling of snake bones in her asson. Josias, her son, stands at the altar behind wisps of smoke. He wears a gauze patch where once he had an eye. Madame Armistead sings, tells Ja Vala that now she belongs to her. She pours powder into a glass of water.

THE WOMAN IN THE CUPBOARD

Explains that she must forever take the powder or death will eat away at her, her skin will fall from her bones.

The nurse is taping fresh packets of powder under the nightstand drawer. She says it wasn't easy to get in to see her. She had to borrow a nurse's scrubs and key to get into the unit and, even then, she has to be careful. She doesn't know that many of the packets she left last time have been discovered and confiscated. She has no idea that Ja Vala has missed three doses, that her mind has become less clouded. That she remembers Josias on top of her. That she has seen Kenny Wadd and learned that he has married someone else. That she recalls Madame Armistead burying her and stealing her soul. That she realizes that this nurse is Madame Armistead's agent, intending to keep her enslaved.

The patient behaves as if she is dull and compliant, as the woman expects. She does not let on what she knows. While the false nurse mixes powder into a glass of water, the patient reaches her hand into her pillow. The nurse assumes that she will obey and drink as the bokor has ordered. The patient takes the glass and raises it to her mouth as if to drink, but at the last moment, she flicks her wrist and splashes the liquid into the nurse's face. While she gasps in surprise, the patient pulls her stolen needle from the fluff of the pillow. The nurse is still sputtering in confusion when the needle plunges deep into her eye. For a moment, the needle shifts, becomes a knife, and the fake nurse becomes Judith Granger. The patient freezes, watching a memory.

The nurse lets out a single cry and sinks onto the bed. The memory is gone, and the patient does not pause. She strips off the nurse's scrubs, covers the body with the blanket. She takes off her gown, hides it under the blanket, pulls on the scrubs. In the pockets, she finds keys, some money, and a phone. She has no plan, but she is strangely calm, allowing herself to be swept away by a current, letting it carry her where it will.

She leaves the hospital, her pockets stuffed with the new powder-filled envelopes. She walks tall like a free woman, a living one. And she is impressed with herself, with how easy the killing felt. Natural, as if she's done it before.

Chapter 70

My phone rang at four on Saturday morning. The caller was hysterical, inarticulate. Female.

"Calm down, Ma'am." I blinked, trying to wake up. "Take a breath and start over."

After the breath, the caller started over, and I realized it wasn't a woman at all. It was Dr. Vogel. He was shrieking high-pitched disconnected phrases. He'd called 911. He'd looked everywhere. Who were they? How had they gotten in? Who was the dead woman? And Mother of Mercy, where had they gone?

Who? "Dr. Vogel, slow down," I sat up, turned on my lamp. Felt a surge of adrenalin. "Tell me what's happened. From the beginning."

"There's no time." He was panting, possibly hyperventilating. "I swear everything was all right when I made evening rounds. I did paperwork, wrote orders for the night and morning shifts. Checked with the unit's security guard like always. Said goodnight to Roseanne, the nurse on night duty. She was fine. She was drinking one of those energy drinks, and I warned her about too much caffeine."

Maybe I shouldn't have told him to start at the beginning. Should have asked for the middle, even for the end. Then again, he was calming down, finally making sense.

"What happened next?"

"I don't know. I left. I went home. My God. Detective, I have no idea how they got in."

I pulled off the covers, swung my legs out of bed.

"The unit was locked when I left. The security guards swear no one came in but staff. Oh wait—The security cameras at the main entrance—I'll have them check the recordings—"

"So, someone came in? What happened?" I looked around for clean clothes. "Dr. Vogel, is our patient okay?"

"Hold on, detective." I heard Vogel yelling at someone. "Stop. You can't go in there. Not until the police come."

"Dr. Vogel?"

He continued talking to someone else, insisting that they leave everything untouched. And then he shouted. "Show me what? A what? What? That can't be. OhmyGod, OhmyGod."

"Dr. Vogel?" I called to him again and again, but he seemed to have forgotten all about me and our call. I heard commotion, voices, rustling. Dr. Vogel keening.

And my phone beeping. Another call coming through.

It was D'Angelo. Calls had come from the hospital to 911. They'd reported conflicting information, but one thing was certain: A woman had been found stabbed in one of the psychiatric unit's beds.

Chapter 71

D'Angelo was going to pick me up on his way. In an oversized t-shirt, I walked in circles, trying to decide what to wear. A woman had been stabbed. Was she Ja Vala? Dead? How could someone have gotten into the unit? Yesterday's clothes lay crumpled by the closet, wrinkled and stale. A mountain of dirty laundry rose from the closet floor. Wasn't there a fresh pair of black pants somewhere? Or gray or khaki? I saw nothing but a limp body lying in a hospital bed. Who could have killed her? The bokor that Kenny Wadd had talked about? No, she was in Haiti. But she had local associates—like the woman who'd shot at us. Maybe some pants were in the dryer. I dashed down the hall to the washer/dryer, found a mass of clean clothes, a black leg dangling down. Yanked at it, knocking the mass onto the floor but retrieving a clean pair of pants. Pulled them on and rushed back to my room for a sweater. Had she been awake when she'd been attacked? Had she died right away? I started for the door before I remembered to splash water over my face, run a toothbrush over my teeth. A hand through my hair.

When D'Angelo pulled up, I ran out to the car.

"Hold it," he stopped me, looked me over, up and down.

"What?"

"Your sweater's inside out."

I looked down. Cripes. "Thanks." I took it off, reversed it while he told me what he knew.

The victim had been found in Ja Vala's bed, a syringe buried in her eye.

Her eye? I saw the gray film on Madame Yveny's eye, the knife wound in Judith Granger's. A patch over a young man's empty socket.

"So, it's Ja Vala? Is she dead?"

D' shot me a look that asked, "What do you think?" but he said, "Apparently."

I pang of sorrow washed through me. Sorrow and guilt. "Could it be that bokor? Afraid she was losing control over Ja Vala, killing her to keep her quiet."

D'Angelo stopped me. "Mo, seriously? The bokor? Even Madam Yveny said that was crap. You believed it?"

"You didn't?" D'Angelo believed that his wife's dreams predicted the future and that he could negotiate with God. But he didn't believe that one person could control another with drugs? "They found scopolamine in Ja Vala's system. The exact same stuff Madame Yveny said bokors use when they create those revenants—"

"Madam Yveny never mentioned scopolamine."

"She might as well have. She said they used a substance to make people compliant and passive—If it's not scopolamine, it's something just like it. And what about Kenny Wadd? The toxin that poisoned him? You don't think it's significant that it was puffer fish, same as Madam Yveny said they use for revenants?"

"You know what I don't think, Mo? I don't think anyone is burying people alive and doping them so much that they become semi-consciousness slaves."

"Then explain why scopolamine was in Ja Vala's system."

"Technically, we don't know for sure that the woman even is Ja Vala—"

"What's going on? Yesterday, you thought she was." I would have gone on, but both of our phones rang.

Another body had been found at the hospital, in a janitor's closet outside the psychiatric unit. This one had been smothered, her mouth and nose covered with adhesive tape. Wearing only underwear.

Chapter 72

By the time we arrived at the hospital, the press had gathered outside, lights and cameras, consternation about more murders. When we got upstairs, we found out that the body in the closet had been identified. A psychiatric nurse, Roseanne Duncan.

The deputy coroner had just arrived but was able to tell us that the nurse had been dead at least three hours because rigor mortis had begun, but not more than six, since she'd been killed during her shift, which had begun at eleven.

Uniformed officers had taped off the area around the closet, and crime techs scurried around. D' and I took a look at the dead nurse. She was probably mid-thirties, her light brown hair coming loose from a bun. Her body was arched backward, wrists taped behind her back. Face wrapped like a mummy. Adhesive tape covered the area from her cheekbones to her chin and wound around her neck. Above and below the tape, her skin was dark bluish gray. Her eyes were wide open, the whites reddened by broken capillaries. She wore a beige bra, matching bikini underpants, ankle socks. Clogs lay nearby.

"Detectives?" a uniform named Brodsky approached, carrying a plastic bag with a medical tweezers. "This was in a trash can."

D' pulled a pair of latex gloves out of his pocket, put them on. Took the bag from Brodsky, looked inside. "Good," he said. "Nice work." He held the bag open so I could look inside. The clothes were balled up, but I saw what looked like a sweatshirt and a pair of leggings.

So, the killer was female. She must have taken the nurse's uniform, put it on, stuffed her own clothes into the bag and chucked it. I rubbed my temples, took a deep breath. Used the nurse's keys to get into the unit.

D's eyes asked if I was ready to move on. I nodded. We moved on, into the psychiatric unit.

Staff members there were hushed, their faces gaunt. I knew the look. Disbelief, fear, outrage, grief. A few were crying. Vogel sat at the nurse's station, staring at the desk. When he saw us, he lifted a hand, waving us away.

"I have nothing to say to you." He turned his head, dismissing us.

D' and I exchanged glances. It wasn't uncommon for crime victims to displace their anger and blame the police.

"Can we get you something, Dr. Vogel? Hot tea?"

He flashed me a glare, looked away again.

"An emergency doctor should look you over."

"No point."

"You might be in shock—"

"Really? Is that your professional diagnosis, detective? Shock?" Vogel stood, leaning on the partition of the nursing station. "Well, I better take that assessment seriously. Just like I took your assessment of my unit's security. Didn't you say my patient would be safe here?"

D' put up a hand. "Hold on, Dr. Vogel. You personally guaranteed the unit's security. You've got guards posted—"

"She was connected to a double murder and had been heavily drugged. Wasn't that an indication that we might need extra police protection?"

D' snorted. "On television maybe. In real life, we don't provide personal police protection willynilly."

Willynilly? I tried to balance D's gruffness with empathy. "Dr. Vogel. Detective D'Angelo and I are upset, too. But the best we can do now is to investigate what's happened."

"Investigate what's happened? What's the point? What's happened is that a nurse was lured out of the unit to be murdered. And my patient is gone." His voice was flat, and he sunk back into the chair. "Just...gone."

"We're sorry." I meant it. The killings felt unthinkably cruel. Just hours after finally being found by Kenny Wadd, Ja Vala had been

THE WOMAN IN THE CUPBOARD

killed. I dreaded going into her room to look at her body, kept seeing Kenny Wadd leaning over her, kissing her forehead. Kept feeling his tenderness, his sorrow.

I ran a hand through my hair, wiping away sentiment.

D' led me toward Ja Vala's room. "You ready?" He looked down at me, seemed taller than usual. Stronger.

I nodded, steeling myself. But I pictured Kenny Wadd and what would happen when we told him about Ja Vala's death, and I lost my footing, actually stumbled. What was happening? How had I gotten personally involved? Murders and victims never affected me, were just part of the job. But now, I was stumbling and D', who usually passed out at the sight of blood, was the steady one.

D' eyed me. "You need a minute?"

"No." I needed a decade. A lifetime.

"You sure, Mo? Have you gotten too close on this?"

I scowled. "Let's go." I barreled ahead, past the officers, through the open door. I took a deep breath, braced myself to see sheets stained with blood.

But I didn't see blood. And when I stepped closer to the body, I didn't see Ja Vala.

Chapter 73

Even with a syringe embedded in her eye, it was clear that the woman in the bed was Alexandra Lambert.

I turned to D'Angelo, confused. Why had Dr. Vogel said that his patient was dead?

And then I realized that he hadn't. He'd said that she was "gone." And, apparently, she was.

I tried to figure out what had happened. In one scenario, Alexandra Lambert somehow got into Ja Vala's room intending to kill her. Instead, Ja Vala had grabbed the syringe, killed her attacker, snuck out. And ambushed a nurse.

It didn't fit. I put myself in Ja Vala's position. Hunkering in the hallway wearing only a hospital gown. Overpowering a nurse, taking her clothing. But killing her? No. Why not just leave her tied up in the closet?

I rubbed my forehead. This scenario didn't work. Ja Vala could have simply taken Alexandra Lambert's clothes.

In fact, she must have. Alexandra Lambert's body was undressed, with Ja Vala's hospital gown beside her. Ja Vala must have undressed her, swapped clothes with her. So, whose were the sweatshirt and leggings found in the trash? They couldn't be Alexandra Lambert's because Ja Vala had put on Alexandra Lambert's clothes to get out of the hospital.

Unless Alexandra Lambert, not Ja Vala, killed the nurse and took her uniform. Of course—she'd needed the nametag and uniform to get past security—not to mention a key to enter the unit. So that meant Ja Vala was now wearing the nurse's scrubs.

"Okay," D' shoved his hands into his pockets. "How did she get in here?"

Was he kidding? Wasn't it obvious?

I told him my theory.

"So," he reasoned, "Ja Vala put the body in her bed so no one would notice she was gone. Bought herself some time."

"And no one stopped her because she was dressed as a nurse."

He nodded, picked up a leather handbag, most likely Alexandra Lambert's. Inside he found some gloves, tissues, cash, a 22-caliber pistol. No phone. But a few dozen small plastic packets filled with powder.

"Scopolamine?" He held one up. "So, Alexandra Lambert was the dealer?"

It looked that way. Did she work for the bokor? And what was Alexandra Lambert's real name? Where was she getting the drug?

"Alexandra Lambert," D' sighed. "Who the hell was she? First, she sends someone to shoot us. Now she kills an innocent nurse. Why? Just to give Ja Vala her drugs?"

I shook my head. I had no answers. But I noticed that, for the first time, D'Angelo had called her Ja Vala.

Chapter 74

She moves stiffly, in awkward spurts like a discarded newspaper blowing from doorway to doorway, alley to alley, resting in spaces between parked cars or behind bus stop shelters. She watches lovers stroll past with their arms linked, their steps and hearts in sync.

Kenny Wadd has walked with her like that under moonlit skies or along sun-drenched paths. Like these couples, they drew their breath in rhythm, and their bodies swayed with matching strides. She thinks of him and smiles, but flames flare in her chest and char her bones. Kenny Wadd has married someone else.

Police all over the city will be looking for a killer. A thin, mocha-skinned woman in nurse's scrubs. She must lose herself quickly, find a haven and swallow some powder before the rotting becomes apparent. She steps into the light of a small all-night market. Wawa, the sign says. She takes out the phone of the woman she has killed. She has never used one of these portable phones, but has seen the Grangers use them continually. She touches the tiny flat screen and pictures pop up. What is she to do? How can she find the number to call? And when she finds it, how is she to operate the phone?

Eyes are watching her. She feels the heat of stares. She must move on. She walks into the store, around the aisles as if her limbs are accustomed to walking, as if being in such a place is normal for her. She remembers that there is money in her pockets. Yes. She will make a purchase, something small. A piece of chocolate? A banana? She must not draw attention. Maybe the man taking the cash has heard that the police are looking for a murderer. Maybe he recognizes that she is the mocha-skinned woman in a nurse's outfit. Maybe she must leave.

He looks away from her, taking money from a man wearing jeans and leather. She takes a powdered pastry from a case, steps over to the cash box. Takes out a few bills. She has no idea how much a small cake will cost. Surely, not much. She hands the man two dollars. He gives one back with coins. "Half price after eight," he says.

She smiles, puts the money into her pocket, takes the pastry, and moves to the doorway. Her body aches. Her heart pounds. She holds the pastry in one hand, the phone in the other. The screen of the phone has gone dark, but when she touches it, it lights up and the small pictures reappear. A tiny camera. A clock. A musical note. An outline of a human head. Maybe this head represents people and their phone numbers? How can she find out? She looks back at the man who sold the pastry. She could ask him, but then for sure he would be suspicious, knowing that she's different, not like normal people who unceasingly talk into their phones or poke at the screens with their fingers. Oh. Maybe that's it—Maybe poking is what she must do? Is that the secret? She pokes the human head and instantly a list appears. Names, numbers. Alphabetically arranged. How is she to move past the A's?

Eyes are on her back. The man at the counter watches her. She smiles at him. He pretends he hasn't been staring, looks the other way. The pastry is crumbling in the tissue paper. In case he is watching, she takes a bite, trying to seem relaxed. Sweetness takes her by surprise. Reminds her of the surprise of the woman she killed, the sound she released when the needle penetrated her eye. She remembers that she must make a phone call.

She pokes the screen again, moving her finger, and the names move at her touch. The A names become B names. B names become Cs. She keeps brushing the screen until she reaches the letter she wants and locates the name, address, phone number. How does she make a call? Does she merely poke the number on the screen? She tries, and the call goes through.

"Did you see her?" the voice sounds scratchy, doesn't ask who's calling. Must assume that the caller is the woman who owns the phone. Who now lies dead in the hospital bed. "Did you give her the powders?"

"She has them."

"Then what's wrong? Why are you calling so late?"

Only then does she realize how late it is. And who has sent the woman to bring her the powders. She thinks of Kenny Wadd. Does he know, too? Is he in danger?

"You sound different." The voice is silent for a moment. "It's you, Ja Vala, isn't it? Ja Vala?"

She doesn't know how to end the call until she sees "end" on the screen and pokes the word. She puts the phone back into her pocket with some of the packets, the money and the other phone. A car drives by with a sign on top that says 'taxi.' The driver sees her at the curb and pulls over. Will he take her to the address she wants? Does she have enough money?

He lowers his window. "Need a cab?"

She opens the door. The handle feels cold, foreign. She climbs in, as if watching herself from afar. She is not sure why, but thick tears stream down her face.

Chapter 75

I needed coffee. D'Angelo drove to the Fourth Street Deli, where he ordered an egg white and broccoli omelet, and I ordered a stack of banana pancakes. He raised an eyebrow at my order.

"You can have a bite." I sipped coffee.

"You know I can't."

"Because? What happens if you break your promise and eat something sweet? You go to hell?" I passed him the cream.

"I bet you ordered that just to tempt me."

"I would never."

"You know that's my favorite, banana pancakes. You're an evil woman, Mo."

"The offer stands. You can have as much as you want."

"That's just what the devil would say."

"Fine. Now I'm the devil?"

He harrumphed, poured cream into his cup. Outside, the city was waking up, getting ready for soccer games and shopping, whatever they did on Saturdays. Maybe watching the morning news, where they'd see a picture of a missing Haitian woman, a person of interest in two overnight homicides and several earlier ones. An all-out search was on for Ja Vala, her photo flashing all over the media, the streets around the hospital being combed. Even so, I couldn't rule out the possibility that she was innocent, victimized yet again. Maybe she'd been kidnapped by the same people who'd stolen her from Haiti. After Kenny Wadd had come here and revealed her identity, those people might have feared that they, and their trafficking business, would be exposed. Ja Vala was only one of their victims. How many others like her were in the area, kidnapped, drugged and enslaved?

"Vogel's going to raise Cain," D' said. Changing the subject. Picking something neutral. "We ought to warn the captain."

He was right. We'd left Vogel in a snit, threatening to expose police incompetence to the reporters, to blame us for the mayhem. Mostly, he was angry with himself and blaming us to cover his own butt. After all, two murders had been committed and his patient had disappeared from a unit under his sole supervision, without as much as an orderly noticing.

Even so, the press would broadcast his accusations.

I swallowed coffee, thought of Ja Vala. Wondered where she was. Our food came. I poured syrup over my pancakes. D' peppered his omelet, and we ate in silence. We were tired, frustrated.

My phone rang halfway through my stack. I answered right away with my mouth full. It was Kenny Wadd.

"It cannot be true what they are saying," his voice was husky. "Ja Vala did nothing. She is the victim—"

"We don't know what happened," I told him. "We're looking for her." I looked at D'. Mouthed Kenny Wadd's name.

"On the news they say that police think she killed two women." It was a question. "A nurse and someone else. Who was the other woman?"

"We don't have the victim's identity. She used a false name."

"Of course, she did. She had to be one of the bokor's agents," he said. "The bokor no doubt sent her to kill Ja Vala. It is because of me. The bokor must be aware that I've found Ja Vala, and she worries that we will expose her crimes. Ja Vala must have fought and run for her life. Detective, we must find her. If the bokor's people find her first, she's lost."

"Where are you?"

"Out. I have rented a car to look for Ja Vala—"

"Stop. Go back to your hotel. Don't go looking for her."

"But I must—"

"Listen to me. If you're right, don't you think the people who took Ja Vala will come after you, as well? You've already been attacked once—"

"It doesn't matter. I lost Ja Vala once. I must not fail her again."

I took a breath, recalled him kissing her. "Where are you going? How are you going to find her all by yourself?"

"I won't be by myself," he said. "I will have help."

Help? Kenny Wadd didn't know anyone in Philadelphia. Except an old mambo.

As if gathered by magnetic force, thought fragments came together: knowledge of puffer fish toxin and drugs, connections to Haiti and Philadelphia, a history as a voudou leader, a friendship with the feared Madame Armistead. And Betiane, a maid who seemed semi-conscious and revenant-like. Maybe Madame Yveny wasn't just a retired mambo.

Maybe she wasn't retired at all.

Chapter 76

The taxi drops her down the street from the Grangers' house. She needs to be sure that no police linger there, that no neighbors are watching. She tries to appear casual as a jogger passes, then a man walks his dog. It's chilly and the sun is not fully up, but she doesn't shiver. Cold bothers only the living.

She knows where the spare key is kept, inside a plastic case shaped like a rock. She walks around the front of the house, back and forth, but does not see the rock. The police have most likely moved it. Nevertheless, she must get inside the house, must find the information she needs. She wonders is the Grangers' son has arrived. Is he in the house? She approaches the front door. Rings the bell.

No one answers. The house is idle, empty except perhaps for ghosts.

She steps away from the door. Another jogger passes, but doesn't notice her. She studies the house, its windows. And notices the narrow gate beside it. Yes. Perfect. When no one is looking, she climbs over the gate and follows the pathway to the courtyard behind the Grangers' house. There, she looks for a rock. Something hefty enough to break the glass.

A few bricks have come loose in the corner of the courtyard, she picks one up, hopes the alarm system is not on. If it is, she will run back over the gate. She throws a rock at the glass door to the courtyard. Glass shatters. She waits. Listens. Hears no alarm. After a while, she reaches inside the door, unlatches it, openes it, and goes inside.

The house smells of dust and dead air. Traces of stale blood. She has no time to dwell on scents, goes directly to Dixon Grangers' study. What she's looking for must be in his desk. Maybe in his safe. As she passes the kitchen, she stops, knocked off balance, holding the wall for support. Dixon Granger stares at her with disbelieving eyes, his head almost severed from his body. Judith Granger lies on the floor, her mouth open, releasing a final gurgle. A woman rushes by, taking shelter in a pantry.

She stands in the kitchen, watching these images repeat themselves. What do they mean? What is she seeing? She herself must be the woman running to the pantry. Detective Sterling has said that she found her there. And that police found her clothes, bloodied, in the washing machine.

She closes her eyes and sees the cleaver in Dixon Granger's neck. A hand removes it. Is it her own?

It can't be. She's taken powders and had no will of her own. She'd acted only on command. But she has no time to consider this, must find the address before Kenny Wadd comes to harm. Kenny Wadd, who has married another. Kenny Wadd who has trampled on and crushed her heart, abandoning her. He says he has come to rescue her, for what reason she does not know. But, coming for her has put him in danger. The bokor will have him killed or worse to stop him from exposing her and her work. He has torn her own dreams apart, but she must protect Kenny Wadd at any cost.

She dashes through the house, turns into a hallway. Stops short. A figure is running toward her. It stops when she does. It takes a moment, but she realizes that no one is there. The figure is her own reflection in the huge mirror at the end of the hall. Still, she is shaken, and proceeds slowly. The image grows larger as she nears it, and she watches the reflection. Gets close enough to study it.

***

Surely, this reflection is not hers. White streaks this woman's hair. Her eyes are dull, without sparkle. Thin lines etch her dusky dry skin. Her lips are covered with cracks. Maybe her flesh has begun to decay.

Ja Vala stands at the mirror, staring, touching her face, her hair. How has she changed so drastically? When was it that she got old?

Her eyes widen, disbelieving. She cannot look away. Her fingers grab at her face, pulling at her features, examining them. Doubting what she sees. She is young, after all—She was about to be married until Kenny Wadd married someone else. She sinks to her knees, her eyes still on her reflection, her hands still tugging at her face. Her mind struggles to understand. How long was she here with the Grangers'? Could it have been years? Has she been lost in her bokor's haze, trapped alone while others lived life? Has time passed without her knowing?

And Kenny Wadd. Maybe he *did* wait for her. Maybe for years.

The loss is too great. It sears her heart, sends her mind reeling. She looks away from the mirror and the empty aging face. She cannot linger on grief or rage. She swallows, feels them roil through her blood, soak into her bones.

She forces herself to stand and makes her way into Dixon Granger's office. She has lost years, but now she counts minutes and seconds, knows that she has none to spare.

She begins with Dixon Granger's desk. She empties drawers. Pores through insurance contracts and legal correspondence. She finds a file labeled "living will." Others labeled "portfolio" and "deductions." One contains handwritten letters. One holds notes from business meetings.

Nothing about the bokor or her cohorts. She moves on, tells herself to be thorough, lest she misses what she's looking for. She opens a file cabinet, scans the tabs. Mostly they are marked with names of people, businesses. She runs her hand over them, reading each one, closes the drawer, opens another. Then another. Finally, flat, buried under a pile of travel pamphlets in the bottom drawer, she finds a folder and pulls it out. Stares at the name on the tab.

Dixon Granger has a file labeled "Armistead."

Chapter 77

D' put the siren on. "We better get there before Kenny Wadd does."

His urgency surprised me. D'Angelo wasn't convinced that Madame Yveny was involved with Ja Vala's disappearance. He was simply concerned about Kenny Wadd.

"Who knows what he'll do? If he thinks that old lady has something to do with his girlfriend's disappearance—"

He stopped in the middle of his sentence. We both knew what he'd been about to say. I didn't comment. I was too caught up in thoughts of Madame Yveny. If she were a bokor, she could have hired Alexandra Lambert. Could have supplied the Grangers with the drug that ensured their servant's obedience. Could be in cohoots with the Haitian bokor, trafficking young women from her native country, selling them as revenant slaves.

D'Angelo swerved, avoiding a van. "What's with people? Are they deaf? Don't they know to move to the right?" He floored it, hurrying because of Kenny Wadd, what he might do.

We crossed Broad Street. Sped along Market. I thought of the Grangers. Their trips to Haiti. Dixon Granger's split with his partner. Was the split because of Granger's involvement with trafficking? Had J. Steven found out that the Grangers actually purchased a slave? Had he been killed because he'd threatened to reveal that secret? It made sense. But what about Sylvia Blake? Maybe she'd tried to blackmail the Grangers.

And the Grangers themselves? My theory didn't explain their murders.

"Dammit." Traffic was jammed at the bridge. D' stuck his arm out the window, gesturing for drivers to move over get out of the way. The siren wailed. D's face was crimson.

"Be cool, D'. You'll have a stroke."

D' cursed. Pushed his way into west Philadelphia. Sped through lights, raced around corners, sped past Drexel and Penn, shot down 48th. Finally, shrieked to a stop in front of Madame Yveny's.

"Ready?" He checked his weapon, adjusted his side holster.

I followed him up the path, looking around for Kenny Wadd. I was probably wrong about Madame Yveny. She was an old lady, half blind, half my body mass. Not capable of masterminding an international drug and human trafficking operation, especially with powerful, high profile clients like Dixon Granger.

Unless she had partners.

D'Angelo rang the bell, and Betiane opened the door, allowing us into the dim foyer. That moment of blindness before my eyes could adjust from sunlight to shadows was the last thing I remembered.

Chapter 78

The file contains a list names and addresses of people in many places—Philadelphia, New York, London, Miami, Washington D.C., Raleigh, Atlanta, Phoenix, Dallas. Each name is followed by M or F. Sometimes both. Who are these people? A double graph shows prices, coded by numbers sixteen to thirty. Are the lines genders, the numbers ages? A chart projecting costs for "s," "t," and "ovrhd and mtnce." Another list includes dozens of names—mostly Haitian, with genders and ages.

What are these papers? And why is the folder named for Madame Armistead? A report is in the folder. A private investigator, giving background on several of the listed names. Assuring Mr. Dixon that none of the aforementioned people had ties to government or law enforcement.

Ja Vala also finds a handwritten letter promising a unique service. Discreet and economical. Providing permanent, compliant, private domestic help. Words are crossed out. It seems to be a rough copy, still being edited. But its purpose is clear: Dixon Granger was offering to supply "help" to people who had no ties to government or law enforcement.

Her mouth is dry and waves of nausea pass through her. She reads the pages over again, unable to accept what she is reading. Dixon Granger was running a business, providing domestic help to customers. Promising workers' obedience and loyalty because of unique "elixirs" that ensure lifelong obedience and commitment to employers. He'd crossed out a section explaining that all the workers come with genuine legal death certificates, a guarantee that no one would be looking for them.

A memory stirs—She is cold, unable to move, alone in darkness. She smells moist earth. Is she in the ground? In a coffin? Icy fear claws at her. Has she been buried? She tries to scream but her throat is rigid and can make no sound. Terror swallows her, and she flails in its belly, drowning but not dying, wondering if she is in hell or merely suffering the bokor's curse.

This memory lasts only a moment, but she knows it is real. She was dead and buried and recovered from the grave.

Kenny Wadd attended her funeral.

But now she has found out that Dixon Granger was planning to provide more servants like her. More who must take their "elixir" powders in water or tea lest they decay. Again, she sees the surprise on Dixon Granger's face. His blood shooting across the floor.

Did she kill Mr. Dixon? Was it her arm swinging the cleaver? Did she do it because she'd found out about this evil business? But no—she couldn't have killed him. The powders blocked her from acting on her own will, even from thinking or remembering. But if somehow, she did kill him, she is not regretful. If he were alive, she would kill him again.

She sits in Dixon Granger's office, digesting what she's read. Considering it. She has lost track of time, has been in the house too long. Hasn't found out what she's come for. Only when she closes the folder does she see the staple on the back. Fastened to the inside of the back cover, she finds a bill of sale with a written guarantee. It is signed by Madame Armistead. It promises the permanent possession of and compliance by the person formerly known as Ja Vala Boudin, for as long the Grangers continue buying and using the powders provided by her local agent in Philadelphia. The name and address are right there, beside my hand.

Chapter 79

Darkness. A crunch, then a splat. Another crunch. Another splat. With each splat, a clump thudded onto me, cool and damp, soft like sand. Like when I was a kid and my friends and I used to bury each other at the beach. Crunch. Splat. Crunch. Splat.

Only I wasn't at the beach. And I wasn't with friends. I strained to open my eyes. My eyelids refused to respond, felt stuck. Glued together. Finally, after a lot of concentration, one lid cracked open, but not for long. Gravelly fragments fell in, and reflexively, my eye snapped shut again. I tried to raise my hands to rub away the grit and shield my face. Tried to turn my head away from the splatter. Tried to yell.

Couldn't do any of that. Couldn't move or make a sound.

Panic shot through me. And questions. Why couldn't I move? Where was I? What was happening? Another crunch. More spatter landed on my legs, my belly. I smelled damp earth, soil. Had no doubt about what was happening. Tried again to cry out. To move. Couldn't. The earth on my legs was becoming heavy. I struggled, focused. Finally forced both my eyes open, squinted into fading light. Saw a figure—no, two, silhouetted in the dusk. Each held a shovel. Each dug up dirt and dumped it onto me. My stomach twisted, flew into my chest. I couldn't breathe. Couldn't think. Couldn't move. Couldn't just lie there and let them bury me.

Crunch. Splat. Crunch.

Okay. I had to think. To figure out what to do. Wiat, what about D'Angelo—Where was he? Hadn't we been driving together? Crunch, splat. How could I think with dirt piling on top of me? Never mind. I had no choice. Had to think. Remembered the case. And Ja Vala. I remembered that she'd gone missing. And Kenny Wadd, her old boyfriend. D' and I were trying to find him and stop him. Stop him from what? Splat. Dirt landed on my face. I'd seen it coming, but couldn't dodge it. I strained again to turn my head so dirt wouldn't fall into my nostrils, between my lips. But my head wouldn't move. The earth was cold, smelled raw. Was this how I would die? Would I suffocate here in this hole, alone with dirt in my nose? Would worms and insects nibble on me before I was dead? Would anyone ever find my body? Would D'?

Oh God. D'—Where was he? Was he even alive? A shudder rattled through me. Were they burying D', too? The figures kept digging and filling, digging and filling. I couldn't feel my feet or hands. Couldn't move at all. And a thought occurred to me. Since I couldn't move, the diggers might think I was dead. Might not realize they were burying a living person. I had to call out to them, somehow make a sound. I concentrated on my throat. Began pushing my breath out hard, trying to squeeze it past my vocal cords. Managed a faint growl, but nothing they could hear above the crunches and splats of dirt. The pair worked methodically, in rhythm. Without talking or pausing for breaks. Never mind. I had to keep trying. Pushed the air through my throat, made short humming sounds as loudly as I could. Hoped they'd hear them.

If they heard, they gave no indication. Just kept digging, quietly. Steadily. Flatly. Mechanically, like robots. Like people drugged into obedience. Like Ja Vala. Oh God. Were these men revenants? If they were revenants, then all of what Kenny Wadd said was true. My mind whirled. Was that why I couldn't move? Because of that puffer fish drug? It paralyzed people, made them seem dead. Had someone given it to me? How? And when? And if I was paralyzed, how come could I open and shut my eyes? I tested myself, lifting and dropping my eyelids. If I could move them, I wasn't completely paralyzed. Maybe the toxin was wearing off, or they'd given me too little. A splat of dirt hit me full in the face. I shut my eyes and let out a shrill high-pitched hum. Miraculously, the digging stopped. Had the men heard me? I listened for more crunches, didn't hear them. Opened my eyes a slit, peered through clumps of dirt. Saw the diggers standing at attention, shovels in hand. Closed my eyes again, trying to decide whether to make another noise. Listening. Hearing a scuffle. Muffled voices. And a woman shouting. Yelling for help.

When I opened my eyes again, the diggers were gone.

Chapter 80

Ja Vala remembers her from childhood, from her village. A tiny woman with an eye like mother of pearl, like the inside of an oyster shell. Not anything like an eye. And yet there it was, a whitish ball where an eye should have been. She was not the size of other adults, so when Ja Vala stood near her, this eye was not far above her own. She remembers watching it in fear.

Ja Vala arms herself with a knife from Judith Granger's kitchen and takes a taxi to the address written on the bill of sale. Madame Armistead took away her life but did not work alone. She had a partner in the United States, Madame Yveny. When Ja Vala knocks, a maid answers the door. Ja Vala recognizes her dazed eyes, her blankness. The maid is who she was. A shell. The maid who is a shell tells her to wait in the foyer and leaves. But, Ja Vala doesn't wait. She moves into the house. In the sitting room, she sees chairs and an altar. So, Madame Yveny is a practicing mambo. On the way to the kitchen, she passes shelves filled with canisters and bottles, supporting her suspicion that Madame Yveny is not just a mambo but a bokor who has been supplying her with powders that keep her under Madame Armistead's control. Ja Vala doesn't have time now, but before she leaves, she will destroy these bottles, even if that means she will rot.

A man's jacket lies on the kitchen table. Ja Vala stops and looks in the pockets. A wallet, a passport. Her heart jolts and her fingers tremble, and she knows even before she opens the passport that these items belong to Kenny Wadd.

Kenny Wadd is already there. She calls out his name but there is no answer. She runs through the house, passing staircases, peering into empty rooms, racing down a long corridor to the back door that leads to the yard. She thrusts it open and sees the maid outside, talking to the bokor Madame Yveny. And beyond them, in the far corner of the property, she sees two men digging.

Chapter 81

They stopped throwing dirt on me. Even so, I couldn't move. Couldn't even brush off my eyes to see clearly. My head throbbed, and waves of nausea passed through me. I had the sense that I was weightless, floating even as my body remained frozen and motionless. Voices rose in the distance. I could make out only bits: "Don't be foolish." Angry words I couldn't quite hear. Then, clearly, "I'll have them kill you. They'll cut you up and devour the pieces."

Women's voices. Not a sign of D'. Oh God, where was he? Was he all right? My mind felt thick. I pushed my brain, thinking back, remembering that D' and I had come to Madam Yveny's house looking for Kenny Wadd who had been looking for Ja Vala. But after we got here?

I remembered nothing.

Thinking wore me out, made me sweat. Linking two thoughts together took monumental effort. Maybe if I rested for a minute, my strength would return. Maybe the paralysis would wear off.

But maybe it wouldn't. Maybe I needed an antidote—Wasn't that how they'd revived Ja Vala? With an antidote? Didn't I need to get it within a certain number of hours?

Except that Madame Yveny didn't intend to revive me. Didn't need an antidote.

Sweat trickled down my temples, into my hair. But wait. They hadn't given me enough toxin to completely paralyze me. If I focused hard enough, I might be able to move something besides my eyelids. Just a little. Just enough to crawl out of the hole.

I opened my eyes, squinted up through small clumps of dirt. The walls of the hole looked high. The surface far away. The sky bright blue.

So, it was still daytime. How long had I been lying there? Minutes? Hours?

THE WOMAN IN THE CUPBOARD

Women were still arguing, keeping the diggers distracted. But maybe not for long. I had to hurry, climb out while no one was watching. Move, I told myself. Get up.

I tried to sit. I grunted, strained. Ordered my abs to contract, my shoulders to roll and rise. Nothing. Not a twitch. I asked again, more urgently. I pleaded with my body parts, bribed them with promises of a hot bath, a day at the spa. A bottle of rye whiskey. But my parts did nothing. I lay flat on my back in a half-filled grave. Sweat blended with dirt, coated my skin with tiny globs of mud. I couldn't move, was going to lie there and be buried alive. I was done. Over. Nobody would even know where I was buried. I'd be considered missing. Odd word, missing. Would anyone actually be missing me? D' would if he was still alive. And Evie of course. But except for them, would anyone care that I was gone? My coworkers might, for about three days, until Reynolds moved his stuff into my desk since it was closer to the captain's office. Some second cousin in Ohio would inherit my big screen tv. Bottom line: my demise wouldn't bother anybody. Since my divorce, I'd kept my distance from people, so now I was nobody to anybody. Tears of self-pity pooled in my eyes, dribbled through loose soil. I was giving up, mourning my own death. Would it take long? Be painful? I lay still, pouting, shedding tears.

Until I realized that I was pouting. Pouting required lip movement. Which meant I could move not just my eyelids, but also my lips. And my voice was working, if grunting counted. Maybe other parts were beginning to come back, too. Small muscles? Could I raise my eyebrows? I tried, wasn't sure. Maybe I was just imagining their upward slide. I needed to try something more definitive. Fingers.

I lay perfectly still, concentrating on moving a finger. Just one, the pointer on my right hand. I took my time, pictured a message shooting down a chain of nerve cells from my brain to my shoulder,

shoulder to wrist, wrist to fingers. And waited, focusing. And wiggled not just a pointer, but a thumb. Then a middle finger.

Tears gushed, unintended, uncontrolled. Mud trickled into my eyesI blinked it out. My fingers could move. I wanted to yell and dance.

But dancing was far beyond my capacity. I worked on my other hand. Moved those fingers more easily. Tried my arms. Concentrated but couldn't make them budge. Rested. And noticed the quiet. The women had stopped yelling. I held still, listening, straining to hear them. Heard only the clanging of tension and the crazed beating of my heart. What had happened? Why had the women quieted down? And the gravediggers—Were they coming back?

Get going, I told myself. Stop sniveling and move. I worked my fingers through dirt. Dug my nails into the walls of the grave, fingers crawling upward, dragging my arms up inch by inch until they were raised high above my body. And then with every bit of my strength, I used my fingers as talons and pulled. I tugged. I clenched my jaw and let out a belly moan.

And nothing. I couldn't lift myself up. Couldn't move my body.

I waited, caught my breath. Told myself not to give up. The diggers weren't back yet. I had time to try again.

I tried again. And again. I couldn't get up the first time or the second or third. But eventually, after I'd stopped counting how many times I'd tried, something clicked. My body responded. Fistfuls of ground gave way and my hands dropped off the walls, but at the same time, my torso sprung upward. Dirt tumbled from my ears, nostrils, lips, hair. It slid off my chest. I almost shrieked with joy and amazement: I was sitting up.

Chapter 82

Moving my legs was still impossible. I dragged myself out of the pit, straining my arms and shoulders. Smelling dirt. Tasting and swallowing it. Lifting myself until I could peek over the edge of the grave. And trying to make sense of what I saw.

The gravediggers stood with their backs to me, blocking my view of two women who appeared to be in a standoff. One was tiny, wearing Haitian garb. Had to be Madame Yveny. The other was wearing medical scrubs. I couldn't see her face. But I saw her hand and, reflecting the sunlight, the glint of her knife.

I didn't dwell on them. All I wanted was to get out of the grave. I looked around to make sure no one else was watching, then pulled myself up over the edge, dragging the dead weight of my legs up onto the ground. I lay on rocks and thin grass, waiting for the others to notice me, but they didn't. They were engrossed in their confrontation.

"Be reasonable, Ja Vala."

Ja Vala—Of course. Ja Vala was there, dressed as a nurse. I closed my eyes, trying to understand. Thoughts swam just beyond reach, slippery shapes in dark water. But a voice in my head—Dr. Vogel's?—screamed at me, furious that Ja Vala was gone. I opened my eyes, squinted at Ja Vala. It made sense that she'd come here. Madame Yveny was a mambo from her hometown. Ja Vala must have come to her for help, not knowing what Madame Yveny had done—Except that she must know. Why else would she be threatening her with a knife? Again, I tried to move my legs, to stand. No use.

"No matter how many times you insist, the fact remains I cannot provide what you demand. No matter how long we stand here arguing, the fact remains you must obey your bokor or suffer the consequences." Madame Yveny's voice was deep and dangerous. "You know what will happen. Your body will rot but you will live. You will be an abomination—"

"Bring me Kenny Wadd."

Kenny Wadd? He was he here, too? Where? And where was D'? My throat clamped up. My lungs couldn't get air. I lay in the yard, struggling to breathe. Was D' even alive?

If she'd done anything to D', I would personally rip Madame Yveny to ribbons. Providing that I could move my arms. My skull hammered, tears welled up. I needed to stop sniveling. Take charge. I was a cop, needed to act like one. I looked around, steadied my breathing. Overcame the sense of floating. Oriented myself. Assessed the threat.

We were behind Madame Yveny's house, in the back yard. Four people stood near the porch: two women and the gravediggers. The diggers didn't move. They stood like sleepwalkers, watching Madame Yveny as she and Ja Vala bickered and hissed.

"Tell them to bring me Kenny Wadd."

"Impossible. I've told you a hundred times. He's gone."

"Stop lying. Do not underestimate me, Madam Yvney. I will cut you. You know I will."

Madame Yveny scoffed. "You think I am afraid of you? You think you're a big-time assassin now?"

"Big enough." Ja Vala clutched the knife.

Madame Yveny spoke quietly, her voice to low for me to hear. But then it rose. "...if I die, no one will provide your powders. They are all that keeps your skin from falling off—"

"Liar. The powder was only to control me. I haven't taken any for some time. Am I am rotting? Is my skin falling off?"

"It will. Soon."

It would? Why would her skin fall off?

"You've stalled long enough. Bring Kenny Wadd or I will slit your throat."

THE WOMAN IN THE CUPBOARD

Madame Yveny cackled. "You can't kill me, Ja Vala. Without me, you will never find your Kenny Wadd."

"You refuse to tell me where he is, so I might as well kill you."

I shimmied away from the grave, testing my legs again, trying to move an ankle, bend a knee. I couldn't. Tried again. Managed to lift myself up and flop noisily, face first into a shrub.

I lay still, expecting everyone to look my way. But no one did. No gravediggers rushed to throw me back into the hole. I hauled myself out of the bushes and understood why no one noticed me. Ja Vala was lunging at Madame Yveny, swinging the knife.

Madame Yveny scooted away, dodging her. "Take her," she barked, pointing at Ja Vala. The gravediggers stepped toward Ja Vala. They continued to approach even as she swiped at them, slicing their arms, their chests. Blood spurted and sprayed, and Ja Vala leapt away from the men, but they kept after her, slowly and steadily, as commanded.

"Call them off," Ja Vala yelled. "I'll kill them."

"Go ahead, Ja Vala." Madame Yveny stepped back. "I have plenty more stored in the cellar."

Ja Vala veered sideways, narrowly avoiding the grasps of the men. She darted around them, agile and light, and zigzagged toward Madame Yveny, grabbing her before the men in their slow stupor could stop her.

"Tell them to back off," Ja Vala growled. She tightened her arms around Madam Yveny's throat. "Make them bring back Kenny Wadd."

Chapter 83

Ja Vala knows he is there. She prays she's not too late, even as she swings her knife at the revenants, drawing their blood. They move slowly, unable to hurry, unable to stop their pursuit. She understands how it is. Just days ago, she was one of them.

Madame Yveny watches, smugly sticking to her lies. Insisting that Ja Vala will be a living corpse. Not realizing that the lies no longer frighten her, that Ja Vala has been without the powder for some days and has not decayed. And that even if she does decay, she doesn't care. Ja Vala has already been destroyed.

But Kenny Wadd—She remembers his lips on her skin. She sees him walking with her, hand in hand, feels the breeze rippling her skirt. Even if he has married another, Kenny Wadd still owns her heart. She cannot allow the bokor to destroy him.

Madame Yveny watches, her blind eye radiating evil. Warning her that on her own, she is powerless. But Ja Vala knows better. She has already had the strength of will power to kill a woman. She will not hesitate to kill again. The gravediggers continue their sluggish attempts to come for her, not able to stop even when she cuts them, compelled to follow their bokor's commands. They will die at Ja Vala's hand unless Madame Yveny orders them to stop.

The wounded men move slowly, and Ja Vala is able to close in on Madame Yveny. She rushes forward and grabs her throat. Holds the knife to her good eye.

"Call them off," Ja Vala demands. "Tell them to bring back Kenny Wadd." The bones of Madame Yveny's neck are fragile. Ja Vala can snap them easily, or plunge the knife into her.

Madame Yveny gasps, or pretends to. She slumps in Ja Vala's arms. Ja Vala doesn't move the knife. Doesn't trust that the collapse is genuine.

"Tell them." Ja Vala's voice is like the ruffle of feathers.

Madame Yveny croaks an order for the men to stand still. They stop where they are, arms at their sides. Bleeding from their wounds.

"You will regret this, Ja Vala."

But Ja Vala is not afraid. Not of the bokor Madame Yveny, or of her friend, the bokor Madame Armistead. Everything she's ever had or wished for has already been lost. She tells Madame Yveny to be mindful, that she has already taken lives and will not hesitate to take another. She presses the knife against her eyelid, feels the tiny body tighten in her grip.

"Get the man," Madame Yveny croaks. The two revenants turn, trudging across the yard.

"Tell them to hurry," Ja Vala demands.

"Hurry," the old woman calls.

The men pick up their speed, retrieving shovels from a hole they've been digging, carrying them a few yards to the left, and they begin digging up a fresh mound of dirt.

Kenny Wadd is buried? Dead? Ja Vala cannot breathe. Her heart plummets as she absorbs this news, and she decides that she will follow him in death. She will jump into the open earth and share his grave. But before she does, she will make Madame Yveny sorry.

Ja Vala drags Madame Yveny to the place where the men are digging. She watches the ground giving way, the growing piles of soil and clay. Blood roars through her veins, and her heart beats its fury Kenny Wadd—Kenny Wadd.

"Tell them to dig faster." She yanks Madame Yveny's head back. Madame Yveny obeys, and they pick up their pace.

"It is no good, Ja Vala," Madame Yveny breathes. "I didn't intend to bring them back. I have no antidote."

"Then you will make it," Ja Vala tells her. "You will mix up something to revive them." And then Ja Vala realizes the bokor has said, 'them.' Has she buried more people than just Kenny Wadd?

The men keep digging. Ja Vala's mind chants his name: Kenny Wadd, Kenny Wadd. She sees his tender eyes, hears him talk about their future life, their children. She waits to see his body emerge from shadows and dirt, so focused that at first, she doesn't notice the voice calling her.

"Ja Vala." It is like the jagged rattling of broken glass. She listens and hears it again, coming from the bushes behind her. Still clutching Madam Yveny's throat, she turns. A figure rises from the ground, camouflaged by hedges and dirt. Madam Yveny lets out a groan. "No. How?"

"Who is it?" Ja Vala holds the knife up as a warning.

The figure stumbles toward them. "Hell be."

Her words are slurred. And her walking is off balance, broken. Labored.

"It's not possible," Madame Yveny shrieks.

"Day berry be," she says. Muddy saliva drips from her mouth. Another of Madame Yveny's victims, rising from the earth.

Ja Vala stares, holding onto the bokor.

"Idiots," Madame Yveny scolds the revenants. "She's moving. What have you done? Didn't you give her all the powder?"

The revenants keep digging. They do not answer.

The woman struggles, lumbering toward them, her limbs stiff, body smudged with dirt, a deep wound on her arm bleeding, clods of soil clinging to her skin, hair and clothing. Finally, under the mess, Ja Vala recognizes her.

"Detective Sterling?"

The detective cannot move anymore and stumbles to her knees. Ja Vala cannot help her without releasing the bokor.

"Madam Yveny has killed Kenny Wadd," Ja Vala tells the fallen detective, but Madam Yveny interrupts.

"I've killed no one."

Ja Vala tightens the grip on her neck.

THE WOMAN IN THE CUPBOARD

The detective struggles back to her feet. Totters, catching her breath. "Wiz Deezhlo?" And collapses again.

Behind them, in the hole, somebody coughs.

Chapter 84

Unable to resist, I felt hands lifting me, arms carrying me. Someone positioning me in an easy chair. I rested there until a familiar smell disturbed me. Sweet like dead flowers. I opened my eyes, saw a kaleidoscope of sparkles. Blinked. The sparkles became glittering sequins on banners hanging over a window. Another blink and I recognized where I was: Madame Yveny's sitting room.

My body was stiff and sore, lungs raw. Lips numb and tongue tasting like dirt. Kenny Wadd lay on the floor by my feet, not moving. Was he dead?

"Kenny Wadd?" I whispered, but what came out was a mangled gust of air. I struggled to get up so I could check his pulse, but my limbs were granite, too heavy to lift. I slumped, exhausted from the effort. Saw his chest rise and fall. Kenny Wadd was alive.

I closed my eyes again, heard women's voices. Sharp and staccato, like the beaks of birds. "Do not rush me, Ja Vala. I must concentrate."

"Hurry. Kenny Wadd will die."

"Step away. Give me room."

"You have plenty of room."

"You're crowding me. I need to think about what I'm doing. I don't have the formula. I didn't plan to revive anyone."

"You know the formula."

"I'm trying to remember it. And I need space."

They argued. I wondered if Madame Yveny was really preparing the antidote or only stalling, waiting for a chance to overcome Ja Vala. And even if she made the antidote, would Ja Vala give some to me or only to Kenny Wadd? Would it occur to her to rescue a detective? Then again, I'd been able to climb out of the grave—Maybe I wouldn't need an antidote. Maybe time would be enough to cure me. Maybe.

THE WOMAN IN THE CUPBOARD

I tried again to move. My body wouldn't respond, felt disconnected from my brain. I started over, as I had in the grave, working on just one hand. One finger. I lifted it, heard Ja Vala demand that Madame Yveny explain.

"Explain what?"

"What you did to me. Why you took away my life."

"I didn't. You sealed your own fate."

"No. You kept me subdued. The Grangers got the powders from you."

"Did they? You know nothing."

"Explain. Tell me why you did it."

I heard a crash like a dish dropping and breaking. Madame Yveny said something, probably a curse in French. "See what you made me do, Ja Vala?"

"It was only a jar."

"Back away. Give me room."

"Tell me why you made me a revenant."

"Me?" Madame Yveny cackled. "How could I? I was here. You were there. You know who it was."

They were quiet for a moment.

"But why? I was defending myself. Josias attacked me—"

"Ja Vala, move away. I can't work this way."

"Should I have simply let him rape me?"

"Why do you persist with this? It's years too late for discussion."

I turned my head, looked at Kenny Wadd. His eyes were open but glazed and unfocused. His forehead was wet with sweat. I turned the other way, looking for D'Angelo. Saw only the back of the two women standing at the table.

"Can you hear me?" I whispered to Kenny Wadd, but my words were gibberish, unclear even to me. His eyes shifted, though, as if trying to see. Where was D'? I struggled to raise myself enough to look around the room.

The women didn't notice. Ja Vala scolded Madame Yveny. "I understand Madame Armistead's anger. But it was you who provided the powders. It was you who kept me enslaved to the Grangers. You are as evil as she is."

"Am I? You are not one to talk about good or evil, Ja Vala."

Ja Vala stiffened. "What do you mean?

Madame Yveny shook a bottle of liquid, held it to the light. "You've done your share of evil, too."

"Another lie." She turned her head. "Unless you mean that I killed your friend at the hospital. That wasn't evil—it was self defense."

Really? Bingo. Even with the self-defense claim, it was a confession of homicide. I could arrest her, if only I had handcuffs. And if only I could move. I tightened my fingers, made a fist. It took all my concentration and strength. Just minutes before, I'd been able to stand. Was I getting weaker?

"And the Grangers?" Madame Yveny taunted. "What about them?"

The Grangers?

"The Grangers?" Ja Vala echoed my thought.

Madame Yveny shrugged. "You might not recall it. The powders cloud your memory."

Ja Vala raised the knife to Madame Yveny's face. "What are you saying? Are you saying I killed them?"

"Oh please, Ja Vala. Don't act so surprised." Madame Yveny scowled.

"I killed them." Ja Vala froze, sounded puzzled.

Another confession? We were on a roll, solving case after case. And we had Ja Vala's clothes as evidence. D' would be thrilled. If he was alive.

THE WOMAN IN THE CUPBOARD

For a while neither of them spoke. Madame Yveny continued mixing her potion, pouring a drop of this, two of that into a bowl. Stirring it.

In my head, D' started discussing Ja Vala's defense. Saying that a good lawyer could get her acquitted, arguing that she'd been kidnapped, enslaved, and drugged for years.

"But why?" Ja Vala wondered the same thing. "After all those years, why would I suddenly kill them?"

"I've thought a lot about this exact question. And there's only one explanation." Madame Yveny kept stirring. "The Grangers themselves must have ordered it. You couldn't have done it otherwise—With the powders, you had no independent will. No, it had to be that he told you to kill her, and she to kill him." Madame Yveny made a guttural sound, like a crow choking.

Could she be right? I pictured it. The couple fighting. Ja Vala in the room. Judith spitting mad. "Ja Vala, just kill him for me, would you?" And Dixon responding, "Actually, Ja Vala. What you need to do is kill my darling wife." Probably neither meant it.

Or maybe both did.

Ja Vala was silent, staring at air.

"I bet they were surprised, too. Neither would have suspected you to take the orders literally." More crow choking sounds. "I'd have liked to see their faces."

"No, it's not true. I couldn't have killed them. Not even with the powders—"

"Oh, please, Ja Vala. It's not like it was your first time."

What? I held still, straining to listen, trying to push myself up onto my elbow, peeking over the chairs.

"You'd killed for them before."

Ja Vala lowered the knife, leaned against the table and put a hand on her forehead. "At least twice," Madame Yveny went on.

Twice? Who else had she killed? I figured out the answer, just as Madame Yveny stated it aloud.

"Dixon Granger's law partner and his secretary."

Was it true? I looked at Ja Vala. She sunk onto a chair, deflated, the knife slumping in her hand.

Chapter 85

Madam Yveny's words reverberated inside Ja Vala's skull, refusing to be hushed.

Has she killed five people?

No. Not possible. She couldn't have. Madame Yveny is not to be trusted. She lies as easily as she breathes. Ja Vala watches her shrunken features, her dead gray ball of an eye. She inhales the hag's sour scent, the smell of deceit. What she says is not true. Cannot be true. And yet, the knife weighs heavy in Ja Vala's hand, and the sensation is familiar. She pictures herself in the doorway of a stranger's building, ringing the buzzer. Going up the stairs, knocking. A woman opens the door. Her hair is red, and she smells of Judith Granger's perfume. Ja Vala tells her that Dixon Granger has sent a message. The woman invites her inside.

And then? Ja Vala doesn't know. She isn't sure. She pictures the woman's red hair splayed on a cream-colored carpet, her eyes shut. She looks almost comfortable, as if she is asleep.

Did this visit happen? Is it merely imagination? Madame Yveny plants seeds in her mind to unsettle her. What about Dixon Granger's law partner? She remembers nothing about his killing. But she envisions him dead. His lips are thin, his nose narrow, his jaw dimpled. The face is unfamiliar. A shiver skips up her back, carrying a question: How can she picture the face of the dead man if she hasn't been there to see it?

Ja Vala swallows. Breathes to steady her pulse. But her hand aches from gripping the slippery knife handle. And Dixon Granger lies on the floor, his blood pooling on the hardwood. Screaming, Judith Granger rushes forward. The knife rises, plunges. Rises again. Is this a memory? Or is Ja Vala's obedient revenant mind merely follow the suggestion of the bokor Madame Yveny?

She concentrates, diving back into the pool of months and years she's spent with the Grangers. It is just a sea of time, days without definition. She recalls scrubbing a floor. Making a bed. Massaging a back. Fixing an omelet. Weeks flowing into weeks into months into years.

And then she hears the Grangers argue, their anger tangible, searing. They shout orders that she must obey. She sees Judith Granger bleeding. Does she let out a wall-rattling scream? Is it Ja Vala's knife that silences her? Dixon Granger's mouth comes open, and he sputters, trying to form words. Ja Vala is not sure if his blood spurts fountain-like across the room or if he tries to grab at the cleaver. She cannot be sure if these snapshots are accurate. But she sees a trail of blood from the kitchen to the study. And the couple lying quiet and still. Neither tells her what to do. She is lost. She has no orders, no place to be. She waits. Dixon Granger's eyes are open, unblinking. Unconcerned.

She turns in circles, not knowing what to do. She tries to move them, make them more comfortable. She drags Judith Granger by her arm along the hall. Judith Granger is heavy, and finally Ja Vala leaves her, one arm extending over her head. Her uniform is covered with blood. She sheds it, puts on a fresh one so she will be ready. Judith Granger will want me to wash the soiled one so it will be clean for the next day. Not certain what to do, she sits in the pantry, out of the way, and waits for orders.

Maybe none of this is true. Maybe her mind is painting pictures. More likely, she went to the pantry to hide from the killers. Madame Yveny is crafty, planting seeds of doubt. And she has reason to cause Ja Vala to doubt herself.

Chapter 86

"You're lying." Ja Vala's voice lacked conviction.

"You know I'm not. You have glimmers, right? Pieces of memory reflecting like shards of a broken mirror?"

"Why would I kill them?"

Madame Yveny tsked. "You know why. The Grangers told you to, and you had to obey."

I looked at Kenny Wadd. Was he hearing all this? His mouth hung open and his eyes drifted.

I tried to keep up with what I was hearing. Had Ja Vala really killed all of our victims? What would have been her motive? No, not her motive—the motive of whoever ordered the killings? And who had that been? The Grangers? Madame Yveny or Madame Armistead? My head was clogged, and my mouth still tasted like dirt. I needed water. Even more, I needed D'. Where was he? Was he out back, buried in a ditch? Was he conscious like I'd been, being suffocated by soil? Was he even alive? I had to go find him, tried to move my legs again. They were wooden, unresponsive. I thought of my gun, my phone. Wondered where they were. Not that I could lift either one.

Madame Yveny opened yet another vial and poured some of its contents into a ceramic bowl. Ja Vala sat expressionless at her side.

"I couldn't have done what you say." Ja Vala sounded unsure.

"Don't worry. Your bokor isn't angry. She was going to have you eliminate the Grangers anyway. You surprised us both, doing it before you received the order. But no matter, as long as they are out of the way."

She shuffled around Ja Vala, reaching for a vial. "The Grangers underestimated us," she went on. "They thought we were simple island people, stupid and naïve. They didn't even try to hide what they were doing, stealing clients from us. Can you imagine? Daring to compete with us? Arranging their own imports?"

Imports?

"They were selling revenants?"

That kind of import?

"They told our customers they could provide equal service to ours without the trouble of puffer fish toxin and burial. They planned to use only the powders that cause obedience. Madame Armistead wasn't going to give them the opportunity."

Ja Vala said nothing.

"Here. I'm almost done. I just have to mix in this extract, and it's ready. Move away. Give me room."

Ja Vala did not budge.

Madame Yveny sprinkled something into the bowl, started mixing. Ja Vala wasn't watching. She sat slouched, the knife slack in her hand.

Chapter 87

So. She is a killer. A stabber. An ender of lives. If Madam Yveny is to be believed, she has taken at least five. And the flashes she sees make sense. The image of Dixon Granger's open, unbelieving eyes. His bloodied wife on the floor, graceful like a fallen dancer.

Ja Vala looks at her hands, the knife she is holding. The hands once belonged to a girl full of hope. Or did they? That girl, the pretty one who walked with Kenny Wadd—The one who was planning her wedding—Does she have any link to Ja Vala whatsoever? What became of that girl?

She asks the question, yet she knows the answer. That girl died and was buried. Her lover mourned and moved on. Only her parents refused to believe she was gone and kept searching. What has been found though is not the girl they lost. It is a creature brought up from the grave. One that relies on powdered drugs to prevent her from decomposing.

Or that is what the bokor has told her.

But it must be another lie. She has missed many doses of the powder, but nothing has happened to her skin. It has not decayed or shriveled. A wave of fire passes through her. For years, she was duped. Convinced by fear to take the very powders that stifled her thoughts, made her subservient. And turned me into a killer.

She watches Madam Yveny who has tried to kill Kenny Wadd. Madam Yveny who has lied about the powders and who is the partner of the bokor who took away Ja Vala's own life. Is Ja Vala to trust her now? Madame Yveny's gnarled fingers, move like spider legs, deft at their work. Her tiny frame hunches over the altar. Together with Madame Armistead, she has pulled people from the grave and sold them. She has provided the powders that deprive revenants of free will. Now, as she mixes the antidote, the air becomes thick and sour. She lights a candle and holds up a vial, melts something over the flame.

She tells Ja Vala that the antidote is almost ready. Nudges her. "Move away and give me room."

Ja Vala doesn't move. Madame Yveny buried Kenny Wadd without intending to give him the antidote, intending to leave him in the ground.

"You wanted to kill Kenny Wadd." Ja Vala watches her reaction.

Madame Yveny doesn't flinch, doesn't deny it. "He went to the police. He would have exposed us."

Ja Vala turns and looks at Kenny Wadd. He lies on the floor, awaiting the antidote. He is so still, Ja Vala is not sure he is still alive, Kenny Wadd, she repeats to herself. Kenny Wadd.

"I have nothing against your Kenny Wadd, Ja Vala," Madam Yveny picks up the bowl. "But my own survival is at stake. Put yourself in my position. I'm an old mambo. Kenny Wadd found out my secret. His mouth was like a leak in a dam. If it had not been plugged quickly, the leak would have become a flood, drowning us all."

She takes the antidote and starts toward Kenny Wadd. Ja Vala repeats her words in her mind and realizes she has been a fool.

"Stop." Ja Vala raises the knife and puts a hand on the old woman's shoulder. Madam Yveny is nothing but bones, but she resists, pressing forward, shoving Ja Vala away. Ja Vala rushes ahead of her and swings the knife, intending only to scare her, but Madame Yveny lifts a defensive hand and the knife tears through it. Her mouth opens in surprise, and she stumbles. The antidote flies from her hand. We watch, stunned, as the mixture rises from the bowl like a dust cloud, falling onto the old woman, coating her skin.

She gapes at the powder clumped on her bleeding hand, then looks up at Ja Vala. Her white eye glows. "No!" She thrashes at her wound. "Get water. Wash it off!" Her voice slashes air.

THE WOMAN IN THE CUPBOARD

The antidote has coated her robe, head, hands. It has covered her open wound. Ja Vala doesn't get water, doesn't move. She watches Madame Yveny rub, swat, blow, even spit, trying to get the powder out of her cut. She continues to struggle, unrelenting, until she can no longer move.

By then, Ja Vala has lost all hope. She is kneeling beside Kenny Wadd.

Chapter 88

Without warning, Ja Vala swung her knife at Madame Yveny, cutting her hand. Madame Yveny stumbled, tossing the bowl of antidote into the air. The contents rose like a cloud and dispersed, floating down like puffs of spilled flour.

"No!" the sound rose from my belly. I needed the antidote, and so did Kenny Wadd. I pushed myself, willing myself to crawl, but my body barely twitched. Why weren't Ja Vala and Madame Yveny trying to collect the powder? Why instead was Madame Yveny slapping and clawing at her knife wound, smearing powder and blood over herself? Shouting at Ja Vala?

I used my chair as leverage and pushed my torso up with halting soil-caked arms. My left arm scraped the upholstery, reopening a long deep cut. My legs were dead, indifferent to my commands. I fought, tried to stand. Sweat poured down my back, my face. My head pounded with pain.

Madam Yveny cursed Ja Vala, swatting the powder, rubbing the cut on her hand with her clothing. Thrashing. Scattering the antidote that was our only chance of recovery. Maybe Ja Vala was waiting for her to settle down. Maybe she would sweep it up and give us what she could.

"Help," I called.

She didn't respond.

I called out again but my voice was weak, my words unclear.

Beside me, Kenny Wadd made a sound. I looked down, saw him watching me.

"Toy suh." His lips didn't move. Probably he was paralyzed, couldn't move them. "Yhenny. Toy suh."

I repeated the syllables. "Toy suh." What was he trying to say?

Poison? With a paralyzed mouth, Kenny Wadd couldn't form a "p" sound.

"Yes," I answered. "Madam Yveny poisoned us both." That was what I intended to say, but my words were indistinct, not any clearer than his. My lips were stiff, my tongue thick. I had no idea what, if anything he understood.

"Zha ala?" he asked.

"Ja Vala's here. She made Madam Yveny fix the antidote." My words were one long syllable.

"Ani oe." He let out a breath. "Nee' ani oe."

I didn't tell him that before either of us could get it, the antidote would first have to be swept off the floor.

His body began quivering, more than a shiver, as if all his muscles were going into spasm at once.

"It's all right, Kenny Wadd," I whispered a blur of sound. "Ja Vala has the antidote."

Despite the slurring of my words, he might have understood what I meant because he closed his eyes as if comforted, and his spasms soon eased.

Near the table, Madame Yveny stopped swatting and scolding. Her body became still, and she dropped to the floor like a dead bird. Ja Vala ran to Kenny Wadd and knelt beside him. She stroked his face, kissed his forehead.

"I'm sorry, Kenny Wadd." Tears rolled down her cheeks. "Madam Yveny was never going to save you—Not with what you know. She wasn't mixing up the antidote—she was preparing more poison to kill you. I'm so sorry. It is all because of me." She sat, lifted Kenny Wadd's head, cradled it in her lap. Rocked back and forth, singing to him, urging Kenny Wadd to live.

I held onto the arms of the chair, struggling to move. Digesting what had happened. Wondering where D' was.

Madam Yveny lay on the floor, her face frozen in a grimace, her white eye protruding like a ball of ice.

Chapter 89

The back door opened. D'Angelo? Had he brought reinforcements? An ambulance? I managed to turn my head enough to see that it wasn't D'. The gravediggers came inside slowly, trudging toward Madam Yveny. I held my breath. What would they do when they saw her on the floor? Would they attack Ja Vala? Try to rebury Kenny Wadd and me? I waited. They plowed ahead steadily, not stopping, not even pausing to look at her, continuing past her body to a door beyond the altar. One opened it, and they both went inside, disappearing down a flight of stairs.

"Zha a'a," I tried to get her attention, but my mouth still wouldn't form syllables. She was the only one of us who could move. She needed to call for help.

But Kenny Wadd was talking to her, and she sobbed, answering him.

"Caw," Kenny Wadd insisted. "Ha'i'y."

"The toxin will wear off, Kenny Wadd," Ja Vala said. "Don't die. I need you to live."

"Kisss," he continued. "Cawl. Loff."

"Don't talk. I can't understand you."

"Tsell. Kisss. Loff."

"Rest," Ja Vala told him. "I have you now, Kenny Wadd. You are safe in my arms."

"Ja Vala," I called again. Again, it sounded like, "Zhaaa."

She didn't respond, kept fretting. Cradling Kenny Wadd.

I tried again. And again. Louder. "Phone. Call 911." I said the numbers slowly. Separately. They sounded like barks.

Finally, Kenny Wadd looked my way. She followed his gaze.

It took a while for her to understand my distorted words. Another while for her to let go of Kenny Wadd long enough to make the phone call. But finally, Ja Vala must have understood that the best hope of saving her beloved was to get him to a hospital. She found a phone—maybe mine? I heard her rifling through Madame Yveny's kitchen while she talked to someone, asking for help. Then I heard her feet going down steps. When she came back, she sat again with Kenny Wadd. If she feared being arrested for the murders, she'd discussed with Madam Yveny, she didn't show it. She held onto Kenny Wadd, singing to him in a foreign tongue until, outside, we heard help arrive.

Chapter 90

Kenny Wadd's eyes reach out, clutching Ja Valas. He tries to speak but cannot make words. They both know she is his only link to life, and in this way, they are as one, together again. His head rests in her lap. She feels its weight and warmth on her thighs. Her fingers stroke his face. She tells him he must not die. Ja Vala sings to him, a song from their home, one that tells their story. The melody is tender, and the lyrics by Coco Rosie tell of fear in the night, of gentle and calming kisses, of a lover's willingness to do anything, even to die for love.

Ja Vala holds him, waiting for help to arrive. She comforts Kenny Wadd with her entire being, and yet she knows that he is lost. Without the antidote, Kenny Wadd has little chance. Already his limbs do not respond, and his breathing is labored. Already his eyes dim, losing their shine, and she watches him fade.

Pain coils around her heart as she rips herself away from him. No hospital or doctor will be able to save him. What Kenny Wadd needs, only she can find. She must hurry. Each step away from him tears at her. Ja Vala still feels Kenny Wadd, the texture of his skin, his feverish heat. After so many years, so much time of longing for him and surviving on faint memories, his presence overwhelms her. She almost staggers as she follows the gravediggers into the basement. The servant Betiane is cowering in the stairway.

"Tell me," Ja Vala says. "Where are Madame Yveny's papers?"

Betiane does not move. She huddles, covering her head.

"Her recipes? Lists of ingredients?"

No response.

Ja Vala steps around her, descending into chilly dampness, hoping to find where the bokor has hidden her secrets. The basement of Madame Yveny's home is dank and dim, lit by a few dangling light bulbs. The walls are lined with bunkbeds. The gravediggers sit on two lower bunks, alert as if awaiting instructions. But others are down here, as well. She counts three women lying on upper bunks, and three men, two of them standing beside a lower bunk where the third man lies.

"Madame Yveny has died," she tells them. "Your bokor is gone. You are free."

They do nothing.

"Don't be afraid. You don't need the powder. It was a lie to control you. You will not rot without it. Nothing will happen to you."

Not one of them moves or speaks. Ja Vala should have expected their inaction. She was one of them, for years unable to make contact with her own will or to act without instruction from the Grangers, whom her bokor told her to obey.

She steps deeper into the basement. It is as if she is unseen, unheard. As if she is a ghost among ghosts.

"You must help me," she begs them. "Is there another mambo? Did you ever see anyone visit?"

She asks. She pleads with them. She knows it is useless. They cannot tell her even if they wish to. They have not been instructed to speak to her.

She feels the weight of Kenny Wadd's limp body, sees the light fading in his eyes. She has little time. The ambulance will come in a moment. She herself has called 911 at the detective's plea even though the hospital can offer no hope. Only a mambo can provide the antidote. She starts for the stairs, and, from the lower bunk where two men stand, she hears a groan. A man calling her name.

She steps over to the bunk. The two men standing there cross their arms, forbidding her to come closer. Madame Yveny must have ordered them to guard the man lying there, and Ja Vala challenges them at her own peril. Instead, she peers between them and in the faint light she sees a bludgeoned, unrecognizable face. The man groans again, and she slowly understand his rasping words.

"Cops. Get cops, Ja Vala."

She bends over, looking more closely, and recognizes the detective by his length and the girth of his chest.

She cannot stay to help him. She is a killer and cannot be found there when the authorities arrive. But as she hurries back up the stairs, she shouts to him that help is coming. She has only moments to search Madame Yveny's house for the name of a mambo who can help. She rifles through the items on the shelves near the altar. On the label of a vial, she finds a faded name and phone number: Madame Sehandieu.

She returns to Kenny Wadd and comforts him until she hears the medics arrive. Her lips rest gently on his for more moment. If this mambo cannot help her, Kenny Wadd will surely die.

Chapter 91

The first night was hell. Violent bouts of nausea, relentless spasms. Sweating. Continued numbness and paralysis. At times, I was certain that I'd died and left my body. That I was drifting above it, looking down. I was vaguely aware of nurses bustling. Intravenous dripping into my arm. A tube in my nose. Sometimes I heard disjointed bits of conversation. But once, I followed an entire exchange.

"...within twenty-four hours."

"What about an antidote?" Was it D's voice? Was I hallucinating, imagining his voice?

"D'?" I tried to call, made only a groan. Listened.

"...doesn't matter what you think, detective. We don't know for sure what they've been given. But if you're right, there is no antidote."

No antidote? Was he talking about Kenny Wadd and me? Because of course there was an antidote. The mambos knew about it. Madame Yveny knew.

But Madame Yveny was dead.

And without her to make the antidote, I must be dying, too. I absorbed the news vaguely, without emotion, too sick to care. Focusing only on listening.

"It was puffer fish—I'm positive. And there has to be an antidote." Definitely, the voice was D'Angelo's. He was alive, not buried in Madam Yveny's back yard. Didn't even sound poisoned. Thank God. At least one of us would survive.

"I'm sorry." The doctor sounded impatient. "Tetrodotoxin is has no known antidote. And according the the police, there were hundreds of vials in the house where they were found, hundreds of possible poisons for us to test for—"

"Don't bother. It was tetrodo—Puffer fish."

"Then, as I've told you, the best we can do is what we've done. We've given both patients edrophonium to inhibit the toxin's enzyme and avoid further organ paralysis. But so far, its effect seems minimal." The doctor went on, speaking rapidly, using unfamiliar words, explaining limited treatment options.

I didn't follow. Didn't try.

"All we can do is hydrate the patients and wait. If they make it through the first day, they have a good chance of surviving. But frankly, even then, recovery will be slow and difficult."

His voice stuck in my head, repeating, "Slow and difficult."

I watched the door, hoping D' would appear. He didn't. Instead, he spoke again. "What about alternative medicine?"

"I'm sorry?"

"The woman who poisoned my partner said she could make the antidote. She used it in a voudou ritual."

"Really, detective—"

"I'm serious. We have evidence that Ja Vala Boudin and a number of others found in the woman's house actually received it."

"Evidence?"

"A few of them are here in the hospital—They can confirm what I'm saying."

"The patients that were admitted with your partner are in no condition to be interviewed, detective. And they've been drugged, not poisoned with tetrodotoxin."

"But they were, before. And they received the antidote. They were victims of human trafficking—"

"They may have been trafficked, detective," the doctor snapped, "but they couldn't have received any tetrodotoxin antidote. What you're claiming is simply mumbo jumbo."

Mumbo jumbo. Was that a medical term? The conversation went on, too low for me to hear. But D' was fighting for me, not giving up. I drifted. Imagined D' wrestling the doctor to the ground, pounding the antidote out of him.

Drifted some more. Lay sweating on the bed or floating over it, unable to move or make a sound. Sometimes while I lingered between the hospital room and nothingness, I saw D' beside me. He had a black eye, a swollen nose, and stitches on his forehead. He stood unmoving, looking at me. Crying.

Chapter 92

I lost track of time and place. Mostly, I felt weightless as if I'd already left my body. Sometimes I was near the ceiling, other times out in the hall, or in a corner of the room. Sometimes I was nowhere. But no matter where I was, I had no doubt that I was dying. I waited for death to come. Would it be violent, like the seizures I'd had earlier? Or would it ease into me gently, taking me softly as a sigh. Would I even notice it? I contemplated these questions without fear or anger. Without emotion of any kind. When I saw D', I felt sorry for him. Other cops came by, and Evie. I saw them in the hall, heard their comments even though they weren't in the room. I was aware that I must have been dreaming, that I couldn't be hearing them because they weren't close enough. And yet I heard them.

"She's tough, D,'" Reynolds said. "She'll beat this."

"Look at her," D'Angelo sounded grim. "Her skin is blue."

"She'll be okay." Wait. That sounded like—Was it Dan? My ex-husband?

"But he's right. She's blue. That can't be good." That was Colby, talking too much, too fast. "But she looks totally calm. So, what is she, like, in a coma now?"

Was I in a coma? I wanted to know, but nobody answered him.

"Please," I heard Evie begging. "Let me go in. I need to be with her."

Another voice asked, "Has she said anything?" Was it Dr. Vogel?

"She tried to talk, but her mouth is as paralyzed as the rest of her, so it was gibberish," D' said. "And then the seizures started."

"And since the seizures, she's been unresponsive?"

"She's just been lying there."

"I'll step inside and take a look at her." Definitely Vogel. "Detective? Any news of Ja Vala?"

"Nothing. She's in the wind."

THE WOMAN IN THE CUPBOARD

I hovered in the air, imagining Ja Vala blowing past.

Dr. Vogel continued. "By the way, those people in the cellar with you? Tests aren't back yet, but their behavior indicates that all of them were dosed with scopolamine. Same as Ja Vala."

"I thought so."

Wait—Those people in the cellar? D' had been in a cellar? When? I pictured his bandaged nose and stitched forehead. Had he fallen down some cellar stairs? Was that how he'd been hurt? My mind hit a wall, couldn't put ideas together. Couldn't remember what questions it was trying to answer.

"So, what happened? They ambush you?"

"The old lady told them to kill me. I fought as best I could, but I was way outnumbered. Passed out. They probably thought I was dead. If Ja Vala hadn't shown up, I guess they'd have buried me."

A door opened and closed. Shoes squeaked on the tile floor.

"So, how is she? What are they doing for her?" Was that the captain? Oh my. The captain was there?

"You're looking at it."

"What's that supposed to mean?"

"Nothing. They tried something but it didn't help, so they're doing nothing. Not a thing. Nada. Zip."

"But she's got an IV—"

"Saline. So she won't get dehydrated."

"Why didn't they pump her stomach?" That was Colby again.

"Because nothing was in her stomach. She got the toxin through that cut on her arm. Kenny Wadd has an identical wound, same toxin powder around it."

"There's no antidote?"

D' sighed. "Apparently not."

Someone stood beside my bed. I was sure it was Dr. Vogel, but couldn't open my eyes to make sure. I was sure he touched my arm, took my pulse, listened to my heart, but I couldn't feel it. My body was numb, already playing dead. He spent some time in the room with me, but I can't say how long or what he did before the shoes squeaked, and the door opened and closed again, telling me that he was gone. I floated under the fluorescents, hearing but not seeing. Unaware of time.

Occasionally, voices drifted along with me. One of them was always D's, husky and swollen with pain.

Chapter 93

Ja Vala refuses to dwell on Madame Sehandieu or her haughtiness. Or her transparent lies when she denied knowing Madame Yveny or anything about puffer fish toxin and its antidote. Ja Vala refuses to think about what she was forced to do to make Madame Sehandieu admit what she knew, or of how she convinced the mambo to create the antidote. No, Ja Vala keeps her mind on the task at hand: getting the antidote to Kenny Wadd before it is too late. Kenny Wadd. She repeats his name in her mind, and her heart beats along in rhythm. She pictures him reviving, the light returning to his eyes. He smiles when he sees her, reaches for her hand. Whispers to her that she has saved his life just as he has saved hers, and that they are linked for eternity, as they should have been long ago.

She rushes along the sidewalk, retracing the route the taxi took. Madame Sehandieu's home is in the southwest section of Philadelphia. She has used most of the money from the nurse's pocket to pay a taxi to drive her there. In the taxi, her mind was on the antidote. She paid no attention to what was out her window. But now she needs to find the way back and has no idea which way to go. She turns onto a tree-lined street where homes attach to each other at one wall. Did the driver pass these homes on the way to Madame Sehandieu's? She doesn't know. The light is dim, falling in speckles through the branches. She keeps moving. Hurrying. She sees signs for the University of Pennsylvania. Streets lined with restaurants and shops. Young people walking in groups or alone without apparent care. As if accustomed to freedom.

She must find a way to get into the hospital where Kenny Wadd is. She heard the medics say Kenny Wadd was going to Hahnemann. It is where Dr. Vogel works. And the uniform Ja Vala wears is from that hospital, so maybe it will get her access to him. Her uniform is stained, but the jacket she has borrowed from Madame Sehandieu covers the blood. Probably, she will get past security. But will she get to Kenny Wadd in time? Will Dr. Vogel be there? Her chest tightens at the thought. If Dr. Vogel sees her, he'll have her taken back to her room, away from Kenny Wadd. She stops on the street, imagining orderlies coming at her. The sting of a needle. Wooziness as she is carried away.

And the unbearable aching knowledge that Kenny Wadd, without the antidote, is dying.

Ja Vala stands still, biting her lip until it bleeds. She decides that Dr. Vogel will not see her. That Kenny Wadd's room will be accessible. That she will get to him in time.

She holds the antidote in the pocket of her uniform, scolding herself. She should have asked Madame Sehandieu how to get to Hahnemann Hospital. She keeps moving across the campus and finally sees a policeman on the corner. Will he recognize her? She turns away, but realizes that he is not searching for her. He is merely watching the campus. She walks up to him and smiles.

His eyes narrow.

"Officer," she puts a lilt into her voice. "I'm new to Philadelphia and I'm lost. How can I find a hospital called Hahnemann?"

"You a nurse's aide?" He tilts his head, looks at me from head to foot and back up again.

She nods.

He points to the corner, where a bus is pulling up. "Take that bus into town. Get off at 15th and walk north. You'll see it."

She thanks him and runs to the bus, trying to blend in among other passengers. But the driver stops her, angry when she holds out a five-dollar bill. "You need exact change."

Ja Vala has no idea what he means. Is he going to throw her out of the bus?

A man offers to make change. He gives her dollars and four coins and takes the bill from her hand. She stands in front of the other riders, holding dollar bills and the man's four coins. And she freezes. Madame Sehandieu's blood is caked on her fingernails. She pulls her hands behind her back. The man tells her to put one of his coins and two of the dollar bills into a machine. Her face is hot, and her hand trembles as she does what he says. Has he seen the blood on her hands? Has the driver? Has anyone recognized her face from the news? Ja Vala lowers her head, manages to pay the fare and take a seat where she turns to the window, watching for 15th Street. She clutches the antidote in her pocket and sings Kenny Wadd's name.

Chapter 94

The first thing I heard was, "Where is she?"

Then, a bustle of confusion. Someone asking, "Who?" Someone else saying he'd seen her in with Mo. "She was there not a minute ago."

Who were they talking about? I opened my eyes, looked at the IV pole with the half empty saline bag. Pushed myself up on my elbows, wincing because every part of me—even parts I'd never thought of ached. A huge vase of flowers on the bedside table blocked my view of the room. It was colorful and lush, not generic enough to come from the hospital gift shop.

"You're kidding? She slipped out?"

"Couldn't have."

"Oh, don't underestimate her." That was Dr. Vogel. "She's good with disguises."

I sat up so I could see past the flowers and find out who was in my room. I saw the backs of four heads: D'Angelo, Reynolds, Dr. Vogel, and a nurse I didn't recognize. No one was looking at me. No one welcomed me back to consciousness and life. They all looked at the doorway, where Kenny Wadd stood with his palms up and eyebrows raised.

"Why are you all looking at me?" he asked. "I just came to see how the detective's doing."

"Where is she?" D' growled, stepped closer to him.

Kenny Wadd stepped back. "Who? Ja Vala?"

"No, my mother."

"I don't know." Kenny Wadd's hand went to his chest. "Honestly. I thought she was in here. Giving the antidote to Detective Sterling."

"Dammit." D'Angelo pushed his way past Kenny Wadd and, followed by Reynolds, rushed out of the room.

THE WOMAN IN THE CUPBOARD

I swung my legs over the side of the bed, hopped off. Fell to the floor. Looked across the room to see Kenny Wadd limping toward me, arms out, calling for help. The nurse turned, seeing me. "Oh dear." She ran over, hooked an arm under mine and helped me up. "You're awake, too? It's a miracle. It truly is."

My limbs were rubbery. I wobbled, leaned on the bed frame.

"Take your time, detective. Give yourself a chance to recover." She guided me back onto the bed.

I resisted. "I have to go."

"No, you need—"

"I need to get D'Angelo." I started for the door, but my legs caved. The nurse grabbed me. I looked at Kenny Wadd. He stood at the door, eyes somber.

"It takes a little while," he said. "Be patient."

"What happened?" I remembered being paralyzed, floating under the ceiling. Thinking I was dead. "Are you okay?"

Kenny Wadd glanced out of the room, then at the nurse. "Ja Vala brought the antidote."

The nurse shook her head. "You're mistaken, Mr. Wadd. You must have hallucinated. There is no antidote for the toxin that poisoned you."

"Nevertheless." He came closer, sat beside the bed, held up his arm to reveal a knife wound. Reached over and picked up my arm. I had the identical fresh wound. "Ja Vala rubbed the antidote into the wounds, the same way we got the toxin. We came back from death."

"Back from death," I repeated. My words were slow, deliberate. "So now we are revenants?" I tried to smile, probably grimaced.

"Technically, I think so. We were even buried first." Kenny Wadd's smile was sad. His teeth glistened.

The nurse ignored our exchange. "Some people survive tetrodotoxin poisoning. No one knows why, but luckily, both of you did. It was close, though. You two had us worried." She poured a glass of ice water. Held it out. "Take a sip." She watched me drink. "Promise you won't get up again. I need to go tell the doctor that you've come around."

When she'd gone, Kenny Wadd took my hand. He spoke in a low voice. "Ja Vala found a label on one of Madame Yveny's bottles. She knew the bottle had come from a mambo, so she went to the address on the label. The mambo was afraid. She refused to help her, insisting that she could not interfere with Madame Yveny's practices. But Ja Vala convinced her to make the antidote and brought it to us, apparently just in time. We were both nearly gone."

Memories surfaced, like bits of mosaic. I saw the dark, open sky from the inside of a grave. The yard behind Madame Yveny's house where I'd crawled, unable to move my legs. I recalled Kenny Wadd's vacant face. Ja Vala, swinging a knife. Madame Yveny slapping at her open wound, falling victim to her own lethal toxin.

I didn't remember getting to the hospital. I didn't remember anything except the awareness of dying.

And now, Kenny Wadd was saying that Ja Vala had saved us.

"But how did she get to us? Weren't they guarding our rooms?"

"She was disguised as a nurse."

Oh. More pieces of memory surfaced. Alexandra Lambert lying dead in Ja Vala's bed. A night nurse tied up in a closet without her scrubs.

Ja Vala must have still been wearing them.

"She saved our lives at her own peril," Kenny Wadd said. "And she rescued Madame Yveny's captives."

D'Angelo flew in, breathless. "It's true? You're awake!"

Reynolds followed. "Mo! Welcome back."

My eyes teared up. "Sorry, Reynolds. You can't have my desk yet."

"Did you find Ja Vala?" Kenny Wadd's eyebrows rose.

"No, but every cop in the city is looking for her." D' came to the bed. Took my hand.

THE WOMAN IN THE CUPBOARD

"Ja Vala saved our lives," I told him.

"She took a few, too, including Madame Yveny's."

"Madame Yveny was a witch. Ja Vala should get a medal for getting rid of her."

Kenny Wadd stood and went to the window. "You're right, detective. She should."

D'Angelo studied me. Leaned over, kissed my forehead. Put a hand on my head. "We still have to bring her in. Ja Vala's leaving a trail of bodies. Alexandra Lambert. Madame Yveny. And that's just today. She's also a suspect in those other murders—You know that."

Four other murders—Another memory flashed. Madame Yveny's living room, women's voices. Ja Vala saying, "I killed them," confessing to the Grangers' murders.

"What." D' saw my mind working.

"Nothing."

Kenny Wadd looked out the window. "Face it. Ja Vala is gone. You won't find her."

"Yeah?" Reynolds bristled. "Why's that?"

"There is no Ja Vala. Officially, she is dead."

"Well, obviously, that's not true—"

"But it is." Kenny Wadd stared out the window. "What I say is true. I was engaged to marry Ja Vala Boudin. But she died years ago."

"She's not dead. She was just here—"

"Believe me," Kenny Wadd said. "Ja Vala is gone." After a moment, he turned and walked out of the room.

Chapter 95

She has never before ridden in an underground train. She looks down at the back of the seat in front of her, but feels eyes aimed at her. She tells herself it is not because they recognize her from television news or a photo in the papers, but because she is a woman whose face is wet with tears.

Kenny Wadd. Kenny Wadd. He has given her money and instructions, told her where to take the train. How to get away. The train is loud, swerving. It smells like filth and metal. She will never see Kenny Wadd again.

Unless they catch her. In that case, maybe he will come to see her trial. She will feel his warm eyes across the courtroom.

But even then, he will be far away, out of reach.

At least he is still alive. Kenny Wadd. Kenny Wadd.

She leans back in her seat, swaying with the motion of the screaming screeching train. She glances around. A boy across from her has earphones plugged into his head. Behind him, a tattooed girl with spiked hair chews gum. A few rows up, a businessman reads a newspaper. Ja Vala's face is on its front page.

The train pumps out: Kenny Wadd. Kenny Wadd.

She sees him as she pours the powder into his wound and rubs it in. She feels his trembling, his ragged breath. His eyes open, and she watches Kenny Wadd stir, coming back to life.

"Ja Vala?" Her name is the first thing he says. Then he stiffens, eyes wild. "Madame Yveny—" he tries to warn her "—is a bokor." His tongue is stiff, his words slow and unclear.

Ja Vala puts her hand on his forehead. She strokes it. "It's okay now," she tells him.

His fingers close around her arm and hold on. "They buried me."

"I know. But I found you. You are safe, Kenny Wadd."

THE WOMAN IN THE CUPBOARD

He lies still, eyes glimmering as she caresses his face, his hands. His chest.

"They stole me from you," she says. "But now we are both free."

He tries to sit up, and she helps him. She puts his arm around her shoulder and lifts him. The arm is warm and heavy. It fits around her perfectly. She holds it against her body and waits for him to say that no one will separate them again. That now they can be together as they were meant to be. She tries not to think of the woman he has married. Of their children. He finally begins to speak, and Ja Vala's heart flutters, anticipating his words.

"The detective," he says.

The detective?

"You must. Help her."

The detective? After all these years of pain and despair, she rescues Kenny Wadd and his first concern is for a detective?

"Kenny Wadd," she says, but his gaze is on the door to his hospital room, not on her.

"Help her," he repeats.

At this moment, Ja Vala does not have his attention.

And she realizes that she does not have his heart.

Her throat thickens and tears flood her eyes. She holds his hand, memorizing its texture.

Kenny Wadd. Kenny Wadd.

The train, like my heart, chugs his name. She looks out the window, sees nothing in the dark underground. Only the reflection of a woman not loved by Kenny Wadd.

A woman not alive. What will become of her?

Without Kenny Wadd.

He is rushing home to his family, and he will visit Ja Vala's parents—What will he tell them? That he has seen her and she is alive? Or that she is dead? And what of Madame Armistead? Will she blame Kenny Wadd for Madame Yveny's death. Because he tried to hide his trip from her, she will assume he is Ja Vala's accomplice in killing her partner and destroying their business.

Madame Armistead will be angry, indeed. Unable to punish Ja Vala, she will harm Kenny Wadd. Or his family.

Ja Vala thinks about this possibility. About his small children. Is Madame Armistead evil enough to harm them? What would she accomplish by doing so? Hurting children will not restore either Madame Yveny or their trafficking business. So, the children are probably safe.

Still, she will want to perform a clear symbolic act to assert her power. Maybe she will kill his wife.

This thought does not bother me. His wife is an imposter. Ja Vala was to have been Kenny Wadd's wife, meant to bear his children. This wife of his is an impersonator, the marriage a fraud that never should have happened.

And if not for Madame Armistead, it wouldn't have.

Heat roils in her chest, along her limbs. Her teeth grind against each other.

The train stops and she slides forward, bracing herself against the seat ahead of her. The man reading the newspaper looks up at her, then back at his paper before he stands and hurries out onto the platform.

For a moment, Ja Vala stops breathing. Has he recognized her? Her face is on his paper. But it's only a small photo, black and white. Probably he hasn't connected it with her. Their eyes met, but it meant nothing, was only a momentary encounter.

She should leave the train. But Kenny Wadd's instructions are to ride it to 69th Street. Kenny Wadd. She hears his voice.

"You must do it." Fire blazes in his eyes. Not with love, with something else. Anger? Or revulsion?

Ja Vala refuses. She says she doesn't have enough for two.

THE WOMAN IN THE CUPBOARD

"Then give her whatever you have left. If you won't do it, I will." He sits up and, though he is still unsteady, tries to get out of his hospital bed.

She clutches the container of antidote to her chest, unable to explain. Unable even to ask Kenny Wadd what he knows. What he has overheard. Maybe he has no idea what was said at Madam Yveny's house. Maybe he didn't hear, or maybe the toxin so sickened him that he heard but doesn't remember.

The detective, though, will be aware. She was trying to stand. Her eyes were open, alert, and she watched Madame Yveny die.

"She tried to save you, Ja Vala. You must help her." Kenny Wadd presses her. His eyes are unforgiving, shocked at her hesitation. If he knows her concerns, he does not let on.

"She'll arrest me," Ja Vala tells him.

"For what? Killing Madame Yveny? That was self-defense," Kenny Wadd says. "I'll tell that to the police. So will Detective Sterling. You saved our lives—and the lives of her revenants."

The train stops again. A bulky man gets on, wearing a jacket with an eagle on it. He stands in the car, looking around before choosing a seat. Another man with an orange cap comes in through the door connecting cars. He steps in front of the first man, takes a seat a few rows up from her. The first man sits on one of the sideways seats near the door. Ja Vala doesn't know why, but she thinks these two men know each other. They don't sit together or speak. They don't even look at each other.

That's why she thinks they know each other. Wouldn't strangers look at each other? Isn't that the normal reaction when someone steps across another's path? These two don't even glance each other's way.

As if they each expect the other to be there.

The train starts up again.

She hears Kenny Wadd saying, "Give it to her."

She can't tell him what the detective will remember. That she heard Madam Yveny list all the people Ja Vala must have killed. The Grangers. The secretary. The partner. By rubbing life-saving powder into her arm, will Ja Vala be allowing the detective to arrest her, sealing her own fate?

Kenny Wadd takes her down the quiet hall, looking in rooms until he finds the detective. Her skin is blue, her face wet with sweat. Her eyes are open, drifting, but they settle on Ja Vala.

"Help me." Her mouth doesn't move, but Ja Vala hears her nonetheless.

Kenny Wadd reaches for the antidote. Before he tries to take it from her, Ja Vala pours it onto the unhealed cut in the detective's arm. Rubs it into the raw tissue, the blood. Soon, she will recover. When she does, she will arrest her.

In fact, Ja Vala doesn't care. She has nothing without Kenny Wadd.

"Listen," Kenny Wadd is writing something. She doesn't know where he got paper or a pen. "Go to this address. If you leave right away, the police won't find you."

He says the police want to find her, so he must know. Has Kenny Wadd heard Madame Yveny say that she's a killer?

Is that why he abandons her?

"Follow the directions on the paper. The man at that home is a friend of my father. You can stay there for a while." He stops writing and looks at her. His eyes are distant, belonging to a stranger. "Take the train to the end. Then connect to a bus. It's all on the paper."

She takes the paper. She thrusts herself at Kenny Wadd and presses her lips against his. His are soft. He doesn't grab her and hold her, but neither does he push her away.

The train emerges from the darkness and rises above ground. Ja Vala looks out the window at traffic. She repeats Kenny Wadd's last kiss and lets tears fall onto her stolen clothing.

THE WOMAN IN THE CUPBOARD

When finally the train stops, she gets up and walks out onto the platform.

A hand grabs her by the shoulder. She is not surprised. The bulky man stands facing me, the one with the orange cap holds onto her. She doesn't resist.

The bulky man says her name and declares that she is under arrest. He names the charges, but Ja Vala is not listening. Handcuffs click coldly around her wrists. They seem comical, these cuffs. As they lead her away, she considers that, in all her years as a prisoner, she was never so lightly restrained.

Chapter 96

D'Angelo tried to dissuade me. "You shouldn't be working, Mo. Technically, neither should I."

I opened a drawer, looked for my clothes. "No one took us off the case, did they?"

"Not officially. But—"

"Then we're still on it." I opened a cabinet door, saw a plastic bag on the bottom shelf, bent over for it and felt my hospital gown slide open in the back, giving D' a generous view of my hindquarters. I straightened up and spun around, bag in hand.

"Mo, you need to rest. Not an hour ago, you were a vegetable." D' wasn't acting right, made no mention of my backside. Not a single jab.

I put the bag on the bed. "I don't need to rest. The antidote worked. I'm fine." I wasn't though. Not even close. I was unsteady and weak, felt worse than the mother of all hangovers. But I refused to sit around a hospital room thinking about how I'd been buried alive, paralyzed, and convinced I was dying. I preferred to get back to work.

The plastic bag held my personal effects. My cell phone and the wallet with my badge.

"Where's my gun?"

"Look at the paper."

What paper? Oh, under my muddied shoes, I found a pink carbon copy of a standardized checklist of belongings. Gun wasn't checked off, wasn't even one of the choices. Someone had written at the bottom that my gun had been taken by Detective Roberto Rodriguez, who'd signed at the bottom.

"Rodriguez has it?"

D' shrugged. "Well, someone had to. They couldn't leave it lying around."

I pulled my clothes out of the bag, held them up.

D' grimaced. "You can't wear those."

No. I couldn't. They were caked with soil and clay, the left sleeve bloodied from the knife wound.

I rang for the nurse. "I'll get some scrubs. I can't interview those guys in my hospital gown."

He leaned back in the visitor's chair. "You're not in condition to interview anyone. Let someone else—"

"Who, D'? Who else can do it?" I faced him, hands on my hips. D' was being obstinate. He knew as well as I did that no one besides us knew the facts of the case well enough to question the people found at Madam Yveny's house.

He met my eyes. "I thought you were gone, Mo." He sat there, battered and stitched, with misting eyes.

I didn't know what to say.

"I stayed with you and prayed."

"Thanks, D'." My throat got lumpy. I almost couldn't talk.

"I promised God all kinds of stuff if He'd let you live."

Oh no. "What did you give up this time?"

He smirked. "Thanks to you, I have to go to Mass for a year. Donate a wad to charity." He mumbled the rest, but I heard it anyway. He had to control his temper, lose weight, and go to the gym.

"Poor D'." I went to his chair, leaned over. Kissed his cheek. "But it's all stuff you should do anyway."

He pouted.

"But just for the record, God had nothing to do with my recovery. It was the antidote."

"God had everything to do with it. Who do you think made sure that the antidote got to you in time?"

"Ja Vala."

D'Angelo shook his head. "I'm not going to argue with you about God, Mo."

"Good."

"I'm just trying to tell you. When I thought you were dying, I prayed for your recovery—" He stopped to rub his eyes.

I leaned over and wrapped my arms around him, felt my backside sticking out again. "I love you, too, D'Angelo."

"So, can't you for once take it easy? Stop racing around, acting like you're fine and none of it ever happened." His body was rigid, tense.

"I'm not." I backed out of the hug, gathering the flaps of my gown. "I'm acting like all of it happened, and I'm going to get the bastards who did it."

"No, Mo. This time you're going to listen—" D' shook his head, but the nurse stepped into the room, interrupting.

"You buzzed?"

Yes. I had. I showed her my ruined clothing and asked for a pair of scrubs. She couldn't consider it because they were color-coded by profession. I couldn't wear dark blue unless I was a registered nurse. Light blue was for interns or students. Burgundy was for social workers. She went on, listing the colors I couldn't wear. And besides, she added, I was supposed to be resting until the doctor signed my release forms, so I shouldn't actually need clothes.

In his chair behind her, D' nodded, smiled. Stood up and walked out.

I argued that I wanted to visit some other patients before I was released, but couldn't with my backside exposed. She offered a second gown to cover my rear. I countered that no matter how many I wore, hospital gowns were unbefitting to my position as a homicide detective.

She was unimpressed. Suggested I call a friend to bring me fresh clothes to wear home. Left me with a fresh gown on my bed to wear as a robe.

Fine. In the end, it didn't matter what I wore. It mattered what I did. What I could find out. I picked up that second gown and was trying to figure out how to snap the sleeves when D' sauntered back in. Tossed me a clear plastic bag containing a pair of pale green scrubs.

Wow. I hugged him again. Had probably hugged D'Angelo more that day than in all the years I'd worked with him. I changed in the bathroom, not sure which profession pale green represented. Not caring. I held onto the sink for support, put on the scrubs. Glanced at the mirror and froze, staring at the grimy, dirt-streaked face reflected there. My hair was filthy, lips swollen, skin ashen, cheeks scratched, eyes puffed. I turned on the water, ducked my head under the faucet. Washed my hair with hand soap, scrubbed my face, ignored the sting of raw skin. When I stepped back into the room, D'Angelo got to his feet, ready to go. Eyes diverted, he clenched his jaw, resigned to go along with me, clearly by no will of his own.

Chapter 97

D'Angelo knew where their rooms were—a row of them at the far end of the fourth floor. D' also knew Bryan McCabe, the officer guarding them. The two exchanged small talk while I chewed my lip and wobbled, eager to get inside to question Betiane or the other poor souls Madam Yveny had drugged and enslaved.

"So, they broke your nose?" McCabe eyed D's wounds. "You ought to thank them—Looks like an improvement."

D' snickered. "Bryan, you ever met Mo Sterling? She's working this with me."

Officer McCabe and I shook hands. "So, is it okay if we have a word with these guys?" My question wasn't a question. I stepped forward as I asked it, and before Officer McCabe could respond, I opened the door to a patient's room and stepped in.

It was a typical hospital room: two beds separated by a retractable curtain. Each bed was occupied by a man with an expressionless face. When I walked in, neither looked up. When I greeted them, neither reacted.

D' came in behind me, stood just inside the door. "McCabe says there's no point talking to him. Neither one's said a word since they got here. They're drugged, Mo. Like Ja Vala was."

I ignored him, stepped closer to the beds, pulled the curtain back so I could see them both. Looked at their faces, one, then the other. I stopped. Took a step back. Heard the scrape of a shovel. My eyes closed reflexively, fending off a slap of dirt.

"Mo?" D'Angelo was beside me, his arm around my waist.

I rubbed my eyes, clearing away soil or memory, and stepped away from D'Angelo. I was okay, no longer paralyzed. Not lying helpless in an open grave. But my arm stung where the toxin had been forced into my blood, and the taste of soil lingered on my tongue.

"I'm Detective Sterling," I made myself tell the gravediggers. "This is Detective D'Angelo. We're with the Philadelphia Police." My voice was thin. I moved my arms, wiggled my fingers, proving to myself that I could.

Neither man as much as blinked when I told them why we were there. They lay in their respective beds, looking at nothing. One had thinning hair and thick eyebrows. The other a short scraggly beard interrupted by a scar across his jaw. Both were scrawny, no match for me. Yet looking at them made my knees wobble.

I took a breath. Squared my shoulders. Ignored the chill in my blood. I was in charge now.

"I'm going to ask you a few questions." They looked helpless and pathetic, no longer armed with shovels. I moved closer to the balding one. His eyes were empty, unresponsive.

"What's your name?" I asked.

The man lay still, made no response. Seemed unaware of the question. I stepped over to the other man. Maybe he'd be more responsive. But before I said anything, the first man spoke.

"Seventy-two," he said.

I stood still, skin tingling, seeing Ja Vala huddled in the Granger's pantry.

"Your name is Seventy-two?" I asked.

I waited, but he said nothing.

I glanced at D'. He'd stuffed his hands into his pockets, was jingling coins. His eyes said that the interview was a waste of time. That we should get moving.

"We found you at Madame Yveny's house. Is that where you live?" I asked.

He shook his head, no, so slowly that the movement was almost imperceptible.

"Then where do you live?"

Silence. D's coins clinked impatiently. Okay, he was right. The interview was getting nowhere. I gave up and was on my way to the door when the man replied.

"I do not live," he said. The words ran together, emerging as a single sound, like a moan.

Chapter 98

"He said exactly what Ja Vala did, D'. That he's not alive." We walked to the elevator.

D' sighed. "Mo. You need to take a break—"

"No, listen." The case was fitting together. "We know what's happened here. Ja Vala's family believed she was alive even though she'd had a funeral and a death certificate—"

"Mo—"

"No. Don't interrupt. All those other people—Betiane and the gravediggers?"

"Sounds like a rock group."

I punched his arm. "I bet each of them has a death certificate and gravestone, too. They're all revenants, just like Ja Vala. Madame Armistead fakes her revenants deaths with the toxin, revives them with the antidote. Then she sends them to Madame Yveny who delivers them to customers and supplies drugs that keep the revenants controlled. Scopolamine or whatever."

The elevator doors opened. We stepped in. I was beaming, proud that I'd put all those pieces together, but not finished yet.

"These people who were in Madame Yveny's house can't be the first group they've imported. There must be dozens—maybe hundreds more. So, Madame Yveny had to have help—People working with her—Like Alexandra Lambert—"

"Hold on, Mo." D'Angelo faced me. "That all makes perfect sense. But here's the problem: We can't prove it. We only found out Ja Vala's name because Kenny Wadd came looking for her. These other people don't remember their names. Seventy-two? Without names, we can't check for death certificates. We can't prove that Madame Armistead had any contact with them, let alone that she launched an elaborate trafficking business."

The elevator opened and we got out. I chewed my lip, replaying our visit with the gravediggers. I saw the man lying limp and indifferent. Heard him say that he did not live. And recalled seeing his soulless his face in the moonlight, shoveling cold earth onto my skin. Even without names and proof, I knew. People were being poisoned, paralyzed and buried, dug up and revived. They were being sold as slaves to people like the Grangers.

The Grangers. A memory flickered: I was draped over a chair, unable to move, hearing Madame Yveny talking about the Grangers. About their murders.

I stopped walking. Recalled Madame Yveny saying that the bokor had been planning the Grangers' deaths. Had been surprised when Ja Vala had killed them before being told to.

"Mo?" D' stood beside me. "You okay?"

I nodded, started walking again. But two questions bothered me. First, if Ja Vala was controlled by drugs, how could she have murdered the Grangers without being ordered to? Second, why had the bokor wanted to kill wealthy customers like the Grangers? My mind was still muddled. I knew I had the answers, just couldn't locate them.

I was about to ask D'Angelo what he thought when we turned a corner and saw Kenny Wadd barreling toward us, hospital gown flapping.

Chapter 99

Ja Vala sits on a chair that is bolted to the floor beside a table that is also bolted to the floor, in a windowless room with walls the color of pea soup. Time does not pass. Like her life, it has come to an end.

Kenny Wadd. Kenny Wadd.

Why does his name resound in her skull even now that she knows he is lost to her? Why does she still feel the warmth of his arms around her, his breath on her skin? No. It is better that she replace these thoughts with others. Like Madame Yveny's dead white eye, or a blade piercing skin. She is, after all, a killer. How many lives has she ended?

She tries to remember, traveling deep into her mind, probing dark portions, seeking lost moments. She revisits the Grangers' home, wandering as if in sleep through back rooms and hallways. As she approaches the kitchen, she hears shouting and a crash, a shattering of porcelain.

The Grangers are fighting again, so she steps back and away. She does not move. If they see her, their rage might target her.

A heaviness settles on her, and a dread of what she might remember. And yet, she persists. She rewinds the memory, backing up to the end of the hallway and walking along it again, as if Dr. Vogel were coaching her, assuring her that she is safe now, that no one can hurt her. She ignores the bolted chair and sickly green walls and tries to figure out what her mind does not want to remember. Is the fog concealing the memories merely from the drugs? Or does her mind resist replaying events that trouble it? Why does she tremble, of what is she afraid?

Inside her head, the Grangers continue fighting. She listens from a distance, and she hears them distinctly as if she has fallen back through time.

"Not with my money." Judith Granger's voice trembles. "I won't give you a penny—"

"You're such a hypocrite, Judith. Acting appalled when you've used these people for years—You even have one now."

"That's different."

"Different?" Dixon Granger laughs.

Something crashes and shatters.

"Feel better now, Darling?" Dixon Granger mocks. "When you can't be reasonable, just smash priceless figurines."

Judith Granger doesn't answer. Ja Vala imagines her pouring her usual bourbon, swallowing it.

"The only difference will be that, instead of paying for these people, we'll get paid for them. Why should we let those old hags get rich when we have the means to run our own ship?"

"You won't run it. You'll go down with it."

The argument goes on. Dixon tells his wife how much money they'll make, adding figures. Judith predicts that they'll get caught. Dixon explains that they won't.

Ja Vala stands perfectly still, making no sound. Even if she did, they wouldn't notice. To them she is invisible, a simple household appliance.

"We've been over this," Dixon fumes. "No one's going to be looking for them. Officially, they'll be dead. And Madame Sehandieu will provide toxin, antidote and drugs."

Judith Granger laughed out loud, a shrill, cutting sound. "That woman gives me the chills. Please don't tell me you trust her."

"Why shouldn't I?"

"You're an ass, Dixon. An idiot. Even if she doesn't put some voudou hex on you, you'll both end up in jail. Unless Madame Armistead gets to you first. What do you think she'll do when she finds out you're cutting into her market and stealing her customers? Have you thought about that?"

"What can she do? She's an arthritic old cow stuck in Haiti. She can't touch us. And nobody's going to jail. Why can't you just for once get on board with me? This is huge. All I need is a hundred thousand to get it rolling."

"Kiss my ass."

"You'll have it back in a few months. With interest."

"Not a cent, Dixon. Not one. You've already squandered your own savings on your brilliant ventures—I'm not going to let you squander mine."

"Fine," Dixon Granger says. "I'll use the trust."

"Don't you dare." Judith Granger is shouting now.

"Just for half. J. Steven's partner, Ted Ames—He'll go in with me for the other half."

"Are you crazy? We can't bring in someone new, not now! And certainly not Ted Ames. Dixon, I went to school with Ted Ames. I know him way better than you, and trust me. He's all posturing, no substance. He won't even consider it."

"Of course, he will. He told J. Steven a hundred times that he wanted in on our partnership."

"And why do you suppose J. Steven didn't let him in? Simple: J. Steven didn't trust him. Neither should you. Ted Ames will turn on you and expose everything just to get his face on the news. Besides, Ted hasn't got the balls to do something risky—He'd sooner vote for a Democrat."

Dixon chuckles. "Funny, Judith. That was really funny." "It was, wasn't it." Her tone warms. Ja Vala hears a smile in her voice.

"What do you say, Darling? Just a few hundred."

"How should I say this, Dixon? Never. Not a frickin' penny."

The air is brittle, ready to crack. Ja Vala backs into the wall behind her. There is silence for a moment. Dixon Granger's voice lowers. "I'm going to do this, Judith. With you or without you. I've got the supplies, the formulae, the prospective customers, even the staff. I just need cash to get us rolling."

Silence again.

"Who are you calling?" Judith Granger sounds alarmed. "Dixon—"

Dixon Granger doesn't answer her. "J. Steven? Hi, Dixon here. Have you got a minute?"

"Don't," Judith Granger insists. "Dixon, I mean it."

"Lunch? Excellent. I have a most interesting opportunity to discuss."

The door to the study flies open, and Ja Vala hunkers in the shadows so Judith Granger does not see her when she passes.

Ja Vala remembers this exchange as if it is fresh, as if the words have just been spoken. And yet, when Judith Grangers comes out, the memory stops. Judith Granger and her home disintegrate into empty air.

Ja Vala's legs are stiff, so she shifts her body on the chair. Nothing has changed in this dull closed space. In her mind, Dr. Vogel exclaims that she has done a marvelous job, revisiting that entire conversation. She imagines him saying that, with time, she will likely remember more. Poor sweet Dr. Vogel doesn't understand, has never understood. Where Ja Vala is, there is no time. There are only the dim, dead-end pathways in her mind. And the name that cuts like a blade.

Kenny Wadd. Kenny Wadd.

Chapter 100

Kenny Wadd barreled into D'Angelo, might have knocked him over if D' hadn't grabbed him and held on.

"Detective, you must explain to them that I cannot stay, I must return home." Kenny Wadd was nose to nose with D', panting into his face.

D' said something but I couldn't hear him because Dr. Vogel ran over. "What's wrong? What's happened?"

"I must go back to Haiti. Immediately." Kenny Wadd was wild-eyed.

Another doctor stepped over. His nametag said Dr. Singh.

"Why did you run away?" Dr Singh was about five inches shorter and forty pounds lighter than Kenny Wadd. He squinted, assessing Kenny Wadd. "All I said was that you should remain for a day because you have only just regained consciousness.

"Impossible." Kenny Wadd looked at D', then at me. His voice was vehement. "I must go home. Now."

"Mr. Wadd, you suffered severe poisoning. It's not clear how you'll—"

"I'm fine. I received the antidote."

Dr. Vogel looked at Dr. Singh, then back at Kenny Wadd. He and Dr. Singh spoke together, saying essentially the same thing. "There is no antidote for the poison you received."

Kenny Wadd rolled his eyes. "There is. It's just unknown to western medicine."

"Neither of you received any such thing," Dr. Singh said. "We had you on saline drips. Nothing else."

Dr. Vogel frowned, rubbed his mustache. "Statistically, some patients do recover. Maybe they were given low dosages of toxin."

"We recovered because we were given the antidote," Kenny Wadd insisted. "Tell them, detective." He looked at me.

"It's true," I said. "Ja Vala brought it."

Dr. Vogel took a step back. "Ja Vala?"

"She gave us the antidote," I told him.

"The antidote that doesn't exist." Dr. Singh scoffed, crossed his arms.

"It exists." Kenny Wadd insisted. "But only a few mambos know of it."

"Mambos?" Dr. Singh echoed.

"It's a voudou term," D' explained. "Means something like a priest."

"Ja Vala found a mambo who would make up the antidote," Kenny Wadd said. "She saved our lives."

I agreed.

"Whatever she gave you," Dr. Singh said, "I can assure you it wasn't an antidote."

Dr. Vogel stared at me. "Why didn't you stop her?"

"Look, I have no time for discussions of Ja Vala. I must go home," Kenny Wadd's eyes darted from Dr. Singh to D' to me. "I need my clothes."

"Stop her?" I snapped at Dr. Vogel. "How? I was barely conscious."

Dr. Vogel glared at me. Dr. Singh eyed me, then Kenny Wadd.

D' stepped forward. "Actually, Mr. Wadd, you're a material witness in our investigation," he said. "We'd like you to stick around—"

"Not possible. I will phone in or email my statement. If necessary, I will come back. But now, I must reserve a flight. Once Madame Armistead learns that Madame Yveny is dead and that I have talked to the police—"

"How's this," D' interrupted. "Why don't you call your family and tell them to leave town for awhile."

Kenny Wadd's eye widened. "Of course." He slapped his head. "Let me use your phone," Kenny Wadd reached a hand out to me.

I didn't have it on me. Wasn't sure where it was.

He turned to D'. "Please! I need a phone—"

"There's one in your room," D' said.

"But Mr. Wadd, you really should rest," Dr. Singh said.

"Rest? Don't you see?" He looked at D' and me. "Detectives, tell them what Madame Armistead will do to my family." He turned to Dr. Singh. "Madame Armistead is a bokor!" He was talking too loud. People in the hallway were turning to look.

Dr. Singh looked at D'Angelo. "Like a stockbroker?"

"Calm down." I moved closer to Kenny Wadd, touching his arm.

"Not a broker. A bokor. It's an evil mambo," D'Angelo explained.

Dr. Singh shook his head, eyed Kenny Wadd.

"He's right," I said. "His family might well be in danger. The bokor will blame him for the death of her business partner—"

"It's not just about Madame Yveny, detective." Kenny Wadd's voice was urgent. "It's that Madame Armistead knows I know about her crimes—What she did to Ja Vala and many others. I know enough to send her to prison for all her life. She will do anything to keep me quiet, including doing harm to my family."

He was right.

Kenny Wadd looked at the door. "I must go."

"You might want to change before you leave," D'Angelo offered. "They won't let you on a plane like that."

"Yes, I need my clothes." He looked at Dr. Vogel.

"Your clothes were beyond repair," Dr. Vogel said. "But your wallet and keys are in your nightstand drawer."

"It's okay. No problem. I have other clothes at my hotel." Kenny Wadd looked around. "Now I must call home. And book a flight." He hurried back down the hall, toward his room.

"I'll see he gets some scrubs." Dr. Singh watched him go. "But he really should take it easy. There might be aftereffects."

"But if he doesn't want our advice, there's not much we can do," Vogel said. "Unless the police want to hold him." He looked at D'.

"No, we don't want to hold him," I answered.

No one acknowledged my comment.

"He needs to get home," D' said. "Under the cirmcumstances, I think we ought to let him."

We moved along toward Kenny Wadd's room, the doctors mumbling between themselves. From the hallway, I could hear his voice.

"Tomorrow? That's the first flight out?"

I stepped into the room. Kenny Wadd was scowling, pacing. Holding his credit card. "Okay. One seat to Port au Prince. The name is Kenny Wadd."

Chapter 101

Kenny Wadd made his reservation, then called a relative in Kennicott, someone he hoped he could trust to warn his family to leave town. He paced, worried his hands.

Dr. Singh stepped over to the nursing station, requested some extra-large scrubs. Then he approached Kenny Wadd. "Since your flight isn't until tomorrow, I must urge you to spend the night here, for observation."

Kenny Wadd looked at Dr. Singh. "I must pack. My flight is tomorrow afternoon."

"Pack in the morning. We just want to be sure you have no complications from the tetrodotoxin."

"Actually, I'd prefer you to stay here overnight," D' said. "You'll be safer than at your hotel. You've already been mugged there."

Kenny Wadd hesitated, watched Dr. Singh. "If you guarantee that I'll be unmedicated, I'll stay until dawn."

Good. It was settled.

Dr. Vogel turned to me, pulled me aside. He looked pale. Dark pouches swelled under his eyes. "And what about you?"

Me?

He pulled out a small flashlight light and shined it into my eyes. Lifted my eyelids with his fingertips. Pocketed the light. "You need rest, detective. I'd like you to spend another day here as well. For observation."

"Not possible," I told him.

D'Angelo stepped over. Good. He'd explain that I was essential to the investigation. That I needed to leave with him.

"The doctor's right, Mo," he said. "You should stay the night."

I kicked him. "I'm fine."

"Nonetheless." Dr. Vogel frowned. "You've been through a lot. Your body needs to recover." He met my eyes. "Let's see how you are in the morning."

I shook my head, vehemently no. I glared at D'Angelo, at Vogel. Didn't they get it? Morning might be too late. "No, I have to go."

"Detective Sterling, don't push yourself. Your mind and body have been affected by a powerful toxin," Dr. Vogel said.

Why weren't they listening? Didn't they care about finding Ja Vala?

"Mo," D'Angelo crossed his arms. With all his bulk and bandages, he looked like a losing prizefighter. "For once, listen. Your doctor says you should stay. That's it. The end."

Dr. Vogel made a note on a chart. "If you feel okay in the morning, I'll sign the release papers, just as I will for your friend Mr. Wadd. After all, detective, it's only a few hours between now and the morning. Really, how much can happen in a few hours?"

Was he serious? I looked at D'. He met my eyes, arguing without words, telling me that he would not back me up. The decision was final. A nurse came in with dark blue scrubs, handed them to Dr. Singh who gave them to Kenny Wadd. Kenny Wadd didn't bother to step into the bathroom. He pulled the pants on, yanked off his hospital gown. His chest and shoulders glowed golden as he slid the top over his head.

D's cell phone rang. "I'm still at the hospital," he said. "Hang on. There's bad reception." He walked into the hall where I couldn't hear what he said.

Kenny Wadd shook Dr. Vogel's hand. "Thank you." Then he stepped over to me, gave me a quick hug. "In case I don't see you in the morning." His eyes were fiery.

I nodded, staring into flames. "Good luck."

"I will contact you soon." When he released me, I couldn't move. Still felt his arms around me.

D' got off the phone and rushed into the room. Said he had to get going.

"Wait a second," I insisted. Since when did D'Angelo have the option of excluding me from our case? "You're saying that you're able to work, but I'm not? I'm in better shape than you are, with all your bumps and stitches—"

"There's been a development."

"What development?" I threw my head back. Not a good idea. The room whirled and I hung onto D' for support as he led me away from Kenny Wadd and Dr. Vogel, lowered his mouth to my ear and whispered.

Ja Vala Boudin had been picked up and taken in for questioning.

I didn't wait for him to finish talking, didn't bother to tell Vogel I was leaving. I spun around and ran back to my room for the plastic hospital bag containing my badge and phone. It didn't matter what the doctors or D' or anyone else said. No way was I going to let another detective interview Ja Vala Boudin.

Chapter 102

It took a lot of arguing, but finally, because of my history with Ja Vala, I got the okay to interview her. But when I entered the interrogation room, for a moment I thought they'd arrested the wrong woman. The suspect I saw was alert and attentive. Not the least like the passive, incoherent and dazed woman D' and I had found just a week earlier. Ja Vala's hair was tied into a makeshift bun, revealing stark cheekbones, strained eyes. She sat with her shoulders tensed, knees tight as if ready to sprint. When I greeted her, she faced me with frantic eyes.

"First of all," I began, "thank you for the antidote. You saved—"

"Where is Kenny Wadd?" She gripped the edge of the table.

"He's safe," I said.

"Where?"

I sat at the table, opposite her. Met her eyes. "Kenny Wadd isn't your biggest problem now, Ja Vala. You're here as a murder suspect."

"Kenny Wadd is all that matters." She let go of the table, laid her hands flat. "I must reach him. He is in danger—"

"He's being looked after."

"By whom? You and your police department?" She shook her head. "You have no idea who these people are, what they will do when they hear the trouble Kenny Wadd has caused."

The trouble *Kenny Wadd* has caused?

"They'll carve out his heart and the hearts of anyone close to him. They'll burn his house with his loved ones inside—"

"Just to be clear," I needed to take control. "Someone has read you your rights?"

"Yes—Detective, please listen—"

"And you understand them?"

"Stop wasting time. The bokors have many followers. Where I come from, even the police are in the bokor's control. Government

THE WOMAN IN THE CUPBOARD

officials are afraid of her and others like her. She will blame Kenny Wadd for everything: my escape, the death of Madame Yveny, the exposure and destruction of her business, and the loss of her inventory."

Inventory? The people we'd found at Madam Yveny's?

"She will make an example of Kenny Wadd. Believe me." Her eyes pleaded.

I sat back, studying her. "You still love him."

She folded her hands, looked at me.

"You were engaged to be married."

"A long time ago. Before I died."

"He attended your funeral."

She smirked. "The whole town went, probably. So what?"

"So, he mourned for you."

"For a time." Her eyes flickered.

"You sound angry."

"Of course, I'm angry. Madame Armistead dug me up and made me into a revenant. You of all people should understand. You were poisoned and buried, too. How did you like it?"

"Kenny Wadd was buried, too."

She turned away. "Yes. But I saved him."

"You saved us both. Thank you." I met her eyes. She looked away. "Where did you go afterwards?"

"Afterwards?"

"After you gave us the antidote."

"Kenny Wadd sent me away." Her mouth puckered. "He said I needed to go or I would be arrested."

"So, he was trying to protect you?"

Her mouth twisted. "Kenny Wadd? Protect me? No, he sent me away so he would be free of responsibility for me. He gave me an address and a handful of money and left me on my own."

I said nothing. Kenny Wadd still could be arrested for abetting her escape. I wanted to change focus, talk about the murders.

But Ja Vala kept talking, her hands clenched. "Kenny Wadd never protected me. I was his fiancée. He knew about Josias and what Madame Armistead might do to me, but Kenny Wadd did nothing. Nor did he question my death."

I didn't defend Kenny Wadd. Didn't mention that he'd brought a hair sample to prove her identity. Or that he'd insisted that we request an exhumation of her grave to prove, once and for all, that she wasn't in it. Or that, because of him, the exhumation might occur any day.

"He simply moved on and married someone else."

"He didn't entirely give up," I reminded her. "He came here to look for you."

"Only all these years later. And only because my family saw my photograph in the news. They paid his way. Listen to me: Kenny Wadd didn't fight for me. He gave in, accepting my death even though he knew about Madame Armistead—Oh, he knew, everyone in our village knew. Even as children, we'd heard that she was a bokor who dealt in revenants. That she sold them to rich Americans. But even knowing about her, Kenny Wadd did not suspect that my death was not final, that the bokor had taken me to avenge Josias. My family had to push Kenny Wadd to find me. And when finally, he came for me, what was there to save? There was nothing—" She stopped mid-sentence. Her hands remained flat on the table. Her eyes narrowed, and she bit her lips.

"There was nothing?" I asked.

"Never mind. It doesn't matter. Now what matters is that Kenny Wadd is kept out of the reach of Madame Armistead."

I nodded. "He is." Well, he was for the night. His room at the hospital was well guarded. Meantime, my captain was talking to the

FBI, trying to get Haitian authorities to cooperate in an investigation of Madame Armistead's human trafficking trade.

Ja Vala looked up at me, her expression sad. Or doubtful.

"Ja Vala, we need to discuss the reason you're here." I folded my hands, leaned forward.

"Because I am suspected of killing people."

"Yes. So. Did you kill them?" I asked it casually.

She shrugged. "How would I know? The drugs gave me amnesia."

I watched her for a moment. Ja Vala seemed indifferent to the idea that she might have committed murder. I pictured her sneaking through the hospital, her hands rubbing antidote into my bloodstream. Probably, her face had worn the same indifferent expression. "Why don't we go through the list of victims, and you tell me what you remember? Let's start with Dixon Granger—"

"You're not serious."

I wasn't?

"All these years, detective, I have been under the influence of drugs that gave me no choice but to obey the orders of my bokor. And the bokor told me to obey the Grangers. Whatever I did—whether it was to make an omelet or cut a throat—it would be because I was told to either by the bokor herself or by one of the Grangers. They controlled me with powders. You saw how I was. I had no choice in what I did and have very little memory of anything that happened during those years."

By contrast, she seemed very aware of her current situation. And of the fact that not being responsible for and not remembering her actions would serve her well.

"Do you remember killing the Grangers?"

She leaned her elbows on the table, gave no response.

"How about Sylvia Blake? Or J. Steven Richards?"

"I'm not sure I should say anything more."

I continued. "What about Alexandra Lambert? She was killed in your hospital room. The Grangers were already dead, so they couldn't have ordered you to kill her."

"I don't believe I should talk any more."

Shoot. "Why not? It's important that we figure out what you remember—"

"But you see, if I say anything else, I might say something misleading that sounds as if I am guilty. My memories are like pieces of pictures, detective, and they confuse me. Possible I saw something or did something. Possibly I heard something, but it is also possible that I only imagined hearing it. I cannot be sure because of the powders. While I was taking them, I was subject to suggestion. So, I might have killed people. But if I did—although I do not say that I did, *if* I did, it could not have been by my own will or intention, as I was in possession of neither. It's not that I don't wish to help you—I saved your life, didn't I? But even so, perhaps I'd better not say more. I think I should have representation. A solicitor?"

She refused to go on, and I had to stop questioning her until she had a lawyer. I sat back in my chair, regarding the dark-eyed woman across the table. She was strong, articulate. Cunning, even. A far cry from the Ja Vala I'd known before.

Someone knocked at the door. I excused myself, stepped outside.

"Great job." Reynolds shook his head, sarcastic. "You got nothing."

"That's why you interrupted? To tell me that I got nothing?"

"I didn't interrupt. You're done. She asked for a lawyer. Besides, there's news: another murder."

My throat tightened.

"A Haitian woman." He looked at a notepad. "Zada Sehandieu, something like that—I got no idea how to pronounce it. She was bludgeoned to death yesterday morning in southwest Philly. But get this—Her house looked just like the place where you and D'Angelo got messed up, full of candles and canisters, vials of dried roots and herbs and whoknowswhat. In fact, it looked like she was mixing up something in the kitchen when she got killed. Some kind of powder got spilled all over, stuck to everything. Lab's analyzing it."

I didn't wait for him to finish. I leaned over and gave Reynolds a kiss on his skinny lips, and headed back into the interrogation room. Ja Vala was no longer tense. She'd settled into her chair. When I asked if she knew anyone by the name Zada Sehandieu, she didn't answer, and her gaze didn't falter. She registered no reaction, certainly not guilt or alarm.

Chapter 103

The walls are still too close, and the flourescent ceiling lights pulse from time to time. But the room is familiar, well known to her in all its surfaces and crevices. All its shadows. She has even found two undiscovered packets of powder behind the toilet.

Ja Vala is back in the hospital, under the care of the esteemed and often strutting Dr. Vogel. The police have released her into his care, since he has convinced them that she has been a helpless, unwilling participant in criminal acts, a defenseless victim deprived of her own will, a sufferer of drug-induced lethargy and amnesia.

What he says is true, and she feels sorrow for what has been done to her.

In fact, she has remembered far more than she's shared with Dr. Vogel or the detective. Why would they expect her to volunteer information that might hurt her? No, she has adopted Dr. Vogel's suggestion, claiming a state of total amnesia. She insists that she has no memory of any killings or victims—At least until Madame Yveny, which was obviously self-defense.

And possibly the woman they call Alexandra Lambert. Also, self-defense.

But Ja Vala says that she does not recall J. Steven Richards. And indeed, she's not sure that she does. His name brings flickers, like an old movie. She sees his Porsche, and his body in the driver's seat. Did her bones tremble as she waited for him in the hedges beside his driveway? Did her hand falter as she ambushed him? She sees his strong, surprised arms flail in desperation. Feels his indignant flesh tightening against the blade.

If she sees these images, she must have killed him.

Ja Vala replays the scene, watching the car pull into the driveway. The door opening. The knife slashing across his neck. Her chest is hot, churning. Resisting the idea that she has ambushed and slain this unsuspecting man. Again, she sees the glint of the blade in the moonlight. She tells herself that it isn't true, that she's manufactured a memory, constructing the scene from what she knows about the crime. The knife rises, strikes. She sees the man, the knife slicing him. But the hand. She cannot see the hand. Is it hers?

She has told the detective that she remembers none of it and has refused to consider her questions. But when the detective mentioned the name Sylvia Blake, Ja Vala smelled heavy cologne, saw a woman's face, her makeup caked and smeared with blood. She said nothing, other than to ask again for a solicitor.

The detective asked if Miss Judith and Mr. Dixon had ordered her to kill those two, and Ja Vala's mind traveled back, behind the closed doors of the Grangers' home where none of their acquaintances could see. Ice cubes clinked, bourbon flowed, hostile voices hissed. Judith Granger accused her husband of cheating.

"It's no use lying anymore, Dixon. I smell her. You stink of your whore."

"Enough, Judith. Sylvia and I work closely in the same office. Her perfume permeates everything—"

"It's not her perfume that I smell, Dixon."

It comes back to Ja Vala in chunks. Not all of it. But slivers. Continuing battles. She sees Judith Granger approaching her in the night, whispering. Is she instructing her how to find and murder her rival?

She remembers Dixon Granger, stunned and ashen, when he understands what has been done to Sylvia Blake. And the way the color returned to his face as he turned to Ja Vala, an idea burning in his eyes.

"Judith." His voice is calm and addresses his wife, though his eyes remain on Ja Vala. "J. Steven knows too much about our new enterprise. I'm concerned that he might expose it. We can't risk that."

"What?" She is distracted. Only half listening, doing something on her cell phone.

"J. Steven," he repeated. "He disapproves of our new business endeavor. Because of what he knows, he poses a threat not only to it, but to us." His eyes gleam at Ja Vala as if she is a newly discovered jewel.

Judith Granger listens to him describe what he wants to do to his partner, but she doesn't say a word. That's all Ja Vala remembers. She doesn't remember Dixon Granger telling her to kill his partner. And she's not sure how she would have accomplished it. Did Dixon Granger drive her to J. Steven's home? Did he tell her exactly where and when to commit the crime?

Did she kill the man?

These details escape her, even now.

She sits in this familiar room, in a chair by the window, wondering if the questioning is finished. Remembering the detective watching her with soothing golden eyes.

But Ja Vala has told the detective nothing. Clearly, she has surmised a lot, including what led to the Grangers' deaths. She asked about their fighting. Their violence. How does she know how they sniped at each other? Does she know about the final fight? Ja Vala see them, Dixon Granger glowers at his wife, insisting that he shouldn't have to bear the entire burden—that she needs to contribute more.

"Why? So you can throw my money away, too?" Judith Granger's voice is flat, indifferent.

"Look, Zada Sehandieu is taking a big risk, going in with us against the Armisteads. She's part of their community, and the Armisteads have a loyal following here. They're like a mini mafia—"

"Sehandieu stands to make a fortune with us—she ought to absorb some of the cost."

"She doesn't have that kind of money, Judith. Her contribution is her expertise. We need her."

"She needs us, too. We're supplying the customer base and the product—"

"Judith. Without her skills, we've got nothing. We can forget the whole thing. Besides, we have other expenses—transportation, warehousing. Supplies—tetrodotoxin and scopolamine aren't cheap. You've got to pitch in."

"Not another penny, Dixon. Not one cent."

It escalates. Ja Vala waits in the hallway to announce dinner. And when she steps into the room, the air stings her skin with crackles of loathing.

That is the last she remembers clearly.

What happened next? Does Judith Granger tell her that, rather than feed his fat face, Ja Vala should cut her husband's fat throat? Do Dixon's eyes bulge and his face redden? Does he sputter, "Never mind that. Go chop my dear wife to bits. Anything to shut her infernal mouth."

Is she inventing these words? Has any of this happened? Did Ja Vala kill them because they ordered her to? How else can she explain the clothing in the wash, her uniform covered with blood? She has envisioned the killings so many times, she can't tell what is memory, what is imagination. She sees blood spurting from Dixon Granger's throat, hears air hissing from his lungs.

No one would blame her for killing them. But she aches, not knowing. She closes her eyes and pushes her brain. It shows her nothing.

Still, she must be the killer. She was the only person in the house, except for the Grangers themselves. And certainly, they didn't kill themselves.

On the edge—No, just beyond the edge of her mind, a lost memory jumps up and down, trying to be discovered.

She repeats the thought that aroused the commotion. "And certainly, they didn't kill themselves." The statement is obvious. Why does it jangle her brain?

She must stop. Must accept the irrefutable truth of her guilt. Perhaps a judge will have mercy on her because of her circumstances. But it doesn't matter. Her life is over, has been for years. A death sentence would be merciful, if not redundant.

Chapter 104

Ja Vala offered nothing more, and Dr. Vogel hospitalized her "for observation." By the time I got home, I was spent. My head felt fogged in, my limbs heavy. But no sooner had I shut the condo door than the buzzer rang.

I slogged over to the intercom.

"Mo? Thank God. Let me in."

I leaned against the wall, pushed the button to unlock the door. Seconds later, Evie burst in, thrust a package onto the kitchen counter, wrapped her arms around me, and pressed herself against me in a breastsmashing hug.

"You're all right? I've been out of my mind. Did you get my flowers?"

Oh. The flowers. They must have come from Evie. I hadn't read the card. "Thanks. They were beautiful."

She pushed away, grabbed my hands, studied my face. "They wouldn't let me see you. They said no visitors and wouldn't give me any information about your condition. I thought you were brain dead."

For a while, I had been. "How did you know I was in the hospital?"

"Are you kidding? The whole world knew. It was on the news. I thought you were dying, Mo." Her voice broke. "I called your office. They wouldn't tell me anything. I was bananas. Everybody was—Cheryl, Lindsay, Maggie..."

She went on, listing names from our high school class. People I hadn't seen in years. I sunk onto my sofa. Even then, Evie hung onto my hands.

"Oh, Mo. What really happened? The news said you were poisoned."

"I was. I'm okay now."

She sat beside me, eyes probing, fingers squeezing. "They said you'd been buried alive."

It was public knowledge? "Can we not talk about it?"

Evie didn't let go of me. She watched me for a while. "I understand if you're not ready. But Mo, you know you shouldn't hold in your emotions. It's good to express—"

"Evie, stop!" My tone was sharper than I'd intended. "I just got out of the hospital. I'm tired." So tired, I couldn't think.

Finally, she withdrew her hands, stiffened. "Okay. I get it."

I'd insulted her. "Evie, sorry. But until the case is closed, I can't discuss it."

She nodded, said she understood. Brightened up and announced that she'd brought gifts. Bounced off the sofa to open a sack containing homemade veggie lasagne, a tossed salad, a chocolate cake and a bottle of cabernet.

I sank back, speechless. Teary.

"It's not just from me," she said. "You have lots of friends, Mo. Cheryl made the lasagne. Maggie baked the cake. All I did was buy the wine."

Really?

"As soon as you're up to it, we're having a girls' night." She went on to update me on our old friends' lives. Cheryl had two kids with her engineer husband Paul. Maggie had had her fourth miscarriage last month so she and Stan were thinking of adopting. Lindsay was in the midst of a divorce from Tom, our high school quarterback. She didn't mention whether any of them worked. Were Evie and I the only ones? Never mind, while the lasagne warmed, I sat back and listened to the news, found it soothing to hear about normal people whose lives didn't revolve around murders. When dinner was ready, I devoured half the pan before attacking dessert.

"Chocolate and red wine," Evie raised her fork with one hand, her glass with the other. "The perfect couple."

She was right. I swallowed wine, savored dark creamy icing. Tried not to think outside the moment. "Thank you, Evie. This was wonderful."

She licked her lips, smiled coyly. "Speaking of perfect couples," she said, "I guess you haven't had time to check your site?"

My sight? For a few eyeblinks, I had no idea what she meant. But then I remembered. I hadn't been online at all, let alone to check the site.

She was on her feet, opening my laptop.

I protested. "Evie. I'm tired. Can't this wait?"

But she was determined. "Let's just look." She remembered my password and signed on. "Oh my God!" she squealed. "You have eighty-two responses."

I did? I sat beside her on the sofa, leaned back. Swallowed the last of my wine.

Evie read names and profiles aloud, pointed out photos. "Okay, no more calls. You have to look at this one. 'Lawman.' Says he works for the D.A. He skis and surfs. And he's gorgeous. You've got to answer this guy. If you don't, I'll do it for you."

I snuggled back under an afghan. Assured her that I'd do it later. As I dosed off, Evie was reading a message. Something about someone wanting to getting together.

When I woke up, it was morning. Evie had put a pillow under my head, and the dishes were all clean.

Chapter 105

The exhumation of Ja Vala'a grave was scheduled for the next day.

D' came in with a box of donuts, plopped onto the chair beside my desk, eyed them. "So, if the coffin's empty, what do you think she'll do?"

"Nothing. What can she do?" I thought he meant Ja Vala.

"With a loyal following in the police and the government? She can probably do whatever she wants."

Oh. Not Ja Vala. Madame Armistead.

"Let's hope they find an empty coffin. Then they'll have to arrest her."

"Think they've started yet?" His eyes didn't leave the donut box.

"Probably not this early. I'd guess we'll hear this afternoon."

D' nodded, rode his chair back to his desk. When he was gone, I grabbed a plain and tried to reread my notes about the Granger murders, review Ja Vala's statements. But my head was still cloudy from the toxin, and I kept losing my train of thought.

D' frowned. "I ought to warn you, Teresa had another dream."

"Don't even tell me."

"A man and a woman were caught in a flood. She saw them get pulled into the current—"

"I don't want to hear it." Did he think he and I were the people in the flood? That the flood was our investigation?

"Fine," he shoved his hands in his pockets. Jingled coins. "Suit yourself." He bounced his knee. "What do you say we go to lunch?" he asked.

It was barely nine a.m. I was chewing a plain donut.

"Change of scene might help us think."

Maybe he was right, but I ached all over, didn't want to go anywhere. Before I could answer, Reynolds came over.

"You guys see the forensics report yet?"

I looked at D' who looked at me. "What forensics report?"

Reynolds closed his mouth. "Oops."

"What are you talking about?" I pivoted to face him.

His gaze shifted. "I guess you two are out of the loop. Captain thinks you both need time off."

D' stepped over to Reynolds, held out his hand.

Reynolds gave him a folder which D' opened on my desk. We read the printout together, almost cheek to cheek. And my foggy mind tried to make sense of what I read.

None of Ja Vala's blood had been found at the Grangers' murder scene. But both Dixon's and Judith's blood had been found on each other's bodies.

Traces of Judith Granger's blood had also been found on J. Steven Reynolds' body.

Traces of Dixon's on Sylvia Blakely's.

None of Ja Vala's had been found at either the Blake or the Reynolds' scene.

On a whim, I'd asked for the Grangers to be tested for scopolamine. Judith Granger had tested positive.

D'Angelo kept rereading the reports, eyebrows furrowed. "All this means is that Ja Vala transferred blood from one Granger to the other. Probably happened when she moved them."

"Yeah. She wouldn't have left her own blood unless she cut herself." Reynolds agreed.

"It's these other findings that are confusing." D' frowned. "Because if I didn't know better," D' said, "I'd think they indicate that the Grangers were involved in those murders. Judith Granger in Richards' and Dixon in Sylvia Blakely's." He paused. "Maybe Judith had something against Mr. Richards that we don't know about."

"But why was Dixon's blood on Sylvia Blakely?" I asked. "If she was his mistress and business partner, why would he kill her?"

Reynolds let out a sigh, sat on the edge of my desk. Shook his head. "Don't ask me."

I picked up the printout, noticed a second report that we hadn't looked at yet. It was on a separate page, issued while I'd been in the hospital.

The hair samples had been tested. Kenny Wadd's sample and the one taken from the maid had come from a single donor, validating Ja Vala's identity. Big whoop. The results seemed almost irrelevant now.

Reynolds and D' jabbered about the blood findings, trying to figure out who did what to whom and how Ja Vala's blood could have been nowhere. I tuned them out, thought about the other test results, the scopolamine in Judith Granger's blood. Then I picked up the phone and called Dr. Vogel. The case was finally making sense.

Chapter 106

Ja Vala hears Dr. Vogel coming into her room just after breakfast and slips her journal under the cushion, hoping he doesn't see. This little book began as his way of finding out her thoughts. Now it has become her private journal. He doesn't mention it, simply asks if she's comfortable, if she wants to talk. She tells him she's too tired. He sits beside her at the window, says that Detective Sterling considers Ja Vala a hero for saving her and Kenny Wadd. He smiles like a proud father and asks if she's hungry. She says no. He tries to rebuild a rapport, reminds her that she's safe in his care, and promises to come back after she's rested.

When he leaves, she lies down, but as she reclines, she recalls a woman lying dead in that same bed, her head where Ja Vala's is now. She hear the woman urging her to swallow the bokor's powders. Thinking the the woman's death, Ja Vala's breath quickens. Her body is oddly energized, as if reacting to scalding soup spilt onto her flesh.

By contrast, the Grangers' deaths seem cool and vague. She picks up the journal again to reread her last entry and tries once again to recall killing them. She sees their bodies in disarray, their gaping wounds. The cleaver. The knife. She has a clear memory of dragging Judith Granger, cleaning her spilled blood. But she sees it all in snapshots. Disconnected flashes.

During the last few days, though, some flashes have joined together like a film clip. She watches this clip over and over, and each time, a few more details appear. So far, this is what she sees: Judith Granger rushes past her into the kitchen, followed by Dixon. She yells at him to keep away, picks up the meat cleaver, holds it up to frighten him. He mocks her. Takes a carving knife from the counter and jabs it at her. She lifts the cleaver, taunts him. You are a coward, she says. A limp-dicked crooked sniveling fraud. He swings the knife across her chest. Draws blood. She looks down at it, amazed. He swings again, cuts her across the midriff.

And then it is a silent dance. His arm rises, swings forward, slices her face, her mouth. Gushing blood, she sways, recovers, leaps backward and sideways, takes two half steps across the tiles. Growls like a wounded tiger. He glides forward, blade extended, puncturing her skin, bending his knees like a swordsman, dodging and ducking to avoid the slashes of her cleaver. They spin, they hop. They slip in Judith's blood. They move into the hallway and their pace quickens, their feet stomping out an uneven percussion. They breathe in rasps, rapid and shallow, circling each other, twirling faster and faster. Until they stop. Panting. Facing each other, each with a weapon raised, ready to strike.

And then, like a jagged torn film clip, the memory ends. Ja Vala strains her mind. She stands. She sits. She forces her mind back to the Grangers. The house is silent, motionless. The kitchen is empty. She finds them outside the study, on the floor, their bodies entangled. Mr. Dixon's knife is buried in Miss Judith's eye. Miss Judith's cleaver has all but severed Mr. Dixon's head.

For Ja Vala, a curtain has lifted and the past been revealed. She sees Miss Judith still standing, even with the knife in her eye. Her husband stares in disbelief at what he has done as Miss Judith gathers her last burst of strength, swinging her cleaver. Ja Vala sees him fall, hears a hiss of air and blood. Miss Judith sinks to the floor on top of him, gasping for help. But only for a moment.

Ja Vala sees herself cleaning up. Pulling Mr. Dixon away, lugging him into his chair. Dragging Miss Judith out of the blood pool. Wiping it up.

Her head aches. She closes her eyes, too tired to think. After a while, a nurse rouses her to measure her vital signs. As soon as she leaves, Ja Vala gets into bed, takes out her journal and goes back, replaying the Grangers' deaths. She hears them arguing, Miss Judith

THE WOMAN IN THE CUPBOARD

refusing to give her husband money. She watches their final moments. And then she closes her eyes, surprised by a new image. Mr. Dixon is at the bar, pouring a bourbon for Miss Judith.

And adding powder to it.

She goes back. Watches the moment again. Mr. Dixon is drugging his wife. Giving her some of Ja Vala's powders. Taking away Miss Judith's will. He waits until his wife has finished the drink, and a while later, tells her to write him a check. Miss Judith obeys her husband without a word of resistance. Mr. Dixon smiles and pockets it.

These moments seem manufactured, as if Ja Vala is imagining rather than recalling them. And yet, they explain the reason for the Dixons' later fight. When the powders wear off, Miss Judith realizes what her husband has done. And she understands that this is not the first time he's drugged her, not the first thing he's made her do.

Images clutter and bump. Can Ja Vala trust these memories? Or is her mind scrambling to invent scenarios that would prove her innocent?

She goes back, sees the cleaver in Miss Judith's grip. Smells her rage. Could she imagine such a scent?

Her mind jumps. What if Mr. Dixon regularly poured the powders into his wife's drinks? Had he have ordered his drugged wife to do more than write checks? Maybe even to kill his estranged business partner?

Ja Vala imagines it. Miss Judith going to J. Steven Richards' home and waiting for him to drive up. He greets her warmly, opening his car door without hesitation, never anticipating the swipe of her blade.

Ja Vala's breath becomes rapid and shallow. Her chest feels weightless. Relieved. The scenario feels true, and a new question arises.

What if Mr. Dixon was not the only one to feed the powders to his spouse? Miss Judith could easily have poured some into her husband's bourbon. And while he was drugged and without will power, she might have ordered him to kill her rival, his own lover. Mr. Dixon would have obediently followed the order, committing the murder and not even remembering it because the powders cause amnesia.

Ja Vala feels like singing. Just as she might not have killed J. Steven Richards, she might not have killed Sylvia Blake. Her killer might be Dixon Granger. He would have gone to her apartment. Maybe she'd noticed a change in him. Reticence. Or indifference. But not in time to escape the swipe of the knife he plucked from his pocket.

Ja Vala sees spurts of blood, stains on Sylvia Blake's necklace, her silk nightgown.

Are these details she's drawn from hearing about the murders? Or are they from memory? Did Dixon Granger hold the knife? Or did she?

She tells herself that it was he.

Ja Vala is cold, restless. She gets out of bed and, wrapping herself in the blanket, sits again in the chair beside the window, writing in her journal. Outside, the day is raw and dark with clouds. Like her mind.

Chapter 107

I was getting off the phone with Dr. Vogel when Kenny Wadd stopped by. His flight wasn't until two, so he had some time before he had to go to the airport. He wanted to say goodbye to Ja Vala, but because she was in custody, he needed clearance.

D' offered him a donut from the box near the coffee pot. "They're fresh," D' eyed them longingly.

Kenny Wadd took a chocolate one, held it without taking a bite. He was calm, not agitated like he'd been in the hospital. "I have decided," he said, "what I will do. I will go straight to Madame Armistead and tell her in my own words what has happened. It's my only hope for my family."

"Not necessarily." I told him about the likely investigation by the FBI and Haitian authorities.

Kenny Wadd froze. He stopped chewing, nearly dropped the donut. "No—Stop them. They mustn't."

"They mustn't?" D' leaned against my desk. "Human trafficking, drug dealing, kidnapping, identity theft—"

"Yes, but please. Don't involve Haitian authorities." Kenny Wadd stood beside me, towered over me. I smelled cloves. "Please. Leave Madame Armistead alone."

D' crossed his arms. Silently told Kenny Wadd to forget it.

Kenny Wadd stood frozen. "Madame Armistead has followers everywhere. Including the police force and the government. They will alert her to the investigation, and if they can, they will sabotage it. My only hope for my family is to convince her that the worst has passed—"

"What do you expect us to do?" I explained, "We can't just allow—"

"No. But if my family is to survive, her followers must not link an investigation to me or to my visit here. Don't you see? It is bad enough that she will blame me for Ja Vala's rescue and Madame Yveny's death. She mustn't think I've also inspired an international investigation."

D'Angelo met my eyes. His gaze told me not to antagonize Kenny Wadd, not to mention the exhumation. To let him believe that the Haitian part of the investigation would be dropped for now.

"We'll do what we can," I said. "But it's not our call."

D' rolled his eyes, expecting an explosion from Kenny Wadd.

But Kenny Wadd just nodded, looked at the half donut in his hand. Dropped it into the trash, wiped his hands. "Thank you, detectives."

I made a phone call to authorize his visit to Ja Vala, and Kenny Wadd was on his way to check out of his hotel, then to the hospital. We said our goodbyes, wished each other well. His eyes seemed muted and he offered no hug, just a perfunctory handshake perfunctory, devoid of emotion. Finally, the man who'd traveled hundreds of miles to give Ja Vala her name, and who'd almost been buried alive for his efforts, thanked us for our help, and, before it occurred to me to offer him a ride to the hospital, walked away.

Chapter 108

I got to Dr. Vogel's office around ten. His eyes were over-bright, ringed with exhaustion, and he looked pale and shrunken. We exchanged amenities. He commented on my quick recovery. I became defensive, assuring him that I was fit to work.

"Let's face it, detective," he sighed. "Neither of our professions allows us to admit it when we need time off. You and I both could use some."

I changed the subject, asked how Ja Vala was doing. "I'm glad you got her sent back here," I told him. "She doesn't belong in jail."

He didn't answer. He lifted his chin, waiting for me to continue. I went on. "She saved my life. And D'Angelo's. And Kenny Wadd's. And all the others at Madame Yveny's."

Dr. Vogel sighed, folded his hands. "And she's left corpses everywhere she's been."

"We don't know what went down."

He tilted his head. "Don't we? You watched her kill—what's her name? Yveny?"

"Like I said. She saved my life."

He nodded. Paused. "I believe she acted to save Kenny Wadd."

"She still loves him."

"Yes. I believe she does."

"Sad."

"Indeed."

We were quiet for a moment.

"Doctor," I began. "I'm concerned about the case against Ja Vala. As you know, there's evidence that she was present when the Grangers were murdered. She had opportunity and means. As well as motive."

He said nothing.

"It would help her case if she could tell us her version of what happened."

"But scopolamine gave her amnesia."

"So, she has no recall at all? Nothing from all those years?"

He unfolded his hands, sat back in his leather desk chair. "Depends on the dosage and frequency with which it was administered—And the quality of the drug she was given. But in my opinion, everything that happened during the years of her captivity is probably lost to her. And let's be clear—that's what I consider it—Captivity."

I didn't disagree. "Any chance memories will surface with time? Maybe with hypnosis?"

"Unlikely." He pursed his lips. "But again, it depends on the level at which she was drugged. In general, scopolamine prevents the brain from recording experiences as they occur, so memories aren't created. But, if the drug is taken over a long period of time—Who knows? A person might become resistant to it, allowing some memories to form. And we don't know how diligent the Grangers were with doses. It's possible they missed some and seeds of memory were formed. She might recall sporadic moments."

Good. "So, there's a possibility—"

"Detective, don't expect too much. Whatever she remembers will be unreliable, as the drug would have distorted her perceptions."

I crossed my legs, digesting what he'd said. "In other words, the last decade—"

"For Ja Vala, those years might very well be lost."

Lost? A whole decade? I thought of the last ten years, how much had happened in my own life. My mother's illness and death. My husband's infidelity and our divorce. The first perp I'd shot and killed. The times D'Angelo had been wounded and nearly died. In a way, amnesia like Ja Vala's didn't seem so bad.

"That is not to say," he continued, "that patients don't think they have memories."

I didn't follow.

"Imagine having no recall of a period of time. And imagine that you hear people describing various events that happened during that same period. The brain is an active organ. When it hears about these events, it pictures them. It might even embellish what it pictures, adding its own presence and participation. Eventually, these embellishments might be confused with actual memories."

So, Ja Vala might believe she had memories when really, she'd only invented them? But she also might have actual memories because she'd been given too low or infrequent a dose of her drug. Was she able to tell the difference between real and invented memories? And if not, how could anyone else?

Not that it mattered, since she claimed to remember very little.

Dr. Vogel was still talking. "As you know, Ja Vala is not my only patient suffering from scopolamine poisoning. The others are being transferred here as soon as they are physically ready."

Of course. The others from Madame Yveny's house.

"For now," I lowered my voice, "I'm mostly interested in Ja Vala. Confidentially, I'm not convinced she committed all those murders. I have a new theory, based on the blood evidence."

His eyebrows rose.

"As you know, three of the murders—Alexandra Lambert, Madame Yveny and Madame Sehandieu—Those can all be argued as self-defense."

He nodded.

"And we've learned that none of Ja Vala's blood was found at any of the other murder scenes. Judith Granger's was found at one, and Dixon Granger's at another. How can we explain that? And then it occurred to me: scopolamine."

Dr. Vogel leaned forward, stroking his mustache.

"Doctor, what if Granger doped his wife with scopolamine and ordered her to kill his partner? Would she have to obey?"

Dr. Vogel rubbed his mustache. "Possibly—The drug makes people compliant."

"And what if Judith Granger drugged her husband and ordered him to kill his mistress. Under the influence of scopolamine, he couldn't refuse."

Dr. Vogel sat back, clearing his throat. "Well. Let me think about that. There are many factors to consider. Dosage, timing and so forth. But, detective, I believe your theory would be sufficient to establish reasonable doubt about Ja Vala's guilt."

I smiled, proud of myself.

"Even so," he folded his hands, "that theory doesn't explain who killed the Grangers."

I lost my smile.

Vogel scowled. "Let me understand, detective. Let's say that we find an alternate explanation to the Granger murders—Are you saying she might get off?"

"I'm hoping so. When a jury hears how for almost ten years, Ja Vala's been enslaved, drugged, deprived of her memory and will power, they aren't going to want to convict her of anything. And when they hear that she killed to protect the lives of others—including two police detectives—I think the jury will not only let her go—I think they'll name a charity after her."

Dr. Vogel grinned. "Too bad you're not a lawyer. You should represent her."

I sighed. "Let's hope it won't even go to trial. If the DA sees the evidence the way I do, it might not."

"But it might?"

"The DA might not buy that Ja Vala had no will of her own. And then there's the part about voudou, mambos, bokors, and revenants."

Dr. Vogel rubbed his eyes. "I see your point."

"On the other hand, Ja Vala's grave is being exhumed. We should get a report from Haiti any time now. When they find it empty, we'll have support for the claim that Ja Vala was dug up and revived and sold to the Grangers."

He nodded. Blinked a few times. "So, what do you think her chances are?"

I had no idea. It was a coin toss. I bit my lip, took a breath. Shrugged. "She saved my life, doctor. I'll do my best to save what's left of hers."

Chapter 109

Ja Vala is dozing when the air stirs and she is roused by the presence of a visitor. A familiar scent of spices. She'd thought she wouldn't see him again except in dreams. But she looks up, and he is there.

"How are you feeling?" Kenny Wadd asks.

"Happy, now that I see you."

He is hurried, distracted. Her body registers the rapid beating of his heart. Kenny Wadd is bruised and scraped, but his eyes glow urgent and determined. "I am going back today," he tells her. "My flight leaves soon."

Ja Vala stops breathing. Her chest goes cold. "Why have you come?"

She knows better, but imagines him saying that he's come because he can't stay away. That he still loves her and always will. That he and she belong together, and that he will leave his wife so they can reunite and share the rest of their lives.

He sits on the chair opposite her. "Ja Vala." It was all he said.

Their eyes meet. Ja Vala has no idea how long they sit this way, saying no words, linked by their gazes. The life they would have built, the children they would have had, the love they would have shared—All of it is visible in the air between them, flourishing under the Haitian sun.

"I have to go," he finally says, and the vision shatters, its particles flittering in the air with the dust. "She will hurt my family."

Ja Vala says nothing.

"You know her, Ja Vala. What she is capable of." His body is tense, his words rushed. "I've ruined her business here."

"No. I did. I'm the one she'll want to punish."

He shook his head. "You killed Madame Yveny but you wouldn't have done it on your own."

Kenny Wadd had no idea.

"None of it would have happened if I hadn't come here and told the authorities who you are. Now her operation is exposed, her partner is dead. Madame Armistead is ruined. And I'm the one she'll blame."

Why hadn't he come looking for her years earlier, before he'd married someone else? Ja Vala closes her eyes, sees them walking hand in hand through their village. Kenny Wadd stops at a vendor and purchases a wall hanging. A silver tree, hand hammered from from an old steel drum, its branches intertwined with flowers and leaves, its roots tangled. "This is for our home," he says, kissing her ear, sending a tickle across her neck. What has happened to this tree? Does it hang now in the home he shares with his wife? Does he think of Ja Vala when he looks at it? Does he regret that he's married another even though he's unable to say so?

"None of what has happened is your fault, Ja Vala. You are the innocent one here." Kenny Wadd's voice is soft. She wants to sink into it and remain there.

But even as he says it, she knows it is not true. She is not innocent. She is a killer. I am a killer. Lifeless, bloodied bodies parade through her mind. She sees a woman's corpse tucked under her blanket. Madame Yveny's iridescent eye. Madame Sehandieu's claw-like fist becoming limp.

"You've been so brave, all these years, surviving what they did to you. You deserve to come home."

Home?

"When your parents learned that the hairs matched, they wept with happiness."

What hairs?

"Your family is joyful, knowing that you are alive."

Her family? Do they know she is suspected of murder? Do the others in the village? Ja Vala's face gets hot. She turns away.

"Listen, Ja Vala." He goes on, talking fast. "I have talked with the detectives. They are optimistic about your case."

She stares at the window. A light beam cuts through the slit of the curtains, slashing the air.

"You were drugged by the Grangers, so whatever you did, you weren't responsible. You didn't intend to hurt anyone, so you might not even be charged with a crime."

Really? "I wasn't always drugged."

His face is a question.

"I killed a woman here in the hospital. And Madames Yveny and Sehan—"

"Stop." He puts a hand on her mouth.

The hand is firm and warm. She wants to grab it, hold onto it. Pull him against her.

"You did that to save lives. Including mine, Ja Vala. I have offered to give a deposition to that effect, but the detectives say it might not be necessary. Like I said, they doubt you will be charged."

What? Is he right? She replays Kenny Wadd's words in her mind. Is there a chance that she might be released, able to live freely?

Freely? What does that mean? How would she do it? Where would she go?

Kenny Wadd's hand is back in his lap, far away from her face. Out of reach. It wears a wedding ring.

"Once my family is safe, I will contact you, Ja Vala. Your lawyer will know how to reach me. I will not forget about you."

She meets his eyes. Isn't his promise a decade too late?

Kenny Wadd stands, looks at his watch. "I have to get to the airport. Friends are watching my family, but Madame Armistead will not be deterred. I have to deal with her in person. You know how she is."

She does.

He bends over, puts his lips on her forehead. She raises her chin, but his lips don't touch her mouth, and his eyes don't meet hers. She listens to his footsteps until she can't hear them anymore. The rhythm of his heart stays with her longer, until gradually, her heart resumes its own. Even then, her skin doesn't forget the pressure of his lips. She has no idea how long she stays seated by the window, watching his empty chair.

Kenny Wadd. Kenny Wadd. Kenny Wadd. Kenny Wadd.

Chapter 110

It was the end of the day when, Robert Durly, our contact with Haitian authorities, finally phoned.

"The grave was exhumed?" I asked.

Yes, it had been, but he had other news as well. The police had been unable to find Madame Armistead, her husband, her son, or any of her personal staff. When they'd arrived at her home to interview her, they'd found it abandoned except for a few chickens. So far, no trace of her had been found.

Beyond that, yes, Ja Vala's grave had been exhumed. A badly decomposed female body had indeed been found in the coffin. The condition of the body indicated that it was Ja Vala's, just as the headstone indicated, and that her death certificate was accurate. The body had been immediately reburied without DNA or any kind of testing, officially declared to be that of Ja Vala Boudin.

I couldn't believe what I was hearing.

"Why wasn't testing done?"

"Testing?"

"DNA testing. To prove that the body is or isn't Ja Vala's."

"We didn't find it necessary—"

"Mr. Durly," I'd wanted to claw through the phone. "The sample of hair Kenny Wadd had brought from Haiti matches the hair of the very-much-alive woman we've identified as Ja Vala Boudin. Both bodies can't be hers."

Durly was unmoved, dismissed the significance of the matching hairs, insisting that there was no proof that Kenny Wadd's sample actually belonged to Ja Vala Boudin. "For all we know," he said, "that man plucked a hair from the woman you have in your custody and told you he brought it from Haiti. There was no reliable chain of custody for the sample, and therefore it must be dismissed."

I sputtered. "What possible motive could Kenny Wadd have for faking the sample?"

Durly assured me most eloquently that one couldn't speculate about what might drive another man's actions. But regardless, the hair would not be considered as proof of Ja Vala's identity.

"But what proof is there that the body in Ja Vala's grave is hers?"

Durly rambled off a list including the body's state of decomposition, its location, essentially saying that he had no proof.

D' ran a finger across his throat, telling me to stop challenging. I knew he was right. I would get nowhere, but I was too angry, couldn't stop myself. "Did you examine the ground around the grave? Had it been disturbed?"

"What are you implying, Detective Sterling? That the body in Ja Vala Boudin's grave is not genuine?"

Bingo. The man was a genius.

"And, assuming this theory is correct, where would this body have come from?"

How would I know? "Maybe from another grave?"

"So you are suggesting that, without being seen, someone dug up a body, took it from its coffin, replaced the empty coffin, and then—without damaging it—transferred the fragile and decomposed corpse to the grave of Ja Vala Boudin, where they dug up the empty coffin, filled it with the corpse, and reburied it."

"Yes, exactly." If someone wanted to hide the fact that Ja Vala was still alive, that she'd been revived and sold into slavery, that might be precisely what they'd do.

Not only Durly, but the Haitian police, and my own department, were reluctant to pursue this idea. In fact, the Haitians dismissed it outright and, with Madame Armistead and her entourage missing, their investigation was clearly coming to an end. As far as her own country was concerned, Ja Vala Boudin was going to remain officially dead.

"Never mind," D'Angelo rode his chair over, put his feet on my desk. "We've got her DNA on file. When she gets home, she can compare hers to her parents' and prove she's their kid."

I shoved his feet off. "Yeah. But why wouldn't the Haitians test the body for DNA?"

D' shrugged. "My guess? Because they knew the body wasn't Ja Vala."

What?

"Come on, Mo. We're talking about Haiti. The home of voudou. Zombies. Stuff like that, right?"

"So? That has nothing to do with our case."

"Maybe it does. Stereotypes like that aren't good for tourism, or the national interests, of a struggling country. They want to quash a story about corpses being revived and sold internationally as slaves who walk around without wills of their own." He raised his arms, zombie-like.

"D'. You're talking about public relations. Who cares about that when real people are being kidnapped and trafficked? Doesn't their country want to stop it?" I almost didn't finish the question. Knew what D' would say.

"Get real, Mo. Kenny Wadd said Madame Armistead has people everywhere. In the government, in law enforcement. No one's necessarily immune to payoffs or threats."

"But she's run off. She's missing."

"Is she? We have only the word of the people who might very well be on her payroll. They might be hiding her. And even if Madame Armistead has skadoodled, they don't want her found. Not if it means they themselves might get busted."

I picked at a hangnail, thought about what he'd said. "So, who do you think is in that grave?"

He took a breath. "Doesn't matter. What matters is who isn't." He stood, getting ready to go. "It's dinnertime. You got plans?"

I didn't, but it was Saturday night, and I didn't want him to feel obligated to invite me over. "Yeah, I'm meeting a friend."

D' said he'd see me Monday morning. In a few minutes, Colby left, then Reynolds. I sat at my desk until after seven, facing the weekend, in no hurry to go home.

Chapter 111

When I got there, home was all I expected it to be. Silent, dark, empty. The flowers from Evie wilted on my dining table, unwatered. Evie had said I should call her any time I wanted company, but I knew Joe wouldn't appreciate me interrupting their Saturday night.

"Try calling Lindsay," I heard Evie nag. "See if she wants to get a drink. You're alone too much. You need to get out there, meet people."

Meet people? I met people every day.

"That's not what I meant," I heard her say. "I mean decent people. You've probably got a ton of responses from the dating site. Why don't you answer some of them?"

I eyed my computer. It eyed me back, daring me to log on.

My refrigerator was more appealing. I opened it, not sure what I thought I'd find there. I hadn't shopped since before I'd been buried, so whatever was in there was old and sour, might as well have been buried with me. Except for the beer. I took one out, opened it. Drank. Searched the cabinets for take out menus. Recalled a new Greek restaurant on Fairmount Avenue, but couldn't remember its name. Athenos? Something like that. Maybe I could find it online.

My computer didn't believe that I was looking for a takeout place. It was sure I was edging toward the dating site, and it dared me to log on. I ignored it, found the restaurant, ordered Greek chicken and a salad. Checked my email. The dating site had sent an email indicating that I had another forty-some connections. And that I had a message from Lawman.

Lawman. I grabbed my phone, called Evie.

"Oh wow. He got back to you?" Her voice was a song. A trill.

"Wait. You know him?"

"So, do you. He said he wanted to connect. We checked out his profile together, remember?"

I had no such memory.

"Well, you were tired. Trust me, he's luscious. What did he say?"

I didn't know. Hadn't read the message.

Evie pressed me. "You're driving me crazy. Read it."

I stared at the screen, at the dating service post that said, "Message from Lawman."

"It's a message, Mo. It won't bite. Do I have to come over there and open it for you?"

No, of course she didn't. I clicked on the box, read the opening line. "Thanks for getting in touch," it began.

What? I hadn't. But all of a sudden, I understood who had.

"Evie. What did you do?"

She didn't even deny it. "I told him I thought we might be compatible and that we should get together face to face."

"You pretended to be me?"

"No need to thank me. So, what else does he say?"

My stomach lurched, my hands were clammy. What was wrong with me? It was a simple computer message, not an armed perpetrator. And yet the hairs on my arms rose. Adrenalin surged.

"Does he want to meet up?"

I took a breath, bit my lip. Read on. He said his name was Ethan Burke. He wrote that he'd found my profile fascinating, and he wanted to meet the actual woman blah blah blah. His work kept him busy, but if I could manage a lunch, he'd be free next Saturday. I stopped reading.

Evie was cheering, offering to help write my reply.

"Evie, what have you done?" I picked up my beer, finished it.

"Just go meet him, Mo. It's only lunch. You might click. And even if you don't, it's a start." She wasn't sorry, didn't apologize. In fact, she was proud of herself, even expected thanks.

It was no use pointing out that she'd impersonated me, fraudulently enticed this guy to contact me. I told her I couldn't possibly accept his invitation. Even so, when we got off the phone, I couldn't help it. I looked up his profile. Studied his photo. By the time my Greek chicken arrived, I'd made plans for lunch on Saturday.

That night, for the first time, I didn't stay awake thinking about Ja Vala and her case. Didn't have flashbacks about being paralyzed and buried alive. No, that night I stayed awake revisiting my message to Ethan Burke. Wondering if I'd worded it right. Or if I could somehow take it back.

Chapter 112

On Monday morning, D'Angelo came in whistling.

"This deal with God is doing me good. I already lost six pounds."

I looked him over. Honestly, I couldn't tell. "Great." I bit into my cheese Danish.

"Teresa says I'm buffed." He posed like a body builder.

I swallowed. Didn't comment.

He kept talking. Described his weekend. His new big screen television. "It shows too much, Mo. You can see the actors' zits." He asked how my weekend had been.

"Fine."

He frowned. "Mo. You need to meet—"

"Don't start. I have a date."

D's face lit up. "Yeah? Who?"

I almost answered, but stopped myself. Ethan Burke worked in the DA's office. D' might know him. "You don't know him."

"See that? Teresa was right again. She dreamed of a family reunion, a big party. Everyone was there."

For once, Teresa wasn't predicting catastrophes.

"You were there, too." He took a sip of coffee. "Along with your little twins."

My twins? My face got hot.

"Mo, it's a sign." He seemed gleeful. "It's no coincidence that Teresa dreamed that the same weekend you met a new guy."

Before I could answer, my phone rang. The captain wanted us in his office. He had news.

Ja Vala was to be released. No charges were being filed. The DA had determined that she'd had no intent to harm anyone and had, in fact, herself been a victim of human trafficking. In addition, there wasn't enough evidence to prove that she had actually committed the murders of the Grangers, J. Steven Richards or Sylvia Blake.

The killings of Alexandra Lambert and the two mambos had been determined to be acts of self-defense. Ja Vala was still under Dr. Vogel's care but, pending his assessment of her mental health, would be released shortly. Free to go.

Leaving the captain's office, D' looked me over. "What's wrong? This is what we wanted. Aren't you happy?"

I answered that I was. It was great news.

But back at my desk, I couldn't focus, kept thinking about Ja Vala. Once she was released, where would she go? She had no apartment. No friends. No passport. No identity. She had a lawyer who was suing the Grangers' estate on her behalf, but for now, she had no money. Until now, these issues had taken a backseat to others. But suddenly, the others had vanished, and she faced the big blank void of her future.

She must be overwhelmed. Frightened. I should stop and visit her. Not that I could fix things for her. Hell, I couldn't even deal with my own big blank void. But at least I could check in, see how she was doing. Meantime, D' and I had paperwork to fill out.

Colby came over, in a hurry. He'd heard about Ja Vala. Soon, all the guys were crowding around, wanting details. "This is one for the books, right, Mo?" D'Angelo began.

As I answered, my cell phone rang. The screen said, "Ethan Burke."

Chapter 113

Ja Vala rises to greet the detective with an embrace as if they are friends. Indeed, the share a connection, even if it's one they have not chosen. Ja Vala is impressed at how well the detective is recovering from her ordeal. She is bruised, but no scars are visible, only the line of stitches on her arm.

The detective asks how Ja Vala is doing. Ja Vala knits her brows to show her that she does not take her situation lightly. She folds her hands to demonstrate that she is composed, then smiles proudly, saying that Dr. Vogel thinks she's become a different person than the silent passive woman brought to him only weeks ago.

The detective is happy for her and agrees with Dr. Vogel about Ja Vala's transition. "You were like a ghost when we found you. And now, look at you. You're vibrant. Beaming with life."

She lowers her eyes modestly. "It's good to be alive," she says. "I owe it to you and your partner."

"Not just to us," the detective says. "To Kenny Wadd, too. Without him, we might never have learned your identity."

When the detective says his name, Ja Vala has to take a breath. "Yes," she agrees. "I owe a lot to Kenny Wadd."

In fact, she has thought a lot about him, has come to understand his failure to declare his love. Being the man he is, Kenny Wadd knows how deeply he has hurt her by marrying another. Having wronged her, he feels undeserving of her, and so has left his love unspoken.

Dr. Vogel joins them, and the detective announces that she has good news. Ja Vala is not going to be charged for any murders. She is to remain under Dr. Vogel's care until he determines she is able to manage on her own, and then she will be released to live as she chooses. The news media have made her into a celebrity. Funds are being raised to help her until a lawsuit filed against the Grangers's estate is settled.

The detective and Dr. Vogel gush information, interrupting each other. Ja Vala absorbs what she can. They talked about a caseworker. About immigration, legalities, deportation, the chance of a green card. She doesn't understand these terms or what they say about money or lawsuits. She knows only that she is to be free, able to move about. To make her own choices.

To plan a future.

Later, alone again in her room, she begins to do exactly that. For the first time since she planned her wedding, Ja Vala is forming pictures of tomorrow. The days ahead open like a fragrant meadow, inviting her to enter.

She cannot wait.

Her years as a slave remain dim and blanketed by fog, but her survival has taught her much about herself. She knows that she can endure, that she is strong. And lately, she has acquired new skills. Dr. Vogel has worked with her on excercising her free will. Setting goals, working step by step to achieve them. He has said that this process—he calls it self-determination—will help her heal.

And so, Ja Vala will follow his advice. She has set two goals and will work toward them step by step. First, when she is released, she will find her way back to Haiti. She will find the bokor Madame Armistead and her family, including the one-eyed rapist Josias. She is certain they are in the mountains among friends, but she will isolate and cut their throats, one by one.

After that, she will proceed to her second goal. She will go to Kenny Wadd's home and wait for him to step out. While he is gone, she will visit the imposter who has stolen her beloved, who was never supposed to have been his wife.

Ja Vala will free Kenny Wadd of his entanglements and obligations, so that he can share his life with her as he was meant to.

Each day, Ja Vala wakes up wondering, if this is the day she will be released. She shows Dr. Vogel that she is balanced and steady, ready to manage on her own. She smiles at him and the nurses, does what they expect. And when she loses hope or becomes impatient, she shifts her focus, looking ahead to her goals.

Soon, maybe tomorrow she will be free. And she will go back home. And reclaim her life. The thought fuels the embers in her heart. They flicker with new flames until she becomes a quiet raging fire.

Kenny Wadd. Kenny Wadd. Kenny Wadd. Kenny Wadd.

About the Author

Merry Jones is the multiple award-winning author of over twenty suspense, non-fiction and humor books whose work has been translated into seven languages. She lives in Philadelphia, PA, where she writes and sculls on the Schuylkill River.

Read more at www.MerryJones.com.

Milton Keynes UK
Ingram Content Group UK Ltd.
UKHW020820200524
442968UK00005B/335